HIS RAGGED COMPANY

A TESTIMONY OF ELIAS FAUST - BOOK 1

RANCE D. DENTON

COVER ART by Sean Martin

(HTTPS://WWW.FIVERR.COM/GRAVYLAUGHBEEBL)

BACK ART by Sandy Butchers

(HTTP://WWW.PATREON.COM/SANDYBUTCHERS)

COLOR STUDY by Marlena Murtagh

(HTTP://WWW.MARLENAMURTAGHPHOTOGRAPHY.COM)

AUTHOR HEADSHOT by Mary Elizabeth Williams

CONTENT & TRIGGER WARNINGS

Ableism, alcohol use, animals harmed in combat, blood & gore, death, dismemberment, drowning, drug use, forced restraint, gun violence, hanging, harsh language, knife violence, racism, self-harm, sex & sexual acts, sexism, sexual assault (verbally threatened, not performed), suicide.

ACKNOWLEDGMENTS

My many thanks—

To Katie, who spends hours listening, suggesting, and pulling my head out of my ass;

To Bob, who holds me to higher standards than anyone else, because a book shouldn't suck;

To Lithia, who creates so tirelessly, she reminds me I should too;

To Mom, who always knows that the value of a story lies in its heart;

To Laura across the sea and Matt down the road.

To you, reading now.

For Dad
who knew enough to teach me how not to be.

A BEGINNING-OF

THERE I WAS, THE GUY WITH HIS HEAD HALFWAY UP A HORSE'S ASS.

Maybe halfway is stretching the truth, but I was close to it. I hung across the rear of the horse. The ground flashed by a few feet below my head. Sand and dirt stung my cheeks. My brain felt like it was close to giving up. Body wasn't far behind.

I heard gunfire. Not close by, but getting closer. The popping gunblasts had a heartbeat rhythm. Woodsmoke was in the air, but I knew it didn't come from a hearth-fire. It was death-smoke. *Town's-on-fire,-get-your-ass-in-your-hand-and-run* kind of smoke.

Welcome home, Elias Faust.

"You mind slowing down a bit?" I said to the rider. "Mind giving me a second—"

Something splashed across my cheek. I thought it was blood. I went to wipe it away. Grains of wet sand clumped in my eyes.

A body went spinning past, rolling along the ground with a slice across its chest that left it resembling more a piece of ham than a living thing. Its black cloaks flapped, *snap-snap*, like a flag. I looked up, thinking it was the rider. It wasn't. The rider still had the killing knife in her hand, poised for another strike. Her face, painted up like a skull, was a mask of stark white shadowed by slashes of coal-black. She hunched over the neck of the horse, melting into it.

In the distance ahead, smoke spiraled into the air like a dirty bandage against the sun. A town was there too, little pockmark of a thing that probably didn't even deserve being called a town. More like a blemish made up of squat buildings, a town hall, and a livery. It all looked like it was burning, but you'd be hard-pressed to see fire with all the sunlight, so I had to imagine it. The smoke made it that much easier.

All around the town, an army of dark figures scurried, some engaged in close combat with townspeople who used everything they had to fight against them: rusty tools, cast-iron, even their fists. Other marauders dashed about on horseback, guns belching out little puffs of smoke, others slicing with keen blades or clubbing heads with cudgels. There was a lot of howling and hollering. It was a big ol' people-killing party. Some of Blackpeak's people had guns, but that didn't help them much – the shadows were faster, more vicious.

Some shadows didn't have guns at all. Just opened their palms and blinding sprays of wildfire spewed like burning fabric from their hands. The figure running the horse turned her head just enough to look at me. She held the reins with her knife-hand and pulled something metal out of her belt.

She spun it in her strange, metal-gold palm, then handed it back to me.

It was my revolver. I grabbed it.

We careened into a group of cloaks just outside the town. They were chasing down a screaming woman and her kid. Skullface, without pausing her horse, leaned down off the saddle and stabbed one of the cloaks in the throat. Our sheer speed tore out the neck in a bloodless spray of dust. The knife wove up like it had a life of its own and came down, cracking into another black-cloak's collarbone. His mouth opened in a soundless yawn, he folded over like paper, and hot sand flew off into the wind.

We swept through the edge of the town and went barreling into it at full speed. The cloaks had themselves a grand time with their wild handfuls of fire, lighting flame to any building within reach. Black-powder smoke burped out of broken windows as the townspeople fired at whatever didn't look like them. Some of the black-clad figures seemed to leap and float, suspended from invisible strings, defying natural rules.

Once we got into the town, Skullface had to let up on the horse a bit to weave through the little fights going on along the main road. "You got any plan here, Painted Wonder," I shouted, "or you just taking a joyride?"

No response. Guess that meant no plan. Ain't a real fan of plans anyway. Most of them go awful wrong.

Then again, I guess not having a plan went wrong, too, because just as she spurred around the corner, the horse bucked. Lots of tattered figures came pouring out of alleys and side streets. Skullface tried to keep control. In the wild moment, she didn't see one of the beings drawing back a hunting bow.

The arrow whisked through the air like a brown insect. Her shoulder jerked. I saw the point come out of her skin, punching through her tattered vest. She collapsed off the saddle just as two other arrows landed between the horse's ribs. It staggered. Its legs collapsed. The world skewed sideways. Skullface reached up, grabbed me by the collar, and wrenched me down to the ground.

Her blood, gray as melted lead, dribbled spirals into the dirt.

I tried to will myself to move, but nothing happened. My legs weren't talking to my brain. The cloaked beasts didn't lend us a second. They started running, firing rifles, hoisting deadly tools above their heads.

"Shit," I said. "This ain't good."

Skullface got a handful of my collar. With her good arm she started dragging me as fast as she could. My limp legs left long traces of blood in the sand. Above the buckle of my belt my shirt was shredded and wet, sticky like syrup. When I breathed, a boiling agony burned inside my guts.

Within seconds, the mob would be on us. We'd be stew.

I raised the Colt. I found the bead of the sight between the trenches machined into the cylinder. Then I looked for one of the creature's chests and drew back the hammer with my thumb.

Had to use my middle finger to pull the trigger. I didn't have the best grip on account of all the blood. My blood. The Colt kicked. One of the intruders jerked back, stumbled, then flopped over.

With Skullface dragging me, all I could do to hold off the group was shoot. They just kept coming. An arrow splashed in the sand next to me. I fired again, but the shot jumped high. I worked the hammer, and this time – even though the ground and hot rocks felt like they were burning a hole through my trousers – I was patient enough to aim. I caught one of the bastards right in the thigh. It stumbled away, leaving three more coming at us.

As Skullface kept pulling me, I held the Colt with both hands.

One of them leveled an old rifle. I could see my fate in its barrel, but I was quicker. *Pop*. He collapsed.

The last two bolted for us. I had two shots left. Only enough time to get one off before they were all over us. I bit down on my tongue, raised the pistol, and fired. A reddish cloud of sand blew out the first one's misshapen head. The other one leaped for me.

It raised a woodcutter's axe. I might have had the chance to get off a gut-shot, but that wouldn't change momentum or the fact that my brains didn't get along well with sharp objects.

Skullface moved in a flash. She leaped over me like a cat and caught the downward-slicing weapon. The cloaked presence hissed.

Without missing a motion, like she was doing some kind of dance, my savior stole the axe from the figure. She spun it in her palm, barked out a cry, and swung. After several thumping chops, the shadow's neck went missing. The body and severed head plopped into the sand at about the same time.

Skullface stood firm, waiting for the next round of raiders. They were coming. I could feel the footsteps like a rumbling train.

We could fight over the burning husk of a town all we wanted, but in the end, no matter who won, there'd be nothing left. Nothing to salvage. "They're on the way," I said, every word sending a new shock of pain down into the bleeding ruin of my stomach.

She nodded.

"And that means we're likely on our way out," I said.

Nod number two.

"Kill as many as we want, we won't come out of this alive."

"You will not," she said.

"Well, I got one more bullet." Skullface turned. Oily paint ran with her mercury blood, with my blood, glistening along the front of her throat. She still had an arrow through her but didn't seem to realize it.

Behind her, another wave of dark raiders swept through the town on foot and horseback, firing and burning and swinging, breaking everything they came across and killing every townsperson who tried to counter them. There was no time wasted on trophies of flesh or bone. The mass of them was a machine, powered solely for the destruction of anything and everything that flickered in front of their eyes.

We'd be next.

I saw a little shift in Skullface's lips – a twitch, like she was about to say something. Instead, she just squatted down over me and threw the axe away. The thunderous crowd came closer. I didn't hear so many people screaming anymore.

Skullface sifted through the dirt. When she found what she wanted, she lifted it up and showed it to me.

"Did it speak to you," she snarled, her words all sharp edges and crude angles. "Tell me. Tell me now." It was a rock, about the size of a fist. Round. Just the right size to—

"The Shattered Well," she said. "Did you hear its voice?"

I tried to remember. I told her. I showed her.

Skullface raised her arm, gritted her crystalline teeth, and swung the stone down at my face.

I fired, mostly on instinct, right from the hip. I felt the Colt jerk, but I never saw what happened. I got clobbered in the forehead with the stone anyway. I was thrown into a black sea and floated further and further away. The cold sensation of wood and metal in my hand started to vanish.

I don't remember my head hitting the ground.

I don't know if my shot landed.

The hot stink of woodsmoke followed me down. Even in death, I doubt I'd shake the smell.

Yeah. Welcome home my ass.

NOW

"*I BELIEVE I ASKED YOU TO START AT THE BEGINNING.*"

"*I did,*" *I tell him. "At least, as far back as necessary.*"

"*Never took you as a man who would cut so many corners.*"

"*Quickest way's usually the easiest.*"

He smiles. If a vulture could smile, I'd imagine it looking something like this. Just like the last time I saw him, he had way too many ivories in too many narrow rows. Give him a side of beef and he could have slivered it into ribbons for you with his eyeteeth. The faster you think a man can mash his steak into paste, the less you can trust him. Meat is meat, after all, whether it's a cow's or whether it's yours.

He flicks his lapel and straightens a wrinkle between his thumb and forefinger. There, set in a gold broach, an eyeball blinks, rolls in its socket, and locks on me. It trembles, disembodied but alive. "Quick or not, Marshal, I'm interested in the details, in the morsels and minutiae. In the truth. Can you give me that?"

"*Never had much of an imagination. Takes too much work to keep all those fantasies lined up in your head.*" *I see only him. Nothing else. The gaslights behind him burn my eyes, blaring like droplets of sunlight. His face is a distorted shadow. "Most people would think them tall tales if I told* them straight, just lies and fabrications meant to impress myself into the company of free drinks and warm thighs."

"You don't have to impress me. You just have to tell me everything you know."

I turn my head away from his breath. It stinks like leather-oil and boiled eggs. With all that darkness around me, I drive my heels into the floor to be sure I'm not being swallowed. I can feel my heartbeat pounding a steady pulse inside my ears. That was a start. I knew I was, just not exactly where. "So where would you prefer I begin?"

"Think of the first time you drew his attention."

"Whose?"

There's that smile again, wide and slippery. Too jovial, too inviting. He knows what he wants out of me.

I tighten my fists. The thirsty thorns bound around my wrists bite deeper into my flesh. Their points cry caustic acid. It takes their juices only a second to find the avenues of my veins and rush through them. Tides of pain explode inside me.

Then the worms come. I see them beneath my flesh, crawling, curling, hatched out of a thousand unseen eggs, lumps of my skin moving like a quilt covering restless legs.

One burrows out from the roof of my mouth, falls right onto my tongue.

"Tell me about him. Tell me about the Magnate."

I suppose it couldn't hurt to be thorough.

PART I

THE GUN

1

BEING A MARSHAL AIN'T REALLY A BIG TASK IN A TOWN SMALL ENOUGH to spit over. It's not very exciting. Not very dangerous. Not very reputable, either. Either way, it's still marshaling. It pays for the whiskey. If I'm frugal, it also makes sure I have a warm body in my bed at the end of a week.

Not much law to speak of in Blackpeak. Every citizen of Blackpeak falls under my watch, no matter who it is. If Paul Fulton thinks someone's snooping around his homestead, then I'll look into it. If Mr. Sloman at the trade shop has a problem with a customer, even if he's nudged up the prices on me once or twice, I'll look into it.

Case in point: Even town drunks like Rufus Oarsdale are my responsibility. My town, my people, my jurisdiction. Most people have probably heard similar talk before, but it's easy to lack creativity when your head's chock full of law and swagger and your hips are heavy with guns.

Rufus came bursting into the marshal's office on a Saturday afternoon. The way his boots scraped the floorboards, I knew he had been drinking before I even smelled his breath. He smashed his meaty fists down on my desk. "Those connivin' sons of bitches," he snarled. "Those pig-stinking, trough-licking—"

"Mr. Oarsdale," I said. "There something I can help you with?"

"Goddamn right there's something," he said, heaving out whiskey-breaths. "Help me dig some graves for the thieving rats I'm about to kill."

I raised an eyebrow. "Talk to the undertaker about the graves. Who you about to kill?"

"Some boys," he said.

"Any boys?"

He said, "'Pacific ones."

"Sailors?"

"No. Pacific ones," Rufus said. "Certain set of boys done me wrong, so it's time for them to get killed."

"These *pacific* boys anybody I'm familiar with?"

"Gregdon Twins," he told me.

Oh, I thought. *Them.*

"Weren't you running with them as of recent, Rufus?"

He jabbed at the desk with his finger. "As of this morning."

"Disagreement?"

"They stole something."

I like to run things in an off-the-spur kind of manner. Situation comes up needs a rule, that means I get to write one. Long as they don't shake up the town too much, of course. That's the agreement Mayor Kallum and I came to. I decide on a rule, and then I talk about it to whoever it applies to. If they don't like it, they get to leave Black-peak in whatever way suits them the best: in a saddle or in a pine box. Like everything else, I had a rule about thieving: Don't do it. Sounds a lot like my other rules. No reason to complicate things.

The Gregdon Twins – capital *T*, as they'd corrected me in the past – were a pair of kids barely out of their teens that had somehow managed to claim Blackpeak as their stomping ground. They were arrogant, crude, and because they could talk a lot of trash and wore firearms at their sides, fancied themselves kings. Rufus, too damned drunk half the time to think straight, had taken right to them. They kept him drunk so they could laugh at him and watch him make a fool out of himself. If you were a scientific sort, you might even call them symbiotic. "You seem pretty heated, Rufus. Must have been something special they took from you."

"It was. It was lucky," he said.

Great.

If there's one thing to know about Rufus Oarsdale: he's full of crap. He'd lie to you to get anything done his way, even if it's not a very good lie. He's superstitious, too. Don't ask me how those two things go together. When you hear Rufus talk about his belongings, he'd say they're all lucky, like a four-leaf clover or a rabbit's foot. Lucky hat, lucky boots, lucky bottle of hooch.

"Well, come out with it," I commanded him, leaning forward in my chair and kicking my dusty boots off of the desktop. "What did they steal?"

"Just *somethin'*. I ain't asking you to retrieve it," Rufus said. "I'm asking you to kill 'em."

"I should at least know what you want me to kill these boys over."

Rufus pulled off his faded hat and wrung it in his hands. Scarce twists of white hair bloomed on his otherwise bald head. "Maybe whatever it is won't mean much to you, but it means a whole lot to me."

"Because it's lucky."

"Because it's mine."

"Fair enough. You want I should go talk to them about giving whatever it is back?"

"Bullshit. I want you to shoot them."

I stood and grabbed my jacket off the back of my chair. It was hot enough outside to fry the scales off a snake, but a jacket's important – pockets and bravado. "Sometimes you can solve problems just as easily with patience and diplomacy. How about I just head on up and talk to them, see if I can ask for whatever it is."

Rufus's bloodshot eyes squeezed almost shut. "And if it comes to shots, you'll kill them boys, right?"

"If it comes to shots, I'll be mighty angry," I said.

"At what?"

"At you," I said. "At them."

He mulled over my response. "Sounds good," he said.

I opened one of the drawers of the old writing desk where I kept sparse paperwork and grabbed a few paper shotgun shells. After filling my bandolier, I grabbed the double-barreled twelve-gauge from where it leaned against the desk. I kept it there most days because I like to think I'm primed for trouble if it comes. I cracked the breach and slipped two shells into it and then draped it over my forearm without locking it shut. Sidearms are one thing, but I don't like walking through the town with a readied long-gun unless it's absolutely necessary. Screams of trouble. Gathers a crowd. Crowds get people killed.

Rufus's beady eyes got wide. "Planning on making a mess?"

"Planning on being listened to the first time. You got a piece?"

"Why?"

"You're coming with me. That means you have to be prepared if their britches get hot."

"I don't got a gun."

I glanced at his belt. He had a worn holster hanging against his hip, but its top gaped like an empty mouth. I turned to the cabinet behind my desk and produced a battered specimen of a revolver – a blemished .38 I'd confiscated a few weeks ago – and slid it and a box of rounds across the desk toward him. He picked it up in a shaking hand. He opened the loading gate and began sliding in a few cartridges. One fell out of his palm and clattered to the floor. "If it comes to shots," said Rufus, "you'll be the one firing first, won't you?"

"Depends on who's quicker."

"You're the marshal," he said. "You've got to be quick, right?"

"Try to be."

"Quicker than them."

"Most times."

"But if you're not..."

I pointed at the revolver. "Might need you to be, Rufus."

"I ain't fast."

"You accurate?"

"I can take a can at ten paces without really aiming."

I studied his face for a minute and then shook my head. Rufus might as well have been a wet goddamn soup-noodle.

"Listen," I reasoned as he fumbled the gun into his holster. "I don't sit at this desk because it's fashionable. It's because I can usually find a way to solve problems, and contrary to popular belief, not all those problems need to be solved with gunfire. But if things start getting batty, you hold your hat and find cover. Unless you want to tell me what it is you're looking to get back so you can stay down here in the office while I take care of this."

"I'm coming," he resolved. "My stuff."

"Fair enough."

"We just talkin' to them, though, ain't we? The guns...they're just for muscle. 'Gotiation." Guns make things real. More real than Rufus's initial excitement had anticipated.

"Negotiation," I agreed.

"But you'll kill 'em if it doesn't work."

"Might," I said.

The hairs of his gray beard fluttered as he heaved out a settling breath. I doubt Rufus had really been looking forward to facing the Gregdons again, but I wasn't going to let him stay behind. If flying lead came into the picture, I just hoped he was steady enough not to shoot me in the face.

I made a mental note to give him and his piece a wide berth.

I checked both of my holstered Colt revolvers and then motioned for Rufus to follow me. As we stepped out of my office and onto the front porch, the sunlight cut a bright swath through Blackpeak's main road. Almost midday. I wanted to get this done and get back to a good bowl of stew.

As a rickety wagon – a tradesman, it looked like, from the pile of nondescript barrels and sacks piled in its back – rumbled by in front of us, I touched the tip of my hat in greeting. His face went white when he saw the shotgun hanging over my arm.

We turned to the stables. "Gregdon boys up at the mine?" I asked.

"Probably."

"We have a stop to make before we talk to them," I told him.

"Why?"

"Rules," I said. "Just rules."

Rufus Oarsdale, who looked very suddenly like he regretted coming to me, didn't bother to ask. I didn't blame him. He's not the only one who doesn't like my rules.

But rules are rules. Best to stick by them.

2

BLACKPEAK'S A POOR EXCUSE FOR A MINING TOWN. OTHER MINING towns have veins literally overflowing stuff – plenty to cook, coke, and con with. Ain't much of that in Blackpeak. Other mines in other places are the heart of the town's economy, but ours was just the asshole of it, shallow and smelly, pitiful to behold.

A ten-minute ride west of town saw us up a winding hill toward a series of small tents where a few folks milled about. Beyond them, set deep into the face of a jagged little mountain, was the black mouth of the mine. Beating picks and hammers echoed deep within.

The six men that stood around the small tents were all dirty and sweaty. Some drank lukewarm coffee while others puffed long pipes. As the two of us drew our horses up near them, they stopped in the middle of their conversation and turned to stare at us.

"Afternoon, gentlemen," I said, leaning over the neck of my horse. They looked at each other. Then they looked at Rufus. I felt the old drunk canter his horse a bit further away from the crowd. "Afternoon," I said again, sharpening my voice.

"Heard ya the first time," said one of the men, his head draped with a wet rag. "You need somethin' or you just here to stare at us?"

"Ain't much to stare at," I said. "Your foreman around?"

"You're armed," he said. "What you want with the foreman?"

"Ask him some questions," I clarified, easing up in the saddle.

The big guy didn't seem to pick up on the relaxation. "What kind of questions?" he asked.

"Questions about the Gregdon Twins is all. You know them?"

"Pretty well. I know that rat behind you, too," he said, swiping the wet rag off his forehead. "You hear me, you pick-pocketing bitch?"

Rufus gave him the finger.

The big boy's feet squared in the gravel and he began rolling up his sweat-soaked sleeves. Just before he started marching in Rufus's direction, I edged my horse around to cut him off. "Oarsdale's with me right now."

"I got trouble with him. We all do."

"I don't doubt," I responded, quiet enough so Rufus couldn't over-hear. "But I didn't bring him up here like a package for you to unwrap. Grudges are grudges, but put whatever you got to the side right now and take it up another day. The foreman," I said. "I want to speak to him."

He flashed his eyes to the shotgun. He turned, shouldered his way through a few of his friends, then made his way into a tent that looked like it would need to grow to accommodate his size. A minute later, the tongues of the tent flopped open. A balding man, shorter than the rest and toothpick-thin, came marching out, wiping his blackened hands down the front of a stained apron. He smiled at me as he came up to me.

"Marshal Elias Faust," he said. I shook his hand. "How do you do?"

"Mr. Bisbin," I said. "Hungry as hell. Got pulled away just before lunch."

"I'm just cooking up some chili for my boys, here. Care to share a bowl?"

"Got some business to take care of, Mr. Bisbin, but much obliged. Wondered if I could speak to you for a moment?"

He clapped his hands together and turned, waving toward his men. "Food's simmering out back of the tent, boys. Help yourselves as you please. I'm going to speak to the marshal here for a few minutes." They seemed to understand that Mr. Bisbin was asking for a bit of peace and quiet. One by one, they stepped into the tent and through it, seeking out their lunch. Foreman Bisbin was a good man to work for – kept his workers fed and happy. If marshaling turned out to be any more a piss-poor way to live, I know where I'd relocate.

When the men were gone, Rufus led his horse a little closer to the conversation between Bisbin and me. Bisbin nodded in stiff greeting to him. Polite, but not cordial. "What brings you two up this way this afternoon?"

"Gregdons," I said.

"Rufus come talk to you after this morning?"

Rufus piped in. "I sure as hell did."

Bisbin, straining hard to make himself sound agreeable, said, "We had a bit of an issue this morning."

"All three of these men working for you? Rufus," I said, "and the Gregdons?"

"Good man to work for," Rufus admitted. Bisbin softened visibly at the compliment.

"I suppose, though I asked them all to take their leave this morning. They showed up at dawn bickering and arguing over some belongings, and—"

"I punched Billy Gregdon in his damn nose," said Rufus.

I didn't look at him. "This happened before, foreman?"

"Pretty regular. Some of my men don't get along, but the Gregdons and Oarsdale here have had quite a number of differences as of late. But Oarsdale hasn't had the finest record, either."

"That true, Rufus?"

"Ain't nothing big," Rufus said.

"What kind of trouble you been causing for Mr. Bisbin?"

"Stole a few things," he said.

"Like what?"

"Watches, some coins, bottle of whiskey or two."

I shook my head for the second, or third, or maybe even the

eighth time of the day. "I take it this has been happening for awhile, Mr. Bisbin?"

"Few weeks. Gregdons thought it would be a good idea to return the favor this morning."

"They started a fight?" I said.

"More or less. As I take it, they took a few things from Rufus's belongings stored away in the tent. They ragged on him something fierce until he struck out at Billy Gregdon and bloodied his nose up. I can't have that kind of fighting in my camp, so I split them all up and told them to skedaddle. Work is work. If none of them want to take part, then they can go where they please."

"Any idea where the Gregdons are right now?"

"Probably down at the old abandoned Simpkin farm gettin' drunk or worse. Least, that's where I saw them head off to."

"Then that's where Rufus and I will be going," I said to the foreman, "as long as I have your permission to do so."

"Why the hell you need that?"

"Courtesy," I said. "Let you know that if anybody does anything stupid, you might need to get yourself a few new workers."

Rufus pulled on the reins of his horse with impatience. "Faust and me are gonna kill those thievin' bastards."

"Rufus?" I said.

"Yeah?"

"Shut your goddamned mouth."

He kept his lips clamped and veered his steed around me, back down the hill we had come up. The heat and the leather jacket were bad enough to deal with without his constant badgering. When he was far enough away, I sighed and took my hat off, letting the hot breeze rush across the moisture in my sweaty hair. It felt damned good.

Bisbin watched Rufus the whole time he descended. "All three of them, a pain in my ass."

"Shame. You treat these boys good, Bisbin."

"Sure, until they start ripping each other off."

"Restless energy," I said, like I knew a thing or two.

"I guess that's how it works." Bisbin paused and then squinted through the sunlight, his bushy eyebrows flattening on his forehead. "You aren't a saint, Faust. You're a man. You should let these dirtbags thin each other out now and then."

"I'd get the chance to eat a lot more lunches if I did."

"Good lunches," said Bisbin.

"Good lunches don't make me money."

"Does marshaling?"

"Just enough."

"More towns would be lucky to have somebody like you," said Bisbin. "I appreciate you coming to me about this. Just..." he added, sucking in a breath that filled him up like a swollen gizzard. "Just don't muck the stalls of this whole situation too clean, Elias. You'll end up with shit on your boots."

I nodded my head and then gathered up the reins on my horse, bringing her to bear with a tug at her bit.

"Them Gregdon boys," Bisbin said. "They won't like talking."

"I get that feeling."

"Yep," he said. "I could tell."

"How?"

"Shotgun," he said.

3

RUFUS AND I LINGERED AT THE TOP OF THE HILL OVER THE VALLEY
where the abandoned Simpkin farm stood. By what means the home
stood was beyond my infantile architectural know-how. The paint
had been chewed away by the elements over the past few years,
leaving gray wood to bleach under a Texas sun.

Gregdon Twins being the troublemakers I knew them to be –
fight-starters, quick on the trigger, and dumb as bricks – it wasn't a
smart idea to go riding down toward the old farm. Not anticipating a
fight doesn't mean you shouldn't be prepared. I wanted to size them
up first, get an idea as to what Rufus and I were working with.

We sat on our horses in plain sight. Rufus got impatient real
quick, got down off his, drank a few slugs from his flask, stretched his
legs. I took out a cigarette, struck a match on my boot, and smoked
contentedly.

"Mostly just whores smoke cigarettes," Oarsdale told me. "You
should get a pipe."

"You gonna buy me one for Christmas, Rufus?"

"Shit," he said. "We gonna go down and get my stuff back?"

"Soon."

"We're just sitting here with our thumbs up our asses."

"That don't keep you busy enough?"

"Like hell," he said.

Meanwhile, I checked my revolvers. Smart gunmen who know their way around a piece like a Colt, they'll tell you not to go around with all six rounds in it. Something stupid happens and you end up dropping the thing, that hammer's liable to strike the primer on the cartridge and fire off into something that doesn't deserve it. Like someone else. Like you. You only put that sixth one in if you know you're about to go wading into some kind of mess that might require it. The Gregdon Twins were enough of one, I guessed. "I don't want to go right down and talk to them. I want to give them time to come to us."

"What'll that do?"

"Let them feel in control."

"And that's good," Rufus mused.

"That's good. They don't feel so quick to defend their territory."

"So if they don't come up..."

I nodded my head down at the old farmhouse. "Then we go down there with the sun at our backs. Gives us an advantage if they want to try something drastic. They'll have a hard time keeping a bead on us with the light in their eyes." When my smoke was done, I ground it out and put the remnants in my pocket.

The sun began to fall into the horizon behind us. The Gregdon boys noticed us not long after we arrived. They came out of the derelict farmhouse and made a point to stay within sight, likely doing much the same as I was. I saw one of them take out his sixgun and play with it, check it, sight it in at an old rock as if he were making sure it would shoot straight. They were flexing their muscles. At that distance they were just blurry silhouettes clicking their heels as they paced along the porch.

When Rufus saw the Gregdon pull out the gun, he stiffened in the saddle and wiped his wrist across his forehead. "Relax," I said. "He ain't gonna do anything."

"How you know?"

"Range," I said. "Too far for him to hope to hit us. 'Course, the bullet could travel that far—" I reasoned, and Rufus grunted, "—but he'd have to be a crack shot to hit one of us. Had he a rifle, I'd probably pull back, but I don't see one."

"Not yet, anyway."

"If they had one, we'd have seen it by now."

We waited until our shadows stretched like long, black fingers down the side of the hill. We watched them like we were hawks – well, a hawk and one half-blind messenger pigeon – and even if they were watching back, being observed makes men nervous.

When it came time, I slipped down off of my horse, hung my jacket on the horn of the saddle, and drew the double-barreled out of its holster. I nodded to Rufus, who slithered down off his horse. "Time to go," I told him. "Just gonna go down and talk to these boys real nice. No cussing, no instigating, just talking. Shut your mouth unless you're spoken to, and when you do open it, you do so easy-like. Last thing I need is to get smoked because you don't know how to harness your tongue."

The valley where the Simpkin farm stood grew darker by the minute. The hills around it were high enough to choke off the sunlight well before the day was at an end. I heard Rufus cursing and stumbling behind me.

The Simpkin farm hadn't functioned in years. Long before my time in Blackpeak, a dispute between landowners had seen the Simpkins killed by a rival. Gruesome stuff, from what I had been told. Husband, wife, two little girls, all shot to death.

Since then, the rotten old farmhouse and the dilapidated barn behind it had become a regular meeting-place for hooligans of all kinds. The fields had been sunburnt into uselessness. Brown weeds overtook much of the land around it. A wagon missing a wheel sat in the front yard, along with a moldering pile of wood half-sunk into the earth. There was a crumbling well that looked about ready to fall in on itself. Two old trees reached leafless arms for the sky. Sad to see a good, productive farm fall into such misuse.

Two shadows stood shoulder-to-shoulder on the porch. Our welcoming party. The Gregdon Twins stared at us as we approached them. As I got closer, I could feel their eyes boring into me. Didn't really matter right then if they could aim for shit or not – I was under the impression they could, and that's what mattered the most.

"Evenin' Billy, Curtis," I said easily as I strode up to them, keeping enough space between them and me so I could see their every move, but just little enough so the shotgun would have an effect if it needed to. I sucked my teeth. "You boys got a real nice place, here. Love what you've done with it."

"What the hell you want, Faust?" snarled Billy, his dark facial hair matted with flakes of blood from his swollen nose. He wore a black vest and a dark hat. Wisps of unkempt blond hung around his ears and neck. He kept playing with the gun in his hands.

"Just to talk. Was wondering if you wouldn't mind sitting down with me to discuss some things."

"What things?"

"Law things," I said. "Breaking rules things. Starting trouble kind of things."

Billy Gregdon pointed over my shoulder at Rufus. "And you brought that pig here to do it, huh?"

"He lodged a complaint. I followed up on it."

"You hear that Curtis?" asked Billy.

Curtis, who stood just beside his brother – and who looked nothing at all like a twin, from his brownish hair to his oversized nose and his too-far-apart eyes – crossed his arms before his chest. Two wooden handles stuck out at his hips. "Thought I heard it," said Curtis, his voice shrill. "Lodged a complaint, Rufus did. Lodged it with the law."

"'Spose that means we go quietly," said Billy, never looking away from me.

"'Spose so," said Curtis.

I held up a hand. "Not talking about anybody going with anybody, boys. Just here to mediate and be sure we can retain the peace."

Billy Gregdon said, "Oh, so you're *rehabilitatin'* us."

"Looks like it. You all take something from Mr. Oarsdale here? He seemed mighty offended."

Curtis's lips and nose curled up in a sneer. "Don't know why he should be. He been stealin' from the boys up at the mine for some time now."

With the hand not holding the sixgun, Billy Gregdon reached back to his other holster, which was filled with a very unorthodox weapon that didn't seem to fit quite right in it. The grip was not the crescent-shaped, flat-ended one you might see on a revolver. It looked longer, gnarled, a little more ornate and primitive. Then he said, "Thought we'd give him what he deserved."

"That's my gun," Rufus blurted from behind me.

Billy grinned a smile with less teeth than I had fingers. "Belongs to us now. Think of it as payment for all the things you been snatching from the boys workin' Bisbin's mine."

"Hard workin' folks," said Curtis. "Don't deserve nothing getting stolen."

I cleared my throat. "Stealing is stealing no matter what. Rules against that kind of thing here."

"You gonna punish Oarsdale for what he took?" snapped Billy.

"Nobody told me he took anything," I said.

"He took a lot," said Curtis.

"Important things," said Billy.

"I ain't took nothing," Rufus shouted, and I felt him surging forward behind me. I reached out a hand and caught him mid-stride. I shoved the old drunk back. "What did I tell you, Rufus?"

"That's my gun."

Trying to stand between thieves and drunks was a lesson in futility. I was more tense than I should have been. My shoulders started to ache. Our shadows grew longer. The sun was setting, and if we talked too long and nothing came of it, then Rufus and I would lose our advantage if things came to shots.

"Between you all and me," I said, "I don't care who stole what. Rufus was the only one who went through the proper channels to let me know. Gregdons, if you'd come to me before today, we very likely would be witnessing a very different situation. But you didn't. The rules don't apply to would-haves or could-haves," I warned them. "I'm asking you kindly, as the marshal of Blackpeak, to return to Mr. Oarsdale what property belongs to him."

"He means the gun," said Rufus, "and the lucky—"

"Rufus," I snapped. I held out my free hand and wriggled my fingers. "The pistol, Billy Gregdon. Pass it on."

"And what if I don't wanna?" he said.

"I get it anyway."

"That a threat?"

"Professional inference."

"What the hell does that mean?" asked Curtis.

"Means that by the kindness of your good Christian souls, in adherence to the values your Mama taught you, and because Saint Nick will bring you sugarplums in your stocking if you do—" I read-justed my hold on the double-barreled, whipped it up with one hand to close the breach, and drew back the hammers, "—you'd be best off handing over the pistol so I don't have to give you both some new leaky holes."

I'm a professional gunman, or something fairly close to it. It's my job to take situations over the line.

"We can talk about this," said Curtis.

"Damned right we can," I responded.

"No," said Billy. He was no longer playing with his revolver. He was holding it tightly, as if he expected to use it. "I ain't giving the thing back. There's a price to pay for stealin'."

"Price to pay for stealing from a citizen of Blackpeak," I said. "Drop your weapon and give me what belongs to Mr. Oarsdale."

I know from experience that it's hard to think when you're staring down two very loaded shotgun barrels. Billy Gregdon shifted his weight from one foot to another. He raised his chin. Instead of staring at the gun, he stared at me. "Just because you're the marshal doesn't mean you can go around killing anybody you want over something as simple as an old man's gun. Laws ain't written with blood," Billy said.

"True, but sometimes it takes a little bit to enforce them. Give me the pistol and—"

"*Elias!*"

Rufus shouted with a timbre in his voice that didn't suit his normal tone. It sprang me into action. If I had followed my instinct, I would have squeezed the triggers and unloaded both barrels at Billy Gregdon, but that would have been an awfully unsolicited mess. I thought defensively. I skittered back away from Billy Gregdon. Just as I did so, I caught sight of Curtis Gregdon drawing one of his pistols. He had the hammer back before it had even left his holster. He aimed across himself at me, between his brother and Rufus.

He pulled the trigger.

I've done this a few times. You still startle, of course. You still flinch. And you react. You react because if you don't, that knife's got your guts, or that lead's got your cheek. Before the first swing or shot, you've already built up a catalogue in your head: where to go, where to aim, who to wax first. When you look at your surroundings, you unconsciously size them up and produce alternate routes to cover and safety. And when it's time, because whether or not you expect it, time'll come sooner or later, your body often moves before your brain, usually recognizing a threat before you even see it.

I pulled the shotgun around as I fell back and gave Curtis Gregdon the left barrel. There was a flash, a roar of flame, and I saw him stumble, clawing at his bloodied face.

"Son of a bitch," shouted Billy Gregdon. He had his revolver poised a second later. I dove for the well. A shot rang. Granite sprayed into the air as a bullet smacked right into a stone beside my head.

One.

"Rufus," I said. "Cover your ass!"

He went for the woodpile. He fired without looking, his thumb working his revolver's hammer between each shot. Dirt kicked into the air and splinters blew out from the side of the busted wagon as his stray shots flew off-course. Billy Gregdon didn't budge. He shifted his aim to Rufus and squeezed off another round.

Two.

"Stop firing, Gregdon," I said from behind the well. "This ain't any kind of solution—"

Another round gnawed through one of the well's wooden posts. *Three.*

I sucked down a breath and leaned out from around the well. Gregdon skittered back to the farmhouse, far more focused on me than Rufus, who blubbered and shouted from behind the woodpile.

I made a dash for the next line of cover – the wagon – about ten yards away. I loosed the right barrel of the shotgun as I ran. The spray hissed across the ground and threw up dust. Pellets slashed into the porch, but Gregdon didn't slow. I slid to a halt behind the wagon just as his fourth shot slammed into the ground where I'd been a moment before.

Four.

I heard the door of the farmhouse slam shut. I cracked the shotgun, kicked out the spent shells, and slid in two more. I drew the hammers back. Curtis Gregdon moaned from the middle of the yard, his boots kicking against the dirt. Not dead. A pang of sympathy rattled through me. "Rufus," I said.

"Yeah?"

"Stay out here. I'm going after Gregdon."

"What you want me to do?"

"Keep a bead on Curtis," I said. "If he somehow manages to go for his gun, finish the job."

Billy was luring me into unfamiliar territory, trying to slice away my confidence. While he might not have had many escapes from within the farmhouse, I wouldn't either, and he knew the place a hell of a lot better than I did. I choked down another breath, crawled to my feet, and then sprinted from behind the wagon, crossing the front yard of the farmhouse as fast as I could.

Billy shot twice – *five, six* – from one of the windows on the second floor. One of the rounds clapped into the peat right in front of me. Another one of them buzzed past my ear. I staggered in surprise and all but threw myself onto the porch and beneath the rotten overhang.

He had fired six shots. As long as my counting was right, he'd be reloading. I had only seen him with one revolver, and there was something about Rufus's gun – the other one that Billy had – that made me think it wasn't worth shit to fire in a gunfight. It was decorative, not likely a battle piece. Bragging rights.

I crashed in through the crumbling front door into a dusty foyer strewn with garbage. Under my feet, empty tobacco-wrappings rustled and broken bottles crunched. With the sunlight coming in through the doors, I noticed there were long, hand-drawn stains scribbled on the walls and floors with messy ink. Most of them looked like triangles. They were all very exact, some sharing lines of the others. They varied in size from ones as tiny as a coin to as large as a man's head. While there were many that seemed as if they'd been scrawled with painstaking, equilateral measurements, the occasional triangle had been hastily swept out of broad, arm-length strokes. There must have been hundreds of them, though counting to six bullets had already strained my brain enough as it was.

The Gregdon twins were budding artists, it seemed.

"Billy Gregdon," I shouted at the stairs, rounding them with the barrels of my shotgun before me. "Put down your weapon and accompany me to Blackpeak. We might be able to overlook the—"

"I'll kill your ass before that, Faust," he bellowed from upstairs.

I heard spent casings clatter to the floor.

Alright, then.

Time to make a move.

I pounded boots up the rickety stairs, praying with each step that my heel wouldn't just punch through the old wood and break my ankle in the process. I shouldered the shotgun and hugged the wall, biting my bottom lip so hard that I could taste the blood seeping into my mouth.

As I crested the top of the stairs and looked down the hall, Billy Gregdon stood as a black silhouette against a window. He was just snapping the shutter on his revolver, cocking it, and raising it as I appeared.

He aimed, grinned, and fired.

A whistling bullet sheared against the wall just to my right. He fanned the hammer for two more shots, but those bullets lanced off somewhere into the hall behind me. Fanning was a stage invention, a showy display more than an effective one. Keeping the trigger squeezed so that multiple shots required only the snap of the pistol's hammer was flashy. Hell on accuracy, too.

I didn't have time to admire my own luck before I remembered that he still had three more shots.

I squeezed off both barrels.

The reverberation of the blast shook the dust off the ceiling-beams. The flash sprayed light across the walls. I caught sight of Billy Gregdon falling to the side, his hand – suddenly red and shredded to ribbons – letting go of the sixgun.

Silence overtook the creaking farmhouse. I heard Billy Gregdon wheezing and cursing just inside of the room. I took the few available seconds to reload the shotgun and stepped into the shot-peppered room to find Billy huddled in the corner against the crumbled frame of an old rope bed. He clutched his bloodied right arm. The shotgun had pretty much ripped the limb off at the elbow. His face was splattered with blood. His pupils gaped.

"Hurts," he said. "*Hurts.*"

"I imagine so," I said, keeping the barrels trained on him. "Stand up, Gregdon." He did, using the wall for support. He left a long, red streak across it.

"You did my brother," he hissed.

"And I'll do the same to you. You hear me, Gregdon?"

He glanced at his ruined arm, then back at me.

"I've got a way about me," Billy said, sneering through his pain. "So does the world, Faust, and you ain't even realized it yet. If only you knew. If only you knew." His mangled arm was a saggy lump of candle-wax. By some will, he managed to lift his shredded hand up to his forehead, slow-like, so I didn't startle.

In his grip, he clutched a piece of folded paper. Then he touched his thumb just between his eyes, pressed his forefinger and middle-finger above them on his brow. Like there was an ache in his head he was going to pinch right out. He left three spots of blood on his sweaty skin.

Then the paper vanished like smoke.

Against my breast, a murmur of heat touched my skin. What had he done?

I poised the shotgun. "You shouldn't take what you know damn well isn't yours. Unholster the gun and give it to me, boy," I finally said. "Real easy."

Gregdon did just as I asked. Only, he did it a lot faster than I anticipated.

My body had started to settle down from all the excitement running through it, so when he yanked Rufus's gun out of its awkward holster, my reaction time had already slowed. I saw a flash and a flare of heat from the top of the pistol before its mouth erupted into a plume of black smoke and muffled flame.

He barely had time to raise it all the way before I fired. The shotgun kicked against my shoulder as a spear of agony pierced through my right leg. Billy Gregdon let out a choked wail. The shots took him in the chest and sent him staggering toward the window. He crumpled against it. The remaining glass shattered underneath his weight and he flopped out onto the overhang of the porch. Then he rolled and fell two stories.

The sound he made when he hit wasn't a pretty one.

I screamed against magma pain in my thigh and fell back against the nearest wall.

My pants were stained with sticky blood. Every time I moved my right leg or put weight on it, the muscles coiled with pain. I bared my teeth and clamped a palm around the wound. The blood kept coming, rushing with every new heartbeat.

Gregdon had dropped Rufus's pistol on the floor. It was an older flintlock, certainly not ideal in the kind of gunfight we'd been waging. He had used its one loaded shot on me at the last instant. I picked it up and examined the barrel, the striking mechanism, and the carvings wrought down its wooden frame. Bronze filigree ran along the wood in a net-like weave, and the black steel of the striker hadn't been touched by a single lick of rust.

"This flying Gregdon boy dead, or just unconscious?" Rufus shouted from outside.

"He making noise?"

"No."

"He moving?""

"No."

"Bet's on dead," I said.

I retrieved my shotgun, dragging my leg and a wide snail-trail of blood behind me. I used the wall to steady myself as I stumbled down the steps.

When I got outside, I saw Gregdon's corpse laying flat on the ground, his limbs twisted at unnatural angles. Blood coagulated in the dry dirt around him like little glass beads.

"Jesus Christ, Elias," said Rufus, rushing to me. "You alright?"

"What's it look like?"

"Like a gunshot," he said.

I stared at him. I held the flintlock out for him. Rufus suddenly stopped being interested in Gregdon's body and took the pistol from me.

With a frown twitching under his beard, he shook the black-powder pistol and said, "It's been shot."

"That's what happens with guns."

Rufus Oarsdale cradled the old weapon as if it was a precious bauble. Even sniffed the barrel. "Shot recently."

"That's what happens with gunfights."

He seemed to put two and two together, and while I doubt Rufus Oarsdale would have come up with anything remotely like four, he definitely understood that there was a correlation between the empty gun in his hands and the bleeding puncture in my thigh. He gave the weapon a kiss on the barrel, and then stuffed it down into the holster where he had been holding the revolver I gave him.

He grabbed up my hand like he was some child on a date. "We need to go back up to them horses. Back to Blackpeak. Can't tarry. Got to get you seen by the doctor."

With Oarsdale in front of me, I staggered up the hill. The sun had almost entirely vanished. The sky was a bonnet of black and blue fading into an orange glow near the horizon. Peaceful, really, if you didn't take into account the sulfurous smell of recently burned powder in the air. Behind us, Curtis Gregdon thrashed in the dirt. "Can't see," he moaned. "Can't fuckin' see!"

I'd send someone out to retrieve him once we returned to Blackpeak. Man who manages to survive a shotgun blast like that probably deserves to have a second chance. Doesn't mean he couldn't hurt a bit beforehand, though, just for good measure.

When we returned to the horses, Oarsdale helped me onto mine. Without any other words, the two of us rode toward Blackpeak by the stark moonlight.

I remembered the heat on my chest.

I found the folded bit of paper in the still-smoking pocket of my shirt just as we crossed into town limits. It was prim and proper, folded tight as a sergeant's bedsheet. Three fingerprints of Billy Gregdon's blood winked up at me from the parchment's corners.

4

WHEN DOCTOR LEVINWORTH ANSWERED HIS DOOR, HE DIDN'T LOOK pleased. "Marshal," said the doctor. But the fellow's eyes shot wide open when he looked down and saw the blood.

Rufus and I had gotten back to Blackpeak sometime after dark. With the exception of the Crooked Cocoon Saloon and the whorehouse, everything was shut down, including the office of Doctor William Levinworth. He had been upstairs, probably reading, probably drinking a gin or two before bed when we came knocking. Blood stops running for no man's busy schedule.

I'd been in that dark office ten times too many. While I'd been to Levinworth for all sorts of problems – all ones that hurt – I'd never been to him for a gunshot. Hell, I'd been to lots of doctors in lots of towns for everything from boils to a bad belly, but gunshots? I'd avoided those. The office was cold, clean, and littered with basins, various knives, clamps, and fabrics. I sat on a wooden table with leather straps on it for struggling feet, hands, and necks. There were stains on it, sunk dark and deep, all relics of frantic operations.

"You kill whoever it was who did this to you?" asked Levinworth as he soaked a few clean linens in a basin.

"You know the Gregdon boys?" I said.

"Regrettably."

"Billy Gregdon," I said. "Body's at the old Simpkin farm."

"It can stay there for awhile," said Levinworth, not hiding the disdain that came to his wrinkled face. He tied on a white apron around his nightshirt. He adjusted the wire spectacles on his nose, brought the lamp nearer to the table, and began to cut through the seams of my britches. The gunshot wound was clean-looking, at least. Pink skin puckered around a welling hole. I hissed as he lifted my leg, clamping my teeth down on my tongue to keep from cursing.

"Easy, Elias," said Rufus, who stood behind me, looking curiously at the procedure.

The doctor placed my leg on a pile of clean linens, folding back the tattered remnants of my pants so he could have easier access to the wound. He reached into another basin and stirred whatever was in it around with his free hand.

He ladled a helping of water and splashed it across the hole. Little pinpricks of pain blossomed inside my thigh.

Levinworth pressed hard at the skin around the little gurgling hole like he was trying to find something. The world spun, and nausea leaped around and around in my belly.

"Brandy, salt, cold water," he said as he mopped up the blood.

"What for?" I asked against gritted teeth. Doctors all do gunshots in different ways, none of them particularly comfortable.

"Distraction, mostly," he said. "Cleaning the wound, too. Maybe some numbing for the next part."

Rufus asked from over my shoulder, "The next part?"

"Removal of the bullet."

"It's still in there?" I said.

Levinworth shrugged. "There's only one hole, Marshal. There'd be two if it had gone anywhere else. The hole you have isn't too deep, either, because if it was, you probably would have been dead by now. Lots of things in a man's leg that can break open and bleed him out. Mister Oarsdale?"

"Yassir?"

"How are you in a barfight?"

"Got a lot of missing teeth."

"Good muscles?"

"Good for raising a drink," Rufus said.

"Ever put a bit on a horse?"

"'Course."

"Ever strangled a man?"

The old drunkard shook his head, but then his eyes got distant. "No man, but that Nabby Lawson, she said she likes it when—"

Levinworth shut him up by throwing him a dry towel. "Make like you know what you're doing, then."

Rufus held the towel for a few seconds and kneaded it as if he was trying to figure out exactly what the doctor was asking him to do with it. Then, victim of a sudden epiphany, Rufus Oarsdale flashed me an almost toothless smile. It was a little too wide and eager for me to take seriously.

"What the hell are you—"

No sooner were the words out of me than Rufus put his arms over me from behind and yanked the towel back against my mouth and teeth. I tried to mumble out a few curses in the process. He pulled me back against him, restraining me. Then metal clicked, and my thigh exploded with pain.

A thousand black and white spots danced in front of my eyes. While Rufus held me still, Doctor Levinworth – maybe with his fingers, maybe with a pair of forceps, I don't know – scoured the inside of the hole punched in my leg.

I squealed against the gag in my mouth, biting hard. If you think getting shot is painful, believe me, getting un-shot is a lot worse. It went right to the top on a list of experiences that I didn't plan on regularly repeating.

A second later, the spots in my eyes stopped swirling and Rufus loosened up on the gag. I yanked the thing out of my mouth while Levinworth pressed some cheesecloth against the wound. I waved him away and applied the pressure myself, leaning forward to take a few much-needed breaths. Sweat crept down my face, stung my eyes.

"Mary and Joseph, Elias," said Levinworth. "What did you go and get yourself shot with?" In the teeth of a pair of bloody tweezers, he turned a deformed ball back and forth. He dropped it down into a small bowl full of water with a muffled *plunk*. "Count your blessings, Marshal Faust. You could have lost the whole damned leg if that thing had hit bone. He was close, wasn't he?"

"Right in front of me, like from me to you."

"I suggest retiring that shotgun of yours and picking up some-thing a little more conducive to longer living. Maybe the piano," Levinworth suggested, wrapping my leg in a few layers of tight fabric.

Rufus leaned over the table to stare at the pink-colored water where the mangled bullet lay. Then, as if he were about to pick up a sweet, he flexed his fingers and whispered, "Come here, you little devil."

He picked up the bullet, which had become a lot less round since its firing, and examined it. He punched me playfully in the shoulder and gave out a thick laugh. "Faust, you're one slick hog, you know that? Tell me, how come you ain't got a hole the size of a wagon-trail all the way through you?"

I shrugged.

"How come you didn't lose your leg when this thing hit you? Flintlocks are strong. Brutal."

I shook my head.

Rufus brimmed with cheer. He hunkered down in front of me, thrust the bullet up so I could see it, and from behind it he whis-pered, "I was hopin' you'd get this thing back for me, Faust. I knew I could count on you. Didn't think you'd believe me if I told you what I was so worried about getting back, but goddamn if you didn't get it back for me anyway."

"The...bullet?"

"Ain't just any bullet," he shouted. "This is my *lucky* bullet."

I swiped my hand down my face.

"Them Gregdon boys knowed I had it packed and ready to go case I ever needed it," Rufus said. "My granpappy, when he was fightin' the Resolution, he kept this lucky bullet loaded and ready for such an occasion, but he ain't ever need it. He got killed quick-like, run through with a bayonet. Since then, it's been passed down in my family for whole generations. This here's an heirloom."

The muscles behind my knuckles began to tense. They tried to get me to make a fist. "What about your flintlock?"

"How much luck is a gun if it ain't got a bullet?" He opened a small pouch at his hip and dropped the ball into it, then pulled a flask out of his pocket and took a long draw. When he finished, he smacked his lips and raised the flask to me.

"To Elias Faust," he said. "Best damned marshal the town of Blackpeak could ask for."

He said nothing more as he clattered out the front door of Levinworth's office. He sidled off down the main drag of Blackpeak, going back to wherever Rufus Oarsdale goes to settle at night.

Rufus Oarsdale had played me like a fiddle all afternoon. All for his lucky bullet.

Levinworth went about his cleaning while I simmered on the table, not yet brave enough to give my leg a try. So I said, "A man's dead because Oarsdale wanted his bullet."

Levinworth was putting his tools away, speaking without looking at me. "Men die all the time. They die like dogs likely because they are dogs. This place breeds them left and right. While it might be you or another good man that pulls the trigger, Elias, it's they who do the job of weeding themselves out. Nothing for you to be ashamed of."

"All this over a piece of lead?"

"Rufus Oarsdale doesn't have much more to him than a few thin superstitions and some old lies he's turned into a family legacy." He took off his bloodied apron and hung it up on a hook on the wall. For a minute, I finally saw the age in the doctor: crow's feet behind his spectacles, a slight shake to his hands when they weren't occupied. From a decanter he poured two glasses. He gave one to me and then tapped his against it. I lit a cigarette and pocketed the burned match.

"I've been in Blackpeak all my life, Elias, well before you showed up. I've seen some strange things come and go. I knew the mines when they used to thrive. But things change. People like the Gregdon boys start trouble, and better men come along and remind the town that, while it isn't always pretty to do and it never really seems right, there's somebody who cares enough to keep it clean. Taking a bullet's worth that much, I imagine. Besides," Levinworth said, hiding a grin behind his glass, "I wouldn't be surprised if there was something to it. The bullet, I mean."

"What makes you say that?"

"No leg should have survived that."

"Boys don't know how to shoot old guns these days," I said, blowing smoke.

"Maybe," he said, though he didn't sound convinced. "Bottoms up, Marshal."

Levinworth was right. Billy Gregdon might be dead, but rules are rules. I stick by them. Somebody has to.

We drank. The gin tasted bitter, burned good, but went down nonetheless.

NOW

THINK SMALL ENOUGH AND YOU REALIZE A SHARP-ENOUGH NEEDLE DOESN'T really pierce the fabric. It just moves the tiny fibers aside, without trauma or struggle, and slides right through. Guess I don't know what I expect of the worms. Probably needles. Certainly not sledges or pick-axes. I clench my teeth until the nerves inside pulse like fidgety jackrabbits. The goddamn pain.

His blurry silhouette leans forward, curious. You could color me surprised he didn't just start poking at me like some bug. "There's still more," *he says.* "I can see it sloshing around inside you."

"You got any prettier way of putting it?" *I say against the pain. I breathe. My innards burn, scream, warn me,* Run, Faust, you dumb bastard. "You see what you want, why don't you just take it?"

But I can't run. Not here. He watches me with every eye, and follows me down into the hot sun of the Blackpeak in my memories.

"How do you open a good bottle of wine," *he asks,* "except very carefully?"

PART II

THE ONE-ARMED MAN

5

"Reckon they've had enough?" I asked.

"They're still standing, aren't they," she said.

"I didn't think you approved of duels to the death."

"Never," she said. "I just like watching white men beat the shit out of each other for the hell of it."

Miss Lachrimé Garland knew that people needed to blow off steam. She knew that if you kept it in long enough, it'd come out in a bad way. She knew that if you didn't fidget, fight, or fuck, you were liable to run through your life like a boil ready to burst. If there's something Miss Garland surely didn't want, it was for a whole town of plug-uglies to fire off like a bad bit of porridge all at once.

So she ran the weekly fights, and you could sign up to swing and bruise – or be bruised, if it so suited you.

And be damned if Blackpeak didn't love it.

She watched over it, arms crossed, a smile carved on her face. "It's a wonder you haven't tried your knuckles out yet, Faust," she told me as she watched two men swing at one another like oversized children in the bloody sand. "I think you might survive a round or two."

"Fists never treated me so good," I said.

She smiled. "You could get lucky. Who knows if you don't try."

"Plenty of people might like a chance."

"Plenty of people might never bother you again," Miss Garland said, "if they saw those fists do the talking."

Miss Garland's kingdom was a twelve-by-twelve sheet of land a few hundred yards outside the city limits where, every Wednesday afternoon, you could toss your name in the hat, make whatever bet you please, and go at someone until Miss Garland called it off. Town had to abide by my rules, but in this tiny province, she ruled. She glided along the outside of the packed dirt ring on bare brown feet, rattling her pocket-watch. The crowds parted for her. A fat purse bounced at her skirt-hip.

I stood by. That was all. I made sure no enterprising, whiskey-fueled up-and-comer tried to start more trouble than was sanctioned. Just a few rules in Miss Garland's Café:

No killing.

No grudges.

No guns. Except for mine, of course.

When the action in the middle of the ring began to wane – one of the big boys reeled back to spit out the blood pooling in his lower lip – Miss Garland thrust a fist into the air and snapped her fingers. "Keep going, boys. This fight won't end itself." So the two shirtless buffoons threw themselves at one another, and the men and women gathered around blew up with excitement. For a few minutes we all forgot about the sun. The sour stink of sweat brushed toward us on the tail-end of a wind.

"Here," Miss Garland said, turning to me as the relentless slapping of fists on cheeks drew every eye to the pit. "I know being here isn't an official duty of yours, but I insist."

A small bundle of bills rolled from her palm into mine.

"If most everyone in the town's out here," I said, "not much to oversee there."

"Good breather," she said. "You know what I heard? I heard the whiskey's drying up."

"Sloman been telling fibs again?"

"His shelves say as much."

"Crooked Cocoon Saloon's still selling it," I said.

"Crooked Cocoon's into making money. You don't have to be smart to make money today. You have to be smart to make money tomorrow."

"And you're smart," I said.

She watched as one of the men hit the other so hard that two of his teeth flew out of him.

"Damned right I'm smart," she said, wearing a grin as wide as a sunrise.

Under her order, a bunch of men dragged the unconscious loser from the ring while the winner scrubbed his knuckles off with a splash of beer. A little girl raked the sand. Her hem left sidewinder trails behind her. Money started changing hands again. Efficiency, efficiency.

Miss Garland was about to turn and say something to me when a large hand stuck itself out between two big shoulders and grabbed hold of her wrist.

My first reaction was to go for my gun, but instead I crammed my palm into the face of a burly fellow I'd never seen before.

"The hell you think you are," Miss Garland said.

I pushed him, freeing up enough space to reach around for my pistol.

"Hey," he said. "Hey, now."

"Let go of her," I said.

"Just trying to get her attention," he said.

"You want to let go of her," I said.

A pistol-hammer clicked near his belly. He understood.

Miss Garland drew her hand up to her chest and held it like a delicate flower. Likely she could have broken this mutton-chopped meatball all on her own. "You got something to say to me, boy," she said, "that requires you manhandling me?"

"I didn't want to let you pass by without talking to you, ma'am—" he said.

Miss Garland's eyes narrowed. "You call me Miss when you want to speak to me. I'm neither a wife nor a weathered crone. I belong to myself and myself alone."

"Christ. You all always so ready to rip a bloke's head off?" It took me then to realize he was speaking in a vaguely English accent. Or what I thought was an English accent. I'd never met somebody with that kind of tongue before. "Sorry," he said, pinching the brim of his road-dusted bowler. "Really, I am. I just arrived a few hours ago."

"You coming to audit the mayor?" I said.

"What?"

"You have that look to you."

"You some kind of bloody moron," he asked.

Miss Garland knew two angry boys when she saw them. She peeled me back like a bit of bread and squeezed her way between us. "No reason to start fires. You want to owe me a week's wages, Faust?"

"Not at all, Miss Garland."

"Then the only time you shoot a man in my Café is when I tell you to. And you," she said, jamming a finger against the broad fellow's collarbone. "You do not demand to speak to me. You wait your turn. You ask permission. I grant you the opportunity."

"She always like this?" he asked me.

"Lion's a lion. You accept her how she is, or she tears you apart."

The people around us started to realize that there was a bit of a commotion. With beer still on his forearms, the shirtless victor snapped his chin in the air and said, "That fellow pissing you off, Miss Garland?"

"He's just fine, Jolly," she said. "Isn't that right, Englishman? Aren't you fine."

He kept his lips clamped shut.

"Permission granted," Miss Garland said.

"I'm just fine," the Englishman said.

Good. We all got to be friends. Sure, I had a gun, but the whole town loved Miss Garland, and if anything disrupted her or her fine chaos, we'd all be held accountable. The man deflated instantly. His shoulders shrunk. He took off his bowler. "I'd like to fight," he said.

"Well, look at you, polite as shit," she said. She flapped her hand. "Look here, Mister—"

"M..." The lump in his throat bounced. "Grady. Grady Cicero."

"Look here, Mister Cicero. While this looks like a simple amusement on the outside, this is a machine: the bets were placed well before today, and the line-up already determined. I refuse to run an enterprise that is anything but my absolute best. You are an unknown quantity, and you've already offended me."

"I have money to bet," he said.

"For as much as I'd like to see an Englishman lose – and *would* I – I can't simply upend the day's roster to shove you in like an afterthought."

He exchanged weight between his feet. "I have quite a bit of money to bet."

"No," she said.

"Please," he said.

She drummed her fingers on her upper arms. "I've made my decision."

The crowd began to disperse.

You look close enough at a man, you can see the thoughts happen. They grow up fast, but unless you feed them with reason, they're bound to be lawless little shits. I witnessed his thoughts come to life, witnessed as he gave birth to *this* particular son-of-a-bitch—

With a rattle of a belt-buckle, Grady Cicero dropped his trousers right there in Miss Garland's Café. His pants and longjohns fell to the sand. He dangled in the breeze, his fists planted on his hips.

It only took one gasp and one surprised, "What the fuck," before everyone – including Jolly, who cracked his knuckles – had their eyes on Cicero like he was the center of the world. A bead of sweat dripped down from underneath his bowler. He thrust his hand in the air, clutching a wad of crumpled dollars. "I have four-hundred dollars. Four-hundred-and-twenty-two dollars, to be exact, right here in my palm. A sum that, if I win, gets redistributed to the whole town. To every one of you men and women right here," he swallowed. "Fair and square."

Miss Garland didn't like it when the rules weren't her own. Her fist tightened in a ball. "And if you lose?"

"Then it goes all to you, Miss. To be given to the winner, or whoever else you deem fit to receive it. I just want to fight."

Sometimes it's hard to not listen to a man with money in his hand. But it's especially hard to listen to a man with that much money *and* his pecker flapping in the wind. Miss Garland took the money and thumbed through it. Her lips darted through a series of additions. "Dollar's missing," she said.

Cicero said, "Bought some beans and a beer at the brothel this morning. Thought you wouldn't notice."

"You want me to chop off your dick?"

"No, ma'—...Miss. No, Miss Garland."

"You owe me a dollar," she said. "You good for it?"

The Englishman uncoiled like a wound-up spring. "Legal exchange?"

"Legal exchange. You can fight."

"Do I get a receipt?"

"Excuse me, boy?"

"You run a business. You run a legitimate business, so I should get a receipt."

I leaned in. "Would it please you if I shot him, Miss Garland?"

Four-hundred-and-twenty-one dollars was a lot of dollars. Miss Garland lifted her left arm and dug around inside the edge of her sleeve. From it she produced a sweat-browned handkerchief. She shook it out in front of his nose. Purple lilies had been stitched into it. She spit into it. She tucked it down into his jacket collar. "Jolly?"

"Yes, Miss Garland?"

"Break him," she said.

"My pleasure," he said.

So that was how I met Grady Cicero, who stumbled toward the packed dirt ring as he tugged his pants up to his waist. Nobody liked him, but they certainly liked the prospect of his money, so they cheered him on and they hoped their beloved Jolly wouldn't last a breath against this Englishman that had come out of the nothing like a wafting bit of smoke.

As they started to fight, I noticed a one-armed man nudge his way toward the edge of the pit. He didn't smile. He didn't cheer. He just watched, and I watched him. Live in Blackpeak long enough – hell, live anywhere long enough – and you recognize faces, even without names. This guy was a blind spot.

The Englishman had brought a friend along with him.

CICERO BARELY MANAGED to rid himself of his glasses before Jolly's fist busted the Englishman's nose like an overripe fruit. Cicero made a sound that I could only describe as "*Geckt*," while the crowd flinched as one. Cartilage popped. His knees trembled like wind-blown scaffolds, but he didn't relent. In the next instant, he surged up, threw a flurry of hard strikes into Jolly's abdomen, and blew the reigning champion back.

"You know there's word about you," Miss Garland said to me out of the corner of her mouth, "spreading like brushfire."

"Just part of the job," I said. "What kind of word?"

Jolly threw a right hook. Cicero bobbed underneath it and punctuated the sentence Jolly had begun with a sharp jab.

"That you did Billy Gregdon in when he was helpless."

"Do they want to see the hole? I'd be glad to show them the hole," I countered. "Who's talking that kind of lie?"

"No one person in particular. Sparrow-talk and shadow-talk never comes from a particular source. It just drifts in like a sand-storm. You don't hear it because you're the one it's about."

Jolly charged Cicero like a steam-engine. He scooped the Englishman up entirely off the ground, then threw him down into the dirt with an earth-shaking clatter. Jolly was quick, but Cicero proved quicker: he flicked a hand up and clapped it across Jolly's left ear.

"Sparrows say you blew Billy out a window," she said.

"He was standing next to it."

"Sparrows say you left Curtis Gregdon there to die something long and slow and painful."

The two men in the pit were starting to get dirty in the mud and the blood. Cicero preferred close, quick flurries, the kind of boxer who whittled down stone like long-running water. Jolly, however, was a shotgun: he loaded up powerful, heavy blasts, unleashed them, and left himself open.

Cicero was on Jolly. But the bigger man had the earth at his back. He bucked a heel against Cicero's belly and threw him off. As Cicero skidded to a halt, he scooped up a handful of sand and dashed it in Jolly's eyes. It sprayed across everyone downwind.

Miss Garland snapped, "No sand, you cheating shit," as the crowd gave out a pulse of confused excitement: cheating, bad; Cicero winning, good.

Cicero threw his hands in the air. "How the hell was I supposed to know? It's not like you said there were rules."

"I took you for a dandy, not a coward."

The two men danced around one another some more, trading careful blows that ranged from sharp and precise to swinging and desperate. I had to hand it to him: Grady Cicero was surprisingly light on his feet. He looked for the right openings and poured into them like beer into a cup, letting Jolly overswing to expose tender ribs or the side of his neck.

The only person who seemed none too pleased with the Englishman's progress was the fellow across the way. He donned a summer linen suit with only a hint of perspiration moistening the collar. His left arm was only half there, cut off perfectly at the elbow. So precise was the edge that you could have mistaken it for being folded behind him. The jacket was tied off in a bow just beneath. In the heat, his face looked more like clay than skin. I tapped my hat toward him. He tapped his. "You know him?" I asked Miss Garland.

"Never seen him in my life."

"Cicero's pal. He's wearing a gun."

"How do you know?"

"Doesn't everybody wear one," I said.

Miss Lachrimé Garland touched the thigh of her skirt, where a patchwork pocket refused to crumple under her touch. A just-in-case, I called it. A pocket special. "How presumptuous of you, Faust."

The fight progressed as fights do: with a hell of a lot of grunting and scuffling and two grown men scraping their boots on the ground and trying to press one another into the dirt.

So it was a bit of a surprise to me when, at an opportune moment, Cicero turned his back away from Jolly and fidgeted with his fingers. I saw a winking bit of brass glinting in the sunlight.

"Jolly," I shouted.

Cicero hauled around and threw a violent, all-or-nothing blow toward Jolly. The brass knuckles gleamed like a crown across the top of his fist. The Englishman made a show of it: a roar, a wide-open swing, the kind that could have murdered a man if it landed.

But it didn't.

Jolly slipped to the side and responded in kind. The heel of his palm landed in a thunderclap against the side of Cicero's jaw. I'd never seen a man turn into liquid before. His hands shot out one way. The rest of his body went in another direction entirely. A swath of mouth-blood cut a spattered arc across the knees of nearby spectators. The brass knuckles fell to the dirt.

He kept his footing though. At least for a minute. Long enough to spin around toward me, grab me by the lapel, and drag me close. Bile and blood swam on his breath.

"Help me," he whispered against my ear.

Suddenly, his striking English accent had entirely vanished.

"I need you to save my life."

He trickled down to the ground, limp in my arms, and collapsed into the sand.

The crowd fell silent.

Miss Garland, limiting the width of her smile within professional courtesy, clutched tight to her purse.

When I looked up, the one-armed man was gone.

6

WHOEVER IMAGINED THIS WAS THE PLACE TO BUILD A TOWN UP FROM nothing, right here in the midst of the Texas drylands, must have been drunk. Or worse. But Blackpeak had its charms. Mayor Kallum's dream had fizzled up and farted out, and what we had left was dirt, sweat, and sand. Blackpeak was easy to forget, and living in it, even easier to forget the rest of the world.

Thing I've noticed about Blackpeak, though, is when you want something, it provides. Of course I don't mean *things* – and believe-you-me, I've spent hours wishing – but *needs*. Can't help but give you what you need. That's the advantage of Blackpeak being the tiny hole in the bottom of this whole bucket of a world: everything drains this way. Wait long enough and your desires will just wash right by.

So instead of going after the one-armed curiosity, I refreshed my smokes and limped to the most popular place in town other than the Crooked Cocoon Saloon: the Horseshoe Junction Inn.

When Grady Cicero had called it a brothel, he'd taken his damn life in his hands. If its owner Aremeda De Santos had her druthers, it'd only ever be an *inn*, a reputable place where one could eat, rest, and just by pure coincidence, lay with a man or woman if the price happened to be met. The beds certainly were some of the best in

Blackpeak long as you didn't mind paying. As long as you didn't mind the noises.

From the Horseshoe's porch I saw the sky wash itself over with orange, then red, then darkness. Candles flicked to life in the windows along the main avenue. Inside the Horseshoe, girls in rustling dresses and ceramic pearls floated by the windows, their fans fluttering, their long cigarette-holders burning bright.

Wasn't too long after when the night lit up with activity down the street.

Doctor Levinworth's door flew open. A broad beam of light spilled out. The man in linens stomped out, kicked his boots with a furious sweep in the dirt, and then started down the street.

Right toward me. Hole in the bucket, like I said.

"Evening," I said as he marched up the stairs to the Horseshoe Junction Inn. This close, he carried the smell of woodsmoke and canvas-oil. A few specks of dried skin peppered his mustache. He gnawed an old bone toothpick.

"This the whorehouse?" he rasped.

"She won't like it you call it that," I said.

"Uh-huh. This where you pay for whores?"

"Yeah," I said. "I take it your friend wasn't awake after the ass-beating he got tossed earlier. It was a fine scuffle while it lasted. In Mr. Cicero's defense, Miss Garland didn't exactly identify the standards of the rules. Name's Elias Faust, town marshal."

I thrust out my right hand to him. He scrubbed his hand off on his lapel, then shook mine. "Keswick Everett."

"Fine night to meet you."

He withdrew his hand after we shook. Wiped it off again.

"Uh-huh," he said.

"Where'd you all come in from?"

That toothpick rattled around against his teeth. "Pickens County, Alabama." When he talked, he sucked in air through the gap in his front teeth. His eyes danced past me. "Been a long two weeks' ride, Sheriff Faust—"

"Marshal," I said. "Appointed."

"Uh-huh. Be that as it may, my bones are tired, and try as I might to have a meaningful conversation..."

"I take it I'm not the companionship you want." I reached down and opened the door for him. The murmur of voices and the cloying scent of sugary perfume and body odor filtered out into the world.

With my open invitation to all the wonders of the Horseshoe Junction Inn before him, the one-armed man drifted inside. But before the carnal promises could magnetize him too greatly, Everett turned in the doorway. "Faust. Elias Faust, is it?"

"Unless it's easier to be something else," I said.

"That lass, the one that runs the fights. Miss Garland? It occurs to me it might do me a bit of good to have a talk with her, if it pleases her. Would you happen to know the right way a fellow could do that?"

"You want to talk to Miss Garland, I can surely make sure she gets word. Keep in mind, Miss Garland ain't much of one to do anything she doesn't choose, so it's no guarantee. You understand," I said.

The toothpick stopped clicking. He smiled, his teeth the color of cork. "Uh-huh, I do, I do. Of course, being a man of keen ambition that also happens to be working within the confines of a very finite amount of time, I've got no mind to be held up by a woman's particulars. You know what they say about us Alabamians."

Frankly, I didn't give a rat's ass. "Sure don't," I said.

"We get whatever we pin our mind to."

"Uh-huh," I said.

His eyes fell. "You a gimp?" he said.

"Leg's in a state."

Then he went inside to get laid. Bit big for his britches, that one. He'd be out of them soon enough in the Horsehsoe, which at least gave me a little bit of time to reason my way through the handful of shit these two newcomers had already tossed on my plate. In the flickering porchlight, I lit another smoke. As I put my matches back into my pocket, I remembered the folded piece of paper I'd stuffed there, marked with three fingerprints of old, browning blood.

I unfolded it. I turned it back and forth, examined it, squinted at it, the way I did every night.

Then I crammed it in my breast pocket and hobbled off to Doctor Levinworth's abode, fighting off one hell of a bad mood.

7

WHEN I ASKED A RACCOON-EYED, BLOODY-MOUTHED GRADY CICERO why he and Keswick Everett had wandered their way into Blackpeak, at least he didn't lie. He was sucking on a glass of Levinworth's gin when he said, "I stole a lot of money from him," and shrugged his shoulders like *that's that*.

"What in the hell is the fascination with stealing people's shit around these parts," I asked, flicking my cigarette in an old bottle. "You know him, then, this Everett?"

"Well enough to know that keeping myself ahead of him is probably the most intelligent choice I can make."

"Did you intend to steal anything from him?"

"No," he said. "A hearty sum of his money just *happened* to appear in my satchel. Please tell me you weren't the only candidate for this position. Is he for real—" a thick finger flicked in my direction as Doctor Levinworth appeared in the doorway with a clean glass cupped in his palm. "Doc, is this *the* town marshal?"

"One and only," Levinworth said. "Evening, Elias."

"Well, he's about as sharp as a bell-end," Cicero said. "Yes, I intended it, and yes, I would do it again. And no, I have absolutely no regrets whatsoever for liberating an absolutely sinful amount of money from that human bit of foreskin."

Doctor Levinworth said, "Gin, Faust?"

"If you please. He been this ornery since he came?"

"Not so much. He was unconscious when they dragged him here."

"Small blessings," I said.

Cicero rolled his eyes behind the wire frames of his glasses. "Like you're a real wonder to behold."

I tapped my glass against Levinworth's and all but ignored Cicero, who sat on the examination table like a slouching child. The doctor had done him some tiny favors: stitched up a gash above his brow, lathered some ointment on his swollen face. Jolly's beating would fade with time, but the scars to pride? Those would linger. "Did Everett try to come in here?" I asked. "I saw him storm out earlier."

"I caught him at the door," Levinworth said. "I only let in who I want to let in."

"He did me that favor," Cicero admitted.

"You only get one of those, Cicero," I said. "Levinworth's ain't no hotel, and you have to pay the piper soon enough. Harboring thieves isn't a habit I pick up lightly. I don't plan to start it with you."

Levinworth finished up his gin, and without a word, he drifted back out of the room. It wasn't so much a kindness as it was professionalism: what he knew was about to go on was marshaling business, and though it might not have been as ugly as bullet-holes or busted boils, his discretion meant he wasn't responsible.

So Cicero and I sat quietly, drinking gin, because why have words when you can have gin.

When I realized he was content to just sit there and say nothing at all, I said, "You scared of him?"

He scraped a bandaged hand over his shorn skull.

"I need an answer," I said. "It comes down to my choice, Cicero: I can deal accordingly with a thief whose actions were both felonious and self-confessed. Or—" I emptied my gin and stood up to stand in front of him like a parent in front of a willful child, "—I can offer temporary asylum to a man who feels his life may be forfeit to someone with poor intentions. One's good for me, and the other's good for you."

The veil briefly fell. Cicero set down his glass and rubbed his palms down his face. "Keswick Everett has been on my heels for two states, nipping like a goddamn dog."

"How much did you take from him?"

His nostrils flared, big as two saucers. "Nearly nine hundred bucks. Don't look at me like that. That turd deserved it. He choked a whole damn village for protection money until they were just about starved and spent, and folks aren't known in his parts for their remarkable amount of brain capacity or frugality. First chance he gets, the minute everyone's back is turned, he'll put a bullet through my temple and not think twice about it. I'm not an easy fellow to scare, Marshal Faust, but that prick's an ice king. When I lodged at Crown Rock for a rest and got word he was on my tail, I came here. Forty miles. Two days. No sleep."

Grady Cicero's bare feet told no lie: outside of his boots, his gnarled toes and heels gleamed with a vineyard of broken blisters and stubbed-in toenails.

Desperate men don't stop to wrap their feet in moleskin.

Cicero told me what he deemed necessary: he'd followed the trade-routes from Crown Rock through the brushlands and over sun-dried hills until Blackpeak emerged on the horizon. Miss Garland's Café had proved the perfect temporary distraction, a busy snake's nest that Everett wouldn't dare to toss bullets into.

These were Grady Cicero's last slivers of hope this side of Mexico, weaving in and out of crowds and hiding himself behind circum-stance. Truth was, I could give him up. This was Pickens business. Private matters between two men. Outside my self-imposed juris-diction.

Squeezing the bridge of my nose didn't kill my throbbing headache. "You want this cleared up, we do this on my terms. The only way I can ensure your safety is to have you under my eye on a constant basis until Everett leaves."

"You going to make him leave?"

"I'll find ways," I said.

"Awful nice," he said.

"Balance, Cicero. Sometimes things are about right and wrong. Sometimes things are about balance. I'll cool off Everett as best I can, but the minute this is done, I'm sending a courier up to Crown Rock for a federal judge to sort this matter out. I can guarantee your life, but not necessarily your freedom."

It was a lot of money. We both knew that. I could harp on Cicero about thieving from a thief, but I wasn't paid this staggeringly handsome salary to moralize at immoral folk. To officialize our little agreement, I thrust out a hand to him. Shake was as good as words, after all.

A small span of hesitation didn't keep his beefy palm from clapping into mine. 'Course, he didn't expect me to pull him close enough so I could jamb a thumb down into the sutures on his brow.

"*Sss - hach!*" he barked. "Son of a bitch, you lunatic!" When he said it, all the Englishman faded away. All that was left was a hoarse, simpering American in his voice as he soothed the blossoming pain on his brow with a few brushes of his fingers. He spat, "You want to tell me next time you're planning on putting me in agony? I'm in a fragile state over here."

"Couldn't just pick you up by the ankles and shake the rest of the lies out of you, could I," I said.

I WROTE a small note to Miss Lachrimé Garland and asked a boy to deliver it. I escorted Cicero to the lone holding cell in my office, where he seemed at once both secure and perturbed. Then I went back to the Horseshoe Junction Inn. Aremeda De Santos said to me, "He's with Nabby Lawson," and escorted me like a special guest to a row of dark rooms up on the second floor.

Being nice gets you favors.

Being town marshal gets you everywhere.

I thumped my knuckles on the door and said, "Keswick Everett," but got no answer.

De Santos, who was thick and powerful and broad as an ox, removed a dull skeleton key from the cavernous split in her bodice. "Nabby's a handful for any man."

Hearing nothing, I knocked again. "Mr. Everett."

"Nabby might'a broke him in two."

"That'd solve my problems," I said under my breath, then took the key from her.

When I opened the door Keswick Everett's face was the most fetching shade of plum, and if he looked any more swollen, you'd have thought he'd pop like a bubble. A neckerchief in his mouth dripped with foaming saliva. A leather strap bit into the column of his neck so tight that I thought I could see his pulse throbbing underneath it. Behind him, half-dressed, stood Nabby Lawson, whose crooked teeth might as well have been the pieces of a jigsaw puzzle.

She loosened her grip on the strap. Keswick's tongue wagged out for air. He collapsed on the rumpled bed. "'Scuse me," she barked, and tapped the ash of a cigarette on Keswick's sweat-lathered back. "You got business, Marshal, or you just watchin'?"

His naked ass arching up like a newly-discovered land-mass, Keswick Everett peeled the wet kerchief from his lips and said, "Look who it is."

Nabby's nose wrinkled up. Perfect imitation of a raisin. "You watchin', Marshal?"

"Nope."

"Because if you're watchin', I damned well better get paid."

"Yes ma'am," I said. "Keswick?"

"Uh-huh."

"Tomorrow evening. Eight o'clock. Downstairs. All involved parties."

Nabby squeaked. "That include me?"

"Shut up," Keswick said.

I closed the door.

I held the key up between me and Aremeda De Santos, examined all its very tiny etchings and curves, and offered it back to her. "That," I warned her, "is the most dangerous object in the world."

"You asked," she said.

8

During the day, Lady De Santos's charming little whorehouse – excuse me, *dainty-room* – served all manners of fine teas and coffees and sweet cakes to any man or woman hankering for sugar and spice. Sometimes it was a two-fer: the same rustling lasses serving little platters of scones and tarts were the same ones that'd stick their fingers up your ass later that night for dessert.

Aremeda was only too happy to allow us her warmth, courtesy, and space for our business meeting. She busted out the silk tablecloth and lace doilies. Lit some fine candles. One of her girls offered us four glasses of cheap red wine, because as she put it, "Mr. Sloman's holding out on our shipment order, the fucker," and swirled away.

Grady Cicero, whose wrist was shackled to the leg of our table, said, "I'd quite like one of those apple things," before arching his head back to call out, "Miss, if you don't mind, I'd be obliged for one of those apple things."

When it came it clattered to his tiny plate like a rock.

"Thank God for teeth," he said.

Ignoring the curling wallpaper and the brown smears of old cigarette smoke on the plaster ceiling, the Horseshoe Junction's party-room was quite a sight. Queen Victoria herself, rumor held, had a visit once and had shit royal finery all over the walls and furniture: ornate upholstery covered the chairs, a hundred gold-trimmed candles sagged in their pewter holders, and decorative plates pocked the walls. A rainy Thursday night, and handfuls of Blackpeak's menfolk were in here, bow-tied and mostly washed, milling about and considering which ladies would lie to them about loving them for an hour or two. They drank coffee and wine, waiting patiently, pants all-abulge.

To my right, Miss Lachrimé Garland sat stiff in her chair. "I dislike being drawn into matters like this, Marshal. You know it," and then to Cicero, "and now you know it. And I won't forget it."

"I would have far preferred more amenable circumstances," Cicero said. "Be that as it may, it was a pleasure getting my ass beat by your resident muscle."

"I think he could have done a far better job."

Cicero tried to touch his brow. The table thumped. He sniffed through the swollen bridge of his nose. "You bring the money, Miss Garland?"

"*My* money. All four-hundred-and-twenty-one dollars of it."

"Consider it a date and I'll let you pay for my pastry." He knocked his sweetroll on the side of the table. "They got a name for this damn thing?"

"Fat Bastard," Miss Garland and I said in unison. Then she continued: "Hard on the outside and moist pretty much everywhere else."

Just then, both their eyes lifted up and someone kicked the back of my chair. That crowding stink of oil and a little bit of minty lather. Keswick Everett stood behind me and clapped my shoulder, giving it a hearty school-boy squeeze. I wasn't his point of attention; I was just his prop. "Cicero," he grunted.

For a long breath there was relative silence. Rain drummed outside the nearby window.

"Keswick," Cicero said.

Keswick knocked a knuckle on the empty side of the table to my left. "This seat reserved?"

Then he sat just the same. Weasel that he was, Keswick Everett had at least understood the unspoken rules of a fair parley. His linen jacket hung loose around him, completely unhindered. He'd left his gun-belt upstairs, a detail that Grady Cicero immediately noticed, because he had color again. "It's a good thing the tail between your legs didn't screw none with your sense of direction, Cicero. If you hadn't happened into the arms of your knight errant here, I'd have gotten you before long. That's luck, I 'spose. And you, Miss Garland. Looks like they let your kind handle all sorts of responsibility 'round here."

Miss Garland flashed a smile at him that could have burned him in his seat. "That mouth, darling, ought to catch itself before it runs too far amok. I'm an interested party now privy to business that, as of this morning, involves one of my fighters. You will speak to me, not down to me."

I cleared my throat. "Now that we're clear, you all drink your wine," which Cicero did, in two long gulps, "and let's take care of the business at hand. First thing's first: Keswick, my town, my rules."

"Uh-huh."

"Until such a time as I say otherwise, you won't throw hands or bullets in Grady Cicero's direction within Blackpeak's limits. We clear?"

"Enough."

"This is a talking establishment. No rowdiness, no loud voices, nothing but soft streams and babbling brooks from all of you."

"So happens this thief gets him a gun or two," Keswick said. "What's the rules on him coming for me?"

"You scared? What a compliment," Cicero said.

"As of last night, Grady Cicero's my prisoner. He's jailed under a charge to be later determined by a judge on account of a confession of thievery. I give you my personal guarantee that for the duration of your stay in my town, Cicero's no danger to you."

Keswick nodded. "So that mean I get my money?"

"Wasn't your goddamn money in the first place, Everett, and you know as much," came Cicero's response through teeth still stained with blood. "Those Pickens folks, you bled them for every cent in their pockets. By the time I passed through, that little town you lorded over couldn't piss without paying you a penny for the privilege."

Everett's rugged face crumpled like paper. "He held me at gunpoint in my home, stole money from me earned legally through my own private endeavors. Who's this prick think he is, fuckin' Robin Hood? I want what's owed to me."

Miss Garland took up her wine, letting the bell of the glass almost float on the edge of her pointed fingers. "As of yesterday afternoon, that money changed hands. It belongs to me, fairly won under the proposition of a social clause."

"The hell's that mean?"

"Texas law. Money won in the course of social and private bets remains the property of the bet's victor. You witnessed the exchange yourself." Miss Garland's voice drew a sharp line, her consonants icy. "You made no dispute, even as the self-proclaimed legal owner of the tender in question, thereby solidifying the legitimacy of the bet."

"You call me here to pull one over on me?"

"For not speaking up," she said, "you gave permission for Grady Cicero to bet that money."

"Won't put a dent in your pocket, Miss Business Lady, to give me back what belongs to me. Every cent of it."

"But I won't," she said.

"And why not?"

I drummed a fingertip on the side of my wine glass. "Because you don't possess any claim to that money other than your word, Everett. Just as fair it could be yours as it could be Cicero's over there. How much was originally taken?"

"Nearly a thousand bucks."

"Pickens business is Pickens business," I said. "I can only determine what I see happen here. Miss Garland, how much was the amount exchanged?"

"Four-hundred twenty-one dollars."

"Hardly sounds like a thousand," I reasoned. "I imagine you got some kind of proof of ownership of such a precipitous amount of money, Everett."

The mustache twitched. "Uh-huh. I got my word."

"So does Cicero."

Keswick leaned over the table and prodded a finger the color of a sun-dried tomato at me. "He had a fine time with that money, plea-surin' himself a wild streak from Alabama into Texas. You planning to take the word of this sharp-speaking vagabond over mine, Marshal Faust, you and I are going to hatch ourselves a bigger problem."

"He's got no need to take his word," came Miss Garland's response. "He's taking my word instead."

The murmuring in the parlor might obscured most tiny sounds like shuffling feet and rustling skirts, but when I heard the clock-work-like click of an iron hammer underneath the table, it wrenched me right back to the situation at hand.

I think before any of us, Miss Garland already had some sense of the stalemate hovering in the air over the table. The issue of who the money belonged to blew like dust into the air. It was stolen money. Lawless money. Anybody's money. Especially now that Miss Anybody had her hand half-crammed in a skirt-pocket, pointing her just-in-case at the crotch of one very displeased Keswick Everett.

The oil-lamps and candles were kind to Miss Garland: not a bead of sweat gleamed on her forehead. "When a man all but puts a half-grand in my pocket, you can be sure I won't give it up just to satisfy some sneering pig's sense of entitlement. Legal exchange, legal right." Her voice swept low, humming with steel. "That money you're aching for? It's now the property of Miss Lachrimé Garland, so if you want it, I suggest you move quickly and *surely* to kill the bitch, Mr. Everett, because at this range, she don't need to aim. She just needs to flinch."

Then, like a traveling magician, Cicero withdrew from the sleeve of his shackled wrist-cuff a wrinkled lady's kerchief, its lilies violet, stark, and royal. His subtle smile was too.

Whether they'd somehow conferred or just come together in the moment, I didn't know, but my hackles shot up against my collar and my guts went cold. "Miss Garland," I said.

"Not now, Marshal."

Breathe. "The last thing Lady De Santos wants in this place is a dead body and the stink of burnt powder and blood stuck to the plaster," I said. Nailed to Keswick Everett, her eyes never moved, never blinked.

"You'd really kill me for it," Keswick said.

"A woman has to take risks to rise up."

"I'll crush your windpipe," he said, "and be happy to do it."

"Don't," I said to him, and then to her: "Please."

But nobody was of a mind to listen. Because Everett tilted his head, said, "Uh-huh," and then lunged—

There's that kind of moment that rings through the air before a glass slides off the edge of a table, like a bell-toll echoing in your brain and body. Whole world floats. Time stops. Wakes up an instinct-deep warning that screams *move!* and you move, not because you want to, but because you have to, because there's no room in the world for the alternative.

Grady Cicero and I? I think we both felt the floor drop out from under us at the same time.

He reacted. So did I.

Keswick Everett's ass didn't get but a hair's width off the chair before I had his right wrist, and with his free hand, Cicero snared the dip of his blunted elbow.

We rocked him back into his chair.

The gun never fired.

The Horseshoe Junction Inn, surrounding our volatile little parley, maintained its perfume-scented ignorance. I heard a woman purr, "Hello, handsome," and heard a man go, "Urp," and scramble for his billfold. Business as usual.

Breathe.

"This," I said, "isn't how it goes. Whatever we do, it happens away from the public. Too many innocents in a place like this. None of this money is worth a single drop of their blood."

Keswick's tense forearm twisted like a screw under my grip. I didn't doubt Miss Garland would blow a divot in his abdomen. I didn't doubt he thought the same way. He licked his lips. "Then whose blood is it worth, Faust? Whose?"

Lady De Santos had some fine wine, though. It did the job. I drank it all at once. "Mine," I said.

———

WHEN HE HEARD MY PROPOSAL, Cicero's face scrunched and he racked his shackled wrist against the underside of the table. "You can't suggest that," he said. "You can't do that. You can't put a human being up as bloody collateral, man."

Truth was, I could do whatever I damn well pleased. Kallum wouldn't care.

You keep a town clean however you got to.

Keswick Everett, whose lone arm was crossed as if it still had its brother, leaned back in his chair to consider the offer. "Uh-huh. I could choose not to take it," he said.

"But it's a solution," I said.

"So is putting a bullet in the head of a horse you don't feel like riding anymore," Cicero tossed in. "This is a real comedy of cowshit if I've ever seen one."

Everett's fingers picked at his mustache. "The money's off the table, then, if this goes down?"

"You leave the money behind," Miss Garland agreed.

"We all come away with something," I reasoned.

The proposal I'd put forward was easy.

No killing.

No grudges.

No guns. Not even mine.

Miss Garland said, "You go until one submits. I call it for nothing. Either a man yields, or he doesn't. And what happens—"

"Happens," I said.

"I want assurance: I keep the sum regardless?" Miss Garland asked.

"Regardless," Keswick and I said simultaneously.

Excitement flickered in the Alabamian's eyes. He'd already made his decision. An unsure man doesn't buzz like a cloud before a thunderstorm. "You happen to win," he said, "you never see my face again. And if I happen to win—"

"You get Grady Cicero."

We shook. Skin of his palm was as greasy as the breast of a plucked chicken.

Cicero threw his unchained arm in the air. "Oh, good. Good and grand. Fucking remarkable. I'm so excited about this I could shit right where I'm sitting."

"Language," Aremeda De Santos snarled at him from across the room.

9

WE LEFT CICERO THERE WITH FOUR GLASSES OF WINE AND ONE SIMPLE command: look, don't touch.

Control was important to me. Couldn't keep your thumb on the heartbeat of a town without it. Sometimes being in control meant drawing a weapon. Sometimes it meant firing one. This time, it meant redressing a long line of wrongs by bartering with a man's life. Chances were that Keswick Everett would do some ghastly things to Grady Cicero in order to visit the displeasure of inconvenience back on him. Probably already had a real carnival planned. While I wasn't keen on putting a man's life up for auction, to be bought and sold with some fists, it afforded me what I'd lost in the Horseshoe Junction Inn: a stake in the situation. Turned it into my circumstance to gild or tarnish. Wrong or right, I'd shaved off all the unnecessary tangles.

Win or lose. That's what mattered.

The three of us strode through needles of pelting rain toward Miss Garland's Café. Blackpeak disappeared behind us. This far out in sheets of rain, you wouldn't know there was even a town at all. Water sloshed in my boots. Miss Garland guarded her face with the tongue of a slouch-cap. Even in a storm, a Texas moon still gleamed like a clean, silver platter behind the clouds. Enough eerie light to fight by.

Surrounded by round stones that jutted up out of the ground like teeth, Miss Garland's Café had become a circle of dark mud. Keswick stepped inside of it, bit down on his cuff, and drew it up to his elbow.

Perched on a stone like some great bird, Miss Garland said, "Clean and fair, gentlemen. And for God's sake, don't take the whole night."

Maybe I overestimated my assumption of the meaning of the word *fair,* because I started shrugging off my jacket when Keswick Everett's lone fist exploded against my jaw.

I sprawled into the mud. Blood flooded my mouth. A plug of foul-tasting snot leaped into the back of my throat.

Hell of a start.

Everett was on me without a moment's hesitation. Before I could gather my bearings in a spinning world, he had my hair in his fist. Rain spilled into my mouth. Apparently, only hoping you still had a fist was as good as still having one: he pummeled the rounded edge of his stump against my skull. Lights popped in my eyes.

"You surrendered that man's life to me, Marshal Faust. What kind of lawman do you think – *hrrk*—" I mule-kicked him from the ground, right in his gut. He was off me. I sucked in precious breath and leaped to my feet.

As he staggered back, I closed the space. I threw a left jab out toward his jaw, not so much to strike, but to distract. It worked. He flinched. My right came in like a wild battering ram.

Fast as a goddamn mountain-cat, he slid in, knocked that hand away, and drummed a tattoo of one-handed blows against my chin like the *tick-tick-tick* of a clock. Pain howled in my head. I fell. My ass struck something damp and hard.

"You forget how to walk, Faust?" he poked. "Is this how you marshal your town, by letting women dictate rules and deciding fates on the heels of fistfights?"

I pushed myself up. The world almost tumbled away again, but I held onto it. "It's a lifestyle," I reasoned, tasting metal. "It works."

"What you need are foundations," he said.

I spit in my palm. Rain washed red away.

"Is that what you called it," I said, "when you bled those folks dry for protection? Foundations? Something to build on?"

He came at me again, shooting through the rain like a bullet. I managed to sidestep him. I clapped a palm across his brow as he passed, sent him spinning. He was on his feet in an instant, shaking off his discomfort. I couldn't take a breath without him being all over me like an old blanket. His feet left prints in the mud as he came again, swiveling at the hips.

His knee darted up into my stomach.

His stump hammered down on the back of my neck and drove me to my knees.

"You don't know the first thing about me, Mister Faust," he said over me, so close that his body shielded the rainwater from my heaving back. "Just because they call you a lawman don't mean you keep it. You're a meaningless title. Pickens folk paid me for what I knew I could do, not what I just hoped I could."

My muscles refused to obey. You either have it or you don't. Everything from my brain to my bones was on fire.

He peeled my head back. The heel of his palm crashed across my forehead. "The money doesn't matter. Money can be made. With enough time, I'll squeeze the paper out of a man's purse and convince him every cent was worth it. Four hundred or a thousand, doesn't matter. Why make it back in Pickens when I could just pick up where I left off, right here in Blackpeak?"

His greasy palm captured my face. I thrashed, but he rolled me over and pressed my mouth and nostrils down into a half-inch pool of mud left behind in the print of a boot.

Then he kicked my ribs.

My mouth opened like a struggling fish's.

I inhaled lungfuls of filthy water. Silt scraped my teeth.

"Problem with you, Faust, is that you let these people run roughshod on you. Little towns like this, they need a figurehead. 'Cause believe-you-me, there are dangers out there that lurk in the shadows that want to eat them up or tear them into ribbons. A few bucks out their pocket means they stay alive, guaranteed."

Stars swam in my eyes. Fire swelled in my lungs. Keswick dug his knee one more time. My jaw hinged open. I could see the future printed on the imaginary papers flashing in my mind: *Blackpeak's Finest Found Drowned in a Boot-Print.* "They pay, and that means they're loyal and expect loyalty. When I walk back in that town tonight to tell your mayor that I'll be taking your spot, he'll smile and nod, because—"

He rammed my face into the mud.

Seconds ticked away in my head. I only had a few left...

Breathe.

"Because I imagine they never respected you to begin with."

Nerves began to scream, desperate and twitching.

Drowning like a fucking dog.

"Just because you can kill a man, Mister Faust," Everett said, "don't mean you have what it takes to make him regard you."

In my last few moments, I heard the muffled demand from Miss Garland to "Get off him," before his weight shifted and something cold, sharp, and all-too-familiar rested across the nape of my neck.

A boot-knife.

"You kill him," Miss Garland shouted, "I'll put a shot in you."

"Uh-huh," Everett said. "You so sure from that distance?"

"I got two rounds."

"Aim true," he said.

My hand jittered of its own accord. I fought back the swelling blackness...

Sand squelched under my hand.

An icy hardness greeted my fingertips.

"This wasn't part of the agreement," she said.

"Fair's relative," Everett said.

"Blood's a vulgar way to repaint a town in your image," Miss Garland said. "You come off him, I'll give it to you. Every cent of what I got and more. Money's not money if it can't buy a man's damned life for him."

The world reduced to a pinpoint.

Last chance. Last...chance...

I closed my hand around the stiff coldness I'd found in the mud.

I bucked my whole body up with a final desperate heave. Burning heat from the knife scraped across the nape of my neck, but terror ensured I felt none of it. Everett faltered. His weight shifted. So did mine.

The moment I scrambled free from the puddle, coughing out ribbons of saliva, I went for him, wielding my found treasure. Cicero's brass knuckles, half-caked in mud, crashed across the side of his face.

Shards of crumbled teeth like pieces of broken soap fell free from him. He tried to keep the knife leveled in my direction. "My town," I spat, barely managing even those two words.

I knew it wasn't my town. You couldn't lay claim to a whole lot of lives and buildings. In the moment, though, I was selfish and wild; I dared him try to steal it from me, like one rabid dog staking ownership of a bloodied hare from another. Wanted to come into my town, drown me in a half-inch of rainwater?

I went for him.

You don't get out of a knife-fight without getting cut. A man doesn't need particular talent with an edge to do much damage. Two gashes snipped across the forearm of my sleeve. The brass knuckles did their work: I hit him again, landing blows on his stomach until I snapped a fist out and cracked the relentless brass against the back of his only hand.

Bone snapped. Everett howled. The knife fell to the mud. His wrist hung loose as a washrag from his sleeve. He dropped.

I kicked the knife away. It vanished in the darkness.

I crammed the knuckles against the underside of his chin, ignoring the smarting ache in my own bones. "Tha'sh *innof*," he bleated. Whatever remained of his jaw sagged like a bag of crumbled ceramic in his chin.

"Yield," I said.

"Doan hi' me, doan—"

"Tell me you yield, man," I barked.

His broken, trembling hand lifted into the air.

"*Yealt*. I – I yealt."

Could have been easy to hit him again. Felt the urge, too, like a thunder under my skin. He breathed, watching me, waiting for me. An ill wind could have chucked my elbow right then and I'd be holding onto a dead man's lapel.

I let him go. He slumped, a half-filled scarecrow. I staggered over to Miss Garland, the old gunshot wound in my foreleg reawakened. I held out my hand.

She regarded me with a long stare, then nodded and placed her dark hand over mine.

The pocket pistol was friendly and warm and dry.

I returned to Everett and leveled it at his brow. "Don't have to kill a man," I said, "to make him regard you. Or your town. Or the rules you set down. I could give a shit less whether or not you regard me. You want your life, you'll get to those feet of yours, and you won't look back."

Like a poleless flag flapping against the wind, he stood. "My gun'sh. In town, it'sh—"

I glanced down at the gun. He saw too.

No more words.

So Keswick Everett turned his back to me, and with the remnants of his pride in more or less the same state as his lower jaw, he left Blackpeak. I didn't know whether or not his broken body could make it to Crown Rock.

Miss Garland took up my arm and took stock of the slices on my skin. "Shallow," she reasoned. "Some long nicks, but nothing we can't wrap. You're a knot loose, I hope you know. He could have had your throat, and he would have been right to have it. He had you from the beginning."

She slung her shoulder underneath my arm and gave me her help. As the moments passed by, exhaustion cycled its way into my body. I paused to retch muddy water outside the circle of stones. She tugged her hem away just in time. "You gonna give me back my gun?"

"Christ, you mind waiting until I'm whole to ask me?"

"Never gonna be a time when you're whole, Faust. You get it all out?"

"Nothing some whiskey won't fix."

We weren't a stone's throw away from her bloody Café when a noise cracked through the air like a distant peal of thunder. Both of us thought it was that, at first, rolling over the hills.

We turned.

Another. And another. Each accompanied by a flash.

Miss Garland and I watched in silence as, in the darkness several hundred yards away, Keswick Everett broke in half and fell to the earth.

10

WE SQUATTED DOWN IN THE MUD LIKE HUNKERING CHILDREN. "JESUS," Miss Garland said. "Faust, was that—"

A tonguelash of fire. Another report snarled out across the flatlands.

"Gunfire," I told her. "Stay low."

"Can they see us?"

I didn't know. The fiery afterimage still throbbed in my eyes.

With my heart punching against the inside of my chest, I scrambled out across the rain-beaten earth, half-crouched, half-sprinting, trying to remember where I'd seen Keswick teeter over. There was time for bleeding later. The hairs on my neck began to prickle through the blood. Tightness gnarled my stomach into knots.

Click.

The zipping-back of a pistol hammer.

I dropped flat.

Boom.

Another blast. This time the light illuminated the world in sickly yellow. In the flash Keswick Everett's body jerked and spasmed on the ground. Around him loomed three brooding figures. Each one of them was a smeared shadow, proportions all jagged and wrong.

Several sensations ripped through me at once:

First, an uneasy vibration behind my teeth, a rattling in the marrow of my bones.

Second, a coil of nausea in my gut, an instinct awakened that told me *stay back, get away.* Every crawling step, I could swear I was tearing my skin off invisible hooks desperate to get me to turn, forget it all, forget what was in front of me.

I slithered across the ground, leveling the pocket-pistol toward one of the faint figures. My mouth filled with the taste of rust and metal and gun-oil. A surge of revulsion rolled through me. My muscles went silent.

The monolithic shadow turned to look at me.

It extended a gangly arm from beneath the cuff of a torn, wind-mangled cloak.

Then it fired one more time. Everett stopped moving.

In the flash I saw the eyes, set like flawless gems in the divots above sagging cheeks. No pupils. No recognition. Just...coldness. Each of them a little ball of silver, mirroring the dark world. Staring through me. The others turned to regard me, too. Sitting there in the mud, I might as well have been naked, just a trembling gumdrop of fear.

I responded how I knew to, like a rat brushed into a corner with a bartender's broom. I took to my feet, leveled Miss Garland's little pistol, and—

"*No.*"

The voice shook through me with an earthquake's force. My fingers jerked open against my will. The pistol fell out. The nearest figure sucked in a wheezing breath. Like dry leather, its loose tongue rolled out. Then it exhaled.

A swirling blast of foul-stinking sand blew from its mouth across my face and cheeks and shoulders. It stuck in my eyes, stinging like broken glass. I raised my hands, expecting blows. I didn't know how long I'd last in this state against those figures, but I sure as hell didn't plan to go without clawing the hell out of them. Of course, that remarkable intent didn't account for the rapid rabbit-foot snare-drum corps trilling away inside my chest.

If my heart exploded, I wondered how long my brain would keep working.

I opened my eyes, expecting to die.

All that was left was Keswick Everett's corpse.

He lay in the stillness of death, his arm across his chest. One of his legs was bent up like a broken twig. A series of bloody holes gleamed on his shirt-chest. He clutched something tight in his palm, holding onto it with the same death-grip a Christian might hold their cross.

Around him, there were three pairs of boot-prints in a triangle, each one of them slowly filling with the run-off of his blood.

I squatted there, trying to silence the sudden rushing windmill of confusion dashing through my head. Amid my gasping breaths, I smelled smoke. I felt burning. I tore at my shirt until a button snapped free.

Billy Gregdon's finely-folded bit of paper smoked in my hand. Each one of his tiny fingerprints burned like a cigarette-ember until I smothered them with my thumb.

Breathe.

I don't know how long I swayed there over Keswick Everett's body, but when Miss Garland came to me, I smelled her rich perfume seconds before her shivering hand cupped my shoulder. "Faust," she said, though from the distance of her voice, I knew she was staring at the body.

"Did you see them?" I asked.

She picked up her pistol and shook off the mud. When she breathed so did I.

"I saw a man get shot. We should go," she said. "Ivanmore can handle this. You know he's discreet."

Ivanmore. Blackpeak's undertaker. A fellow who found himself flush with cash in a town where people like to keel over and die of boredom or because they said something wrong to the wrong set of guns. Ivanmore. Right. Rarely asked questions, rarely said much, just found proper spots for bodies that no mother and father cared to visit.

I stuffed Billy Gregdon's confounding paper into my back pocket. Then I stood. "We have a problem. I don't think I can trust Ivanmore with this, Lachrimé."

"Why not," she said. "He won't say anything. We should go, Elias. There's *badness* here, and if you don't feel it floating in the air and picking at your skin..."

I turned and showed her the object I'd pried out of Keswick Everett's stiffening fingers. "Oh," she said. "Oh, Christ."

Pristine. Well-polished. A pride piece.

A bronzed star affixed in a circle.

On it, engraved with an artisan's care:

Alabama
Northern District
U.S. Marshal

After we both stood there for some time basking in the weight of shadow and rain, wondering if maybe we didn't move that this whole problem would resolve itself, Miss Garland touched my elbow. "That's...not the only problem we've got," she said, before she shrunk away from me and Keswick Everett's steaming body. She looked small. Like if the world turned sideways, she'd fall right off the whole thing.

"Okay," I said steadily. "What's the other?"

"Did you see his eyes? Oh my God, Elias. Who plucked out his goddamn eyes?"

———

I KICKED Cicero's chair to wake him up. All at once he sprang to life like a wooden puppet. His eyes might as well have been two pissholes in snow. "*Shee*sus Christ," he whistled. "You look like ten pounds of shit in a five-pound bag. Took you long enough. I had a birthday while you were gone. Raised up a few kids. Got married, settled down." Sunlight crept in through one of the parlor's slatted windows and slashed across his face. "The hell time is it?"

"About eleven."

"I'm about overdue for a piss," he said. "And you for a bath and a shot, looks like."

I reached out my right hand, which I'd wrapped up to the elbow in cloth, and took up someone's long-abandoned, half-empty glass of wine. It stuck to the sides of the glass like silty molasses as I drained it. "You know you could have slipped that cuff off the leg, and hightailed."

"Sure could have. Sure should have."

My fingers left muddy prints on the glass. The wine hit my stomach like acid. "But you didn't."

"But I didn't."

Pressure-blisters smarting on my palms screamed like sin. I clenched my fists to silence them. "So. Everett," he began.

Had nothing to say on that front, though. So we just sat for a bit.

Truth was, we could bandy words back and forth all we wanted, but we'd just circle all around the things that either we needed to say or couldn't dare to utter. When Aremeda De Santos floated downstairs in a dressing gown to find two ugly men seated in her parlor, she boiled up some coffee and obliged us with unnecessary courtesy. "You two haven't much more than an hour. And Faust," she said, "you tracked mud in on my rug."

That one cell in my run-down office was enough for a bag of skin like Grady Cicero. Officially, story was that I kept him there so that a judge from a nearby district could process him accordingly. For trafficking illegal monies. And for public indecency, of course. But whenever it came time to minister to the paperwork, the words fled. I spent my time digging dirt out from under my fingertips. It never seemed to get any less.

Almost a week later I sat on one of the gray stones on the outskirts of Miss Garland's Café and watched as a ham-fisted Jolly got pounded so hard by a barrel-shaped girl named Peg Winters that a tooth came out his left nostril. I smoked cigarettes. The sun blared down on the back of my neck. Everett's knife hadn't but scraped the skin raw. A final and unexpected kindness.

"You ever done much fighting before," Miss Garland asked her new girl.

"Naw, nodda lot. Jes bet up my brodders awful. Fer fun."

"You got a good pair of fists on you, girl."

"Shaw do."

"You think you can perform that well a few more times today?"

"Shaw do."

"And if you do – Peg, is it?"

"Paiggy Winters, ma'am," Peg said.

"Word on horseback is that Crown Rock's got itself a fledgling strawfloor circuit up that way. I like you. You're solid. You're fast. You aren't afraid to scuffle with a fellow."

"Fellas is jes girls with dicks, ma'am."

Miss Garland wore a smile that could cut the world in two.

Peg Winters was something else. She shed a lot of blood. It covered up almost all the scuffs we'd left last week in the muddy center of the Café. Just like that, everything vanished. They drank their beer and they shouted and no one knew any the wiser. Black-peak's got a short memory. It has to. You live this far out on the outskirts of civilization, most goings-on aren't good. So people drink and they cause a ruckus and I suppose somewhere on that timeline they up and die, too, and that's that. All that for nothing.

I went into my pocket for a smoke. Paper crinkled.

I withdrew the folded piece of paper. The bloody fingerprints in their fine little triangle still bore flecks of ash. I blew them away.

Peggy Winters had just more or less turned a man inside out when the paper came to life in front of my eyes.

Black ink began to draw itself in long hooks and sweeping arcs along the note's center crease, right between the burns.

Look behind you, it read.

My shoulders tightened. I stopped breathing. In a gust of too-hot wind I ran suddenly cold.

It took me what felt like a lifetime to turn my head.

Flatlands stretched on for eternity. Mountains danced yonder and wriggled in lines of heat. A bird whisked by. Tiny illusions tried to trick my eyes. Every time I glimpsed what I took as a meaningful stir, it proved itself anything but: here, a rustle of long-scorched brush; there, the scamper of an animal darting out of the sun.

The ink rolled down the paper like water off canvas. New words bloomed to life on the page, each appearing in the casual scratching flicker-flack of an unseen hand.

This town will choke for what it did to my Billy.

Flicker.

Choke and burn.

Flicker.

And so will you, Elias Faust.

PART III

THE EYE

11

"POINDEXTER," I SAID TO THE FRENCHMAN BEHIND THE BAR. "I'D LIKE some of that stew and a biscuit with gravy if you don't mind."

He gave me a glare that ate right through me. He swabbed out glasses with a rag, slammed them down, then disappeared into the kitchen. I don't think he liked what I called him, but I couldn't pronounce his real name, so Poindexter it was.

I returned to the table where I sat with company. The Crooked Cocoon Saloon was barely active this early. The dust and stains in the wooden furniture stood out in the scouring sunlight like badly faded tattoos. Old booze and old blood look a lot alike. The place smelled of too much drink, too much sweat, and not enough washing. Regardless, it was the only place I could think of meeting for breakfast in Blackpeak. The only people in the place besides Poindexter, me, and my company was a lonesome fellow drinking coffee at the bar. He munched on a Fat Bastard. White powder snowed down to his lap.

"Biscuit and gravy on the way, Mrs. Fulton," I said as I took my seat. "Paul, you sure you don't want nothing?"

"Just fine, Elias," my friend Paul Fulton said from across the table.

"Thank you, Marshal," his wife said. "There's something about not needing to cook a breakfast in the morning that appeals to a lady."

Paul Fulton and his wife Eliza were a pretty cute pair, as cute as anybody could ask for in a roughshod place like Blackpeak. Paul was a thin as a ramrod, tan as a keg of ale, and wheat-field blond. Forty-five, give or take a few years. Eliza was a little younger, always smiling and talking about God and all the good He did. She toted her Bible and rosary everywhere, ready to sweep away every little bit of sin like dirt out the door. "Glad I could catch you for a quick meal," I said. "How's that new barn of yours coming along?"

"Quite nearly done," he said. "Foundation, roof, frame, and walls are all up. Now I'm just trying to get the stalls raised so we can start moving the horses in. If I had *help*..."

"'Whatsoever thy hand findeth to do, do it with thy might,'" recited Eliza. "The boys usually want to spend the day doing fun things."

"Them boys of yours need to learn the nature of hard work," said Paul.

"Boys will do what's in their blood," I said.

"Seems to be every time I catch you, Elias, you're on the mend. You look run ragged. You alright?"

Poindexter brought two platters, beef stew for me and a biscuit and gravy for the lady. "Best a body can be with Kallum in one ear and the rest of the town in the other. What you up here doing this early?" I asked Paul.

"Looking to talk to Mr. Sloman at the trade shop, see if he doesn't have a few plots of land open to sell near us. I'd like to expand our fields, give the horses we raise a little more of their own grazing area. It's picky living out in the drylands. Wanna plant crops, but my boys couldn't be caught dead helping."

His wife stabbed another chunk of biscuit off of her plate. "The three younger boys don't have a problem lending hands. It's Joshua, our oldest, that Paul's got his little rivalry with. It's just natural. As boys get older, they'll do as they desire—"

"Even if it means sleeping in the loft of the new barn, reading books by lamplight and getting intimate with nature. Whatever that means," Paul said.

"Still just a boy," said Eliza. "He's learning, sprouting his own leaves, reaching out his feelers for something special to him."

They talked about feelers and sprouting things, so I chose to get real interested in my stew. They raised good boys – even that Joshua they talked about – and knew how to keep a solid family together even in a godforsaken place like Blackpeak. They were horse farmers. They bred and sold them. Good stock, Fulton horses.

When I finished my stew, I wiped my mouth and stood, pushing the chair out from behind me. "Paul. Ma'am," I said. I tapped the edge of my hat.

Eliza said, "It's nice to see you again, Marshal. God bless you."

"And you too, Mrs. Fulton."

"Don't go pissing off any knives today, Elias," Paul said.

"You didn't bring me any coffee?" said the man behind the rusted bars as I entered the broom-closest I called an office.

"Do my hands look occupied?"

Grady Cicero reached his hands out between the bars and let them hang. Long strips of rusted paint flaked onto his sleeves. "Maybe you're holding out on me."

"More important things to do than bring you treats."

"If by important you mean smoking cigarettes, thumbing through yellow-backs, kicking your feet up, and polishing the old Yellowboy over there." He nodded to the lever-action Winchester rifle leaning against the wall near my desk.

"Need to care for a gun if you want it to work," I said.

"It's a gun, Marshal," said my prisoner, "not a trust fund."

Grady Cicero was going on two weeks under my watch. In his free time, he tried to keep himself in impeccable order: he polished his jacket buttons, and every other day, he shaped up his mutton chops like a damn topiary. He'd mostly straightened his spectacles after his run-in with Jolly. Despite his expensive, road-weary clothing, I'd long dodged my belief he was an accountant. When I'd booked him, I'd found a dog-eared Shakespeare collection and some crumbled cake-makeup in his left pocket.

In this place, only two kinds of men dress like Cicero did: men who don't know how to survive, or men who are trying too hard to do so. "You mind if I stretch my legs, Marshal?" he asked.

I grabbed up a match and one of my hand-rolled smokes from the desk drawer. Cicero's nicked-up pair of brass knuckles rattled around inside. I tossed a rusted key to him. He caught it in his palms between the bars. "Any word on when I can depart?" he asked.

"When I can get a Crown Rock judge to grace us with his presence."

"I've served plenty of time already. It was just a few hundred bucks, and I doubt your judge is going to make heads or tails of any of it by the time he trundles his ass on down here. People get shit stolen all the time," he said. "Make an exception."

"Principles, Cicero. Principles."

When he managed to unlock the cell with the key, he stepped out and tossed it on my desk. He sat across from me. He leaned back in the seat and the whole frame creaked beneath him. His face had mostly knit back together. Mostly. "You want to play a game of dominoes?" he asked me.

"Nope. Just want to smoke."

"Got some whiskey?"

"Nope."

"You ever going to give back those brass knuckles of mine?"

"Nope."

"That's thievery," he said.

I smiled at him through a plume of tobacco smoke.

"A man asks a question, he at least deserves a dignified response, especially when he's been stuffed in this rusty cesspit you call a cell for the past two weeks." He waved a hand at me. "Give me a smoke, Marshal Asshole."

I pushed my tin of rolled cigarettes and matches across the desk, from which – with an obvious amount of indignation – he took a smoke and lit up. I said, "You planning on staying here in Blackpeak, Cicero?"

"If you ask nicely and let me go."

I flicked my cigarette, tapping it at the air like I was teaching a grammar-school lesson. "I'm a champion of your preservation. If I let you out of here, I'd probably find your body in a trough soaking for the pigs. Rough types around here don't take kindly to seeing a man's bits flapping out in the air."

"Just my luck I happen to stumble into the asshole-nest and piss off the no-fun crew in the process." When he smoked he blew it out the side of his mouth like a steam-engine.

Cicero went through the pile of dime novels I kept by my desk and frowned at each one. "You have absolutely nothing of any literary merit in this bunch of smut." He tugged a thinner book out from the middle of the pile. He adopted his temporary Englishman's accent as he read the title. "*Mistress of the Plains* by Edward F. Puntney."

"It's a good one," I said. "It's got a farmer in it who befriends this runaway lass from a rich family, and they bond over sowing seeds while sowing a little bit of their—"

Three gunshots – *crack, crack, crack* – rattled in the air outside my office. I put a palm to one of the guns on my belt and leaned forward, as if at any moment expecting a hail of lead to pop through the walls like angry bees.

Another gunshot rang, sharp and fine, breaking the quiet morning. Then a voice.

"*Elias Faust!*"

Cicero frowned. "Sounds like you're cordially invited."

I took out one of my Colts and half-cocked the hammer so I could spin the cylinders. I checked to make sure I saw brass in each one. I started to hate the thought of my name being regarded in full. A clatter of bothersome thoughts I'd buried over the past week or two started to flare like embers in the back of my brain.

"You going to go check what's happening?" Cicero asked.

"Not yet."

"Could be people getting hurt," he said.

"Nobody shouting or crying."

That's the thing about gunshots: they have very fickle personalities. They're intimidating but captivating at the same time. If a gun's discharged into a crowd, then sure, people are going to scramble and scream because fear motivates. But if they're just being fired in the air for show, to get attention? People will come watch. Ineffectual bullets don't achieve much but to get innocent folk more damn interested.

"Elias Faust," the voice bellowed again. "We needs to have a talk, you and me."

I caught myself refusing to breathe.

Cicero raised an eyebrow over his glasses. "You're a popular man. You should go."

"You ever seen someone run *at* someone shooting a gun?"

"Just heroes or madmen," said Cicero.

"Both good candidates for being dead," I said.

Two more gunshots in rapid succession. That made six. I got to my feet.

"Only takes one bullet to kill a man," Cicero added, grinning from beneath his bushy mustache. "I imagine he's got more where those came from."

I grabbed my hat off of the table. "Cicero?"

"Yes, Marshal?"

"Get back in your goddamn cell," I told him as I headed for the door.

12

In front of Blackpeak's town hall, it looked like there was a party of suits and skirts and sooty suspenders. People filled the corners of the square like a big horseshoe, lingering in the shade on porches. I knew some of those faces. Picked them out from among the ones I didn't. Paul and Eliza shrunk behind a feed-cart, trying to watch and disappear all at once. Miss Garland, rarely far from events of note, had her arms crossed and stood beside her prized Peggy, who'd brought all her jowls to the gathering.

In the middle of the crowd, holding a dull revolver high in the air, there was a rider on an impatient horse. He sauntered the animal back and forth in the crowd, making circles. He shouted at the top of his voice when he saw me.

"Took you long enough, Faust," he said.

"Could you have picked a cooler day," I yelled back. Old boy wanted to make himself obnoxious, visible, apparent. He wasn't looking to kill me, because if he was, he would have pardoned the whole process, come to my office, and laid me out.

He donned ratty clothes and dirt-caked boots. One eye followed my every movement, but the other was hidden behind a leather patch and complimented by a splash of dirty bandages from his ear to his nose. A few raw, moist strips of red went uncovered just under his chin and along his throat. Tracks where skin used to be before it'd been shredded away.

"Problem?" I asked.

"Leg's looking good," he observed.

"Working," I said. "It healed up nicely, barely a scratch. But I imagine you don't know how that feels, Curtis."

I heard his teeth grind in his mouth. "You get paid for your sense of humor, Faust?"

"No. Just makes what little I'm paid that much easier to appreciate."

What remained of Curtis Gregdon's face resembled mashed pork and gravy. Staring at the mutilated face of one of my most recent mistakes turned the morning from fine to foul.

My stomach turned and twisted.

I remembered the paper.

My Billy.

Only one name.

I should have known. Goddamn loose ends. Goddamn sloppy work.

I said, "Good to see you dropping by, Curtis. Minus most of your face."

"If I wanted to hear snarky shit, Faust, I'd go to the funny-shows."

He broke open the top of his revolver like a shotgun – Smith & Wesson, probably – and emptied out six spent rounds. He proceeded to slip cartridges into each chamber from his belt. The horse tromped in a circle below him, widening his space. "What do you want," I said. "You're interrupting a perfectly peaceable morning."

"What do I want?" Gregdon asked me, closing the top-break. "I want you to know that I'm comin' for your ass, Faust. I'm comin' for you when you least expect it, and if you wake up with a bleeding hole in your head—" he tapped at my forehead with a finger, "—you can be damned sure the bullet belongs to me."

The barrel of his gun swept across the crowds. They surged back.

"Put the gun away, Curtis."

"And what are you going to do about it, Faust?"

"Depends on how soon you put the gun down."

He leaned off the horse and put the mouth of the gun right against my forehead. I felt a ripple of surprise rustle through the crowd, carrying them all back a step or two more. Town law was being held at gunpoint by a vengeful criminal; they had no reason not to take it seriously. When he lifted his thumb and drew back the hammer to cycle the newly-filled chambers, neither did I.

"You pull that trigger," I warned, trying to keep my voice steady, "you probably won't survive very long."

"You think these people give a damn about you, Faust?"

A battered, eyeless face snapped to mind.

Problem with you, Faust, is that you ain't established any system here. You let these people run roughshod on you.

I realized my muscles were tight. Even if I had wanted to go for one of my Colts, I would have never gotten it out of my holster. My mind entertained a series of stirring images involving my brain flopping around in the dirt like a suffocating fish. Afraid? Damned right I was afraid.

Curtis saw. Curtis knew. And like a wolf, Curtis leaned over me, his mossy teeth gleaming. "A reckoning is coming. Give you a chance to rethink what you did to my brother." He pushed the barrel against my head until I could feel the pressure growing in my skull. "I won't have a chance to see you like this again, so I wanted to take the time to do it now."

We locked stares. I saw a fire that wanted to burst out of him. Gregdon was doing his best to stay his hand.

"Who's telling you not to kill me, Gregdon?"

His lips tugged back like an animal's. "Billy didn't deserve to die."

"He could have cooperated. You could have cooperated."

"We ain't bitches."

"Really? Then who's filling your pockets?"

I put my hand on the revolver at my left hip. I wanted to stretch the boundaries, but not far enough to get a brand new hole. The tension danced in the air like the sparks over a hot bonfire. I stared. He stared.

He pulled his second gun and pressed it against the other side of my forehead.

"You pissed some people off good and well," whispered Curtis Gregdon. "They gonna give you a chance to make it right. Tonight."

"Where?"

"You'll get the message. Trust the ink. 'Hamstring their horses, and burn their chariots with fi—"

He didn't get through the sentence before the whip-sharp blast of a gunshot interrupted him.

My hat went flying off of my head as Gregdon's pistols discharged wildly not two inches from my ears. I didn't hear their shots as much as feel them, as if they'd crushed my head in invisible hands. All the sound in the world got sucked away. My legs went weak and shaky.

The crowd rushed away, sinking into the alleys and disappearing into buildings. One of Gregdon's pistols fell to the ground. His hand was clamped against his left ear, trying to catch the blood spilling out of the black hole where skin used to be. He swayed in the saddle. Red droplets splattered to the dusty ground like beads from a broken necklace.

Somebody had shot him.

The commotion scared up Gregdon's horse. Though I couldn't hear the hooves, I felt them beating against the ground as the beast whirled around. Gregdon steered it down one of the streets, almost sagging off the saddle. In a scattering spray of dirt—

(Dirt? Or sand? Black figures. And sand, like that storm of breath...)

—he managed to control the horse enough to rush off into the distance.

When Gregdon vanished, I turned toward the source of the shot. Grady Cicero stood on the porch of my office, his cheek pressed up against the butt of the old Winchester, its barrel still smoking.

Note to self: Don't leave prisoners unattended near powerful weaponry.

I leaned over and picked up the Smith & Wesson that Gregdon

had dropped and tried to ignore the bloody tangle of skin that lay next to it, which was all that was left of Curtis Gregdon's ear. Paul Fulton came bursting out of the thinning crowds and over to me, barely reaching me by the time I stumbled against him. Time and sensation came disjointed.

That intense surge of nausea revisited me. Sprang up out of nowhere. Flooded over me like a storm.

What I felt rising in me, I realized too late, was panic, springing up from a tiny pocket beneath my heart. Were these sounds – the gurgle of rushing blood in my ears, the *da-dum, da-dum* of my frantic heartbeat – just illusions? Or was I deaf?

Balance failed me. Then Cicero was there, all but wrangling me like a cow. He dragged me into my office and slapped me down in my chair. I caught a glimpse of Miss Garland standing in the doorway, her face holding to some secret like an iron trap. The world spun, the orchestra inside my ears still howling.

Can you hear me, I said, feeling the vibrato of the words in my chest.

I pulled my hands away from my ears, examining my palms. No blood.

Stitching words together, I said, *Will one of you find Curtis fuckin' Gregdon and tie his ass to a pole...*

Paul's lips clapped and flapped about something or other next to my face, so close his spittle hit my cheeks. I turned away.

About that time, my eyes danced past one of the windows of my office, where a perfect avenue of sight cut between the rooftops of Blackpeak's squat skyline toward a hillock beyond. A flashing wink of silvered mirror caught my eye. I saw them: shadows on horseback, some regular, and others misshapen, looking like robed scarecrows...

A fistful of imaginary sand clogged my mouth.

A whole roomful of hands pinned me down into a chair. I clamped my eyes shut.

I owe you, I told Cicero.

13

THE MOMENT THE GAGGLE OF FOLK IN MY OFFICE REALIZED I HADN'T actually been shot, they crept out one by one to tend to their own needs. Or to drink.

Soon the muffled noises of the office around me began to introduce themselves again, from the creaking moan of the wood to the rattle of an occasional wind against the window's frame. I nursed a pounding headache, the kind that felt like it was trying to punch its way out of my skull from inside. The light of the day was more fierce than before. When I stood, the world tilted around me, off-kilter.

I looked outside. Up on the hill beyond town.

No lingering shadows. Just blots in my memory.

"He stirs," said Cicero from the cell, laying along the cramped bunk. "How are you feeling, Faust?"

"Like someone ran a herd into my mouth and out my ass," I said.

"He hears," Cicero proclaimed.

"Fortunate for you. Would have held you liable."

He frowned. "Where's my damn compliment?"

"You've got a good eye. Or did you aim for his head?"

"Figured you'd want to do the honors yourself one day. I just grazed him."

"You could have hit one of those townspeople."

"But I didn't," he said, bearing the grin of a proud child.

"How thoughtful."

"Just doing your job," he said. He slid the keys across the floor and out of the cell. They clicked to a rest against my boot. "That fellow seemed particularly interested in you. What'd you do to him, Marshal?"

"Killed his brother."

Cicero's face crunched up.

"He shot at me first," I added. "Bullets just get personal."

I sat back down, hoping to ease the wardrums trilling behind my eyes. I picked up the gun Gregdon had dropped. I stared at it, rocking back and forth in my swiveling seat. It was a Schofield, a thick-bodied revolver with a pin-hinge just past the guard of the trigger that could drop the cylinders open for quick loading. "Nice gun," I said, and crammed a thumb-knuckle against my ear.

"Not good enough to kill you," Cicero said.

"He didn't plan to." I worked and worked my jaw, trying to free that nutshell of hollow noiselessness out of my brain.

I dragged my tongue against the front of my teeth. Fucking sand.

Through the widow the fading sunlight burned my eyes.

"You good?" he asked me, voice soft.

Oh my God, Elias. Who plucked out his—

"Yeah," I said. "Yeah."

"So then maybe you can explain who I saw off in the hills beyond the town hall, looking like a goddamn Greek chorus when this all transpired. I thought about throwing them a warning shot, but I wasn't going to make a mistake on presumption alone."

So he'd seen them too.

Gregdon had friends that didn't take kindly to rules. Take away most every other desire, vengeance proved to be a mighty powerful motivator. Opium for the heart of the ill-at-ease. It'd ushered Keswick Everett a few hundred miles in pursuit of a purse of cash, had driven Curtis to launch himself like a cannonball into the middle of a town he knew I was in.

Good afternoon for a glass of whiskey. I took an old bottle out of my desk. When Cicero saw it, he lost interest in his paperback.

"Liar," he said.

Night fell. Eventually I started to hear the tinny music from the piano at The Crooked Cocoon warbling its way down the street. *You'll get the message*, Curtis had said. Thanks to him, I kept a Colt in my lap and my senses sharp.

"You're starting to look more like an owl than a sick turkey," Cicero said.

But nothing happened. Whole town seemed to forget the afternoon. No flickers of movement in the night.

I was out on the porch thumbing a cigarette out of my shirt-pocket when a familiar piece of paper crumbled at my fingertips.

Which is when I realized—

Trust the ink.

Frantically, I opened it, flattening it against a railing so I could see it in the lantern-light. Sure enough, there it was: a new series of slices and slashes in black, reading *11:6*.

Over my shoulder, Cicero whistled. "Alright, come clean: which is your bank balance and which is your age?"

But my brain was already winding through wordless paths and possibilities. First, a sinking sensation. I'd been too late. Then a furious, gut-wrenching anger. Stupid tricks. Stupid wit. Stupid smart people, playing subtle games. I hated being rocked back on my heels, shoved into corners.

I flew inside. Seconds later, I shoved the Winchester against Cicero's chest. He cradled it like a baby. "You're coming with me," I said, and dangled the Schofield on a finger for him.

"Hello, Yellowboy, old friend," he said to the gun, before squaring his stare on me. "I thought you said you owe *me*."

"I hope you enjoyed your whiskey."

"Is this conscription?" Cicero slipped the Schofield uncomfortably into his left pocket — I had no holsters for it — and opened the Yellowboy's loading shaft, sliding a handful of .44s down into its tube magazine. When he was done, he racked the repeater and placed it over his shoulder. "You're going to owe me more than just some damn whiskey."

"A nice gravestone, then."

I stepped out of Blackpeak with Cicero on my heels and my shotgun at my side. I focused on the horizon, walking fast but not fast enough. At night the lands were faded monochrome. The grasses and dirt shone almost white, but the distant mountains were scribbled with charcoal. I looked out for shadows within those shadows, expecting at any moment that they might come alive.

"Why aren't we riding?"

"Reasons," I said.

"Which ones?"

"Tell you when we get there."

"Why then? Why not now?"

As the ground crunched beneath my boots, I imagined I was walking on ashes. "Because I don't want to be wrong when we get there."

14

As much of Blackpeak lived outside of it as lived within. Those with the money and wherewithal owned land in valleys where sunlight dared to turn the dry hind-quarters of Texas into something lush and viable. Blackpeak was, on the best day, just a spoke in the center of a wheel, an anchor of life and business. A means for whiskey and feed.

We walked for ten more minutes in silence. By that point, the moon was a silver pendant in the sky.

Even though the Fulton home wasn't a decrepit husk of wood and wallpaper like the Simpkin farm had been, a certain familiarity started crawling along the hairs on the back of my neck. Another farmhouse, another inopportune circumstance. Paul Fulton had built their wooden home with months of his very own sweat and industry. It was a squat home amidst a number of fenced-in fields where horses milled about as dark lumps against the backdrop of the night.

In the moonlit lawn out in front of the Fulton residence were five shadows, two on horses, each with a rifle, and three others milling about on foot. Huddled at their feet was the family. Paul Fulton sat with three small boys leaning against him. Eliza Fulton had her head bowed, no doubt snapping out a constant litany of silent prayers.

I closed my eyes and listened to my stomach.

No wave of nausea. No twisting.

I crouched down behind a dry bush. "Keep your head down," I whispered.

"This is a hell of a first date," he said.

"You sure look nice," I said. "I was right."

"Right about what?"

"11:6. Chapter and verse. There's some damn Bible school still left in this old boy."

"Or maybe it's the corporal punishment."

"See that barn over the way?" I nudged my shotgun toward the towering wooden building just beside a wide, gated field to the left of the home. Stacks of squared hay leaned against its side. It rose up high, its roof a hard spine of angled slate. "Paul and Eliza Fulton's barn. My friends, Cicero. They're starting shit with my friends."

"I don't see Gregdon. Probably nursing his ear," Cicero answered, flashing me a grin in the moonlight. "Let's do this thing, Faust. What do you have in mind?"

As I ignored the nervous rush of my heart behind my ribs, I explained to Cicero the plan I percolated. It was no strategic brilliance, but it'd do in a pinch, and this was indeed a pinch. I scampered back the way we had come, wanting to backtrack away from the bush. I circled around a few hundred yards and came toward the house more from the east.

I think I took the group by surprise, because I was only about thirty feet away from them when I flicked a match with my thumb and flared up a cigarette. The horsemen and footmen all turned. Guns clicked and cocked. I felt sights on me, a cold rush of fear that came only with leveled steel and the promise of gunpowder. I adjusted the shotgun draped over my arm. "Evening, gentlemen."

One of the men on foot – he had an old Army cap-and-ball revolver – took a step forward. "You Elias Faust?"

"If I'm not, can I go home?"

"Don't be a smartass," he said. "You got the message?"

"Sure did," I said.

They all wore dark clothes. Dark hats, dark pants, dark scowls, as if they were part of an exclusive club. The one with the old revolver aimed from the hip had a thick, graying beard. "You made a bad choice, Elias Faust. Heard you're the one killed Billy Gregdon."

"Killed and dropped him," I clarified.

One of the horsemen let out a little giggle. "He's trying to soften you, Partridge."

"He don't scare me," Partridge said over his shoulder, still watching me.

"Not trying to scare you," I said. "Just reliving past accomplishments."

"Well, Billy's why we're here." Partridge turned around and motioned to the Fulton family. Paul looked at me, begging me to help. Eliza never looked up. Partridge reached over and grabbed her by her red hair, wrenching her against him.

"Let her go," shouted Paul. The nearest horsemen jabbed a rifle into his collar. Eliza's fingers kept dancing over the rosary. Her eyes squeezed shut. She prayed louder.

The horseman said, "You gonna fuck her, Partridge?"

"Maybe," he said.

"I'll find you and tear your guts out," snarled Paul from the ground. Though his gentle hands were comforting vices around his children, I saw fury in him, ready to be unleashed. "You do anything to my wife and I swear to God, I'll hunt you down and—"

"Knox?" said Partridge. "If you'd please."

The horseman named Knox promptly spun the rifle and bashed the butt of it down into the top of Paul Fulton's head. Fulton dropped. One of the children wailed.

"Knox?" Partridge said. "You mind if I fuck the farmer's wife?"

The rifle pointed back to me. Knox said, "Not at all, darlin'. You plug who you want to, just as long as you do me when you're done."

I urged every muscle into silence, kept myself reserved in the face of my friends being rounded up like cattle. When Partridge spoke, the barrel of his cap-and-ball revolver swayed in the air. "Gregdon clan's a lot larger than you assume, Elias Faust. You killed one of our

brothers, and we don't take kindly to that. You mangled Curtis something awful. We don't approve of that neither. Some are born Gregdons, while others—" he motioned to Knox, to himself "—are just
accepted in through other means."

"Big family you got."

"It'll get bigger. The Magnate will see to that in his own way.
We're always growing. It's just what we do. The Gregdon family
understands that you're just doing what you think is right, Faust, so
that's why we want to give you a chance to actually do something
right. You disarm yourself, give us your guns, and we'll let the pretty
thing here go free—" he shook Eliza, who cradled herself, "—along
with the rest of her family."

"That's all you want? My guns?"

"And for you to come with us. Boss wants to see you."

"The boss?"

"Magnate Gregdon. You killed his son," Partridge said. "Least you
can do is come speak to the man."

Knox said from above me, "Hey, Part?"

"Yeah?"

"He got something in his hand."

Partridge's stare felt like oil on my skin. "Give it to her, Faust."

"Gimme," she said. I slapped the tin into her gloved palm. She
opened it carefully and then let out a quick laugh. "Smokes. Our
marshal comes with a gift."

Knox took a rolled cigarette from the bunch along with a match.
Partridge pushed Eliza harshly down to the ground and then caught
the tin as Knox threw it. He proceeded to pass it around to his friends,
who all happily took a free cigarette. Matches flared. Knox let out a
choked cough and all of the other gunmen snorted or chuckled.
"Shut the hell up," she snarled.

"Good smokes," Partridge said, savoring his, the pistol still
pointed at me.

"I have good taste."

Just about then, the cigarette that had been dangling from my mouth finally died out. With a careful, obvious motion, I took it out and flicked it, showing no threat.

"Drop the guns," said Partridge from behind a twisting serpent of smoke. "Shotgun first. Belt second. I don't want to take you off to the Magnate with you thinking you can blast your way out of the conversation. Kill a man's son, no matter what for, no matter the reason why, you owe him a visit."

"And you're the welcoming party?"

"I wouldn't call us welcoming. We're your escorts to be sure you don't try anything we don't approve of."

I did as he asked. I laid the loaded coach-gun on the hard ground and then unbuckled my Colts. I reckon this Partridge was right. You take the life of a man's boy, whatever the reason, he's probably earned a chance for you to tell him straight. Courtesies and all. Of course, it wasn't until this moment that I'd thought of the Gregdon Twins as anything but motherless swindlers in the first place. Pretty bad when you begin forgetting that everybody's subject to certain biological truths – like being someone's child – no matter how heinous they are.

There's another biological truth, too.

Without excitement or grandeur, I clapped. Twice.

I saw the damage before I heard the noise.

Knox was taking in another mouthful of smoke when she jerked in the saddle. The thunder of a distant rifle shot drew the attention of all of the gunmen away from me.

The bullet took her in the throat just under the hand she raised to finger her cigarette. Warm blood splashed on my cheek. Knox gargled around a mouthful of liquid. Curls of half-inhaled smoke wisped out of the hole in the front of her neck. She slid off of her horse and crumpled lifelessly to the ground.

"He's got a gunman," Partridge yelled. He fired at me. His pistol bucked and a flash lit up everything around us.

The sudden pressure of the report throbbed in my eyeballs. A round whistled off just over my shoulder. I dropped to the ground, ripping both of my Colts out of their holsters and firing simultaneously. I wasn't as interested in Partridge as I was his goons, so the first shot was meant for one of the footmen behind him, and I guess it hit. I heard a yelp of pain and the shadow began to stagger, trying to find cover.

Another greeting from Cicero's rifle. Just as the other horseman tried to rear his horse away, his head whipped backwards hard enough to cause something to snap under his skin. Burning sparks from his cigarette sprayed across the ground. Both of the horses ran in separate directions, spooked by the noise.

They had taken the bait. With the cigarettes, Cicero had an easy time aiming for faces in the dark.

Partridge was only two or three yards away, but the children, Paul, and Eliza were so near that I didn't want to risk further gunfire. Just as he was about to shoot again, I threw myself forward and slammed a shoulder into his chest, knocking his revolver into the air. I heard the breath whisk out of him.

We landed in a heap on the brittle grass. With his suddenly unoccupied hand, he punched me across the jaw. He shouted, "Harman, you know what to do. Light the goddamned place up." With the riflemen dead and one other goon wounded, the only still-mobile member of the Gregdon crew sprinted for the barn, leaping sloppily over the wooden fence.

I laid into Partridge, bashing my fist across the side of his head. He hammered one into my kidneys, but I kept trying to crush his head into the dirt. He started laughing.

"This is just like you, Faust."

I hit him in the nose. It crushed under my knuckles. Blood ran fresh.

In the corner of my eye, Eliza was trying to usher her children away. Partridge reached for one of my Colts, but before his fingers could touch it, I smashed them under an elbow.

He let out a cry of pain. He thrust up and threw me off of him, managing to roll me over just enough so he could stagger to his feet. Instead of going for a gun, he slammed a foot into my ribs and blew the air out of me. Then the side of his boot caught me in the teeth. Stars exploded in my eyes.

My mouth closed on something hard. A tooth. I spit it out with a mouthful of blood.

"Killed plenty of lawmen in my time, Faust."

He balled his fist up and punched me in the left eye. For a moment I went blind. My arms flailed in the darkness before I fell back on my spine. My hands patted the ground frantically, trying to find one of my guns. Partridge found his first. He stomped on my knuckles and aimed at my face.

"Billy Gregdon was your last mistake," said Partridge.

"Thought your Magnate wanted to talk to me."

"He did, but exceptions can be made. Harman?"

"I'm trying to light it," shouted the last standing outlaw.

"Then do it!"

"I'm trying," came the response from near the barn.

Partridge turned back to me. "You got rules and so do I, Faust. Always have a contingency. I was hoping I wouldn't have to go through with this part, but..." he shrugged. "It's not that simple now."

Right after Partridge stopped talking, I heard a victorious howl from near the barn. Then, out of the corner of my eye, a flicker of fire caught my attention. Harman's black silhouette waved a match and then dropped it.

With a bloody grin, Partridge said, "'Hamstring the horses, and burn their chariots with fire.' Joshua 11:6. Magnate's taking a Promised Land back by force, Faust."

Blue and orange fire lit up the night, streaking in a liquid beam across the grass. It rushed for the nearly completed barn, eating up a line of kerosene all the way to the stacked hay.

"No," I heard Eliza cry.

In a great explosion of brightness, the haystack went up. The fire didn't take long to latch to the new wood. It spread wild and unhindered across the wall, flicking toward the roof. Partridge said, "You could have just dropped your guns and come nice and easy, but that would have been too hard for a righteous man like you, wouldn't it? Wouldn't it, Marshal Faust."

"Probably," said someone in the dark. "But that's Marshal Asshole to you."

Partridge spun, his gun at the ready. A whole rifle swung over me and smashed him in the busted mouth. Teeth clattered to the ground like rain. Partridge pitched over.

Cicero set the butt of the Yellowboy on the ground and pulled me to my feet. "You owe me twofold," he said.

I shook the confusion out of my head and pointed toward Eliza, who was huddled over Paul and the children, sobbing hysterically. "You take care of the Fultons."

"What are you going to do, stomp on the fire?"

I picked up one of my Colts and started to run for the burning barn. "Kill someone," I yelled.

I raised my Colt shakily as I sprinted. The man named Harman was still surveying the damage he had done, watching the flames spread.

I was twenty feet away when I started to fire.

The Colt bellowed. I worked the hammer and fired a second time. Harman spun, almost leaping, going for his own holster. My third shot went high, but it scared him. "Jesus Christ," I heard him hiss to himself. "Oh, God."

The muzzle of his revolver flashed. The round fell short, punching into the grass. I ran until the muscles in my legs burned.

I was five feet away from him when I recognized him.

I still think he had some of the powdered sugar from the Fat Bastard on his upper lip. He had been the other patron at the Crooked Cocoon when I had eaten breakfast with the Fultons. Realizing who he was was akin to being bucked off a horse.

He knew the Fultons were my friends.

He knew how to make the Gregdons draw me in.

I knew why burning the barn was their backup plan.

Harman dropped his gun and raised his hands.

I jabbed the barrel of the Colt into Harman's stomach and pulled the trigger. His body quieted the blast. Even through the blood, I flicked the hammer and fired again. I kept working the hammer until my fingers were too slippery, until the gun just kept clicking when I squeezed the trigger.

He fell to the side, squealing, trying to scoop whole pieces back into himself. I sprinted for the burning barn. A crown of fire already danced on its roof. I holstered my guns and pulled a handkerchief from my back pocket before throwing myself willy-nilly into the fire.

Heat blasted into me as I shouldered through the main doors, tossing them wide. Billows of smoke already roiled restlessly within, desperately trying to find a way out. Flames licked up along the inside walls. Just like Paul had said, there were no stalls. Just bare soil on the floor, covered with some hay, and a tall ladder leading to a loft about ten feet high.

I saw a figure up there, standing at the lip. I knew exactly who it was.

"Joshua," I shouted.

I crossed the barn floor in several great strides and threw myself onto the ladder, clambering to the top no matter how many splinters slit into my hands. The smoke fogged my vision, magnified the heat. I coughed into my handkerchief and rushed toward Joshua Fulton, who stood perched on the edge of an old chair.

"Come on, kid," I said, reaching for him.

He turned his head to look at me, and his eyes – one sharp and blue, the other a faded green – were afraid. He didn't have much to say around the gag pulled tight into his mouth. Carved on his forehead, the word *HORSE* gleamed red.

They had him tied up like a hog for slaughter. His arms were strapped behind his back with laces of hemp. A noose was around his neck, drawn just enough to touch his skin. The rope had been tied over one of the beams above. I looked at the chair, thinking I could have stood on it to pull the noose off, but no luck: Joshua was balanced on three out of the four legs because one was missing. Sick bastards.

"Joshua," I said. "I'm going to get you down out of there. You hear me?"

He nodded, his feet wriggling on the chair to keep it steady.

The loft was just as empty as the downstairs save a pile of old books that Joshua must have brought up with him. An extinguished candle sat beside them. There was nothing to cut him down with. I had left my knife at the office. My eye caught something shining in the fire on the loft floor.

Liquid. It ran a trail from the wall of the loft to the weak chair on which Joshua was balanced. The burning haystack was just on the other side of the wall. Smoke and fire poured into the barn through the slits in the boards.

Without a sound, flame crawled along the line of kerosene, racing for Joshua's chair.

The kid could either hang from above or burn from below, and given enough time, one or the other was going to happen.

The heat and smoke and fire grew worse, spreading fast. I had enough light to see by, at least, but it only revealed that there wasn't anything to use.

Unless...

I ran at the wall burning from the haystack outside and began to kick the boards. Suffocating sparks sprayed each time. If I could get one loose I might have a chance. After a few kicks, the smoldering wood broke.

I needed to be quick. The place was all structure and no contents. The only thing to burn was the barn itself, and that wouldn't take but a few more minutes.

After breaking the wood, I grabbed one of the adjacent boards and tried to pull it free. My fingers burned, searing fast. I hissed but kept pulling even when the fire began to crawl into the new hole and spread up the inside wall.

When the board came loose, I staggered and fell on my ass. After getting to my feet, I dragged the edge of the board through the line of burning kerosene and wielded it like a torch. Joshua's stare was wide and frightened.

"Duck your head," I said, pressing the burning board up against the rope from which he was hanging. Joshua's feet kept dancing on the chair, trying to avoid the spreading fire. It started to lick at his pantlegs.

The ceiling of the barn was a wild storm of smoke and orange-and-black flames. The moaning of the fiery barn was as loud as a steam-engine. Tongues of fire peeked up through the floor of the loft. The smoke rolled over us. Little strips of braided rope began to snap free as my makeshift torch started burning them. As each fiber broke loose, Joshua jerked.

He was almost loose when the burning chair gave in.

It crumpled beneath him into ash and embers, sending him into a spinning swing. I heard him gag. His cheeks bulged and his eyes looked like they were going to burst from their sockets. His feet kicked like broken clock-hands.

Joshua's tongue whipped out. Spittle dripped to the floor, his legs jittering left and right.

Then he went slack.

I couldn't see anything, not anymore. The world was all distorted. I thought I heard a crack of thunder through it all, but rather than rumbling, it bellowed, the roar of wood and structure finally giving into its own weakness.

A black beam fell down to the loft just beside me, its one end giving way. It smashed into the wooden platform and sent up a searing geyser of fire. Joshua fell right beside it. The rope had been tied to it. His eyes snapped wide open, his mouth spasming for breath.

Even through the gag, I heard him scream. His face contorted in pain. The beam lay across him, and I couldn't see his legs underneath its edge. From his left hand, something tiny and forgettable fell. It clattered to the loft's floor, found a gap between two boards a little too small for it to fall between, and began to roll away from us.

Gleaming. Perfectly round. Like a musket-ball, polished to a mirrored silver.

I tried to lift the beam. Lightning shot up through my shoulders and back as I tried to push it off. My hands cooked, but I didn't care. If I could move it just enough, I could drag him out from under it...

I heard the floor under us belch, crack. It started to fold inward. The loft gave way.

It shattered with a deafening crack and dropped us down, sucking us into a hole made out of burning wood and hot, hot hell. I think I screamed. I only wished Joshua could have done the same. As we tumbled, I kept reaching out for him. I found nothing but handfuls of scorching cinder.

The burning debris collapsed on us, covering our bodies. Hot sparks seared my lungs and boiled in my eyes.

I read somewhere one time that death was supposed to be dark, but I guess the genius who wrote that had never been caught in a collapsing barn. White hot relief followed the burning pain. Beside me, Joshua's tiny artifact fell into scorching ash. I closed my hand over it.

Darkness.

15

MOUTHFUL OF ASH. FLICKERS OF CONSCIOUSNESS. A FLOOD OF relentless pain. Dragging, dragging, scraping, being dragged...

"Ma'am, please talk to me. What's your name?" a man said above me.

A weak little voice said, "Eliza. Mrs. Eliza Fulton."

"Mrs. Fulton, I know you feel like what you're doing is the right thing, but I can assure you—"

"Shut up," she said.

"I understand what you want to do, but I don't believe—"

"Shut your mouth," she said.

Another voice, too. But this one wasn't spoken. This one awakened itself in the darkness and wound itself like a snake around my brain. *Dodging death only remains so practical. After awhile it becomes exhausting, doesn't it?*

"You don't want to do this. It won't fill the holes, Mrs. Fulton."

"What do you know about holes."

"Enough to know what won't fill them."

The heartbeat. The pulse. All these systems working away like a wound-up clock. And for what, really?

"He burned my baby. He burned my baby," Mrs. Fulton said.

The stars spun in circles, like someone had plucked them all out of the sky and tacked them to a pinwheel.

It's tiresome, watching it all play out. But balance is worth it. A man loses a boy, a woman loses a boy...

Eliza again. "Who the fuck are you to teach me about holes?"

"Nobody, ma'am."

"Then get out of my way—" I heard the zip of two gun-hammers being drawn back, "—before I blow your teeth out of your head."

We all lose something, Mister Faust, the whisper said.

I reached into the air with my fingers. I could feel the cool wind of the night brushing across them. Two silhouettes stood above me, facing each other. Eliza looked little and scared and pale, almost dwarfed by the long shotgun – my shotgun – with its butt tucked into her shoulder. She stared down its shaking barrels at Grady Cicero, whose big hands were flat in front of him.

When I stirred, they both stopped what they were doing and looked at me.

"Faust," said Cicero. "Holy hell."

I lapped up lungfuls of chilly air like it was cool, life-giving water. After coughing myself ill, I swiped a mouthful of black phlegm on my sleeve. "Mrs. Fulton," I groaned, grimacing as I sat up. "He's with me."

"Doesn't matter, Marshal Faust. God as my witness, I'll put him in a grave if he doesn't move out of my way."

I looked around as I staggered to my knees. My clothes were burnt in places, creased with sooty black. My guns were still miraculously tucked in their holsters. A series of fat blisters and wet, pink sores adorned my knuckles. Burns. How had I gotten out of that?

The minute I balanced, the world crashed back into me. I stumbled against Cicero, trying to regain my center. Behind me, fire flared on a massive pile of smoking wood. The barn used to be there. Partridge was still unconscious on the ground several feet away from his molars. Harman squirmed on the ground behind Cicero, holding his guts.

"She wants to kill them," Cicero said.

I reached out one of my scorched hands to Eliza. Cold silver still rested in the other. "Cicero is a friend of mine, Mrs. Fulton."

"I'll kill him, too."

"I'm sure he'll get himself killed good on his own one day. Where are your children?"

Cicero said, "I got them all inside when you ran for the barn. Eliza insisted on coming back out."

"That man burned my baby," Eliza said.

"I want to talk with you, Eliza," I said.

"Tell your friend to leave."

"Cicero? He's not a bother."

"Tell him to leave."

I nodded. I turned to look at my associate and motioned to the farmhouse. "You good with children?"

"Good enough," he said.

"Mrs. Fulton, you mind if my friend Cicero goes and talks with your children until your husband wakes up?"

Her fingers flexed on the wooden stock of the gun. She licked her lips. "Children need someone to watch over them," she said.

I nodded.

"He's a good shot," she said. "Like lightning."

"Like lightning."

She said, "Alright."

Cicero took the command for what it was: a chance to let Eliza win this round, to give her something of a victory even if her world felt like it was falling apart around her. He adjusted his spectacles and then turned, approaching the farmhouse with a tired canter.

Harman kept squealing, grabbing at grass and pulling even though it didn't do him a damned bit of good.

"Jonah came out of the belly of the whale when all was said and done, Marshal Faust." Eliza never watched me, just looked through me like I didn't exist. "He was on his way to Nineveh, where he would have brought God to those who needed Him. But he never got there. He fled God's purpose for him. He threw himself into the seas."

"So the whale got lucky?"

"Three long days," she whispered, barely audible. She searched in herself for something. Her eyes were wet. "You came out. My baby didn't."

There were pieces she was putting together – pieces of other puzzles – while still trying to pick up her own. I couldn't imagine what it had felt like from the outside, watching the fire spread, waiting every long, dragging moment. I hurt, but by the grace of something I wasn't yet willing to consider, I was alive. I couldn't imagine what it felt like inside of little Mrs. Fulton.

"I need you to move aside, Marshal Faust."

I eyed the struggling Harman. "He's already going to die, Eliza."

"It'll be my choice."

"Is that God's law?"

"God has no part of this. But now He has my son. We'll have to talk, He and I."

I wished Paul was there. Paul would know how to talk to her. He likely knew how to pluck all her little strings. I just threatened to break them. She looked up at me like she had never seen me before. I told her, "It's not so easy for warm folk to be cold-blooded."

"My child, Marshal. My Joshua."

"You're not a killer."

She kept swallowing down hard like she was trying not to throw up. Her tears were like little crystals on her face. "I need this from you, Marshal Faust," she said to me, softer than she had before, hawk inside a sparrow. "Not so many things Paul and I ask for. Not help for the barn, not free meals, not anything. But this..."

"This is big."

"I need it," she mouthed to me. "Give me this, Faust."

"It'd be best if I had someone alive to put on the bench, Eliza. Sometimes I can swing it, but this time?" I didn't say it to her, but this time, a boy was dead, and that could make things problematic. "This time, I need a living face for the judge to put a name to. Somebody he can look at and hate just as much as you and I. Otherwise, it's just our word to vouch for a whole wagonload of corpses if somebody comes asking questions. In the end, we feel good and avenged, but nothing gets done. Blood for no reason."

"What about Joshua?"

She cried loudly now, grunting through a storm of sobs that threatened to tear her apart from inside. She stood, because standing, in that moment, was everything. She needed to balance the scales. It was the only thing that would feel right to her. To turn a man into a dead thing.

"Don't talk to him," I said. "You'll remember he's a man."

"He ain't a man to me."

"God will tell you otherwise."

She nodded.

"Don't overthink it. Don't look at his eyes. Aim the gun, look away, squeeze the trigger."

"And it'll be done?"

"He will," I admitted. "You won't be."

"It'll always be there?"

I nodded.

"I want it," she whispered. "He burned my baby."

"Anybody asks you, Eliza, things got hairy here."

"How?"

"Bad turn. He had me down. You were deputized by the moment."

"You were going to die," she said, understanding.

I stepped away from the barrel of the shotgun. She stiffened when she saw Harman again. The coils of bloody sausage he juggled in his hands didn't seem to bother her. He started to hobble to his elbows, trying to stand up, to say something, but she did good.

The deep, throaty howl of the twelve gauge echoed out over the mountains. Smoke swept away in the dry wind.

Eliza dropped the shotgun. She lowered her head and didn't look up at me, but when she reached out and fell into me, everything came loose. She screamed as she cried. She bit my shoulder. We stood in the field, smelling the burning wood, listening to the crickets mourn for her.

We turned away from the barn. Away from the bodies.

16

A WEEK LATER IT RAINED. THE DROPS WERE BIG AND FAT. THE WIND CUT sideways. The water didn't care. It went on for hours at a time, turning everything misty, gray, and dull.

Cicero and I sat outside my office, avoiding the rain by sitting under the awning. We shared a small bit of whiskey, not enough to get drunk, but enough to get us thinking. There was a lot to think about, but like all other things, likely not enough time to think it.

A few blocks down the street, Blackpeak's church bustled with life. People came and went, men dressed in nice suits, women in long dresses that they had to keep up from the mud. Umbrellas stuck up like mushrooms from the crowds. Some people stopped in the street and gave *how-do-you-do*s and *God-be-with-you*s.

"Think we should go?" Cicero asked me.

"Maybe. Maybe good to give them some room, too."

"You their friend?"

"I am."

"It's their son's memorial. You have every right to be there. You tried your best to protect him."

I nodded, sipping whiskey.

"You risked your life for his."

I kept watching the people. "He's not alive."

"So?"

"I tried. I didn't succeed."

"And that matters because?"

"Because they know."

Because there'd been nothing left of Joshua to find.

I poured us both more whiskey. The people eventually swarmed into the church and the road went silent except for the rain pooling in its dips. Inside the chapel, a booming voice praised the Lord and said some things from the Book. I couldn't hear what, exactly.

I was surprised Cicero was still around. We never spoke much after the incident at the Fulton farm. I nudged him some gratitude money and invited him to finish out the rest of his sentence in a comfortable room. The next day he came back, and the next, even though I didn't tell him he needed to. I owed him something for his riflework. For dragging me like a lump of half-cooked beef out of the burning remains of the barn.

I turned the glass in my hands. "Where'd you learn to shoot?"

He squinted at the church but didn't give me an answer.

"You got an eye that can put a bullet into a target a few inches out of a cigarette at a hundred yards. You've got no problem killing a man."

"Or a woman," he said, both out of playful pride and out of something else. A hint of ruthlessness.

"So you've done it before."

"When I've had to. I'm just an actor," he admitted. "Shake-spearean. Deal with a bunch of actors and Englishmen all day and you'll learn that you don't get any acknowledgment in a pair of suspenders and dirty long johns, and even less with shitty aim."

"What did you do that's bad enough to send a Shakespearean actor halfway across the country into a shithole like Blackpeak?"

"You didn't mention Gregdon's ear."

"Huh?"

"You can't leave that off of my list of credentials," he said, taking on his fake British accent. "I worked bloody hard at that. Don't you forget it."

Ten minutes or so went by. Father Steward stopped shouting inside the church. The doors didn't open yet, but I expected them to burst at any minute with the mourners looking to fill their bellies. "I appreciate what you did at the Fulton place. So do they."

"What you're saying, Marshal Faust," Cicero clarified, still tapping his hat, "is that I can leave when I'm ready. I've paid my due."

"Judge is coming now, just not for you."

Partridge wouldn't be going anywhere any time soon. The rifle had knocked something out of place in his head. Ever since the night at the Fultons, he'd been under guard at Doctor Levinworth's, fading in and out of consciousness. Citizens of Blackpeak jumped at the chance to be deputies for a few hours at a time, even if it just meant keeping a beefy old prick like Partridge in his bed at gunpoint. "I never asked: the third man on foot – not Harman, not Partridge, but—"

"The one you shot, but didn't kill?" Cicero smiled at me. His mustache twitched. "Found him bleeding next to the house. I was going to knock him out, but he sort of took care of things for me." He put two fingers in his mouth and flicked his thumb like a pistol-hammer.

"He was scared."

"I guess so."

"Not of you, though," I said.

"I was the only person with a gun around."

"Not the gun," I said. "Of the Gregdons. He'd rather die than face their disappointment. Or the Magnate's, whoever the hell he thinks he is."

"I take it they won't like you much after this, Faust."

I heard the joyous sounds of hymns emanating from the church. They got louder as the front doors opened and a small figure dressed in black swept her way out, ignoring the rain. She seated herself on the front stoop of the church and buried her head in her arms. Eliza

Fulton looked like she was trying to escape the noise, the praise, and the memories. "I'll be back in a bit, Cicero," I said.

"I might not be here, Marshal."

He leaned forward and extended a hand to me. We shook. He adjusted his glasses and placed his bowler back atop his head, peering out along the landscape of Blackpeak. "It's been fun."

I walked in a brisk stride toward the church, hoping every step would carry me further away.

———————

I SAT DOWN NEXT to Eliza Fulton. She wore a thick veil around her face, but even through it, I could see the tears working their way down through the caked makeup she wore. "You're getting wet, Mrs. Fulton." I put my elbows on my knees, cupping a cigarette to keep it from the rain.

"It's suffocating me in there."

"That's not like you."

"Things have changed."

"You two have that talk yet?"

She picked invisible burs on her skirt, trying to find something to do with her shaking hands. Normally, they would have had something in them – a Bible, a rosary – but they were unoccupied, and she seemed particularly restless. When she turned her face to look at me, I saw an Eliza Fulton I had never really seen before. There were dark bags under her eyes, liquor on her breath. "I asked Him to protect you. Did you know that? I asked Him to protect you both when it all came crumbling down. Why He'd only do half of what I asked," she wondered aloud, tugging at fabric, "I can't ever understand. What did Joshua do that God didn't like, Marshal Faust?"

"Being your boy, I'd bet everything I owned that he did everything the way he was supposed to."

"How can you be so sure?"

I still had the blisters on my hands, but they were fading every day. I blew out smoke into the rain and watched it get sliced apart. "I can't. I can just hope real hard."

When I finished my cigarette, I flicked the remaining paper into the street and let it drown in a muddy puddle. Before I walked away, her tiny hand reached up to grip mine. It squeezed. Her muscles felt colder and harder. "Your friend, he found your hand and pulled you out of the rubble and the fire. It was like God had put you in a little papoose and made sure you wouldn't get burned so badly. Did you feel Him, Marshal? Did you feel His favor?"

"I don't remember, Mrs. Fulton. It was black and hot. I was scared."

"You must have known He was there with you."

"And if I didn't?"

She'd scraped up her sleeve by then, until the tender skin beneath showed its face to the world: a series of half-healed gashes glistened on her wrist, some fresher, some more angry and red than the others. Under her breath, she said, "I can just hope real hard."

Paul came out into the rain a few minutes later, decked all in black save for the gauze bandage wrapped around his head. He said nothing to me. His pupils were just holes, empty and vast. He leaned down next to Eliza, took her hand, helped her stand.

"He did what I wanted, didn't He," Eliza said to me. "He protected you. So why don't it feel right?"

"Come on, Eliza," Paul said.

"Why don't it feel right at all?"

I walked away from them. He could pick up the pieces better than I'd be able to.

———

SEVERAL MORE DAYS PASSED. Away from the town where the ground was soft, Harman, Knox, and the other two members of the Gregdon clan were stuffed in a shallow and unmarked grave. Nobody would remember them. Ivanmore did good work.

Things began to trickle back to their normal ways. I breakfasted at the Crooked Cocoon Saloon every morning, trying to avoid the pastries at all costs. And despite his say-so, Cicero never left. I suppose he liked the girls, the booze, and the fights.

"Thought I'd stick around," he told me over a pitcher of cold coffee I'd made the night before. It tasted like oil and dirt. "Enjoy this place a little more without getting the hell beat out of me. Fulton situation's on everybody's mind. I'm old news. Thought I'd do my part and vouch for Partridge's being such a piece of shit when the trial comes. Never been a witness," he reasoned. "Sounds exhilarating."

Trial came and went. Barely an hour's time out of the town's morning. Guilty, guilty, guilty. Wasn't much fuss. Couple of Crown Rock lawmen with stiff jackets and even less exciting senses of humor came to collect Partridge up. Didn't matter; speaking wasn't his forte anymore. The only mouthpiece to the Gregdon situation rattled off in the back of a cart, and justice being what it was, it left without satisfaction – and without the last bullet to put everything back to balance.

"How long are you staying in town, Cicero?" I asked as we played dominoes in my office.

"As long as it stays interesting."

I clicked down a double six-pip. "You're a pretty good shot. You want a job?"

He tapped a domino against his lips. "You want me to be a mercenary?"

"I want you to be my deputy," I clarified.

"That's sweet of you, Marshal Asshole. All your job offers this unceremonious?"

"Take it or leave it," I said.

Grady Cicero quirked a bushy brow underneath his spectacles. He watched me for a few minutes, now and then his temple twitching or his mustache flicking like it was trying to whip a fly. A hard sell.

He clicked a tile down. A six-and-two.

"So," I said, clearing my throat, "when you want to start?"

"By the way I showed you up with your own rifle, I think I already have, Marshal Faust."

We finished our game. I figured in the future I might be needing help. Maybe not, though. Maybe the Gregdons would stay in their hole. Maybe they'd forget I existed. Maybe they'd go back to their normal ways: simple thieving, simple bullying, easy to kill.

I doubted it, but I hoped.

Suppertime came and Cicero went for beef. I lingered behind with whiskey. I rolled back in my chair when he was gone and considered my desk drawer. After enough thinking and not enough doing, I pulled it open.

Rattling around inside one of the knuckle-holes of Cicero's brass knuckles, Joshua's perfect silver sphere winked in the dull light of my desk's oil-lamp. I saw my face distorted and reflected back at me in the silver ball.

On my desk, Billy Gregdon's half-burnt piece of paper began to darken. New ink bled into it. *I see you*, it read. In a flash, it burned to nothing.

I slammed the desk shut.

NOW

BEING'S A FUNNY THING. YOU TAKE IT FOR GRANTED. THAT'S NATURAL, *really. Look too far into the crevices of what we don't know and can't fathom – like what you are when you aren't – and it starts getting too bright for us to handle. What's unknown isn't a dark room. It's a blinding ball of fire. But turn your head to acknowledge it, it shines light on all those bleak parts that make up who you are: your doubts, your weaknesses, your inadequacies, all your mistakes.*

So most of us don't think about being. We just are. No questions, no answers. Easy. Breezy.

But with that legion of worms writhing inside of me, I wasn't.

At this moment, I am not.

Fear rattles me. Inside me. Shakes me like cornhusk doll.

They're eating the time out of my bones. They feast on fibers under my skin. What could have been but one minute stretches out into an endless bootlace of time. Now and then I become vaguely aware of the agony of the thorns in my wrists, but swarmed by these burrowing beasts, I imagine pieces of myself falling away: slivers of skin, and with it, tidbits of memories and sensation and weight...

"Hold on," I growl to myself through my—

(Do I still have teeth...did I ever have teeth?)

"Tell me this doesn't unravel you that much, Elias Faust. You're made of more resilient stuff, or so I was led to believe." His voice thrums with quiet pleasure. He's enjoying this; he's loving it.

The worms, they're in my brain. Gnawing at the meat in my skull. Driving themselves like nails underneath my muscle and curling around my organs. When they suck at me, parts of me start pulling away from the here and now, like a blanket pulled apart thread by thread...

"Why are you—"

(Think...words. Find them. God, are they...are they eating those, too?)

I glance down. The slithering little parasites feast under my fingernails. My nails are like cloudy glass. They thrash underneath. "Why is this so important to you," I manage to ask.

"Because it is imperative that we know every detail exactly as you experienced them."

"Why the worms," I say. "The bugs? Is it really..." (What's the word?) *I find it eventually. I might as well have needed to wrestle it out of a worm's slimy mouth. "Is it really necessary?"*

"Necessary? No. Amusing? Highly. Testing your resolve, though, is part of the process."

"Well, your process is a real pain in my ass."

Just then, in front of the sickly gaslights over my questioner's shoulders, I watch him lift a hand into the air and clench it into a violent fist. An invisible hook snares me by the stomach and yanks me forward. Inside me the worms chatter in a heinous symphony of noise, squealing and screaming and screeching in discomfort, burrowing deeper into my conscience to get away from whatever danger they sense, like rats fleeing fire.

I'm face-to-face with him. There's blood and rot on his breath.

Every one of his eyes – all thirteen of them – stare through me. His face is a whole array of them, bulging and large, beady and small. They gleam on the cheeks like pustules and wink and blink across the misshapen brow. They don't open and close in unison. When he speaks, the cavernous mouth gapes and there is a lone eyeball resting on the back of his tongue, as if it might roll out at me any second. The worms are screaming. I feel it. They're terrified.

My whole body goes numb.

The fisted hand tightens. I lurch closer. I'm inches away. "Even under this kind of duress, Faust, your cooperation is essential. There's still quite a lot of ground to cover, and letting yourself be misguided by small distractions will only extend our inquiry. The choice is yours: you can wallow in your pain, or you can agree to tell us what you know. That means everything. That means—"

The worms peel the image out of my brain. They unstitch it out of my memories, and I see it flash like a quick burst of lightning in front of me: a face of stark white and black, like bone formed on flesh. She's small, she's powerful, and I...

(They're going to eat what remains of her right out of your mind...)

"You want me to tell you about her?" I ask.

Thirteen. His name's Thirteen. I remember it now.

"Absolutely everything," he says.

PART IV

THE GIRL MADE OF GOLD

17

I was having a really good night until, twelve-and-a-half minutes before all the bloodshed, Miss Lachrimé Garland stormed into the Crooked Cocoon Saloon, gasping like a well-pump and looking about ready to bust a few whale-bones out the side of her corset.

"I think you need to come see this," Lachrimé told me, and they were the most sobering damn words a body can hear.

I was halfway through a very good beer. It was Saturday night. I was enjoying myself, mostly. "It can wait," I said.

Next to me, Cicero pinched his bowler. "Maybe we should burn that into the office door. The age-old motto: *It can wait.*"

"Well, this absolutely can't, with a big motherfucking emphasis on the *absolutely can't.*" She never raised her voice, just thrust her chin forward and glared holes through me. "You do get paid to do something."

"A lofty presumption," Cicero said.

"This is something," I said, raising my beer.

Which she snapped out of my hand and chugged to solve the problem, leaving a mountain of foam under her nose. Then, her hand as hot as a furnace, she grabbed my lapel and yanked me to my feet. "I swear to Christ," she said and wrenched me for the door.

People parted in front of us, but were altogether too busy to care much about anything except their games of cards, their warm drinks, or the tinkling mutter of the off-key harpsichord trilling away in the corner. Cicero sat back at our table and raised my shotgun from where it'd been leaning against another chair. I shrugged as loudly as I could.

Sure, you lazy bastard, I thought. *Keep enjoying yourself.*

When Lachrimé tugged me out the front door, I immediately felt the cool air of the Blackpeak night against my face, knocking my head free of smoke and commotion. She pushed me into the street and started walking in front of me like a hasty pigeon, the tail of her skirt sweeping a paintbrush pattern in the sand and rocks. "If I come to you, Elias, it's because I'm choosing to be careful, and you and I, I think we've come to learn the importance of discretion."

"There something wrong?"

"Not wrong," she said. "Just not quite right."

That was enough, whispered with just enough careful coolness that having any more scruples about Miss Garland's judgment would have been willing ignorance. A lump of anxiety jumped into my throat. We whisked past the Horseshoe Junction, past the general store, down a muddy path that led to the tailor's storefront and a gaggle of two-floored residences. Here, the noise of the night died away and if you stood still enough, it was like nothing in the world moved at all.

"Down there," Lachrimé said as we came to the mouth of an alley. She withdrew a crumpled cigarette from her sleeve-cuff and lit it with a match struck against her boot.

"When'd you start smoking?"

"When didn't I?"

"Never saw you partake in such a habit."

"Never buried a man before sunrise, neither."

I stared into the alley, seeing blackness, smelling nothing but stale piss and old brick. "This some kind of—" I waved a hand in the air,

"—birthday surprise, like folks are gonna come leaping out of the woodwork blowing confetti at me?"

"Is it your birthday?"

I shrugged.

"What a shitty birthday this would be." Her cheeks darkened as she sucked in smoke. "All I know is I *saw* something, and it wasn't normal, and since the Everett fiasco, I'm sure not willing to traipse into a dark alley by myself."

"So you want me to do it?"

"I got things to live for," she said, haughty about it.

"Seems about like your only purpose in life is making mine hell."

"To you it's hell," she said. "To me it's pure joy."

I rested a blistered palm on the cold handle of my Colt. A chill shot down my spine. I searched the darkness for silver eyes. When I tried to breathe, my chest refused to expand all the way. My hackles shot to attention. A hum in the air. Nothing you could hear, nothing you could barely even feel, just a dull sense, the same one that lights a fire under a kid's ass as he stares into the darkness of a cellar. "What is it exactly I'm looking for, Miss Garland," I asked.

"I think you'll see."

I damn well had no room for secrets, but I pulled my Colt and she *shoo*ed me forward with her hands. Regretfully, I started creeping forward into the alley, begging my eyes to adjust.

The alley held nothing more than the discarded garbage of human business: some busted casks, rotted boxes, glass bottles. An old wheel missing its spokes. A broken trough someone had planned to dismantle but never got to. People clung to the presumption that garbage would just vanish after awhile, and that's the way it seemed to be with most things.

I did what any sensible fellow would do: I started nudging at objects with the mouth of my revolver.

I turned my head. Looked back at Miss Garland for guidance.

I damn well had no room for secrets, but I pulled my Colt and she *shoo*ed me forward with her hands.

The alley held nothing more than the discarded garbage of

human business. Busted casks, rotted boxes, bottles. Old wheel missing spokes. When, I thought, was someone going to take a hammer to that crumbled trough? I supposed garbage might just vanish after awhile, sink away, become nothing. That's the way it seemed to be with—

I turned my head. Looked back at Miss Garland for guidance.

I certainly didn't have *time* for secrets, but I pulled my Colt and—

She pinched a cigarette out from her sleeve and lit it.

We talked about something. About...

"I got things to live for," she said, haughty about it.

Whiplash. Back. Back there. Standing.

Miss Garland retrieved a rumpled cigarette from her sleeve. She struggled lighting it because cold rain punched the match-light out. "Oh, fuck off," she said, and flicked the useless paper.

"When'd you start smoking?" I asked.

"When didn't I?"

I tripped over something, stubbing my boot-toe against it. I pitched forward in the alley and fell hands-first to the mud. "Would you believe some lazy prick," I shouted back to Miss Garland, "just dumped their old trough back here, like what, it's going to sprout wings and just fly away?"

Her face lit up with fire as she sparked a cigarette pulled out from the cuff of her dress-sleeve. "I never liked smoking," she announced.

"Then why'd you start?"

"To you," she said, "it's hell. To me—"

What? I thought.

"—it's pure joy."

Whiplash. Back. Back there.

Trundling into the alley, there seemed like there was just so much trash: a wagon-wheel rolled across in front of me, and boxes stacked themselves like puzzle-pieces in front of me. I thought *Christ Almighty, how much garbage do these people make?* I kept walking deeper and deeper until, out of nowhere, my ankle busted through a weak piece of discarded wood and I lost balance, pitched forward...

Forward and *through*, pushing through some unseen blanket. A fog in my brain blew away. I fell...

Fell, like a sack of bricks, at a pair of feet half-sunk in the mud.

I followed them up to protruding ankles, knees bent, to a figure huddled like an oversized child in a crease of alley-cast shadow. What I saw there stared back at me, with eyes that gave off a wild array of green sparks, and when they blinked they went *flicker-flack, flicker-flack* like loose-hinged shutters, a sideways blink.

A naked woman stared up at me through unclear layers of the world. A furious pounding began in my skull, pushing at its every corner. Up came her hand, a graceful but powerful hand that pushed at me, pushed toward me, trying to encourage me to...to...

I needed to leave her be. Needed to ignore her. Needed to...

I mean, after all, I supposed garbage might just vanish after awhile, sink away, become nothing. That's the way it seemed to be with—

I turned my head. Looked back at Miss Garland for guidance.

Then I slammed my eyes shut and I barked, "Stop," with all the ferocity of a trembling cat. It fizzled out from me, pushed out from deflated lungs. "Stop, *stop*," I gasped, my heartbeat starting a relentless stampede. I was about to scream it, too, when the membrane cleared, as if wiped away by a careless palm.

The strangeness melted away from the world.

Clarity crashed back into me.

I stared down at a frail but peculiar specimen of a living thing: a woman-that-was-not, hairless and more a living gem than a fleshy thing at all, with skin polished-smooth, shining gold and jade in an array of map-like patterns. When I tried to look at her, the air and wind and even the cigarette-smoke tried to drag my gaze away, shift my attention to something else.

Lachrimé's feet crunched down the alley. With a pale cigarette bobbing in her mouth, she tugged up the lap of her skirts, squatted down, and offered a hand to the hidden woman before us.

"I watched it happen," Lachrimé whispered, afraid Blackpeak would overhear. "I saw a star break out of the sky, clear as day, and fall to the ground. It was her, Elias. It was *her*."

18

"And the first thing you thought to do," I asked Lachrimé, "was come to get me?"

"No, the first thing I thought to do after the impact was to get new britches, because I just about pissed myself."

The woman, hunkered in the mud, shot her gaze back and forth between me and Lachrimé. Her shape had all the strokes of an artist's exaggeration, her legs and arms all lanky and overlong. Her skin smoked like an oiled pan, and her hairless head leaned back so she could take stock of both of us. Her body, the wild pattern of shining gold and green, breathed out its own subtle glow. More like a pieced-together antique than a woman at all. Could have flicked her and shattered her to a thousand pieces.

With her hands scraping like crude tools, she tore at the wet soil. She exhumed whole handfuls, scanned them, then threw them aside.

We just watched. If not for all the mud, I could have sworn she shone like a jewel. This woman, if woman was even the word for her, stood out like a swollen thumb in the filth. "How did you come across her, Miss Garland?"

"Exactly as I said. I noticed a spark in the sky..."

"Yeah?"

"And I was just about on the verge of doing what you do with shooting stars when I heard a whistle, *phewpt*." Lachrimé took two fingers on a comet journey through the air and landed them in her opposite palm. "When I came out to check, here she was, glowing like a sparkler."

Miss Lachrimé Garland had never misguided me, and as we stared at this wiry geode-girl, I wondered why it had to be *me* dragged here to this shit-stinking alley.

"You think we'll encounter as much resistance going out as coming in?"

Miss Garland reached back toward the invisible membrane, waved her fingers in the air, and shook her head. "I think whatever she put into place lost its purpose when you buffaloed your way in here."

In here. The words made me painfully aware of what I was missing here: the murmurs of voices through the thin walls, the sounds of night, the distant winds, howling things, hooting things, crunching footsteps, all the usual ambiance of a restless world. But not anymore. She'd cupped us all up inside some great invisible hand and muted the world to us.

A fool's advice: accept what you see in the moment, fill in the blanks later, preferably over a gallon of something foamy.

With strangeness afoot, I found myself eerily calm. Heartbeat slowed to normal. Skin didn't prickle with that *get-your-ass-in-your-hand* fear that comes with gunshots and knife-tips. I crouched down in front of the lost girl.

She didn't look at me. Just kept digging, her face set in frantic determination.

"You think she can walk?"

"She's got legs," Lachrimé said.

I stage-whispered to our new charge from behind a hand, "Atrocious bedside manner if you ask me." Then, very carefully, with the same soft-motion approach you take with bitey animals, I held out my palm. "Hey."

She stopped, solid as stone, and regarded me.

Then, after her chin jerked to the side, she looked at my outstretched hand.

The girl placed her dirty hand in mine.

Fingers brushed the inside of my wrist. Little digits of metal, cool like bullet-heads. The hairs on my neck and forearms shot to attention.

Not a gentle touch. A grab. She tugged me close.

A blossom of light blew wide open in front of me. I tried to speak, but nothing came out: just a stammer, pulled off my tongue, down through my throat, driving like a train along the veins of my arm, and then leaping out of my palm and into hers. I watched in frozen surprise as a flipbook flash of reason poured across her face. When she opened her mouth, teeth like cloudy glass clacked together. Then my words came out of her: "Atrocious bedside manner if you ask me." A hoarse and yet oddly musical collection of creaks and whispers.

Lachrimé crushed her cigarette between two fingers. "We should get her somewhere that isn't just a well for disease, Faust. Get her some clothes, get her something to—"

"Get her some clothes," the woman repeated, in a remarkable echo of Lachrimé's voice. "Get her something to—"

"Eat," Lachrimé concluded.

Leading her out to the mouth of the alley was a journey in itself. Her gangly legs stretched in long strides, but her feet slid with all the uncertainty of a newborn calf. Tricks played out in front of me: in the alley she towered, stretched long like taffy, but by the time we were at the street she seemed smaller, meeker, as if she'd shrunk herself into the best imitation of *normal* she could manage. Between Lachrimé and me, she could have turned sideways and disappeared.

Her hand gripped mine. Seeking reassurance. Or so I told myself, to avoid just how possessively powerful her grip felt.

Lachrimé asked, "Levinworth?" and I nodded, because when you didn't know what to do, you went to someone smarter, someone sharper. At all costs, we avoided lamplights and visibility and I hoped we could shuffle her off in due time.

We passed by the Crooked Cocoon, skirting the span of light from the windows and porch. Tension shot through her stickfigure limbs, hard as steel. Her chin jerked left, right, and the jewel-like eyes began to seek out some kind of answers in the darkness. "Wrongness," she said. "There is a – a wrongness here, like a failing heartbeat. You feel it. You must."

"You're giving my senses more credit than they deserve."

"Why have I come," she said, "but to fill myself with its – its prodigious *stink*? It is dying."

Lachrimé's lips tugged into a line. "And so am I, listening to this. You got some kind of name, Stargirl?"

"Do you not smell it? It weakens. It falls to pieces, pieces, *pieces*, and drags the clouds down with its cries. You—" Turning, she pulled her gaze from Lachrimé and pinned me to the wall with it. "You do. I know it." Her nostrils flared. "You're jumbled and misplaced, tangled and discarded and tossed aside, forgetting and forgotten."

Her hand opened. A brief surge of power like wind almost sent me ass over teakettle. I steeled my heels.

It occurred to me, perhaps too damn late, that I was dealing with something *else* here. Something you don't measure with yardsticks or pray about in church, something gone uncategorized in little books and catalogues. *Human* was just a familiar word, but not one that applied to her. Her jaunty, carved form turned away from us.

Not knowing the etiquette of the unfamiliar, I asked, "Do you have a name?"

"Everything has a name. I am not an exception."

"Then what will I call you?"

"Can you not find it in yourself? I have left it there, in the space where I took the knowledge of words from you."

"*Oo*-kay," Lachrimé breathed. "It's been a nice walk, dear, but whatever you decided to smoke tonight has messed you up something mighty." She reached out for the woman's jade wrist, her fingers a kind invitation. "There's a fellow we're on the way to see by the name of Doctor Levinwo—"

A sweep of her arm sent Lachrimé back, back, in a banner-flap flutter of skirts and sleeves, until she struck the side of the tailor's building.

I tugged the statuesque woman away from Lachrimé, away from the porch, shoved her out into the street with a firm proclamation of, "Back the hell off," before I gathered any damn sense at all.

Stargirl, still infantile with her feet, would have splashed right down into the street if it weren't for crashing into someone else entirely, and almost collapsing against him.

There was a kerchief wrapped around his head. Streaks from black coal were smeared down the front of his shirt. Despite the dark, I recognized him. He worked at the mines with Mr. Bisbin, the foreman. He was as big as a locomotive.

"Well, goddamn, Faust, don't mind if I *do*," he said, giving the girl a twirl. When the light struck her it scattered in a hundred different rays. "And I'll be, you're one odd-looking duck if I say so myself. Ain't that right? Ain't that right. Hell, Marshal, look at you sneaking out to round up the circus freaks after hours."

His attention seemed to waft over her for just a few seconds before a dull glaze filled his wet eyes, and she slinked away from him like a crude afterthought. A vein on the right side of his temple bulged ferociously against his skin. He blew out a breath, reeking of hot whiskey. Behind Big Boy – I couldn't remember his name for the life of me – a stumbling posse of shadows emerged: some of his friends, all faces from the Crooked Cocoon, stinking so strongly of Poindexter's cheapest booze that I greeted their sweat before I ever saw their faces.

Big Boy started rolling up his dirty cuffs. The universal sign of being drunk enough to toss an ass-whooping. "It's a good Saturday night, wouldn't you say?"

"Good enough," I said. "Great for enjoying a few deep breaths to clear the mind. How much have you had to drink?"

He laughed. "Plenty. Plenty enough to do something stupid." The miner's fist tightened into a meaty sledgehammer.

"But not enough to not reconsider, I hope."

"You make a habit of souring the mood, Marshal Faust? Soured the mood right up when you killed that Gregdon boy," he said. "Seems like there's twice as much work up at the mine now that he's dead."

Behind him, his friends blew up their shoulders. "You think this is a smart idea?" I asked.

"Nobody around to say it isn't." I kept my place, never moving, never shifting my weight. Though I knew he could have crushed me into the earth with barely any effort, letting him see that fear would have been a bad idea. "You love that shotgun of yours, Marshal. Hide behind it a lot. Last time you and I talked, you were hugging it like it was gonna suck you dry.

"Shame you left the shotgun with that other cocksucker. Certainly makes a body wonder if you're just as good with those revolvers."

One of his friends had the battered handle of a revolver hanging out of his pocket and a knot of rust-colored hair. The one in the middle was short and bald and so smeared with coal that he looked like he'd had a run-in with a tar pit. The third one stumbled drunkenly, a Four of Spades still stuck to his sweaty forehead from an unfinished game of liar's poker.

This was not going to go well.

If girls falling from the sky were the start of the sentence and drunken miners with vendettas the period, I was the dumbass comma crushed in between. When Big Boy broke conversation and decided to break my face, I should have been ready. *Should* have. "Ya ain't nothin', not you, not that pussy-ass bitch of a deputy you got, either."

He swung. I scuttled back.

"Miss Garland," I said. "Could you ask Deputy Pussy-Ass Bitch that his company would be greatly appreciated?"

His friends converged, intending to leave me in a heap. They came too, all at once. I barely had the Colt's mouth cleared of the holster's leather before they were close enough for me to breathe in, all their stink and sweat, all their spit and rage. I jacked my thumb back on the hammer. The gun chirped like a cricket, ready to fire.

But in the next instant the pistol was gone, knocked away. It hit the sand. Suddenly, the woman of gold and green was a wall between me and the oncoming threat, her hand ringing with an odd, metallic echo where she'd struck the pistol out of my hand.

Keeping me from shooting.

I tumbled back. The moment rolled back, too, like a pulley in reverse, the world stuttering the way it did before: little slivers of time staggering over each other, vying for control.

In one, I drew, I felt the gun jerk, I felt blood—

The next, I never had time: Big Boy crushed me, a wall of pain, behind his swinging fist...

Another, we all simply walked past one another, eschewing offense, ignoring conflict, a proper Saturday night.

Did Lachrimé feel it all, too? Did Big Boy and his goons? I gasped for breath.

Her name poured into me, dragged out of *nothing*. Her name was—

"Nycendera," I shouted.

When Big Boy moved, I couldn't help but shout out, trying to warn her about what she clearly saw: the miner balling a fist as thick as a hamhock, then swinging it *down*, as if to crush her into the earth.

She moved like a dancer made of starlight, her expression indifferent. She slid effortlessly out from beneath Big Boy's falling fist. When it swung by her, she snapped her right hand out at her side, and a shock of green light flashed, wispy and thin, at the edge of her fingertips.

A knife, or the likeness of one, sprang into being, just like that.

A sliver of jade-like geode, perfectly arched, ready to stab.

She reached up, grabbed one of Big Boy's ears, and pulled him down so that his neck was just a breath away from slicing itself on the jagged edge.

I sucked in a breath. I waited. The knife never moved.

Something swam under the surface of Nycendera's face.

Confidence. Ease. Hardly a disturbance.

Red Hair pulled his rusty gun and yelled something, pointing it at her. The coal-stained one – Tar Pit – balled his fists up and prepared to pounce. The drunk one – Four of Spades – staggered toward the threat, fumbling at the back of his belt for the handle of his own knife.

Four of Spades swung his blade in a wide, lazy arc. When Nycendera pushed the Big Boy out at him, Four of Spades stumbled over his big friend and collapsed into the dirt.

Tar Pit was on her next, jumping and swinging, throwing fists that were surprisingly fast. She slipped back, her bare, metallic feet kicking up not a speck of dirt. When she found her chance, she lashed out a bare hand.

It struck. It struck more than once. It struck four, five, six times, with such rapidity that I thought I saw two, three, four ghostly fists flutter in right behind it. Tar Pit's head snapped back several times – *thunk-thunk-thunk* – and his nose burst.

Red Hair took aim, ready to shoot.

The green knife snapped out like a scorpion's tail. There might have only been one knife, but several after-images leaped into being, the arm leaving traces and memories of itself in the air. Dark blood spilled from Red Hair's wrist. She twisted the cut wrist at such a wild angle that she managed to point the revolver up into Red Hair's chin while it was still in his hand.

A too-long second was all it took for her to assess the machine, understand it, and manipulate it.

Before I could intervene, a flash.

Red Hair's skull hung open like a nutcracker's jaw as he flopped to the ground.

"Shoot the goddamn thing, Faust," said Big Boy.

As Nycendera turned, Four of Spades was there again, punching at her with the tip of his blade. She sidestepped, twisted, dodged. Never seen something move like that. Maybe wildcats. Maybe snakes.

The next instant she was behind him, and the crystal knife pierced him time and time again, punching brutal holes in his back like a sewing-needle.

He belched up a mixture of hot blood and sour whiskey, fell, and said no more.

Tar Pit was still trying to get to his feet. Nycendera leaned down, picked up Red Hair's revolver, examined it for a moment, then blindly pointed it at the miner and squeezed the trigger.

Tar Pit went still.

She dropped the weapon and began to stride toward Big Boy, her smooth feet silent on the grainy earth. Another knife flashed to life in her grip.

The big miner was quick, too. He leaped to his feet and grabbed her forearm as she sliced.

I could have interrupted. Should have.

With my feet locked into place, just the reminder, *Breathe*, drifted to mind.

When the miner punched, she flickered, moved aside, and when she stabbed, the miner swayed, avoiding the blurring edge. They struggled on like that for several moments, scuffling in the dirt.

But a body tires quick. In seconds. In less than that. Big Boy did. He tried to pull something out of his belt, and I hissed, "No," maybe at him, maybe at her, but it was too late.

Her fist fell so hard on him, blasting against his chest, that I *heard* his heart just...stop.

When the dust settled, there were four dead men. My Colts didn't matter then. I had seen what had happened to four miners in less than ten seconds, and in two more, I'd be afraid to know what would be left of me.

Nycendera simply dropped down to her knees in the bloody sand, surrounded by her handiwork. She put her palms on her knees. She watched me.

"Ours is going to be a very strange future," she said, surveying the scattered debris of bodies around her. She lifted her hands. Turned the knuckles, admired the curves, as if seeing them for the first time. "What wondrous things."

Then, the air seemed to *pop*, and all the air from the night around us poured in. Like a bubble had burst.

It was Cicero's voice, breathing hard, that I heard first. "Holy mother of God." He stood there in a half-buttoned vest, cradling the shotgun. Miss Garland was there too. The two of them saw me, saw her, saw the corpses, like a curtain had lifted before them.

Lachrimé covered her mouth.

Cicero threw me my shotgun.

I caught it in both hands, tugged back both hammers, and tucked it into the crook of my shoulder. As the world drew in around us, I noticed swan-necked children looking down from open windows. Men in longjohns and women in dingy nightgowns came out onto their porches. The street came alive with sleepy murmurs, and there was me holding a clothingless, hairless woman at gunpoint with dead men all around us.

She turned her palms upward, showing no threat. Obeying the rule of the shotgun angled at her, I suppose.

This wasn't obedience on her part: it was a truce, a willingness to submit because she *chose* to.

"What the fuck am I looking at," Cicero asked, reaching for his pistol.

"They intended to take your life," Nycendera said.

"She tore them to ribbons," Lachrimé said.

Nycendera tilted her chin to Big Boy's corpse. "Theirs was a cruel intent worth intercepting."

Staring down the barrels of my shotgun didn't allow me to feel any more powerful than I had before. I felt small, insignificant, even fragile, all ways I didn't exactly like to feel when faced with something greater than me, or that I didn't understand.

"Was this," Nycendera said, "a miscalculation?" As if finally noticing the bodies for the first time, in all their breathless wonder, looking like smoking lumps of meat.

"You could *say*," Cicero said, shoving his forearm against his nose.

Nycendera lifted both her hands, those weapons of hers, and kept staring at me. She crossed her fingers behind the crest of her bald head and lowered her eyes to the earth.

"Then I submit myself to you freely, Elias Faust, on penalty of destruction: I, known as O'uluth ar Nycendera, called elsewhere the Herald, have overstepped her boundaries to a grievous degree and from this moment, shall fully obey your tenets."

She knew my name without me ever having given it to her. A sour knot of disgust clogged my throat. Had she...taken it out of me, the way she'd first given me that strange name of hers?

Cicero held his sights steady on the silent creature as I slid forward and nudged her to stand with the barrels of my shotgun. We angled her toward my office, where the only jail cell in Blackpeak awaited its new resident, and Lachrimé Garland, with a handkerchief shoved against her mouth, leered down at snake-trails of blood.

I turned to her. "Can you brave the alley one more time?"

"Could. Doesn't mean I want to."

"Find what she was looking for. Don't let it get into anyone else's hands."

Her stare could have sliced me into four different pieces. "You better fancy pinning a question mark onto the end of that, Elias."

"Consider it pinned and nailed," I said. "Sorry."

She jerked around in a whisk of skirts, grateful to look away from the blood, and moved toward the alley. Leave it to Miss Garland to keep my manners in order, even at times of pure tribulation.

Cicero whistled at the crude human wreckage behind us. "So I missed the party, but I can definitely tell that wasn't your mess."

"What gave you that idea?"

"The problems aren't breathing anymore."

19

IN THE ABSENCE OF BOOKS OR LOGIC ON A SUBJECT, YOU GO WITH THE
next best thing besides bullets: the gut. Granted, this was unexplored
territory, so Cicero and I did the only thing that seemed logical when
faced with the unfamiliar. We drank about it.

He poured glasses for both of us while I guided Nycendera to the
lone cell. It'd seen its share of drunks and fools and fighters. At the
rusted door she stood, gazing blankly at the rusted bars. "Is this the
consequence?"

"One of a few."

"Must I enter?"

"Make this easy on me," I said. "This is the way it goes."

"A Herald abides by no metal box," she said.

"You killed four men."

"They tried to kill you," the strange woman countered.

I readjusted my grip on the shotgun. "And then you gave yourself
up to me, so this is just the next step in the process."

A haze of misunderstanding clouded her face. "I wished to show
you that I meant no harm. You would call it a courtesy."

Cicero snorted, sipping whiskey in liberal gulps. He leaned over to look out the window, squinting at the street. "A remarkable display of discretion. Faust, heads up: the curious eyes are starting to gather."

And they always did, sooner than later. Sometimes it was the cleanup that became the hardest part: the organization, the fixing, putting everything right before too many questions arose. "You exploded like a stick of dynamite out there. I'm growing used to handling volatile quantities, whether it's folks with drunken vendettas or women with gold in their veins. If you don't want this to get any messier—" and I sure as hell didn't, "—then the best place for you is inside, pride be damned."

"And if I refuse?"

She tightened her fist around one of the bars. I locked up, but kept my finger ready. Cicero touched his holster. Whatever she was, we were nothing. She could make us nothing. I said, "You already wrestled one chance from me to perform my duties. I won't let it happen twice. I'd prefer it not happen twice. Whatever your claim to fame, I'm asking you to be human in as many regards as you can manage. Give me a chance to do my work *my* way, because you've not even been here a damned half-hour and I'm already cleaning up."

Whether it was the lamplight shifting or my own perceptions playing games, her whole temperature changed: the gold of her skin softened, a crackle of brightness flared in her eyes. Her tension, her strength, it all rolled out of her and she picked her way into the cell like a beleaguered child.

She found the bed, sat down, and like the arm on an unwound watch, she went still.

Cicero's hand grazed my shoulder. "Where's she from," he asked.

"Hell if I know. Just showed up, no ceremony, no warning, just...was. Miss Garland found her." I avoided the falling part.

"Right," Cicero said. "But I mean, where's she *from*," as if asking the question a second time would somehow change the answer. Because hell, I didn't know; I didn't really care to know, except that this peculiar woman, this so-called Herald, had just played mud-pits in the guts of four men out in the middle of town.

"You got that drink?" I asked.

"Thought you'd never ask." He put a smooth glass in my hand.

The whiskey tasted like old rust. I put my forehead on the cool bars of the cell. "I need to know if you'll do it again, what you did to those men."

"If such men require it," Nycendera said, not looking at me.

I didn't know what questions to ask or if there even *were*. I could have gotten more progress shoving a thumb up my ass. A shadow crossed the front window. Cicero took a preparatory swig and muttered, "Oh, lookie. Here comes the Fuck Patrol."

Right on cue.

Just as I turned, the door flew open, admitting one of the most unpleasant men I'd ever had the misfortune of seeing. A strange mixture of fragile-thin and burlap-sack thick, he looked like a bag of curdled milk wearing a pair of tiny spectacles. His thick hands, purple and flaky, clutched in modesty to a sleeprobe. He rattled, "There you are," with an edge of accusation.

A smaller figure, leaner and stronger and silent, entered just behind the huge man and leaned against the wall next to the door.

"Mayor," I greeted the living sack of cream. "Whiskey?"

"Stuff your whiskey straight up your ass," said Mayor Morgan Kallum, his words inflating his cheeks with rage. "Be a great night indeed if I could sit back and drink whiskey to my heart's content, but I happen to think that with four dead bodies laying out in the street, there's more important things to be done."

"One of them's sort of slumped, actually," I corrected him. "That means there's three laying and one sort of sitting."

"So I hired a marshal and a comedian at the same time," said Kallum.

"And an actor," I said, motioning to Cicero. "Shakespearean."

"Word from the saloon says that you hauled away a woman who did the killing."

I pointed with my half-filled glass at the figure lounging behind the bars.

He frowned. "What in God's name is that?"

"Definitely not a dead body," Cicero said.

The mayor snapped the glass of pale whiskey out of Cicero's hand. He threw it down onto the floor, shattering glass and spraying whiskey across the floor like bad art. "You mind shutting your mouth for a minute, you degenerate shit? I don't remember you giving permission to hire this clown, Faust."

"Didn't think I needed your permission," I said.

"You did."

"Noted for future reference," I said. On any normal day, Kallum annoyed like a swollen pimple. No matter what he wanted to call himself, Mayor Morgan Kallum wasn't a real mayor. He was just a lucky monopolist who happened to have cash at hand and managed to turn Blackpeak from a dingy little mining town into a dingy little mining town with some whores in it.

Still staring at her, he said, "You need to go to Undertaker Ivanmore and move those corpses out of the street so they don't start smelling to high hell. Already got a crowd gathered, like they're going to pop up and do some kind of talent show."

"They ain't starting anymore trouble, ain't pissing in the troughs," I said.

"Corpses," Kallum repeated.

"Cicero," I said. "The Mayor wants me to tell you that he wants you to go to Ivanmore and move those corpses out of the street so they don't start smelling to high hell."

The actor threw his hands up. "I didn't make the damn things. Why should I need to have them cleaned up?"

Kallum said, "Get out."

Cicero squared his ox-like shoulders. "This is horseshit." He pushed past Kallum and stormed out of the office, leaving me alone with the mayor.

When Cicero was gone, I took my hat off my head, tossed it on the desk, and crossed my arms. "You said it yourself when you hired me on, Mayor. This is my town to supervise as needed, so long as I keep the shit from flying too much."

"The shit's flying, Faust. Things you're doing are making this town uneasy. You killed off one of the Gregdon boys over a dispute he was having with a drunk. You let an untried convict accompany you on a clean-up mission at the Fulton barn where you thought you could make some difference." The beady balls of his eyes narrowed into bulging slits. "Innocent boy got burned to death because you miscalculated. Now this."

Something sparked in me, like a thumbnail to a match. My right hand clenched around the whiskey glass. My left went to my Colt.

The mayor's man reached for the revolver tucked in a tight cross-draw holster in front of his belly.

Kallum raised a hand. "I'm talking to the marshal," he said. The small fellow nodded and sunk back against the wall. "Touched a nerve? Mistakes do that, Faust. They make you act a fool when somebody calls you on them. When you misjudge, families like the Fultons have nothing but a few smoldering wood-ashes to stuff in an urn."

A boy hanging from the rafters of the Fulton farm, kicking his feet like a rag doll.

My mouth full of fire and ash.

Sorry, kid.

I gnawed on the inside of my cheek until I thought my teeth had pierced the skin. "They came for me, Kallum. Not just for fun, either. Ready to slice me apart, raging drunk and mighty pissed."

"Do you blame them? You going to go up there and do their job, Marshal? You going to fix that up too? I don't mind you needing to break some skulls if it keeps this place running, but if men keep dying, who am I going to have buying whores and drinks? Corpses don't fuck, Faust. Corpses don't make me money."

I took my hand away from the Colt. It was easy to go for the pistol sometimes. Sometimes too easy. A hot surge of anger rose up in me as I flicked my eyes toward Kallum's hired fellow.

Find words. Diffuse the situation. Better choice. "She took care of them too fast for me to do a thing about it," I said.

"She fast enough to dodge bullets?"

"Maybe," I said.

"You fast enough to dodge bullets?"

"Fast enough to catch them," I said. "Just maybe not with my hands."

Kallum drifted closer toward the bars of the cell and looked in. A living trophy in a skin-tight suit of gold and jewel that she couldn't peel away, she turned her chin, stared at Kallum, stared through him...

He stepped back until his ass struck the desk.

Without looking away from her, he said, "Give me your keys, Faust."

"What is this about?" I asked.

"I want you to take a day or two and reassess yourself. You find what edges of yours you need to tie up, and you tie them up tight enough so they never come apart. I can't have sloppy work in this town. You've pissed off enough people that there's no other option but for your work to be shoddy."

His friend hitched a ride on a floorplank and came closer, drumming his fingers on his gun-handle.

Muscle. So that's what this was. Made sense now.

"Give me your keys," said Kallum, "then I want you to take your shit, find a room at the saloon, and piss off for a few days. You and your Shakespearean darling can buy a hooker and take turns for all I care. Just get out of my sight."

If I wasn't his marshal anymore, then what kept me from laying him out? I slammed the keys into his upturned hand. "What's your plan with her?"

Only men with money to burn manage to look at others like novelties. Kallum rapped his knuckles against the bars. She didn't startle. She didn't look.

"I'll do as is done with all rabid beasts."

"How you intend on doing that?'

"Trial. Judge Fairchild's still around after your Partridge fiasco." He smiled. "Two days from now, I'll gather the court in the town hall and let Blackpeak all see this too-fast-for-Faust piece of work before we hang her strange ass."

He went for the door, but stopped with his hand around the handle. He stared into the woodgrain for a few long seconds.

"I want you to bring yourself down a notch or two, Faust. I want you to know what the price of pride is. Killing doesn't bother me except when it's out on the streets. I don't want some young gun who thinks he knows the world like the back of his hand getting a hard-on every time he gets the chance to determine right from wrong. This is my town, Elias Faust. I have the final word."

Kallum held out the ring of my keys to his compatriot, who took them up and latched them to his gunbelt. Kallum pushed his way out of my office, each board creaking and bowing beneath the weight of his puffy ankles. When he vanished, I closed the door and lit a cigarette.

Through the gray smoke I looked at the man still standing beside the door. He looked back at me. He stepped into the light of the oil lamps. There were wisps of black hair on the bottom of his chin. He couldn't have been more than maybe nineteen or twenty.

"You got a name or something?" I said.

One of his sharp eyebrows raised. He made a wriggling motion with his fingers at the bottle.

"No name, no whiskey," I told him.

His upper lip curled. "César."

When he caught the bottle, he just popped it open and took a few quick swigs out of the neck. Trained drinker, I supposed, or just a hard-ass kid trying to put on a good act. He ambled toward the cell. He knocked the bottle against the bars. This time the Herald stirred. César rubbed his stubble like an oracle does a crystal ball. "She's a strange one," he said, then raised his voice: "You hear me, Goldilocks? You a strange one, showing up out of the blue."

"Same could be said for you," I said.

"*Señor* Kallum pays good money. Better than Díaz and the Army. Little tasks, fat wallet." The Mexican pressed his face against the rusted bars. "Plenty of dealing with the strange. Unlike gringos like you, first instinct isn't *pew pew*. Patience," he said. "You want something dead, you do it smart. Where she come from?"

"Found her wandering on her own. Wait, does Kallum know something?"

"He knows a thing or two. Sometimes more." He smacked his heel against the bar, rattling the iron. Her bald head rasped against the bed as she turned to leer at him.

"He barely spent ten seconds looking her over, and he thinks she deserves to die?"

"Barely spent ten seconds looking at what was done outside. Knows enough after that."

"So why don't you just shoot her now?" I said.

He shrugged. "Why didn't *you* shoot her then, *amigo*?" When I didn't immediately respond, César snapped me a thumbs up. "Remarkable! Intuition. You got it too. A miracle, ah? Sense enough to know you when you do it one way, sense enough to know when you do it another. You didn't act quick, so he's gotta."

She hadn't come seeking trouble. Regardless, even if she had just been defending herself, she was going to get hanged anyway, and probably sooner and harder when they discovered there was *something else*.

Then again, looking at her told anyone all they needed to know.

Nobody would need to miss lunch the day of the trial, at least.

"Place is all yours, Emperor," I said. I grabbed up the tin of my hand-rolled smokes and some matches.

The Herald Nycendera did not look at me as I left.

By the time I got halfway up the street toward the Crooked Cocoon Saloon, the bodies had already been moved away and rake-lines ran snaking paths through the gravel.

For everything I'd lose by the time this situation was over, the Herald had landed herself in the most expensive mud-puddle imaginable: in a few days, she'd have lost her life, and nobody'd bat a goddamn eye about it.

20

WITHOUT MY OFFICE, I WAS A TRANSIENT. I HAD OPTIONS, BUT THEY weren't much to speak of. With a few bits you could lodge in a room at the Crooked Cocoon. When you did, you slept upstairs where the beds smelled like sweat and smoke and booze, where threadbare sheets were crusted with the musty odors of old sex and sour feet. Say you were hankering for some pleasure, there were bound to be some freelancers of every persuasion.

That wasn't for me. Least not tonight. So to Lady De Santos's I went.

Aremeda's common room was packed. The rugs had been cleaned since the last time I came. The candles in the glass on the walls gave a warm feeling to the halls. Her ladies could almost have been confused for proper belles if it weren't for the stains on their dresses and the stink of their armpits. Classier than the Crooked Cocoon and more expensive. High maintenance, fake accents. If saloon girls were the *whores-devores*, then Horseshoe women were the main course.

"Rumor has it that whenever there's blood, you're somewhere not far behind," Aremeda told me as she found the key to a room. "I'm not going to have much business if this doesn't relent. There's only a few hundred people in this pesky town, my friend. If bodies keep dropping around you, this town's fixing to go under in just two years' time. You looking for company tonight?"

I shook my head.

"Nabby's available," she reasoned, looking at her books. "And Phillipa."

"Nabby'd ride me to oblivion and back if I let her," I said.

"That's why I call her the Troubles-Killer," she said. "Or Salted Earth."

"Ha."

"Got others who can coddle you if you want it, maybe give you some soft love. Pet you 'til you purr. Come on, my boy, don't wallow. It's goddamn sad. Cornelia's free."

"I think I'd rather not."

"Not even Nathaniel?"

"Not tonight," I said.

I forsook indulgence. Instead I drank. You ask me how much I drank, I wouldn't really be able to tell you. It just seemed like a good idea at the time, because alcohol has a habit of convincing you that it's the best way to alleviate a problem. Sometime in the night, whiskey might as well have been water.

Night slashed by me in a blur. There was an argument at some point with someone – God knows who – and I sang something off-key and I spat at somebody in the street and pissed some silly patterns into the dirt near the Horseshoe hitching-post, and I thought of the Herald until her face was a drunken blur in my head and a parade of corpses and the sockets of Keswick Everett's eyes...and whole fields full of those black, leaning figures and their shoe-leather tongues...

...and that boy – Joshua, *HORSE* himself – staring at me, just about to burn—

Mouthful of bile, and I swayed and

(*I don't need no goddamn friends.*)

couldn't hardly shake myself dry without stumbling into the—

(*...how do I fix this. How do I set it right-side up?*)

And everything went black and I fell with a head that wouldn't stop spinning

(*You don't make any sense.*)

into a throne of cold, stone-hard pillows, clutching a silver ball.

THE NEXT MORNING my mouth tasted like an ashtray. The bed was an ocean of sweat under me. I thumbed a film of half-dried saliva off my cheek. "Jesus Christ," said Cicero from a chair in the corner, a cigarette in his hand and *The Collected Works of Shakespeare* opened in his lap. "Looks like you spent a good part of the night wrestling with two dogs in heat."

I sat up and cradled my head in my hand.

"Two *big* dogs," he said, then howled at the ceiling.

I staggered to the chair next to him. There was coffee. The smell of biscuits and gravy filtered up through the floorboards of the tiny room just big enough for the two beds and the morning table we sat at. "We're out of a job," I told Cicero when the first cup lubricated my voice enough to speak.

"Assumed as much when I saw that César asshole spinning your keys around his finger outside your office this morning. You know, there really ought to be a rule against it."

"Against taking a man's job out from under him?"

"No, against a man gluing pubic hair onto his chin until it looks like a beard."

Coffee brought life. A tiny burn in the middle of my palm smarted when I touched the hot mug. A rogue cigarette wound, I reckoned. I squinted at it with disapproval.

Cicero closed his book of Shakespeare and thumped it down on the dusty table. "So, at least that first part's done."

Then I squinted at him.

"The explosive part. The inner riot. When something burns you up and you just can't fathom spending a night any other way than wanting to destroy everything big and small – and yourself in the process. That's how you let it out. How's it feel, being glass?"

"What's that supposed to mean?"

"I can tell something's bothering you. It isn't the job or the lack thereof. Doesn't take much to tell something's going on inside a man who drinks himself stupid when stuff goes to shit."

"Ain't that what everyone does?"

Cicero refilled coffees for both of us. "It's the boy, Faust."

I looked down at my hands and tried to remember where the burns and blisters had been. They hadn't been there long; they'd mended and healed quickly enough, leaving little more than pink and scabby blotches in their wake.

Cicero continued. "You try to push it aside and act like nothing's wrong, but if anyone here can see through a veil of lies, you're looking at him. Trying to get that Fulton kid out of there before it fell took a lot out of you. You didn't succeed," the actor admitted, slurping beige coffee he'd filled with cream, "but that doesn't mean that you have to shoulder that blame."

"Ain't letting it eat at me."

"Look at you. You're a stinking, sweaty, hungover sack of dogshit, Faust. You don't think I'll see the correlation between an innocent boy dying on your watch and this sudden burst of binge-drinking and self-disappointment? You're a window and I can see right through you."

"I'd as quickly blame it on Kallum."

He shook his head. "I reckon you're just about approaching the second phase of your personal reflection."

"Which is?"

"Human puddle," he said.

Things you do as a marshal – hell, as a human – stay with you, no matter how small or big they are. But usually it's not so much the things you do as the things you *don't* do.

I remembered how Joshua's mother cried. I remembered how the Herald tore those men to pieces and I just stood there. I just fucking stood there.

"Doubts are a heart's poison," Cicero said. "You can't do a damned thing but bear them because you're the only one that was there and the only one that could have done anything to prevent it. She killed those men quick as can be. They're going to put her on trial and kill her. You and I are both painfully aware of how unfair they'll be. You're looking it right in the face, and you think you're responsible for that."

"My prisoner," I said. "My responsibility."

"There's the human puddle I was expecting to meet."

"Kallum doesn't have any right taking me off my post."

"Power's what he makes it to be. When the dead bodies stacked up after Partridge, he certainly could have, but it wouldn't have afforded him any advantage. Getting you up-in-arms about this random woman, that sways public opinion in his favor and away from you."

I made it my business to keep things in Blackpeak safe, wholly outside of who benefitted or who it broke down. I'd never wanted Kallum's position, never yearned for it, and sure as hell never breathed even a word of that idea to anyone. "Couldn't ask me just to step down?"

"Looks bad on him. This gives him impetus. Makes you look an impulsive fool."

"You think he's trying to play at something?"

"I barely know him, but he's big-fish,-little-pond material. He's just the self-proclaimed mayor of a dusty little town most people would rather forget. Worst part about not mattering a damned thing is knowing that when you die, you'll just get tossed in a grave without a name on it and nobody will remember or care. That scares a man."

"Explains his bodyguard," I said.

"A man threatens you or Blackpeak, Faust, *you* lead by example. *You* shoot and you kill. I think Kallum might be afraid that he could be one of your next, especially with someone as dangerous as Miss Murder at your fingertips. He's got to stifle you any way he can."

"So he's afraid I'll take his town."

"The minute bodies started stacking up around you, you flashed your alpha hackles. Rules of nature and all."

"He takes away my sway for awhile," I considered, forgetting about the war-drums slamming between my ears, "and uses Nycendera to cement his own mercilessness."

"Power without needing to raise a gun or pull a trigger to do it."

I pulled on my trousers, strapped on my suspenders, gathered my vest, and brushed the dust off of my sun-bleached hat. Washed and shaved and dressed, I felt sort of alive again. Thoughts of burning barns and scarecrow shadows faded to a whisper. If I did nothing, then that woman was going to die. "Kallum told me he was going to get Fairchild to try her tomorrow. I want to go to that trial. I'll more likely than not need your help."

He picked at the side of his teeth, trying to find pieces of breakfast. "Every time you want help, Faust, people go belly up. No offense."

"She should die to cement his authority?"

He licked his thumb and turned a page. "You look at what she's done and tell me if the small part of you that isn't crammed up your own ass doesn't think Kallum's entirely wrong. She's no innocent, Faust. Four men. Yeah, four real assholes, but four living, breathing bodies—" he snapped his fingers, "—just like that."

"She protected me. It's only right."

"Some stupidity I'll stand beside," Cicero said, before shaking his head. "Just some."

Blackpeak might have been subject to Kallum's authority, but for the past few years, it had been kept safe by my eyes, my guns, and my law. To lawyers and judges, law might have been words on pages, lines of ink to be debated and crossed out and rewritten. To me it was a hard border, something you stood beside and, come blood or fire, you upheld. A foundation to be built on and preserved. A matter etched in stone.

I asked Cicero for his black string-tie.

21

THEY GAVE HER CLOTHES, AT LEAST.

Just before nine the next morning I watched as César escorted the Herald up the dusty street. With a pair of dirty trousers cinched around her waist, a flowered tunic, and a pair of cracked U.S. Cavalry boots, she looked almost normal. Almost. Rusty chains heavied her golden wrists and ankles. They disappeared into the old hall's tall, black doors. Place was packed. You don't need to post signs about a trial. Dead miners do their own promotion.

I pressed my head against the doors and listened to the commotion inside the town hall. A bunch of voices bantered back and forth. Folks packed in hot, impatient crowds gasped and awed at *her*.

They'd never seen anything like her.

They'd never known such a thing could exist.

So they were damn happy to do what too-proud white people normally do with those who look different. I rolled Joshua's little steel ball back and forth between my thumb and forefinger, feeling its polished surface and perfect curves. Good order in a wild world.

"The gravity of the loss of human life is indeed hard to measure," said someone I recognized to be Judge Fairchild. He sounded like someone's sharp-witted grandpa, his words coming out in whistling breaths.

"Four industrious citizens, scraped up out of the gravel like undercooked griddle-cakes."

"Any motivation?"

"A woman of whatever fascinating origin can still be a creature of destruction, Your Honor. No cause here but chaos and hate."

"Prosecutor Bromley, does it seem plausible to believe these murders were premeditated?"

"Absolutely. This was mutilation and dehumanization."

Judge Fairchild rejoined with, "Can men not walk the streets in Blackpeak safely anymore?"

"Not with vagrants such as her alive and well," said Bromley.

Mayor Kallum's voice rose up over the conversation between judge and prosecutor. "I will not allow this town to become a haven for the cruel and the peculiar, gentlemen."

"What in God's name has she done with her flesh?" Fairchild asked.

"An aberration of nature," Kallum said. "Nothing more."

Bromley said, "Mayor Kallum, what cannot and should not be ignored is that this is an illness in your community, this violence that ever seems ingrained in it. How did she come to be here? How do any of your people thrive with the shadows of ruin hanging over their heads?"

Kallum's voice softened so much, I could barely hear it through the door. I closed my eyes, as if shutting out the world would make it easier to hear. "Judge Fairchild, Mister Bromley, establishing a town and ensuring its survivability on so few resources is no easy task. We often find ourselves appealing to the most...*frugal* type of citizen. And the most enterprising."

"And the most lawless," Bromley returned. "Crown Rock thrives quite well, and without the chaos bred here. We have established ourselves as a town of some repute."

"You are a municipality governed by a board, protected by a

willing militia, and aided by the writ of local constitution. I am but one man aided by a citizen marshal."

"Where is Mister Faust this morning? Was this not his responsibility to prevent?"

Kallum wielded patience like a knife. "I have removed him from his position in dispute with his methods. In his absence, I've installed Corporal César Salgado, a former member of the Mexican Army and my personal friend, with the expectation that we enhance our practices from this point forward."

A load of horseshit had more integrity. Dispute? It had never bothered him until now, so spoke his silence and my salary. The fair-weather bastard took any chance to elevate himself.

Judge Fairchild said, "Is Mister Faust present?"

Kallum said, "No, he is not," with the closest thing to speed he'd ever known.

It was Nycendera the Herald who spoke next, because her voice seemed to hum like the teeth of a fork striking stone.

"This man lies to you," she said. "For the being of whom you speak stands right outside the door."

Maybe if I stood still long enough, she'd laugh it off like some kind of poorly-timed joke. That'd be just fine with me. I felt every single eye — the straight ones and the crossed ones — turn to the door, and about the only thing I could hear was the hissing rush of blood in my inner-ears. Did she mean me?

Shit. She meant me.

Don't give Cicero the credit; I'm an avid contemplator of the *the-a-tuh* myself. I took the cue and threw open the doors to the town hall with both hands.

I kept my chin down and marched up the center aisle of the town hall. There were townspeople sitting in chairs on either side, staring me stupid. Judge Fairchild was a little fellow, his head covered in wispy hair and his body almost invisible under his faded black robes. He held a shingler's mallet over the nicked-up table he sat behind.

"Your Honor," I said, taking Cicero's bowler off of my head and squeezing it between my hands.

They all sat stiff as gravestones, staring at me so fiercely I wondered if they knew just how tightly-puckered my asshole was. Meanwhile, Nycendera the Herald, her glass teeth shining behind crown-gold lips doing their best imitation of a smile, seemed pleased as punch.

The prosecutor named Bromley, a man in a bulging brown suit and glasses thicker than a bullet, leaned toward me. "You are interrupting a trial in progress. Do you have anything to say for yourself?"

"Probably so," I said. "But nobody saw fit to ask, apparently."

Mayor Kallum sat with the crowd in the hall, leaning against a wall and smoking a thick pipe that never seemed to run out of tobacco. His eyes were on me like flies on shit. Good he smoked, because his rage boiled like an overheated pot just under the surface.

"Marshal," Judge Fairchild said. "Word has it that you were present for this grotesque display."

"You mean the killings, or this lovely courtroom pageant of yours?"

Bromley barked, "He ought to be held in contempt."

"Good to see you too, Bromley," I said.

I knew these fellows. Not intimately, mind you, and not at the whims of the same kind of fancy bureaucratic relationship they shared with Mayor Kallum. The Judge cleared his throat. "It wasn't too long ago that we were all in here to see Mister Partridge get put to trial. Pageantry or not, the same process applies this time."

"Partridge hurt some good people," I said.

Bromley ground a fist into his table. "This monster tore fathers away from their families, Faust."

"Different trial, different situation."

"Are you questioning the legitimacy of this courtroom, Faust?"

"I'm just saying that it might smell a little bit like a traveling sideshow," I said. "Or just bullshit."

The crowd of townsfolk erupted into a murmur of whispers and gasps. I took a long minute to gaze at Mayor Kallum where he sat like a blister. This was the type of game he liked: he could watch on from afar as pieces moved, not because he lifted them himself, but because he slipped dollars into the pockets of folks who moved them for him. For Kallum, visibility was legitimacy.

But I'd heard him loud and clear, and it sat wrong on that little shelf above my stomach where feelings had one hell of a time staying still. "This woman is already as good as dead in your eyes. But Partridge, a white man, he's still alive, ready to rot away in Huntington."

Bromley's throat fizzed with frustration. "Citizens of Blackpeak are dead and you expect what, exactly? Clemency for their killer? This isn't about what she *is*—"

"Hell it isn't."

From the chairs, Kallum said, "Sit down, Faust."

"You mean to tell me you all don't see?"

"Sit down, Faust."

But I went on. "Of course you see." I swallowed. Cicero's string-tie bit into the skin of my neck. Maybe I'd planned to come in and start shit. I'd dressed for the occasion, after all. I lifted my sleeve and let it roll down far enough to show off the flesh of my wrist. "Something about her looking far different from *this*," I gave my skin a few slaps of the forefingers, "turns your guts into soup, and most everybody in this room is just waiting to see what kind of juicy mess you plan to make with someone that couldn't blend into the crowd."

"Marshal," Judge Fairchild said. "You're derailing the trial of someone about to be sentenced to death."

"Elias," I said. "Just Elias. I'm on holiday for the time being according to Mayor Kallum. But there's words I'm meant to give, because I was right there when those four miners got some leaks put in them."

At that point, Kallum stood.

"She did it on my behalf. She did it for me," I said.

Bromley sucked in a ribbon of air through that gap in his front teeth. "Explain this."

The room tightened up harder than a rawhide knot.

"They had beef with me. They got drunk. It was a bad decision from the start. They found an opening. So they capitalized."

The Judge asked, "Did you ask her to intervene?"

"I'm one man. They were four," I said. "If anything requested her action, it was numbers alone."

Bromley shook his head. "Elias Faust, protected by strangers in the night. First Miss Eliza Fulton, now this. No wonder Kallum heeled you like a dog. You ask too much of others."

Nycendera, from her chair, jerked once, as if struck. "He did not ask this of me."

"From the outside," Bromley continued, "it's easy to see the patterns at work. The women do a better job at cleaning the rabble out in your name."

"He did not ask this deed of me."

Bromley's voice trembled with severity. "Yet you turned those men inside out. Whether or not Elias Faust requested this, you performed it. You willingly murdered, and should hang by the neck for the act. Do you deny ending the lives of those four men?"

"I do not."

"Did it please you?"

Her hard lips remained closed.

"Bloodthirsty bitch," someone muttered in the benches.

Which cemented it for me, really. Bromley was the mouthpiece, and Judge Fairchild the means. Around these parts, being American meant hating anything that wasn't like you, and my God, if this woman of gold and green was anything, she wasn't *us*. When white men died, not even other white men paid that price.

Because for men like Partridge, men like us, the laws glanced right off or just melted away like ice beneath a sunbeam.

These people would all stack their blame on whatever shoulders weren't their own. Exactly what Kallum wanted, too. Tight ship. Ensured his little world saw him at all times for all he could offer.

And that's why I shouldn't have been the least bit surprised when, standing just behind him, I noticed Lachrimé Garland giving him something wrapped in a little handkerchief square. She caught my gaze for just a little finger-snap second. Then it was gone, and I thought she flew a thousand miles away.

Judge Fairchild, sensing loss of control, lifted his shingler's hammer. "What has become tremendously clear, Mister Faust, is that you possess little control over yourself let alone the firebrands and vagabonds in your town."

"So she'll die because you want to make an example?"

"She'll die," Bromley added, "because that is the law."

"Partridge gets Huntsville," I said, "and she gets the noose? Just *because*?"

The judge held his hands out to his sides. "Do you expect me to change the norms of society, Faust? This creature is going to die, whether it be by the terms of my verdict—"

"Or at the hands of men and women in Blackpeak who won't cease to lynch her before she can skitter out of town," Kallum barked from his corner.

You could feel the angry static crackling in the air like an oak fire. I felt the sudden urge to hold the Colt tucked underneath my jacket. I saw César in the corner thinking about his gun. We locked eyes. At least we agreed on something.

Kallum had everyone's attention now. He brandished the wrapped trophy.

The object he shook free looked like smoke-filled glass, glowing and brilliant. As long as a hand from palm to fingers and as sharp as a fang, it looked almost unreal: a see-through artifact, shaped like a witch's finger.

"She came to murder," Kallum proclaimed. "She came to destroy."

The point of her strange, green-stone knife gleamed in Kallum's hand. It looked just like the ones Nycendera wielded in the street, but stronger, more vibrant, more real. Like the others had been but drawings, or hastily-formed copies. It pulsed, a blinding beacon, flashing like some just-awakened eye of the world.

Nycendera leaped up from her chair, cast her shackled hands out before her, and snarled, "Mine!" like a damn petulant child.

And the shard damn near obeyed.

Almost.

We all watched like bug-eyed crows as the sliver of jagged gemstone tore itself away from Kallum's hand and flew toward Nycendera.

Or tried.

Morgan Kallum had no reputation as a physical being. Despite skin as loose as an old shoe and some pockets of age that sagged him down rather than wrinkled him up, he reached out with a young man's quickness, and as the artifact shot out, he caught it again.

Holding it tight like a man fiercely clutching a kite in the wind, Kallum said, "César."

The young man snapped into action.

He jammed his gun against the back of Nycendera's round, shining skull. The hammer clacked like a beetle's legs.

Bromley launched to his feet.

Judge Fairchild smacked the head of the foot-long mallet four times on the table. Each smack sounded like a smaller-caliber gunshot.

People began to get to their feet, some filtering out of the town hall like scared rats, others flattening to the walls. My heart beat a thousand gallops a minute, and my hands shook in little sweaty fits.

"You cannot have what is mine!" Nycendera said.

Kallum stared over the precious jewel. "You present a clear and viable danger to our town. Look at you, trying for a weapon in plain sight."

"It is no weapon," Nycendera began, her skin flickering like wild flame.

Kallum nodded his head. A command.

César's arm jerked. Wood struck Nycendera's scalp. She teetered, half-turned, then crumbled.

What ran out of her wasn't blood, but quicksilver, syrup-thick and pouring out of her broken skin like a melting mirror.

"Order!" Judge Fairchild cried. Right. Wishful thinking.

Because really, once people started running past, it didn't matter what was up or down anymore. They'd seen something strange happen in front of them and their minds began to create reasons, explanations. Control blew out of Fairchild and Bromley's courtroom like the hairs of dead dandelions.

It wasn't smart, going for my gun. Gunmetal was a comfort. I drew and stared down César, but kept my finger just outside the trigger guard.

"Are we really doing this, Faust?" Kallum asked.

I shrugged. "Step back away from her, Emp," I told César.

Kallum began to wrap the gleaming shard again. "I knew you'd fuck this all to high hell." The light faded from his face as he tucked the object, bound in Miss Garland's napkin, in a pocket near his heart. "You find ways to basically shit in my wallet every day, even if you haven't even unbuckled your pants." I didn't see it all. I couldn't. Whatever Kallum had tangled himself up in, Nycendera had all his ire. "Why do you honestly care if she's safe?"

"Why do you care if she's dead?"

Bromley and Fairchild did their best imitation of statues. With guns out, the two of them were paper-thin problems at best. Bromley, the underarms of his brown vest stained with hot perspiration, slumped down into his designated chair.

Kallum sucked on his teeth. "Alright, Faust. This is an easy game to play. I don't like it, but I'll abide. Getting things ugly in the town hall is a damn bad habit. César?"

"*Sí.*"

"If you'd please."

He turned his barrel away from the golden woman's head.

Slow, slower than molasses, so I wouldn't flinch, he poised the barrel in my direction.

Tightness invaded my throat. I lay my finger across the trigger.

Kallum, cooler than a pig's muddy underbelly, patted the lump beneath his jacket. "You shoot him, you're just another disposable stiff that deserved a bullet. I imagine Salgado's had his share of men pointing guns at him in his time, so I wouldn't chance that particular game of chicken. He's the law right now. Come off it, Faust. I don't want to smell gunpowder. Shit makes me sick."

César had glare heavier than a bag of ingots. Maybe it was

because he knew he had the upper hand. Maybe a streak of hard-ass authority. He didn't shoot, though, and I didn't either.

I loosened my fingers one by one and let my pistol hang from my fingertip. I lifted my arms. César approached me and yanked the gun out of my hand. He stuffed it in his belt.

In front of Judge Fairchild and Bromley, the Mexican soldier locked a pair of stirrup-like cuffs on my wrists and drove me down to my knees.

In my closed left hand, I rolled a silver ball-bearing around in my palm.

22

ONE CELL. TWO PRISONERS. CÉSAR SHOVED NYCENDERA INSIDE AND locked my wrist to the bars. I yanked on general principle, *click-clank, click-clank.* The gold woman crumbled to the hay-stuffed mattress. Still shackled, she cradled her skull, its surface cracked like a polished eggshell. I sat in a sweltering ray of sun squeezing in through the window and boiled inside and out.

Whatever she was, it wouldn't matter once Bromley and Fairchild meted out their judgment behind closed doors. Kallum had tugged those fucks like jittery puppets, and the whole town hummed with excitement and fear. I could feel it rattling through the windows, pouring down the streets, because without something to hate, most folks just drifted around like ghosts and filled the air with complaints about time and money.

I spit on the office floor in front of César Salgado's boot-tips and said, "You happy with yourself, Emp? You knocked her to high heaven."

"Just good to know she bleeds."

At my desk, César pulled open a drawer and brought out the bottle of unlabeled whiskey I usually kept there. He pushed a ring of rusty keys aside with the bottom of a glass. He shoved my gun in a drawer for safe-keeping.

"Thought you were a responsible marshal," I said to him.

"Was a responsible soldier, too. And soldiers drink." He poured a glass.

"She needs medical attention."

"You plan to give it to her, *señor*? Because nobody except you seem to care about this mess. Bad habit, caring too much. Same old song, eh? Gringos roll in here, think they can change the world for the better just by looking at it. She bleeds," he reasoned, "she dies. Mayor will see to it in time. Or maybe she dies right there, and that's alright too."

Newly-appointed Emperor César grabbed his keys and went out to sit on the porch, whiskey in tow. All in a day's work. With one boot on the rail, he wiped fingerprints off his sixgun.

The sun leaned closer toward the horizon. Christ, I had to piss. Nycendera's gold hands, segmented like a suit of armor, were covered in silver muck. She rolled her thumb down her cheek and stretched herself up like a creature unfurling into light. "What was it," she asked, "that you expected to accomplish, interrupting their trial?"

I squatted down, rested my wrists on the cross-rails of the bars, and leaned my head into the cool metal. "It was just a parade for them."

"Then let them parade if they so choose. If that is my end, then I shall meet it."

"So you hang your hat up, just like that?"

"When you found me in the alley," she said, "I *tried* to keep you away. You refused to obey the signs."

"You didn't exactly do a damn good job of putting them in my language."

She gritted her glass teeth so hard I heard them squeak. "When the rules of the natural world begin to fall away, most creatures flee. Smart creatures flee. They survive. They obey an instinct to preserve themselves. It is either by design or by sheer stupidity that you lack the ability to understand."

Being lectured in natural fundamentals by a walking, talking antique. Nice. "So this is what I get? I pull your ass out of the mud, I basically throw myself at Bromley and Fairchild's mercy for you--"

"I did not request to be the tool of your misplaced heroism. You have undone precious works, Elias Faust, just by *being*. Now your Mayor has an object of great value merely because your friend put more trust in him than in you."

"You mean your knife?"

Her hands, still shackled, lashed out. They struck the nearby wall. She barked, "It is *not* a knife."

If I thought about Lachrimé too much, I'd feel something — and right now, I didn't have space or time for feeling. "Then why'd you use it like one?"

"I did not use *it*. I used a—" A pause, to search inside for the right word, "—a *memory* of it, brought to the forefront of my mind and made whole. A simulacrum."

"So these spikes, you just...think, and they're there?"

"You have your bullets. These?" A wisp of light sprang from her fingers, took on a green, tooth-like shape. It flickered, then vanished. "These are mine, and I use them as I must. They are a likeness, an object made of substance and will, and nothing more."

"Then why not use them to set yourself free? Fight your way out of this all?"

Her reptilian eyes fell on me. They softened like jelly. For a minute, behind them, I saw...

An ocean of stars...

A shifting sky of quicksilver tides...

Breathe, man.

"Bending reality to free myself does not give me freedom to break the rules of the world in which I find myself living. I ended those men. If I am to die for the misdeed, it is best. You were not supposed to know of me, Elias Faust. Compromising your awareness is not a mistake I will make again, whether I am destroyed, or whether I have fled."

She peddled riddles, and though questions formed like smoke in my brain, they fell apart by the time they got to my tongue. I wanted to know things, ask questions, demand answers. Ask too many, though, shit gets real. Those are trails you can't track back. Bridges out of ignorance burn quickly underneath a man's boots and land him on unfamiliar shores.

For now, she was just a woman.

One made out of gold and secrets.

Everything in its place. That was easiest.

Outside, the world became red and dull and night fell on it like a shadow.

"Will they kill you too?" she asked.

I shook my head.

"Why not?"

"Some folks have it easier here."

"In Blackpeak?"

"And beyond."

Sure, I'd be done in Blackpeak. They'd wrap me up in a nice bow and give me a nudge into the Texas badlands. West of the Pecos River, that was where you threw your skeletons and bad decisions. But I'd still have my skin. Clean slate. Kallum, Fairchild, Bromley, they'd consider it a victory. They'd say things over their cool lemonade like, *Sure, we might have killed that girl who fell from the stars, but at least we kept that white man alive.*

Why, of all the specks in the sky, did Nycendera choose this one to land on?

"When Lachrimé found you, why didn't you push her away too, and avoid all this bullshit in the first place?"

"Because I did not believe humans to be so petty. Because I was not sent here—" Nycendera's head dipped toward a shadow out front, "—for *her.*"

Outside, a familiar voice nettled César Salgado. "I want an audience with him," she said.

"No."

"Who are you to tell me no?"

"Marshal."

"My ass," Lachrimé Garland said. "Nothing more than a mustached hotspur to me. So how about you get up and go bring him out here so I can have a word or two with him. Kallum's orders."

"Welcome to go inside, *mi amiga*."

"Oh, we're *friends* now?" She snorted. "I'm not talking to him in there where *it* can overhear. Play me for a fool all you want, sweetheart, but don't confuse me for one."

Nycendera's cold lips creaked back and tightened into a line. "I will be very happy to hit her."

I whispered, "That's what got you into this situation in the first place."

"*Hit*, not maim."

César came in a moment later and thumbed through a series of rusted keys, squinting drunkenly at them. "Other one," I reminded him, before he found the right one. He grunted when he worked the key, and my shackles fell away in a clatter.

He pushed me outside with a few sharp jabs from his finger. There stood Miss Garland with her dark hands on the hips of her dress, pacing like a metronome, buzzing with tension.

Just as I was about to say something, her rigid finger shot out and crammed itself against my lips.

"Don't," she hissed. "Just don't. Because some stubborn garbage is liable to fall out of you like buffalo shit."

César flashed a pair of fingers. "Two minutes."

"Two?" Lachrimé's eyes flashed. "Nothing worthwhile ever got done in two minutes, but I wouldn't expect a boy like you to know that one way or the other. Don't worry, he's coming back." She grabbed me by the upper arm. "Frankly, he's too daft to run anywhere and too clumsy to capitalize on the urge even if it struck him."

Miss Garland led me through the tight crease of a nearby alley. I waited for it to fold over and over on itself the way the world had when we'd first found Nycendera, but it never did. Blue night had mostly taken over the sky now. Just when I expected Lachrimé to stop, maybe shove me against a wall, rip into me about what a fool I was, she kept pushing, pushing, until we came to a pathetic excuse for a fence. Nothing but the flat, purple lands lay beyond.

"Leave," she said, "just for a few days. Maybe take a sabbatical in Crown Rock or give yourself a few nights under canvas. When I turn my back, just make sure all that's left are footprints." She didn't ever look me in the eye. She clutched herself, reached in and found that simple steel in her, that matter-of-factness that Lachrimé Garland always wielded.

"You should have come to me," I said.

"Some things just aren't as easy as you want them to be, Faust."

"Yeah? You belong to Kallum now?"

When she struck me open-handed across the face, it left fire on my cheek. Howling started in my ears. Ringing. I shrank just about to the size of a penny.

She wiped her palm off on her skirt and cleared her throat. Her voice plateaued, something cool and rock-hard. "Kallum doesn't know I'm here. He'll be beside himself when he finds out. You don't seem to understand, Faust, that it's a matter of picking the right battles at the right times, and for every one you start with your gunpowder, there's twenty more I'm fighting otherwise. You've got the whole wide-open world if you want it, just snap your fingers and it's yours. But Blackpeak's all I got, and if I've got to hold onto it until my skin's rubbed raw, I'll do it. I'll do it however I must, blood ot not."

Breathing hard, her shoulders lifted and fell like a bellow. I didn't doubt her. Not then. Hopefully not ever. Violence wasn't always gunshots and knife-wounds. Sometimes it was a stare. Sometimes it was the cold quiet, fragile as glass.

In that moment, the world fell still enough for me to hear voices in the distance, carried on the breeze, chanting "Kill it, kill it," with every falling boot.

23

SHIT.

They were coming for the girl made of gold.

"No, Faust. You can't go back there." Lachrimé grabbed my elbow, dug her nails into me like I could have shed oil. "You have to leave."

"You serious?"

"As a grave."

The bottom fell out of my stomach. I tasted my own breath, hot like smoke and acid. She didn't want me to be there. She wanted me out there somewhere, feet planted firmly in useless soil, somewhere I could do nothing at all. "How much did Kallum pay you for it?"

"It wasn't about the money."

"Just because you're a good businesswoman doesn't make you a good liar," I said, and tightened my fists. I'd been rolling that silver ball bearing around and around.

God, I knew; I knew I should have just stayed back.

It wasn't my job anymore.

"You know what men can do when the world shows them something that could be a danger to their power, their status, their bodies." Lachrimé went for my hand, but I yanked it away. I struck myself over the heart, a few heavy blows to convince me my blood was still pumping, that my heart was still there. "Doesn't make it sound, but my God, you saw what she's capable of. Doesn't some part of you fear it, what this invites into our world?"

The men grew louder.

Which is when someone shouting my name came thundering on a horse up the middle of the street, a breathless Paul Revere in the night.

"Faust," they shouted. "*Faust!*"

I turned from Miss Garland, hoping she'd stay here. Hell, half-hoping I would, too.

My feet clapped up the alley as the figure emerged from a cloud of blue dust thrown up into the moonlight. The horse frothed white hot. Grady Cicero all but crumbled out of the saddle. "There you are," he heaved. "We need to move – and fast."

César stood on the porch, thumbs in his belt-loops, giving me a hard stare. "I'm in custody," I said.

"Yeah, I heard. But we've got problems far bigger than that right now, and Mexico here's going to have to make some fucking concessions." Cicero threw the reins over the hitching-post, scrambling frantically. "I ran back as quick as I could the moment I saw them. They're coming, man. They're coming, so we've either got to haul ass or do something really stupid really quickly, because..."

Over his shoulder I saw *them* rounding the corner in the town square, all moving as one mass, and my blood ran as cold as Montana winter.

I saw the torches first, tossing yellow light into the air. Smelled the kerosene-soaked rags. Felt the earth trembling underneath countless feet. Waves of disappointment and anger washed over me all at once. Their faces glowed like beacons, some obscured by kerchiefs and hats and hoods. The whole crowd moved like a single entity. If a hand didn't carry a makeshift torch, then it held some kind of weapon: pitchforks jabbing at the air, pick-axes, some even with bottles held by the neck. I started hearing their voices, too. Curses. Shouts. Unintelligible. Righteous.

Laughter, too.

"They amassed right outside the town," Cicero said. "I saw them lighting torches, went to take a gander, like I had some business knowing. You see what kind of righteous shit you've gotten into me? Heard them talking among themselves. Bad shit. Make your blood run cold shit. You think they really mean this?"

I went for the Colt stuffed in my pants, wanting that comfort that only cold steel could give.

Wasn't there.

"No time for bullets," Cicero said.

"Ring out a shot or two, the cowards among them will scatter. You could do the honors, Emp." I nodded to César.

"And leave the ones who *really* want to put a dent in your skull? Don't let your pride be a bludgeon, Faust," Cicero said. "You're a good man, but you're a *man*. Don't underestimate the overwhelming power of people doing foolish things in large groups. Bullets frighten crowds, not conviction."

Their call-and-response billowed up in the night.

"We don't stand for God-forsaken murderers."

"*Kill it,*" the crowd said.

"This is our town. This town belongs to us."

"*Kill it,*" the crowd said.

"Our town, our land, our people. It killed our boys—"

"*Kill it, kill it, kill it.*"

"—so we kill it, if we gotta."

There must have been twenty or thirty of them, shoulder-to-shoulder, carrying their fire. They didn't so much stomp or storm in as ooze like burning oil through the streets.

In seconds they'd be on us, and probably tear us into ribbons if we stood in their way. The horse Cicero had borrowed from the livery gave a tremor. I glanced at it, then at Cicero. He said, "Bad idea," as if he could read the words on my brain like one of my folded-up novels. "No time for posturing. You're not a marshal anymore, Faust. You're one of them, and if you aren't one of *them*, you're an obstacle."

"Someone has to do something." I reached for the horse.

He yanked me back by the collar.

"I'm asking you," said Cicero, before putting himself between the crowd, the horse, and my poor ideas. "You're not a city boy, Elias, but I am. I can sure as hell read a crowd. You have nothing on this. Knock you right the hell out if I have to. I'm begging you. Riots destroy men's senses, boils them down to beasts."

A fireplug of a figure came swirling out from a nearby building, crashing into a collection of men with torches. "The hale you doin' marchin' through heah lie' dat?"

"Get out the way, bitch," someone said through their teeth.

Which the *bitch* promptly knocked out.

"No place for this, for y'all, for any'a dis—"

A throng of firelit shadows converged on her.

"Ya wanna speak it," I heard her spit, "then you godda backet up wid sompin', boy." Another blow, and another man fell into others.

I started to move. Cicero threw me back.

"I'll get Peggy," he said. "Get the prisoner. Just *go*."

He unreined the horse and gave it a hauling crack across the ass. It darted toward the crowd. They all splashed against the buildings on either side of the street. Cicero descended into the crowd without any additional sound. They poured in on him.

None of them would listen. None of them, in their hoods and their hate, would have time for noise like mine. Torchlight crept toward my feet. I scrambled back, grinding my teeth together as – *shit, shit, shit* – I stormed back up the stairs, past César, and blasted into the office...

...just as the voice leaped into my brain.

It's a pity what unchecked fear can do to people, isn't it?

César followed me and watched the procession through a window. He pressed his face against the glass. Firelight danced on his cheeks.

As far as motivators go, though? Fear's a poor one, the voice said.

Nycendera was up when I got near the cell. Her sharp stare pierced through the bars. Her body moved like a wiry feline. She gleamed brighter, almost blinding.

As far as catalysts to action go, do you want to know what I prefer?

"Emp. Key. Now."

Humility. I think humility's one of the strongest motivators there is.

The front door flew open.

I realized only then why the voice had found me again. I looked down into my palm. At some point, I'd dug the tiny mirrored ball-bearing out of my pocket and clutched it like a precious gem. If the cold metal of a gun couldn't help...

Two figures exploded into the office, one donning a loose sack with sloppily-cut eyeholes, the other a kerchief across his mouth. Emp reacted immediately. He lashed out for one of the intruder's temples with a pistol-handle. It cracked across an upraised forearm. He moved into their space, driving one of them back against the wall with the heel of his boot. In the same motion, he yanked the keys off his belt and tossed them in my direction.

They skittered across the desk, hopping once, twice.

I caught them in my free hand.

While César traded blows with the sack-head, I fumbled the key into the lock. The Herald grabbed the bars, looked at me, then thrust her face out between the rusted iron. "Why?"

The key turned. "What's right," I said, "is right."

"*Why.*"

"Nobody deserves to die just to make other people comfortable."

Frustration mounted. She shot a hand through the bars and grabbed my wrist. With iron fingers, she turned my palm upright and pried it open. I saw myself in the silver ball. She saw herself too. It lay perfectly in the canyon between the lines in my skin. Right atop of that burnt patch of skin.

Oh, he said in my head. *She's got a sense, that one.*

"Why," she demanded again.

She pushed me back with a vicious palm. I barely managed to keep hold of the bearing.

I fell into the kerchiefed figure right behind me, blowing the air out of him.

His palm engulfed my face. He threw me back into the desk. I collided with it, all sharp edges hitting sharp edges. Meanwhile,

César and the one in the sack wrestled over the Mexican's gun. I tore the desk open, grabbing my Colt.

Classic Faust. Killing. And why? Because it's easy?

In the corner of my eye, I saw César go for a boning knife sheathed in the back of his gunbelt. His assailant tore the pistol away, then cracked him across the side of the brow with it. César dropped.

Then the gun was on me, and Edward Sloman, the owner of the general store, said to me from under the sack: "Sorry, Elias, but I can't let you shoot my friend. Slide him your gun, nice and easy. All we want is the gold one."

I put the Colt on the floor, nice and easy, and nudged it toward Kerchief with the edge of my boot. It slid and spun.

"This what you really want?" I asked Sloman.

Kerchief picked up my Colt. He leveled it on the Herald. Outside she could have probably had a chance, but behind bars and surrounded by brick, a bullet was bound to hit its mark.

With all those mysteries at her fingertips, she summoned none of it.

The rusted cell door moaned open, and Kerchief stood right in the doorway, blocking her exit. "Knees," Kerchief said. "Now."

Nycendera's chest rose, fell, rose, fell. With her fingers interlaced behind her head, she kneeled. From his belt, Kerchief took a length of rope.

His knee nearly cracked her jaw in two. She folded. Mercury drooled to the floor in long strings. He lashed the rope about her neck, once, twice, three times, and just as she tried to twist and fight against it, he yanked. He dragged her from the cell.

No. Not like that. God, not like that.

"You want to be stained by this?" I said to Sloman. "Associated with it for the rest of your days? You want to grow old with this?"

"I want to grow old," Sloman said.

Flopping and twisting like a hooked fish, Nycendera's body scraped across the floor. I saw her eyes in a flash: bloodshot, corners gone red, almost squeezing out her sockets. Whatever secrets lingered in her veins either refused to leap out right then, or simply couldn't.

One of her fingernails snapped free of its base as she grabbed hold of a floorboard.

Kerchief wrenched her out the door.

It's out of hand, Faust. This whole thing, it's simply gone awry.

Every time he spoke it was an anvil screaming sparks and fire in my head. Edward Sloman crammed his weapon into the small of my back. "This isn't about you, and it's not about me. We'll do what we have to do. Town's got no beef or trouble with you, but any friend of a problem like that is a problem for all of us."

"Don't cross this bridge," I warned him.

"Just don't interfere. That *thing's* not got much of a life after what it did, but you still have one. This is your voucher – for all you've done for us before now, you hear?"

He shoved me aside and stormed out.

If I went out there, they'd tear me to pieces. They'd have their corpse. That much hate, it scorches and scours and slaughters; I'd have no sense to talk into them. Not that they'd hear. But I couldn't handle that hellacious cackling, that teasing, that joy—

"Bring her on over here," someone bellowed.

"Look at me, you fuckin' monster."

"Christ, boys, she's petrified! Sling her round this way. No, *this* way."

"That horse. Get that horse."

I tightened my fist around Joshua's silver ball until my fingernails tore into my skin.

Out the window, a small resistance pulsed from within the torchlit crowds. I saw Cicero's too-red face as he barreled, bloody and exhausted, into two men who beat the hell out of him with blunt sticks. Then there was Peggy Winters, holding her own, throwing enough elbows that the sleeves of her dress were torn and red.

Then I saw her. Nycendera. Thrashing. Being dragged by one man toward another two who held the horse – Cicero's horse – by its reins.

It would only take a few seconds, if the horse ran fast enough...

The torches would do the worst of the work afterward. Melt her, even if they couldn't burn her.

"What will this cost," I said to the silence of my office.

Very little, really.

Nycendera managed to slip the knot. She took on *all* of them. They came down on her with torches and bludgeons. The girl made of gold never tired, though her graceful motions collapsed. She became a lunging, lurching mass. She broke one man's nose with her forehead.

I swallowed.

"Help me," I said. "Please." The words rang out in the air, reaching for nothing and everything all at once. Disembodied and fragile, almost like they weren't mine. They echoed off the corners of my office before settling like dust into the cracks.

See? That wasn't so hard. Sometimes all it takes...

"...is a little bit of resignation."

In my palm, the silver sphere shuddered.

It leaped out from between my knuckles and shot across the room, right between the bars of the cell, where a waiting hand snapped it out of the air. The palm – old, craggy, covered in a mass of liver spots – turned upward. The ball rolled into its new owner's grip.

Where there'd been nobody but moments before, now *he* was.

"Elias Faust," Magnate Gregdon said. "There you are in the flesh, murderer. And now, so am I."

HE SAT shirtless on the bunk in the jail cell, his spine bent like he was reading a book. When he stood, I saw how age had chewed away at him. His arms were twigs, the flesh of a once-hale man hanging like rooster-waddles from his elbows. A sunken chest peppered with hair looked more like parchment than skin. "Looks like you've got something of a problem on your hands."

He wiped off a bit of lather from the underside of his cheek. A spot of it still clung on.

It was some morsel of knowledge garnered from the silver ball that told me this was the Magnate, the man whose voice had played interloper in my skull. He wore a pair of loose pants that only stayed upright by virtue of frayed suspenders, one strap on, the other hanging free. A hayfield of whiskers covered the left side of his face, but the right was red and angry, freshly trimmed.

I found it hard to look at him. My nerves shot to the ends of their registers. The din from outside became a murmur. "It's *you* been talking to me? From—" it sounded crackers, "—beyond?"

"One and only."

"How," I said. "How does it work?"

"Don't start jabbering stupid questions you and I both know there's no time to answer. All I had to do was knock you down a few rungs so you could admit there was something you couldn't handle. Was that so hard?"

"Can you help me?"

"Fine question to ask the man whose son you shotgunned out a window." He peered outside, his gaunt face wearing the color of fire. "Goodness, Faust. Blackpeak's quite a sight, and here you are calling me during my weekly ablutions."

"That woman doesn't deserve to be torn apart like a dog."

"You have a shirt around this place anywhere," he said.

"They're killing her."

"Maybe a splash of aftershave—"

"You going to just stand there?" I said.

They pulled her down to the dirt. They kicked at her ribs.

"Dash of cologne, maybe?"

They lashed rope to her throat, heaved the end over a wooden lamp-pole, then tied it to the saddlehorn of the horse.

"No," I screamed against the glass. "Fuck *this*. Goddamnit, old man, aren't you going to—"

His hand shot out. The liverspotted skin of his palm split open like a slash-wound mouth.

A swarm of black insects flew in a cloud and struck my face. I screamed. Their stingers jabbed into my lips and gums. The skin swelled. I clawed them away, but only pulled away handfuls of sand. My lips melded together and refused to move.

"Composure," the Magnate said, "is as essential as silence. You pick one or I pick the other for you. For Chrissake, boy, if you can't manage to keep your heart from skipping a beat at the slightest hint of danger, I don't know how you managed to survive this long."

Nothing about him made sense. Not how he'd been speaking to me, not how he'd emerged from the walls, not how he'd called trickery and corruption right out of his own skin.

"Problems aren't choosy. Wavering on the threshold produces no result. You want this problem fixed, then wrap yourself in it. I know you tried." He stepped over César's unconscious frame as he approached the door. "You let your associate talk you down. He saved your life. Granted, it only evens the scales. They'll just take her life as a result. That's the rotten fruit of hesitation. You're either in, or you're out."

He knew. He'd heard. *I see you*, the paper had said.

Without a shirt, the spindly fellow went right outside, into hell. I followed him.

From his pocket, he produced the strangest little item: a golden artifact roughly the size of a fist, covered in countless spikes and thorns. He clenched it, until tiny spots of blood sprang out on his fingertips.

Then, with red palms, he pocketed it again, and observed.

The cruelty just kept dragging on and on, as all awful things do. The Herald's heels scraped long canyons in the soil. Seconds clicked away like hours. Kerchief laughed and they were all laughing and it was so loud and in her last moments, right as Edward Sloman slapped the ass of the frightened, wide-eyed horse, Nycendera chose to watch *me*.

The horse neighed and shot like a bullet from a gun.

The rope slithered like a snake up and over the lamp-post.

Hooves pounded out an earthquake.

"Now or never," Magnate Gregdon said. "Time's right."

He shook out his hands like washrags. His fingers snapped to attention.

Then he clapped.

Our world is in constant motion. Everyone's moving, shuffling, breathing, heaving, coughing, shaking, scratching, walking, creaking, yawning; it's this stream of going-going-going, never truly starting or slowing down to its ending, because that's life. People bicker and dance and swoon and kiss and laugh and crumble. The wind beats, the sky slides, the earth does its Copernicus waltz. By chance we don't fly off it, but we sure as hell crash against one another trying to hold on. It's all deafening noise.

When it all stopped moving, the silence could have broken me in two.

The lynchmob stood stark still. On their torches, the fire froze in its hungry dance. Their faces, locked in stupid fury, refused to move. The town square had become a wax-sculpture museum, an unmoving testament to this terrible moment in time.

The horse, half-stride, still sought freedom, but without motion.

Nycendera, two inches from death, might as well have been an artist's drawing, suspended midway through a yank. Her spine bent at a grave angle, her neck at odds with it.

Her bones wouldn't have lasted but another breath.

When the Magnate walked, his boots crunched craters into the gravel. "Hardly any rush in watching time move by when you can just slip between each second and give the world the nudge it needs. You might not understand this, Elias Faust, nor do I expect you. Simply accept it, do not question it, and consider it the favor I provide you."

I strode between the bodies of men consumed by rage. I was afraid if I touched them, they'd awaken. I found Cicero. He'd been driven to the ground under heavy fists.

Instinctively, I reached out to touch him. To help.

"No," the Magnate said. "Not him. He will take his beating. That's the price one pays for nobility, wouldn't you say?" From his left pants-pocket, he withdrew a handful of dried peanuts. He cracked the shells. "Pushing against the tide always hurts, even if it's the proper course of action.

"And look at this one. B*iiiig* drink of water," he said, circling the mid-swing Peggy Winters, whose dusky skirt flared out around her ankles like a ringing bell as she put her elbow against a lyncher's chin. Blood on his face looked like red gems.

He crunched a peanut.

The swelling around my lips subsided.

The Magnate took his handful of broken shells and carefully deposited them in one of her skirt-pockets.

We continued on, moving our way through the stilled chaos. I passed my hand through the air near some torchflame. "Don't chance it," he warned. "It would still burn. Nothing here stops, exactly, despite being stopped."

"Did you stop—" I stuttered. "Did you stop time?"

"Hardly. Time doesn't stop," he reasoned, peeking at me from underneath a lyncher's elbow. "It marches on. Tomorrow and tomorrow and tomorrow, petty pace, all that. Think of it like..." He popped another peanut in his mouth, then sought out words simple enough to explain the inexplicable. "Time didn't stop. Watches still tick, minutes still pass, hearts go thump. Nobody's got the juice in them enough to stop the world spinning, Faust. Trying that would pop you like a boil, and probably everyone in a twenty-mile radius." He laughed. Good laugh. I could have liked that laugh.

"Then – then how?"

"I stopped the perception of time," he said. "The way their minds understand it, the way their bodies react to it. Theirs—" he pointed at the few people around him, "—and ours, a little bit."

"How'd the fire stop?"

"It's still burning bright and dangerous. Better to uphold the aesthetic. Brains are fragile things, Elias. It's better we believe it, too, as much as we possibly can. I'd hate to bust that skull of yours with mere ideas before having the chance to do anything else to it." He dug into his other pocket and found a folded straight-razor.

He tossed it to me. It soared over the still-life of the Herald.

I caught it in both hands.

"About three-and-a-half minutes before this clever bit of work falls apart around us," he said. "Time to nudge."

So with the straight-razor unfolded, I began to saw the rope like hell. I cried and I didn't know why; I couldn't not cry, with this pressure hammering inside my brain, fierce as a rail-driver. Sweat poured out of me, so much that my grip almost slipped right down on the razor.

Her eyes hadn't ever left that place where I was standing.

I think they hated me. God, I hope they did.

I said, "What do you get out of this, other than some kind of one-up on me?"

He grinned. "Come on, Faust. Choke this town as I might want to do, Blackpeak's best interest is still my main priority. I want this town. It harbors secrets. I'll have them as time and circumstance allows. Watching the snake eat its own tail over something as petty as bigotry and fear? You can't do any spellwork fine enough to suck out *that* poison from a place."

Spellwork. The word, foreign and strange, hung in the air.

"You know this place?" I asked, the rope almost halved.

"Hell if I don't. I lived here too. Well before you took away one of the two sons God gave me. Two minutes, ten seconds."

"Yeah? These folk have never mentioned you before. Just knew your boys," I said.

Some peanut-skin fell and got caught in his chest-hair. "You know how legends come to be?"

"They do legendary things?"

"They get forgotten first." He chewed another peanut. "Then, as legends do, they rise up out of the dust of history, and they leave their footprints in the paths they tread through culture. The present forgets them – sometimes by happenstance and sometimes by force – and the future carves their name in stone, to be remembered long into new centuries."

"By...force?"

"Why wait for them to forget you," he said, "when you could

make them? Just to prove to yourself that you can?"

It was only from Partridge's lips that I'd ever heard word of him. Nowhere else had I ever encountered any mention of Old Man Gregdon, of a Magnate. The name Gregdon had barely been a fart in the wind before the Gregdon Twins with their carousing and drinking and their capital-fucking-*T*. This man was just a smear on the window of the whole town, washed away by a bit of clever rain.

"One-minute, thirty seconds," he said.

With his razor, just one across his throat. Just one...

It's why I never played cards. My poker face was shit.

"Not a good idea, whatever you're thinking, Faust."

A pale finger lifted. He waved it at the top of a nearby building.

There, perched like a gargoyle, was a misshapen figure in a flapping cloak. Another one stood on the crest of the town hall. Yet another crouched on the awning over Edward Sloman's general store.

Staring at me, silver-eyed, ready to pounce.

"You came prepared," I said.

I clicked shut his straight-razor and chucked it to him. He caught it.

"Had plenty of time." The Magnate smiled. "You really don't remember, do you, Faust?"

He threw me the ball-bearing. I snapped it out of the air. It landed smack-dab in the middle of my palm, right where the little burn smarted—

A little burn. A little...

...*burning, that whiskey, going down and coming up too. My feet dragged like bricks through the sand. Who did Kallum think he was, canning me in favor of some bristle-chinned little shitshoe. And that goddamn walking gold-nugget slithering her way into town, she was going to die. But there were options, there had to be...*

I shouted at the ball bearing, "You wanna pour your words into my head, you invisible motherfucker? Then do it. Do it, righ' now, b'fore I fuckin'...before I fuckin'—"

I reared back my arm to throw.

Which is when that ball-bearing started to burn like a sun in my fist.

Is this what you really want to do?

I hissed. Opened my palm. It glowed hot as a cigarette cherry. I tried to shake it free.

"Ged'off me," I barked.

The impossible isn't impossible, Faust. There are ways.

"What, you my goddamn friend now?"

A mutual beneficiary.

"I don't need no goddamn friends," I shouted, and drank.

Not every problem can be shot at. Some need to be finessed.

"Or some jus' godda get thrown out."

That voice sighed as I spent my time kicking like a mule at a trough because why the hell not, boots were tough, and feet were stupid. You going to spend your night arguing at me?

"Argue at whoever the heck I want to, Mister Brainbabble."

I've had more charming conversations with rocks.

"Yeah, well." *Another swig.*

Faust. The girl's life. Do you want it saved?

"What's it matter to you?"

Nothing.

"Fuck you," I snapped. "Yes," *Pause.* "Yes. Christ, absolutely. How do I fix this. How do I set it right-side up?"

I will give it to you.

"At what cost?"

None.

"You don't make any sense."

Unnecessary blood is unnecessary blood. Despise you as I do – and I do despise you, Elias Faust – I still possess a heart. But you need to ask. You need to bend a knee.

I swallowed vomit. I ground at my nose, burnt from snuff and cigarettes. What else did I have to lose?

You need to ask, and I'll be ready.

And then all that whiskey had to come back out from somewhere, so it did...

...and like a sky having its clouds wiped away by a barcloth, I remembered.

I'd already asked. The other night. Drunk as a loon.

It was the Magnate's final cracking peanut that broke my reverie. That, and the way he said, "Forty-five seconds," and snapped his fingers in Nycendera's direction.

Motion poured into her. She crashed to the ground and clawed with abandon at the rope, her motions from minutes before bleeding right over into these. Frantic. Unyielding. She swiped at air, at anything and everything, then promptly wrenched at the rope and doubled over to draw in precious air.

When she found the frayed end, she looked up at me. At us.

I said, "Go. Now. There isn't time. You need to go."

She licked at a trickle of silver that had welled in the divot above her lip. I helped her to her feet. Or tried to. Her forearm slashed out in the air and knocked me away. "Do not *touch* me."

"This is your chance," I said. "You don't get another."

"You were not meant to give this to me."

"I didn't," I said. "He did."

Between the statuesque figures frozen in the midst of their hate and murderous schemes, she glanced at the Magnate, who looked almost fragile among the immobile crowd. Their attentions met.

It was Nycendera who unraveled first. She lunged forward, her arm snapping out like a whip. At the edge of her fingertips, inhuman light exploded: out of some sort of greenish rift or split gouged in the air, a jagged tongue of jade appeared as if withdrawn from a tiny pocket in reality. The magical blade slipped into her palm, humming with power. One of those damned conjured things.

She threw it at the Magnate.

He swiped a hand into the air.

The weapon stopped mid-flight, barely a hair from his nose.

And there it hung, quivering, its momentum fighting against whatever wonder he'd worked.

"We have mere seconds," he said. An outbreak of perspiration gleamed on his half-shaved face. "Whatever intents, aims, or discomforts you possess, abandon them."

"I will owe my existence to no one," she said, never taking her stare from the Magnate.

"You don't," I interjected. "Consider this an apology. For all this."

"Carried on the back of dark company, that means very little," Nycendera said.

"I take it you two know each other?"

The Magnate's whole throat tightened. It was beginning to wear at him, this extended exposure to whatever-the-hell he called it: his craft, his magic, his talent. "Names on the wind, Faust. The minute you break out of your very limited scope of reality, you need never meet someone – or something – to know of it. Ripples in the water, Herald, am I right?"

Nycendera's narrow features gave a twitch of recognition.

"Ripples in the water," she said.

Jesus, it was like watching snakes rear up and flare at one another. "I don't want to shake my dick in the middle of this little pissing contest, but this is not the time and definitely not the place. I asked for his help. *Me.* We need to leave it at that."

She passed by Kerchief, and with a petulant swipe, tore the bandana from around his mouth. "This is mine, now," she proclaimed.

Touching her throat where the lashed rope still dangled like a necklace, Nycendera crept back, sliding between the outstretched arms, grasping hands, and surging legs of her captors. She jabbed a finger in my direction and said, "Below our feet lingers that which should be claimed by no man. This one yearns. He *knows.* I smell it on him, like sickness. Do not be just another fool. *This is your chance.*" My words came from her like an echo. "*You don't get another.*"

The woman turned and fled.

Fled, but with an unnatural speed. Blurring like a slow-moving bullet.

Or a fast-fading dream.

The Magnate's vitality crept out of him, leaving him frail as paper. He balanced this tiny morsel of the world on his fingertip. It began to fall apart.

"What does it cost you," I asked, "to compete with reality like this? It's got to cost you something." A heavy wind could have torn him asunder. Maybe if I huffed, and I puffed…

"There's always a cost, Elias Faust." He held the golden object again, with all its edges and barbs. Clenching around it, his fingers looked like tiny tubes of paper. "The costs must be paid. Sacrifice. Of the self, of others. Payments of pain and blood. Do you know how much pain there is, truly? Do you fathom even a fraction of it? Blood drying in the dirt of plantations in Georgia and South Carolina. Agony festering in cities, polluting the earth. Pain to be gathered up, taken back, and breathed out into the world as something better.

"And you've put so much of it there, Elias Faust. You killed my boy. I helped tonight, with parlor tricks," he said, his lips peeling back from his gums like bits of tanned leather, "but you already made sure the blood-price was paid for them, well before you even realized it."

Crackpot philosophies and machinations. The shine in his eyes was a devil's: he believed every word. I stared into the face of a man forgotten by a town, a wraith that had ejected himself out of time and memory and humanity.

"What price did I pay?" I breathed.

"Ask Keswick Everett. Ask Joshua Fulton." The Magnate's grin split a canyon across his face. "I'm sure they'll help you see."

Which is when everything exploded.

Exploded into motion, into screams, into shouts of "Hang her, hang her," like a bonfire full of noise and color and movement. Cicero got pummeled to the ground. Peggy Winters thrashed several men like wheatstalks. Horse kept sprinting like a bat out of hell, and it carried its way off through the town on a wave of dust, a flapping tail of rope unwinding up over the wooden lamp-pole and *snap-snap-snapping* off behind its hind legs.

A hellacious cheer of victory and satisfaction flew up from the crowd.

Until it simply stopped.

They realized.

"The fuck she go," somebody asked a friend.

I saw Kerchief just a few feet away, starting to discover his disappointment. He and Edward Sloman stood together like lost children.

I went for Kerchief. I punched that sonofabitch right in the jaw.

I stole my pistol from his sweaty hand, and in the middle of the crowd raised it, fired right into the air. Once, twice, three times. Four, five—

The sixth shot I fired into Edward Sloman's kneecap.

He didn't drop so much as he formed into a howling puddle on the ground. He grabbed at the wet remnants of his pants.

"Enough," I bellowed.

The whole town made me sick. I despised their smug, confused, and questioning faces, their coal-stained stubble, their damning eyes. I wanted to burn their ragged clothes, tear each one of them down. A gaggle of bigots and wishers. A crude collection of unlikable souls purged from the rest of the world. The crowd spread from around me. I stuffed the ball-bearing into my pocket.

Edward Sloman looked up, teeth gritted. "How'm I gonna walk?"

I crunched the heel of my boot into the damp beef of his knee. His scream split the night.

I reloaded each cylinder in my Colt from my belt. I took my time. Blackpeak watched. Give them a show, they'd watch.

Sloman's grungy hair shone with sweat. I grabbed a handful and dragged him like a doll across the ground.

Toward the floating knife.

Nycendera's spell-forged blade still hummed in the air. Perhaps with a flick, it would have kept flying until it hit the horizon. By what means it trembled there, suspended, I wasn't sure, but it didn't matter. I heaved Sloman's face up until his lips grazed the point.

"This never happens again." *Breathe.* "This. This?" I pointed with my barrel toward the scrabble-marks in the sand, the hoof-prints, the hints of blood and spit. Toward Cicero dragging himself up off the earth, and Peggy Winters putting her broad belly between him and a group of lynchers whose steam had started to fade. "Never again. Not tonight, not any other night. Any man or woman that thinks their hatred is enough reason to rewrite law forfeits their right to citizenship in our town.

"Do it, and I will drive you out without hesitation, and without question. I'll break you if I have to. There are limits and there are lines. I'll observe them, I'll keep them, and you sure as hell won't cross them. If I saw your face tonight, you know I know who you are. I'm glad to know who you are." It just kept coming and coming. "I'm glad to know what you're capable of and what shade of cowardice boils inside you. I'm glad to look you straight in the eye and never forget what torch you held, what pitchfork you raised, and what a brave soul you swore you were as you just about dragged a woman to her death.

"And if you wore a mask," I warned, glancing at one man in a crumpled hood, "wear it for the rest of your days. Stitch it to yourself for all I care. Whatever face you decide to show the world, you bury this foul shit so far underneath yourself that you pray it never surfaces, never dares to leak out, because I will see it, I will smell it, and I will bury it with you. Tell them, Mister Sloman," I said, staring not at the crowd, but at the knife as I pressed his teeth up against the jagged point. "Go on. Tell them."

His lips hesitated. "Never again."

"Louder."

"Never *again*."

"Am I clear," I said, finally cutting my eyes across the lot of them.

A wind snapped through the town square, daring the silence.

You'd have thought the whole planet went to sleep.

"Am I *clear*?"

You could see the questions bursting in their faces. What had happened to their prey? Where had she gone, here one moment and then, like a flash of lightning, vanished the next? I wondered what it had been like for them, whether that span of time-that-was-not-time had been a long, sleeping eternity, or whether it had been just a blink. Hiccup-quick. Hardly anything at all.

I threw Sloman to the dirt. I stepped away.

The moment I did, the knife caught up with time, too.

It flew across the town square and sunk with a shaking *thud* into the door of the town hall.

I waited a painful long time for them all to disperse, giving each one of them a chance to meet my gaze as if to tell them I knew, I *knew*, and dare them to puff themselves up. Silence followed them. The crowd slinked back to their shadows, to their homes, to their beds.

Cicero spit. It was pink. It hit the moaning Sloman on the lapel.

"Jesus," he said. But that was all.

The truth of it lay stretched out like a book in front of all of us: Grady Cicero and Peggy Winters both wondered in relative silence why one odd minute had crashed like an axe-edge against another, why there was once a golden woman, and then no longer one...

I surveyed the alleys, the awnings, the rooftops. No shadowed figures.

No Magnate.

We all stood there and packed secrets away in our pockets like precious jewels. It felt nice to say nothing at all.

24

Cicero and I had to hoist Emp between us. Peggy Winters managed Edgar Sloman on her own. She threw him across her shoulder like a sack of feed. "Bet'cher ass you go t' chapel inna few days, all them folk be there prayin' up sompin' powerful, they will, God is good'n all that."

Sure as hell if she wasn't right.

Next Sunday morning, by half-past eight, Father Steward stood at the pulpit and waved his hands and went about his *Hell's got endless room for sinners!* and *Temptation is the Devil's ruse!* and on and on until you wanted to burst into flames just to end it. When the whole church sang a dead-sounding hymn, I worked through pews toward a familiar wide-brimmed hat. "Miss Fulton."

"Oh, Elias," she said between bits of melody. "You're a church-man now?"

"No bad time to start," I said.

"You're interrupting the song."

"Best for all of us. I'm hell with a tune."

She had a small drink from a flask drawn from her purse.

I rested my hand over hers where it clutched the pew in front of her. Her knuckles shook with a hellish tremble. Her voice dropped, bitter as coffee. "What the hell you want from me, Mister Faust, that you need to bother me at prayer?"

From my pocket I removed my tiny ball bearing, polished and silver. I asked her if it looked familiar and her eyes instantly welled up with leaden tears. Her skirt hem crumpled closer to the floor. She sat. So did I. "I don't remember where he got it. I just remember he had it. It concerned me mightily, but Paul said a boy's apt to find baubles and things."

"Did he ever mention where he found it?"

"Some man he met. Said to him – my God, what did that boy say he said? – it'd show him *real family*, or something of the sort. Can you believe it," she whispered.

"Happen to know what this fellow looked like?"

"Goddamnit, Elias, I never saw him. I don't remember," she said, raising her voice to a bark. "You expect me to remember and I can't, I just can't, so you ought to be just fine with that. Who are you, bothering me in a house of God about my boy?"

I tapped my hat to her and began to slink away.

"I hate you," Eliza Fulton said to me underneath the din of the song, words spoken so hard that a bubble of spit gleamed on her lip. A gaggle of women surrounded her in a protective shell. I listened loudly to Father Steward guide them into another proclamation of brimstone and hellfire. His gaze never met mine. He avoided it, rolling his attention to this person and that person, but never to me.

Without a handkerchief covering his mouth, I suppose he thought himself invisible.

WATCHING Morgan Kallum eat was an exercise in resilience. We'd agreed to meet at the Crooked Cocoon Saloon under the pretense of business. We sat beside a window. Emp, whose face looked like a battered side of steak, sat there too.

"You got some big balls to want to talk to me face-to-face, Faust."

"Runs in the family, I guess. Good breakfast?"

"Tastes like shit."

"Good to see you, Emp," I said to the Mexican.

Kallum glared mineshafts into me. I don't know what the bastard relished more, my absolutely charming company, or the sloppy meal he could stuff down his gullet. "You want to explain to me why there ain't a woman hanging from the steeple? Rumors are burning this town alive about you, Faust. About how much trouble you're liable to cause from here on out."

"Laws don't count for anything when a town stomps all over them."

"Laws don't count for anything when you stick your nose into a situation it doesn't belong in, Faust," he said, a bead of milk dripping off his lip. "There's a fucking murderer prancing around in those plains. I've got a district judge and a snot-nosed prosecutor hounding my ass to correct my marshalling inadequacies. You expect me to be *calm?*"

I wiped my hand across my forehead. "I expect you not to spit milk on me when you lecture."

"I tried to keep you separate from it," he said. "For your own damn good."

His supposed charity made my guts go to ice. So I told him what happened. The lynchmob, Emp getting overpowered. A slip of the noose. A moment of distraction.

I'm pretty good at bullshit. About as good at it as I am at banking and dress-making.

"You'd swear to that in front of a court, Faust?"

"'Course I would. Even if it turned out to be a whole pack of lies, I'd swear to it anyway."

I unholstered my Colt, pulled back the hammer, and laid it down on the table between the three of us.

He stared down at the gun, his eyes like rocks, his clay-like hands almost crushing the corner of the tablet. He licked his lips. "What do you want to talk about that requires a gun sitting here?"

"Ain't nothing much worth talking about can't be talked about with a gun around 'lest you say something that'd piss it off. Truth of the matter is, Kallum, you need to yank your head out the bankrolls and take a look at the big picture around you. You aren't a king or a president. You aren't royalty. Blackpeak is Blackpeak."

"You fucked with the process," he said.

"Sure. But anybody in their right mind either gets out of this place or dies. The ones who stay are either drunks, outlaws, or people like you and me—" I lifted the gun and pointed it at him like a baton, "—that think there might be something worth salvaging in this shithole town."

Me. Kallum. The Magnate. Peas in a pod and all, arm-wrestling over a pimple in the Texas drylands.

"I'll have you arrested," he said.

"Emp, you gonna arrest me?"

He sipped morning whiskey.

"Let's not complicate this, Kallum. I bet if I were to look hard enough, this town ain't even official. It ain't on the books. Nobody cares about it from the outside, and barely anyone who cares about it from the inside.

"Money ain't forever," I continued. "One day, like water, it'll dry up. Your bars will stop getting customers. This place will tear itself apart from the inside. By that point, what little semblance of law you have will have crumbled, and there ain't gonna be nobody around – not me, not Cicero, not Emp – to keep you from getting mauled to death by the very people you paid to lynch a golden woman."

I could smell his sweat. He stank like old chicken soup.

"I want things back the way they were," I said. "I want marshal back."

"César's my marshal now."

"César's a good kid," I said. "Pay him as your bodyguard. Marshal ain't his bag. No offense, Emp," I said.

Emp raised his hands.

Kallum took in a breath. He stared at the gun.

"Last night fades, Kallum. We move past it. We have that privilege. I want Cicero as my deputy. And when things go down," I said, real quiet, making sure he could hear each damn word, "I want you to

206 RANCE D. DENTON

keep your blinds closed. I don't want to hear you questioning how or why I do my job. All that should matter is that, at the end of the day, you still got a place to lay your head and some money in your pocket."

"That's all you want," he said.

"Let's call this Herald situation a bust. You talk down the judge and the prosecutor, send them back home. This ain't something we need to pursue anymore."

The veins in his forehead bulged out against his skin as if they were going to burst.

"You are a remarkable fool, Elias. You don't know what she – it – is. You haven't a clue. You're too busy playing your little black-powder games, but if that suits you, it suits me. In time, you'll know I was right. Better off dead," he said. "Better off dead."

Before I stepped out the door, Kallum found steel in his heart.

"Only tyranny goes unchallenged and only fools rely on morality. What happened last night will come out in time, Elias Faust. When it does, I'll be there to smile from across the courtroom."

"Holy shit," shouted Grady Cicero. "Did you see that? It was like tossing a pebble at a cockroach's ass a thousand yards out!"

Shards of the green-dyed bottle rained down to the hard Black-peak soil. Cicero tapped the edge of his bowler with the barrel of his .44.

"Did you see that?" Cicero asked again.

"Even if I was a blind man I'd have seen it, with all this yelling you're doing about it. Don't take much skill to shoot bottles fifty yards out," I said.

"Stage is yours, Marshal Asshole."

I squinted my eyes down the mast of the Yellowboy. I lifted my elbow and poised the sights on the colored drink-bottles sitting on the rock downrange.

Cicero whispered, "Pressure's on, muffin."

The rifle twitched. A quick crack sounded out over the dry fields. Somewhere back behind the bottle, a little volcano of dirt shot up from the earth. None of the bottles moved. Cicero started laughing so hard that he had to clutch his belly with his hand.

And I'm the asshole?

I worked the action. A smoking cartridge leaped into the air and plopped into the brim of my hat. "Between you and Emp," I said, "I think I'm going to become a full-time drunk."

"Make sure you hit your mouth with the alcohol."

"I've got a gun," I warned him.

Cicero raised his revolver in one hand, turned a bit to the side, and then fired off a round. The very same bottle I had been pointing at burst into a glassy cloud. He sucked his teeth. "How many minutes was it?" he asked, dancing his question out the side of his mouth.

"About three, give or take."

"That's enough time to change the world."

"I hoped so."

"You want to talk about it?"

"Nope," I said.

He emptied spent brass onto the ground. It gleamed at the end of his boots like bits of powder-burnt treasure. Eventually time would crush them down into the dirt, into fossils, into the past. *Now or never. Time's right.* "I take it they'll hide for a long time, those men. One speech doesn't fix all the ugliness in the world, Faust. One speech, one bullet, or a thousand. Doesn't put a dent in any of it. So you're going to have to ask yourself whether it was worth it, whether three minutes and a fistful of seconds pulled the veil off the world, or whether it just tied it down tighter. Whether or not you were the same person at the start of that ticking clock," he reasoned, "that you were at the end of it."

We both had our secrets. They filled up holes. Personal and precious.

"You need to figure it out whether you want to be Caius, or whether you want to be Kent. For Blackpeak, for Kallum, and for yourself."

"Friends of yours?"

He pulled a brick of a book from his breast pocket. *The Collected Works of Shakespeare.* Small enough for the pocket, and thick enough to kill a man. "You need to read more, Faust."

He took my cigarette tin out of my shirt pocket and stuffed the book in. It weighed damn near a thousand pounds. Then he lit a cigarette and seemed mighty satisfied with himself. "From me to you," he said.

The black and faded mountains seemed like a thousand miles out. The heat on the badlands threw mirages in the air. I wondered where exactly Nycendera had gone off to, but I imagined I'd never really know. That was fine with me.

I lifted up my shotgun from where it leaned against a rock.

You're either in, or you're out.

Breathe.

The shotgun roared. Bottles vanished, sending the broken teeth of shattered glass out into the dirt. I cracked open the shotgun, ejected the two cartridges, then turned and smiled at Cicero.

Cicero flipped me the bird.

"Show-off," he said.

PART V

THE MARK

25

Nobody touched the gemstone knife in the town hall's black door. Nobody wanted to. You'd have thought they'd burn their damn fingers off if they did. Suited me just fine. Town hall dances happened and there was the knife. A wedding happened once, and there was the knife as they threw rice and dead flowers, *hip-hip-horray*.

One day Cicero and I stood outside the town hall to observe a cattle-trade. Men poked at cows' ribs and women lifted their hems over lumps of cowshit. He said to me, "You ever see a bunch of animals this damn useless-looking?"

A little boy came darting up to us, maybe six or seven, and he said, "Mister Faust," and spit brown tobacco at my feet. "You gonn' care if I take that knife?"

"You'd split yourself wide open."

"Aw, you serious?" the boy said. "It's just been stickin' there for weeks."

"And it's just gonna keep sticking there for weeks," I said. "You can't have it."

The boy's packed lip pooched out. A dribble of brown rolled down his chin. "So why cain't I have it?"

"Yeah, why cain't he have it?" Cicero said.

"You ever met Peggy Winters," I asked the boy.

"Yassir."

"You ever seen her punch somebody's lights out," I said.

"Nosir."

"You won't see it either when she knocks your lips right off your face for stealing my knife."

The boy's face tightened up. "That's a demon knife. It ain't *yours*."

I squatted down. I put my palms on my knees and thrust my face out to meet the boy's dirty stare. "Damn right. Full of all that gold demon magic, the kind that'll peel your skin right off your bones you decide to mess with it. Why else you think it's still there?"

His attention flicked to it. "Would it really do that?"

"It's full of bad magic," I said. "Whole town knows it. Now you do, too."

"When you gonna take it down," the boy asked.

"When the bad magic's gone."

"How you gonna know?"

"Don't suppose I ever will until it happens," I said. "I ever catch you even thinking about touching that knife, whether it's right now or the middle of the night when nobody's around—" I pointed two fingers at my eyes, and then pointed at his and whispered, "—just remember, *I see you.*"

The cattle-sale came and went. At least Blackpeak was consistent: they worked their days, they drank away their nights. Since the incident with Nycendera, the town settled into quietness, people lived on, and most seemed happy. Mostly.

When the last cow trailed off, Cicero and I walked toward my office. "There a science to explain why everybody's been on such good behavior lately?"

"Don't tell me you don't know," he said. We stood outside my office. The sky broke open. A night-time rain started. It knocked like falling knucklebones on the tin roof. "It's no secret."

"Full moon?"

He looked over his shoulder toward the town hall.

Toward the knife.

"They're afraid of you," he said. "They're *all* afraid of you. Maybe only somewhat afraid of you. Maybe mostly afraid of what they don't understand. Only two things spread quicker than gossip: brushfires and the clap. You and Sloman—" he paused, then snapped his collar up along his neck to guard himself from the downpour. "We had our reality bent just a little bit, Elias. What happens in this world happens because it makes sense. We're several weeks out from *nonsense*, still reeling, and treading carefully. You understand."

You understand. Wielded with the careful courtesy of a schoolmarm with a switch.

I jerked my chin toward the door. "You want a drink?"

"I have an appointment with Nabby Lawson."

"You don't watch out, there's gonna be more than just reality getting bent."

He tapped his bowler. "Don't I know it."

Then Cicero was gone. The silence had been hard-bought; if Blackpeak found order, then far be it from me to disturb that precious balance for as long as it'd last. I reckoned not for long, of course.

But I wasn't a very good bullshitter, especially not to myself.

The only light inside my office came in slants and slashes through the barred windows. I'd gotten so familiar with the layout, though, that I could have wandered through it with my eyes closed. I kicked off my boots near the door, dropped my trousers, and emptied my pockets on my desk. I went for the matches and an oil-lamp.

The pistol jabbed itself into my spine.

"Don't move," the voice said from behind me. "Don't breathe. And whatever you do, don't speak until I damn well tell you to."

26

"WHERE IS IT," CAME THE FRANTIC VOICE. "THE EYE. WHERE'D YOU stash it?"

I squinted at the silhouette as it drifted from behind me toward my desk. It still had a gun on me. The intruder reeked of hot sweat and salt-lick. "Everything I own's in that top desk-drawer," I said.

The gun didn't move away. The figure yanked out the drawer by the handle and dumped it on my desk. A bottle of whiskey, some shackles, and the Shakespeare book all clattered out.

The silver ball-bearing almost rolled away. I heard it. So did he.

The free hand clapped down on it.

"Light the lamp," he barked. "Now."

So I carefully moved, took up the matches. Lit one. The brief flare blinded me. I touched the lamp. Warm light flooded the room.

Curtis Gregdon stared at me from over the barrel of his lone pistol. Underneath the brim of a lilting hat, he resembled more a child's drawing of a man than a real one at all. His face was half-covered by a dirty bandage gone brown with old blood. In the three months it'd been since I'd clipped half of Curtis's face with shot, he'd taken to the crusty facemask like a signature. "Uncap the whiskey. Put the bottle down. Step back. No bullshit, or I'll put a hole through you, no hesitation."

Did as he asked. Had no intent to die over a bottle of hooch.

He dropped the silver ball-bearing inside the bottle. It plopped into the amber fluid and clacked against the glass at the bottom. A wave of emptiness surged in my stomach. "No listening, no whispering in minds. No intrusions. Just you and me, Faust."

The black mouth of his pistol stayed firm on me. I said, "Ain't the first time we've been this close with a gun between us, Curtis. This going to be the last?"

"You don't shut your smart-ass mouth it sure as hell might be." His lip curled up to reveal a broken tooth. "I came to talk."

"You and I ain't exactly friends, Curtis."

"Nobody else to talk to."

Bullets tell all truth. My brains were still intact. Was he lying with that gun of his? Eventually everybody's wrong at least once. "I killed your brother, Curtis. Don't think there's much that I could say that you'd really give a shit about."

"It's got no bearing on what tonight's all about."

I jerked my chin toward the whiskey. "Is he watching?"

"The whiskey'll keep it asleep for the time being. Enough for you and me to do what we gotta do." Curtis Gregdon reached back to where my tarnished shotgun leaned against the bars of the empty cell.

I expected him to level it at me.

Instead, he threw it over the desk. I snatched it out of the air.

"Point it at me," he said.

"What?"

"I said just *point* it at me. I need you to."

"So you can have an excuse to put a round in my—"

"Point it at me! Just point the goddamn thing at me so we can do this right, Faust."

I didn't have much choice but to do what the man with the gun told me to.

From the hip, I waved the barrels in his direction and wrenched back both hammers. With every passing second I saw the theatre of the moment in front of me: Curtis's pistol wavered, so I shouldered the butt of the shotgun. "Lower the gun," I said slowly, "or you and this shotgun can get intimately reacquainted with one another."

Curtis's good eye flicked down to the side-by-side barrels in front of him. Relief flooded his mangled face.

In the whiskey, the silver ball – the Eye – jumped, spun, and ricocheted like a loose bullet, tinking against the glass.

"Ain't nothing," Curtis said. "Just spasms. The booze and the charm, they don't like each other much."

I didn't like this much. "Gun," I said.

"You ain't serious."

"You told me to point at you, man. Trying to correct the fellow with the shotgun is not normal survival practice."

He pulled it out, turned the handle to me, and I took it.

"You got a second one?" I asked.

"You got my second one," he said.

"Cicero's got your second one."

I cracked open my shotgun and draped it over my left arm with the two unused shells still winking from the breach. I half-cocked Gregdon's .44, opened it at the top-break, and emptied the cartridges into my palm. I gave back the weapon. He took it with a frown. "You really gave my other gun to that fruitbasket?"

"He earned it," I said. "Curtis, you're a fugitive of Blackpeak. Last time we encountered one another, you threatened my life in front of the whole town. You ain't supposed to be here unless you're locked up for hanging."

"Which is why I wanted you to point the gun at me. So you knew you was in control."

"You had to point a gun at me to do that?"

"You would'a shot me the minute you saw me if I didn't," he reasoned.

"Have faith."

"I *do*. If it walks, you shoot it. You wanna be marshal of a graveyard, Elias Faust, that's damn fine by me, but I don't plan to be in it."

He paced around behind my desk. Sometimes he gnawed on his nails, biting them bloody. "Truth is, this ain't about turn-ins or hangings or any of that. Ain't here to get hanged. I come as...as—" he tried to pull the word out of the air, "—a neutral party." He picked up the whiskey bottle, shook it, and quieted the Eye. "I need to talk to you about things. We can't do it here. Ears in the walls. People might be listening. Creepers in the dark," he breathed. "I'm not supposed to be here."

"Then where you supposed to be, Curtis?"

"I'm 'sposed to be hiding, but I can't fuckin' take it anymore, Faust. All this shit, it's just digging into my head and it won't let go." With the bottle picked up in front of him, he jammed his face against the glass and leered at the dormant ball-bearing inside. Sometimes it jerked, leaped, last vestiges of life. "I need you to come with me. Marshal Faust, there's things you gotta know. I can't sit here with these thoughts in my brain anymore."

Struck me then that I'd never looked directly at the kid before. Behind blonde stubble and his coal-dirty face, he could have been *someone*. The poor bastard simpered in front of me like a shaved lamb.

That's when I saw it on his forehead: carved deep, still red, gleaming wet. A triangle.

"I could choose not to help." I rolled the .44 cartridges around in my palm. "I don't have any obligation to you. I got too many issues with you. You got too many issues with me. You could be drawing me into a trap."

"It don't matter if I am or if I'm not at this point, Elias. Because just by virtue of me walking through that door, I drew you in. Trap or not, the minute he knows where I am, he'll send them to collect my ass."

"Send who?"

Curtis fell still. "You know damn well," he whispered. "You seen'em."

I flicked my gaze to the stilled Eye.

Christ, even thinking of them – of them squatting on the buildings, of them around Keswick Everett's mutilated corpse – threatened my evening meal.

Knowingly, Curtis jerked his chin in a nod. "Sandshades."

Abruptly, a spark of movement suggested itself to me: I wanted that whiskey bottle. I wanted to shatter it. Maybe crash it across Gregdon's chin. Maybe across the side of the desk. Get that sphere, hold it in my hand, feel the cool metal...

Curtis slid the bottle to the edge of the desk, where he took it and set it on the floor beside his boot. "You'll get it back soon enough. You feel it, don't you? Bone deep. That's the charm. The – the *spell*. Minute its invisible hands start squeezing your brain, they change how it works. Not in big ways, but subtle-like. You like it. You *want* it."

I imagined the Magnate's voice coaxing itself out of the shadows of my mind.

And you'll get it, he would have said.

"I need you clear," Curtis told. "Clear the way I am. Clear as water."

"Your life in danger, Curtis?"

That he didn't respond and just stared off at the horizon on the edge of the desk told me everything I needed to know.

"If I find that whatever it is you want to show me turns into a trick, a problem of some sort—" I angled two fingers at his wrecked face, "—you're first. Got it?"

He blinked, swiped at his visible eye, and agreed. He looked a hundred years old. A thousand.

I had half-a-mind to call Cicero out from underneath Nabby Lawson's skirt to grade this boy's acting ability. But instead I did the stupid thing: I trusted that little acorn of instinct in my gut instead of that hunk of logic in my skull. "I can help you," I said. "Where the hell is this thing you feel compelled to show me?"

"Thirty miles north. South of Crown Rock, just near the Western Elbow toward Rouseville. A shack. A little place don't nobody else really know about 'cept me and all the other Gregdons."

"Which means it's a dangerous place for me."

"Ain't nobody gonna know you're there, Faust. I can show you

what I got to show you, tell you what I got to tell you, and we can go
our separate ways. Then you and me never see one another again.
Ain't nothing left in Blackpeak for me. I go, and you and I act like we
never knew each other."

"I'm supposed to forget everything else?"

"I'm asking you to, Faust. A favor. Regardless of all that other
bullshit."

People who ask for favors are usually the same ones won't ever do
you one back, and Curtis Gregdon was no different. Yet, sitting there
in my longjohns, an outlaw in front of me and a half-living silver ball
snapping away inside a bottle of whiskey, I thought about how much
I could gain. If he held his word, I'd be free of a Gregdon. If things
didn't go the way he told me, I'd probably have to kill a Gregdon.
Either way, the situation seemed like one that was going to end on the
upswing.

Just depended on how much I was willing to risk based on Gregdon's vague invitation.

He lifted the bottle up. He extended it to me. When my skin
touched the glass, it gave out a soothing coolness. For all the times I'd
left the damn Eye in my desk-drawer, I hadn't been so desperate, so
needful...

It'd been mine, though. No matter where it was.

"Please," Curtis said.

I needed him to leave Blackpeak. I'd give him the next few days.
Least I could do for killing his brother.

"Get in the cell," I said. "I need to set some things in order before
we go."

So I got dressed. I buckled on my holsters.

Felt good. Felt normal. In Blackpeak, it's good to have a gun. Just
in case.

I shook free my canvas duster from the office closet. Found my
oiled hat. I took to the streets of Blackpeak. My boots got swallowed
to the ankles in the puddles. Each raindrop felt like a pebble falling
from the sky.

———————

Before my second knock, the door flew open, and Grady Cicero stared at me with his cheeks all flushed. His mutton-chops stood straight like a cat's hackles. He was breathing really hard, peering at me from around the door. Several candles flickered behind him, some shorter than my thumbs and skirted with melted wax. "I'm a little hurt you didn't invite me to your shindig," I said.

The door swung all the way open, and there stood Grady Cicero in a pair of short pants, shirtless enough just to show me how insignificant my own physique really was. He held his pistol and a cigarette. A short woman with yellow hair latched onto him like some kind of leech, sucking up and down on his chest. "Miss Lawson," I said.

"Elias Faust," she said, standing from the floor to lean back against Cicero's bear of a body, giving me full view of everything from the waist up. "Thought you might want to see what you interrupted."

"Something you need, Faust?" asked Cicero, easing the hammer down before he stuffed the .44 Russian into his pants.

Miss Lawson giggled and bit a small tag of Cicero's skin. "How 'bout you invite him on in, Cissy? We can put on a show for the marshal, then give him a drink and some smoke."

"Something you *need*, Faust?" asked Cicero.

"Who shit in your boots, Cicero?" I said.

"Cute boots," Miss Lawson said.

"Miss Lawson, you mind giving Cicero and me a few minutes?"

"Ain't nothing you can say to him you can't say to me, Marshal."

"Maybe not, but I'd prefer the illusion of privacy."

"I could just suck your dick while you talk," she offered. She reared up and slapped one of her long-nailed hands across Cicero's ass. Her feet tangled themselves drunkenly in her discarded blouse as she staggered toward the bed. She tried to pour a drink on the bedstand. She spilled half the brandy on the sheets.

"Class act," I said.

"I'm not marrying her, Faust."

"Quality kind of man," I said.

"You're a quality pain in my ass," Cicero said, pulling the door almost all the way closed behind him as we stood in the hall. "Faust, can it wait until the sun?"

"Not for me. For you, maybe. Striking out for a few days. Don't know when I'll be back exactly," I said. "How's Marshal Grady Cicero sound for the next several days?"

"Fits," he said. "Just not permanently."

"Need you to watch over things for awhile, sling lead if lead needs slinging, keep Poindexter's bar from getting too much blood on it."

Miss Lawson shuffled around inside Cicero's room. "Cissy?"

"What?"

"Get done out there," she said. "You ain't paying me just to drink."

He said to me, "I'll handle Blackpeak, but I don't have it in me to do it too long."

"Even if you're getting paid?"

"You know what I mean, Faust." He leveled his eyes at me over the rims of his spectacles. "If you wanted help, I know you'd ask me. You come back in a pine crate dragged on a horse's ass, though, and I might just celebrate. Get that through your thick-ass skull before you go do something like get a mouthful of bullets, yeah?"

Miss Lawson interrupted again. "Cissy!"

"I'll be back before you know it," I said.

"In one piece," he said.

I thought about coming back in one piece as I walked to the stables. I thought about coming back in two or three. Might be able to survive that. Hard to tell, dealing with secrets coming from a Gregdon. The less pieces, the better. Two or three wouldn't be so bad.

IN THE GRAY morning Curtis and I packed our horses: coffee, beans, blankets, all mine. He stationed his foot on the stirrup and jumped up. His horse was just skin-and-bones. I slung a Winchester, checked my pistols, and saddle-holstered my shotgun. "You bringing a damn armory?" he asked.

"I like to have lots of options. Your brother knows."

"No more talk about my brother, Faust."

"He tried to kill me, Curtis. You were there. You saw it."

"Don't hold it over my fuckin' head, alright?" he said, spitting over the side of his horse. "We ain't always accountable for what our blood does, Elias Faust. You ever put it through your rabbit-shit brain that maybe blood don't make all the bodies it's in act the same?"

"Gregdons are still Gregdons."

"Gregdons are still Gregdons, but I'm Curtis." He yanked his reins hard and spurred his horse down the street, sloshing through the mud in front of me, leading the way.

We didn't talk. Gregdon was sour. He could lead the way and not talk to me once the whole trip toward the Western Elbow and I'd be perfectly happy with that.

Wrapped in a rag soaked in whiskey, the Eye sat like a lead weight in my breast pocket.

Close, but not too close.

27

By the time we were seven or eight miles out from Blackpeak, the downpour had turned into a mist. Come morning the sky was thick as smoke. The flatlands seemed endless, sprawling out on all sides. Gradually, ranges of hills and flat shale mountains rose up on either sides of us, formed from slanting rock and layered earth. The canyon must have been a riverbed a few thousand years back. Good path for horses. Makes it easy for them not to stray.

Also makes it easy to get jumped on from onlookers above. At least, that's what the corpse we found in the middle of our path reminded me.

We drew our horses up on either side of the shadow. The rain pelted the dead skin and had likely been doing so all night. Bloated and fat, the canine's body was open to the elements, cut from chest to groin. Dark blood ran in a river between my horse's hooves.

"Dead dog," said Curtis.

"Coyote," I said. "Spindly legs. Long nose. Big ears." I leaned down, took a wary sniff. "Pretty new. Don't stink yet. No big organs got cut."

Curtis must have seen me reach over and draw back the hammers of my shotgun where it hung at my saddle's side. "Tense, Red Riding Hood?" he asked.

"Not too familiar with the wilds, Curtis. I usually don't get much of a chance to travel."

When he grinned, half of it disappeared behind his face-wrap. "Big bad Marshal Faust shakin' in his boots about a dead dog and a bit of blood."

"It's been cut longways. That normal to you?"

"Rough area around here, Faust. Used to be Apache grounds. Now it's lawless land. Cults, zealots, runaways."

I tried to ignore the prickling feeling of eyes on the back of my neck or the way I shifted to make my Colts more accessible to my hands. "That don't explain the coyote body." As unsettled as I was about Gregdon being my only key to surviving a bunch of pissed ne'er-do-wells staking claim to the wilderness, it wasn't them that bugged me. Something else... "What you trade these undesirables for passage through this place, Curtis?"

"Guns we take, shit we steal."

"And the Gregdons get free rein?"

"Information and knowledge. Cooperation, and if necessary, some of their help. They got the whole damn world mapped out, seems like," Curtis said. He looked up along the slopes. "And the Well. Some of them know where the Well is."

I gnawed on a piece of dried meat. It hit my stomach like steel. "The hell's so important about a well?"

Underneath his dripping hat, he had the look of a kid who'd shared a secret he wasn't meant to – expecting leverage, perhaps, or praise. "I take it Mayor Kallum's not been very forthcoming, has he? I met some oblivious bastards in my time, Elias Faust, but I think you might be among the worst. You know what my old man would say about you? That's the short-sightedness biting you in the ass. How you 'spect to live into the future if you can't see the present?"

"Kallum and I have our agreement, and that's about where it stands. We don't spend much time in one another's company." We circled the coyote's shredded body, leaving hoofprints in the blood. "I reckon if he hasn't told me anything about a well, he doesn't have any plans to."

"Nope," Curtis said. "I reckon he don't. Mayor Kallum might be an inhospitable bag of shit, but what he ain't ever been is stupid. If the man's got money and bodies, he'll dispose of them in the general direction of whatever it is he wants. How long you been in Blackpeak, Faust? Three years, give and take?"

"Along those lines. What's that matter?"

"You got no idea how it works," he muttered. "Christ, you just as daft as a mole-rat. Your head's floating up so high over that town, you haven't even taken a chance to see what's happening under your feet. You got no idea how it works, but you'll learn. Believe me, you'll learn. The Well, that's all that matters."

He tightened his grip around the reins of his horse, dug his heel into its ribs, and sauntered up a few paces away from the corpse of the coyote.

I looked at the coyote, and the uncut guts waggling out of its belly and laying like spilled meat on the hard peat. I looked into its dead eyes. The black pits reflected a message at me that didn't come with words, but instead with feelings, instinct, and intuition. I kicked my horse into a canter.

The coyote wasn't a fluke. We were supposed to find it.

It was a warning.

———

We pushed the horses almost twenty miles that day, putting a big chunk of the trail behind us. We leveled out into easy-riding plains where both of our horses could be let to run when they wanted to. Come sunset, the sky looked like the inside of a blood orange sprinkled with stars. Curtis and I found a dead but sturdy tree with branches like sky-bound snakes. We tied our horses to it by the halter. Tinder, branches, and four matches later, I cooked beans. "Western Elbow ain't but a few hours off," Curtis said as he shoveled beans into his mouth with his knife. "I put us there by mid-morning."

When we were finished eating, we hunkered down over the fire. When I got bored, I read *The Collected Works of Shakespeare*. I read about Hamlet and guessed he'd turn out to be a pretty good king in time.

When I was distracted, Curtis removed the dirty bandage from around the side of his face, finally revealing his other eye and the damage that had been done to the skin there. One side of his mouth sagged like a loose bag. A permanent splash of scar tissue darkened his neck and face. "This is what you did to me," Curtis said, tapping at the skin.

I closed the book. "You expect me to feel sympathy for you?"

"I 'spect you to feel responsible for turning me into a fuckin' freak, Faust." When Curtis sneered, the side of his mouth that looked like ripped ribbons and wet fabric revealed the shards of teeth. "Out here you're just a cold turd with bad aim and nuts the size of a jack-rabbit's eyeball. Out here—" he motioned out to the sprawling plains, "—you don't have any of the comforts and laws and clever little rules. Best bet for you, Faust, is to get out of Blackpeak before that place gets its fangs in you and starts pulling. You don't know the place like I do."

"I know it from a different side," I said.

"I'm tryin' to help you." With calm hands, Curtis pushed aside his slicker and drew his revolver. He worked the action and pointed it over the fire at me. "Get out of Blackpeak, Faust, before it drags you down like it did for all of us."

Have a gun pointed at you enough by Curtis Gregdon and it starts not really frightening you. It uneases you, sure, but you don't exactly start fearing for your life when you've stared enough times down a cold, black barrel. "Why so adamant?"

"Shit I don't want to *tell* you," he said. "You won't believe me."

"What I got to believe from a lunatic?"

"You stay in Blackpeak long enough and you're going to die, Faust."

"That's marshaling," I said.

The gun shook in his hand. "I know what happened to the marshal before you, Faust. You didn't see that. I bet you didn't even hear about it." He waved the barrel at me and tightened his fingers on the handle. " You're going to run out of clever quips and witty words one day, Faust, and then you'll sit there and think to yourself, 'Curtis tried to warn me,' and you'd have wished you'd ran when I did."

"Get your gun out of my face, Gregdon."

"Not until you tell me you're going to run. Until I know I did something good for once."

"Tell me about the last marshal, Gregdon. Tell me what's got you so scared."

"He saw something one day unhinged him bad, made him lose his mind, Faust. I ain't always been a fuckin' lawbreaker. I ain't always been like this." The gun dipped and waved little patterns in the air. "What's it worth, fighting over a place this small, huh? What's it worth, pulling coal out the ground day-in and day-out, when we barely even live long enough to light our own furnaces? Shit. Kallum ain't in this for no coal or riches. Best it suits him that everybody stay drank up and fucked up and don't pay attention." He swam for his words. He tried to pick them out of the air, piece them together. "Kallum wants it, the Magnate wants it. Hell, there's... there's other people want it, and they'll tear this place to pieces just to get at it."

"This all a bunch of talk about that Well of yours? You can sit here all you want and talk in circles, Curtis, but as it stands, you still ain't told me shit. I'm taking this all on faith. Taking *you* on faith."

"You think there's something special about this place just naturally calls people?" the outlaw snapped. "You think Kallum picked *this* spot to drop a town on, what, 'cause he threw a rock and that's where it landed, like, 'I proclaim thee Blackpeak'? There's power in this sand and dirt—" and he scooped it up between his fingers, "— because the Well is somewhere beneath it all, and men'll wade in each other's blood and guts to be the first one to find it. I know, because—"

I saw the flash of glowing eyes over his shoulder before he ever would have.

A high-pitched wail. A growl. I slipped one of my Colts from the holster like it was a second part of me, reached across the fire, and pushed Gregdon out of the way.

A sack of bricks smashed into me, landed on me with four paws. Hot, sour breath blasted in my face. My Colt was in its mouth. Teeth clacked against it. I fired. A subdued flash of fire exploded out of the back of the beast's head. Fluid splashed down onto me. The body went limp.

Maybe a wolf. Maybe a mountain-cat. *Something.* I wrenched the crumpling body off of me and scrambled to my feet.

"Curtis!"

He was already spinning around, his pistol clenched in both hands. From just outside the firelight's reach I frantically counted at least five pairs of eyes watching us, reflecting our fear back at us. Beastly shadows stalked there, their claws dragging bad omens through the dirt.

One of the pairs of eyes vanished. Curtis got blasted back, expelling a gasp of breath. He splashed down into the fire, spraying sparks. A canine figure ripped at his slicker, ignoring the storm of embers. I raised my pistol and squeezed off a shot, but the beast leaped away the next instant. Curtis rolled out of the fire, his jacket glowing orange. He beat himself like a dying fish on the ground to put out the fires.

"Don't fucking shoot at me," he shouted.

"So get eaten faster next time," I said.

I tore my other Colt out of its holster, unfocused my eyes to ignore the blinding firepit, aimed as well as I could at two of the figures – one at my left, one at my right – and fired.

A yelp. Another ran for me. Its paws hammered the dirt. I caught sight of a shock of bristly fur, a coned snout, pointed ears. It closed the distance almost too fast for me to react. I belted it across the face with both of my pistols. The iron sights tore its skin. It skittered to the side, unbalanced and distracted, blood spilling.

A rattling bark from my left. I cussed and threw myself down to my stomach as one leaped over me. Curtis's half-bandaged face flared yellow as he unloaded three quick shots into the beast's side.

The one I'd smacked was still trying to clamber to its four paws. I squeezed off a shot at its snout and it dropped. On the end of my pistol, matted fur smoldered and smoked.

Curtis and I stood back-to-back. We peered into the darkness. The horses were pounding the ground, shuffling, neighing.

"Goddamnit," Curtis whispered over and over. "Goddamnit. Goddamnit..."

"You see any of them?"

"They're still out there." He shot. The gun bucked wildly. I heard bullets whip into the dirt in the distance. "They're still out there."

"Wasting shots," I said. "Don't shoot any of the fucking horses, Gregdon, or—" he fired again, as if he was trying to scare whatever was stalking us, "—we won't have anything to ride. Steady hands, steady hands."

"Goddamnit," he said. A mantra.

I heard Curtis frantically fumbling to reload. Meanwhile, I caught sight of another pair of eyes in front of me, hovering like floating gems in the darkness. It bared wretched teeth. One of Curtis's cartridges fell into the dirt.

When I took a bead between those two flashing orbs, I didn't hesitate to shoot. Not knowing exactly what we were fighting, I didn't want to take chances on being dinner. The revolver jerked in my hand. One of the creatures yelped and fell backwards, dead before it could ever approach. If I went off the five sets of eyes I saw after we first got attacked, that meant that three of the bastards still lived.

Three animals.

Three shots in my left-hand Colt.

Three shots in my right.

Wait. Scratch that. Two, right? Shit.

I ain't had much experience fighting things that don't cuss or splash piss on the pot-side, but I guessed animals weren't going to be too different than men. A distraction for us meant advantages for them. I immediately spun around, aiming around Curtis. Can't aim too good in the dark, but I saw what I expected to see – a shadow bounding at him, rearing up, leaping. Left Colt, two shots in quick succession – *bang*, hammer, *bang* again – and the furry blur slammed snout down into the ground. The body skidded to a stop right in front of Curtis and me, its mouth sagging open, its neck bent awkwardly to the side.

A coyote.

"Goddamnit," sputtered Curtis, still fumbling to reload. With his shitty gun skills, I started to realize why Curtis Gregdon had run from his fears in the first place.

And that gave me an idea.

"Gregdon," I said, barrels still pointed, waiting for the next attack. "Make a run for the horses."

"You're crazy."

"Better than being dead," I said, and I kicked him in his ass.

Sure enough, Gregdon's wild flight drew the beasts out of the darkness. One of them came thundering out at him. It was followed by its partner, but that one only tailed Gregdon for so long before it pinwheeled its paws in the dirt, spun around, and began to rush for me.

I raised my right gun. The angry-ass coyote snarled. I squeezed the trigger. It kept coming. I fired again. The bullet-soaking beast just kept running.

The body careened into me, swept my feet out from under me, and smashed me back into the ground. I knocked my skull on the hard ground and felt my hat blow away. The coyote went straight for my throat, but I rammed my forearm between its jaws. It crunched down and my vision exploded into stars.

Few things ran through my head while getting love-bites from a coyote. Is that blood or saliva running down my arm? Is Curtis dead? Would a damn rug-mutt actually be the lucky one to do me in?

And how does a fucking coyote survive two bleeding gunshots in the middle of its chest?

I pounded on the coyote's snout with the butt of my empty Colt. My pistols tumbled from my grasp as the coyote snarled, peeled back its lips, and struck again.

I balled a fist and cold-cocked it right across the snout. Just as it was about to go for me again, I went for its mouth. I grabbed the top and bottom of its jaw with both hands. Its teeth cut like razors. Those wild eyes wanted to kill me. I managed to throw the hackle-necked bastard off me and rolled with it, pinning it between me and the ground. I rammed my shredded forearm down into its mouth.

As I wrestled with the furious coyote, I noticed its gaze kept straying away from me. Flicking, flicking, toward something else.

My pocket.

Where the Eye sat in a whiskey-soaked rag.

Did it sense it?

I reached to the back of my belt for my knife, which I'd promised myself never to forget after the Joshua incident. I drew it out and hacked. The blade scraped between two of the coyote's ribs. I turned my wrist to gut it, releasing the musty stink of blood and fresh shit into the air. The coyote's breaths came out of the new hole in its side. It suffocated in its own blood.

"Faust," I heard Curtis cry out.

I stumbled away from the coyote's body, falling just enough to cake my ripped arm in loose dirt. Curtis and the coyote he'd drawn out of the darkness tumbled around in the weeds. I sprinted for the horses, who shifted uneasily away from me. I slid my shotgun out of the saddle-side holster.

I sauntered to Gregdon and his furry pal, reared back my boot, and then kicked the animal right in its throat.

Gregdon rolled away and quivered in the dirt.

I jabbed the barrel of my shotgun down against the coyote's neck, its rigid paws trying to claw for purchase on the ground.

"Fuck me," Curtis cried. "Oh, fuck, I'm all ripped up."

I thumbed each hammer back, put my foot on the coyote's head, then blew the mangy creature to bits.

THAT WAS the last of them. I reloaded.

I followed the trail of glowing coals to Gregdon's writhing form.

He was still rubbing at his face, leaving smears of red in the dirt. "They're gonna kill us," he said.

"The dogs?"

"We're gonna be fuckin' dead."

"Aren't yet," I said, kicking one of the dead coyotes. No white foam around its mouth.

I crouched down next to Gregdon and pressed the brain-stained shotgun down against his forehead. He stared at me, the burnt half of his face freshly bloodied where a coyote's claw had torn lines in his skin. "Faust," he gasped.

I pulled back the right hammer. "I want answers."

"I don't have any—"

"Bullshit. Before I get fed up enough to blow your brains apart and pick out the info I want, I suggest you start talking." It struck me then that most of our relationship had been shared overtop the barrel of a gun. Curtis and I thought too much alike. "You want to know what scares me, Curtis?"

He glanced at the shotgun, raising the burned skin where no eyebrow remained.

"Coyotes," I told him, twisting the tip of my boot in a squishy piece of gore, "Especially ones acting out of sorts."

"Wild coyotes. Wild."

"I'd have thought so, but wild coyotes ain't so stupid. I don't imagine they'll prey on humans by choice."

"Maybe they had no choice."

"They did," I said. "The horses."

"Maybe they didn't want no horse."

"Feeling I get is that if they *needed* to eat, that would've been their first option. They wanted us." I pulled back the second hammer. "They wanted you."

"You're making shit up."

I ignored him and continued on, narrowing my eyes, keeping him pinned beneath the weight of the double barrels. "Only thing I can assume is that maybe they're trained. Maybe tamed, at least enough to kill when instructed in ways their nature won't otherwise encourage."

I saw a veil come over him, a thing of realization and discovery, as if I'd just put together things he'd never wanted to admit.

He wasn't afraid of me. He was afraid of whatever it was he hadn't revealed.

"They all want it," he breathed. "The Well. Kallum, the Magnate, and hell, anyone else that knows about it. And my Pa says they find it – we find it – we get to ask of it anything we want. If we got gaps in our life, it fills it in with pleasures. If...if there's somethin' in life we want, it gives it to us. And if there's somethin' we done we want to take back, it lets us, quick as a flame or a gunshot."

Some words, no matter how many strange things you've seen, still beggar understanding. His eyes leaked and he covered his face with a pair of trembling hands. What sat in front of me wasn't an outlaw; it was a boy scared by stories, someone who'd had unreal promises dangled in front of him for far too long.

Then he sputtered, "I haven't done a goddamned thing. I haven't done anything..."

Scared child. Scared little boy. Had he ever seemed so small before?

"Ten minutes," I said, storming past him to the horses. "Wash up, patch up, and saddle up. We're due for the Western Elbow."

I left him alone amid the coyote corpses, their blood, and the scattered curlicues of their brains drying in the sand. I used to think the dead coyote in the pass was saying *turn back, turn back.*

It was really saying *We're coming to get your ass.*

We're coming to kill you.

28

TRAINS DON'T GO IN OR OUT OF BLACKPEAK. NO TRAIN WOULD WANT to. There ain't a single thing Blackpeak has of value unless the rest of the world wanted the syph, bedbugs, and bad alcohol. The closest thing any resident of Blackpeak would ever get to a train is the Western Elbow.

It was right near nine in the morning when we arrived, looking down on the rickety train-tracks from a series of bare rocks above it. The Western Elbow was where southbound tracks coming from Crown Rock curved to avoid the mountains and shoot off west toward Rouseville. Enterprising trains would sometimes stop and sell extra cargo to people who waited at the Western Elbow. Usually cost a shit-load more, but not-exactly-legal transactions weren't known for fairness.

Quick exchanges, quick escapes. Take your pick.

"So here we are," I said. "You frequent this place a lot, Curtis?"

"If it weren't for the Western Elbow and the Gregdons, that piss-ant town wouldn't be around and you wouldn't have that fat star on your chest or the salary that comes with it."

"Really rolling in it," I said.

"Always beer in the Crooked Cocoon and the Horseshoe Junction.

Always feed at the feed shop. Always coffee in your mug when you want it. That ain't Kallum at all. You think any of those so-called businessmen gonna hump it all the way out here? That's a Gregdon job. We buy all the goods from the Western Elbow, maybe sometimes we take it, and we sell it back to Sloman and the Frenchman behind the bar and whoever else wants it."

"Black market."

"Mutual business interests," he said.

"I take it Kallum knows?"

"Kallum doesn't give a fuck as long as business is good. Miners mine, outlaws scuffle, drinkers drink, and the marshal marshals," he said, stifling a grin. "God, you some damn fool, sliding right into the general plan."

"So what, Kallum constructs this town to work like clockwork so he can—" I spun my hand in the air like a windmill, "—spend his days searching for your so-called Well?"

"Now you're not so stupid," Curtis said. "Enough talk. The seven-fifty from Crown Rock makes its way through here in about twenty minutes, and all goes well—"

"That's your ticket out of here?"

He tightened his hand around his horse's reins. "Let's get this shit done with."

Curtis traced his way down to the tracks. His horse's hooves knocked stones down in front of it. Once we both hit the flatland, Curtis motioned for me to follow him along the tracks.

I didn't pry into Curtis about this Well. I rathered he tell me what he wanted to. Whether or not I was dealing with high-strung stories or low-brow rumors, you couldn't toss a question at Curtis and expect a clear response: he thought more like buckshot than straight bullets. Before Nycendera, before seeing the Magnate bend the rules of the world like some cheap bit of leather-work, I would as soon spit as I would believe a single sound that rolled off Curtis's greasy tongue.

Nycendera's warning came alive in my memory: *Below our feet lingers that which should be claimed by no man. He yearns. He* knows.

So Kallum and the Magnate. Was it some kind of race, then? A dash to whatever end this Well allowed them? And how the hell had I managed to go all this time ignorant to it?

We rode for a thousand yards, keeping the rocky hills on our right and the tracks on our left. Gregdon halted us when he got to where he wanted to be. He leaped off his horse and led her a few more paces up, where a hitching pole had been driven sloppily into the earth. I dismounted and tied mine up too. "Up this way," Curtis said.

Set against the side of the stony hill I saw an outcropping. I climbed up after him, my boots scraping against the dust and my fingers finding every crack. Tucked between two large boulders, made out of wood the same dull brown as the dry earth itself, there was a tiny shed with a slanted roof and a single boarded window. The tiny railhouse overlooked the tracks. Wasn't no bigger than those fishing shacks you see in winter paintings. It hovered, held up by frail supports between the rocks. I imagine you had to know it was there to see it in the first place. Curtis helped me up the rest of the hill.

"We're here," he said.

"This is what you wanted to show me?"

"That's inside." He swallowed. "It's good of you. To do this. Most wouldn't have. Not for me."

He reached forward and pulled open the door to the shack. All the wood creaked.

The first thing I noticed was the stench.

The rancid smell punched me in the mouth, stabbed my nostrils, made my ears start to ring as my senses all exploded inside of me. It reeked like pools of stagnant blood, thick as milk.

"Inside," said Gregdon, who covered his mouth and nose with his hand.

"Shit no," I coughed. "You first. No fish, no barrels."

"I wouldn't have brought your ass out this far if I just wanted to put you somewhere you couldn't escape and shoot you full of holes, Faust. In. We ain't got time for this."

Order didn't matter. Gregdon *could* have shot me if I went in first, but he wouldn't, just like I wouldn't shoot him. Thought about it, of course. He did too. Our eyes said as much.

Lawmen, outlaws, all the same mold at the heart.

I slipped inside.

He yanked the door shut. There was a bundle of burlap on the floor, curled up like a pillbug. In the darkness, cut only by slants of dusty light coming in through the boarded window, I recognized the shape as well as I could. Could've been blind and known enough by the stink. "How long has it been here," I asked.

"Few days. Didn't know where else to put it. It's why I came to get you. What I wanted to talk about."

"You want some kind of investigation?"

"I want you to look at it. Go ahead," Curtis said, sweat running down his face. "Go ahead, Faust."

The burlap had just been draped over the corpse. I slid the tip of my knife underneath the cloth and lifted. The skin had almost gone gray, wrinkled like a grape left out in the sun. A new blast of stink hit me, made my mouth water. The sweltering little room started to spin. I caught a glimpse of knotted white hair crawling with white slugs and a wide, gaping grin, toothless and laughing.

Rufus Oarsdale was just as ugly dead as he had been when he was alive.

"Goddamnit!" I lunged back on reflex.

"Had to show you the body, Faust. You had to know. You had to know, because if you didn't, fuck, who was going to?" With a cold and deliberate hand, Curtis drew his .44 Russian and placed himself against the single door to the small hut. He cocked back the hammer and pointed it at my gut from his hip. "Keep your cool, Marshal. I need you to."

"Did you do this?"

Rufus Oarsdale's stony face didn't tell me shit. He just kept staring at the ceiling. A fly perched on his upper lip, then crawled curiously into his left nostril. The old wound in my leg started to act up, the scar spasming with every heartbeat. I had taken a bullet for Oarsdale. His lucky bullet.

Curtis took off his black hat and threw it down on the floor between the tips of my boots. "I've been running for three days, Faust.

After three days, there ain't many other places you can run when you know the world's on your tail. Sooner or later, you have to find a place that feels right to be, turn your back, and close your eyes to it all.

"This is my place. This is the place where I'm going to turn my back to everything else."

"Why bring me this far," I said, "if you only plan to tail it out of here? You want *me* to clean this up and not ask questions? Not demand you answer?"

"I done this for Rufus. Wanted to clear my conscience."

Gregdon thrust the gun down toward Oarsdale's dead body and discharged three quick shots. The gunshots sounded like flat boards being smacked together on the inside of my skull. "I didn't know where else to stash the fuckin' body, Faust. Three days ago I lured him here, 'cause the old man always liked cheap trades, because he didn't have much, you know? Man, you should'a listened to him babble all the way here, apologizing to me for what you done." Curtis wiped his mouth. "When he came inside, I drew and put two slugs in his back without him ever knowing."

"So you did him," I said, "for some kind of revenge?"

"I don't give a shit about revenge, Faust."

"You gave a fuck when it concerned me."

"I was told to go for you," he said. "Hell, before Rufus here, I ain't ever killed nobody. It scares the shit out of me, idea of killing a man." His shoulders shook as he tried to pull a laugh from somewhere inside. "You'd think all the ways I'd played around the past few years, totin' guns and threatening people just because they breathed, I'd actually have the balls to do something."

"You didn't have any issue drawing on me."

"Ain't the same as squeezing the trigger, Faust. You know that."

Somewhere in the process, my knife had found its way back into its sheath and I'd slid one of my Colts out of its holster. I'd already cocked the thing and was aiming at him from the hip. Some things come natural. Almost too natural.

While Curtis tried to keep his seams together, I spoke. "I think it's time you start telling me why we're here, Gregdon, besides clearing your pretty shoulders of all that hard burden."

"Can't. Nervous. 'Fraid of saying what I got to say."

Maybe it was the reek of death thickening the air, maybe it was the trickle of sweat sliding down my neck, but I was restless, ready to flee. I wanted it all over with as soon as possible. I tapped a finger on the bridge of my nose. "Raise that revolver of yours, Gregdon. I want you to take aim right on this spot."

His eyes flicked left and right before he raised the gun and steadied it.

"Take control, Gregdon. You're not ready to say shit because you're too much of a child to be responsible for what you do or what you say. Find the irons and put them right between my eyes."

His hand jittered. The metal frame of the gun started to rattle. "Faust, you're pissin' me off."

"Take control, you little shit," I said. "Aim at me. Cock the hammer."

His teeth chattered like an off-time clock."Yeah," he said. "Yeah."

"You're the man with the secrets," I said, "but you're the man with the gun, too. You could tell me you still suck your thumb like it was your Mama's tit and still be in control, because that's *your* gun, and I'm *your* target, and if I don't play shit straight, that'll be *my* bullet."

I saw little flashes of light in his eyes like thoughts coming to the surface. A gun can make any man feel stronger, and with Blackpeak's sole authority pinned down under his sights, Curtis Gregdon started remembering his boldness.

Training an outlaw how to be an outlaw. You learn to do new things every day.

"I didn't want to kill him," said Curtis with a steady voice. "Faust, I ain't no killer. It don't take no killer just to be an outlaw. It's always been easy, doin' shit that ain't always right, but killing?" Then his tone fell flat as a sheet. "Pa, he told me—" He shook his head. "The Magnate, he wanted him."

"Dead?"

"Alive. Rufus Oarsdale was the only one who knew the way to it.

To the Well. To that end-point all these power-hungry dipshits are fumbling over themselves to find. Magnate might've thought him just some two-bit thief and a drunk that couldn't do anything that wasn't worth being fixed right again, but if it meant having Rufus Oarsdale lead him to the Well, he'd kiss his ass.

"Pa told me, he told me—" Curtis's words became frantic and breathless, a broken-dam rush of rapid whispers. "'The Well chose Rufus Oarsdale to be its Arbiter.' He divined it, right out the air. Did his spells, called on his spirit broker, discovered through whatever dark avenues he travels that there was somethin' special about old Rufus here."

A tickle in my brain. A little spark, blown in from far, far away.

There was *something special. Until Curtis spilled it...*

I gritted my teeth.

Shit. I realized too late—

I hadn't re-soaked the whiskey-rag.

"You could dig and dig and dig for centuries to find that Well and never find it. Dig yourself straight to Hell and back, never get a glimpse unless the Well wants you to. Shit, Rufus barely even knew, too damn drunk and blasted out his mind to ever be of much use if the Well called on him. Can you believe it?" The outlaw laughed, a loud and barking noise. "An Oarsdale. Rufus fuckin' Oarsdale, special inside and out. How you 'spose it picks some pimple like him to be its Arbiter?"

You weren't supposed to know about this, the Magnate said.

Curtis began to tromp in a wary circle, shaking the edge of his gun like a maddened baton.

I asked, "If the Magnate wanted Rufus, why'd you plug him, Curtis?"

"Because he wanted him," he snapped.

The Well protects itself. And if putting the knowledge of its location in the mind of a drunken half-wit is how the Well fortified against prying eyes and prying minds...

"Two shots to the back. Dropped dead. No mess, no crying, nothing to come back and haunt me, Faust."

...then I suppose I'd need to play whatever game the Well had in store, even if it meant ripping that title of Arbiter straight out of Rufus Oarsdale's veins.

"One minute he was alive, the next, there was smoke, and he was still."

He blinked twice, then wiped sweat off his runny forehead.

"If fate lined up," Curtis sputtered, "and fuckin' Kallum could find the Well, and if...if the Magnate could find the Well, then who says I couldn't? If I killed Rufus—" he knocked his pistol against his chest, "—maybe *I* could be Arbiter. Maybe it'd choose me. Maybe I could find that goddamn Well, and ask it to bring my brother back, ask it to put back together what you fuckin' took away from me, you blood-thirsty sonofabitch!"

His gun reached out to me.

My son, the Magnate muttered. *Such a greedy little prick. Avarice is a child's call to action.*

Curtis had started to light up like the sulfur head of a match. "None of it's fair. None of it was ever supposed to be fair. My own father put his own sons out to do his filthy bitch-work, and for what? To put them under his heel? Make'em do whatever the hell he wanted? Billy's dead. Billy's dead, and there ain't a damn thing in this world that's worth going through it all feelin' like I'm half-put together without my brother near me.

"So fuck the Magnate, and fuck Kallum and the Well, and all these little otherworldly games. And you too, Elias Faust. Fuck you too." I thought his teeth would shatter in his mouth. "I put two bullets in this old bastard's back to hope I could be the Arbiter of the Well. Just one chance to make a wish and set the world in reverse. For once, let Curtis Gregdon be at the top of it all. The Well didn't want that, though. World didn't want it either. Faust, how do you do it?"

"What," I said.

"Kill," he said. "I've seen you do it. You don't ever stop, don't hesitate."

"I'm good at it," I said.

"Only until you die. But there's something else," he said,

realigning the sights with the spot between my eyes. "There's gotta be something else about you. Some reason it's so easy…"

Faces started coming to mind, hovering inside the black pistol-mouth like pictures in a metal frame. Billy Gregdon. Harman, who still felt enough like my own kill. The memories didn't bring with them the quick pangs of belly-weight you usually get when you feel connected to something. No happiness, no sadness, nothing.

"I just don't linger on it much, Curtis," I said. "I don't think about blood or pain or bullets or dead things. I don't think about how there could be other options. I sort of think of it like a circle, one just between you, my gun, and me. Have to complete the circle."

"A circle," he said. "You just make a circle."

"All it seems to ever need is—"

"A bullet?" Curtis said.

"A bullet," I said.

"So," he said, "who's going to close our circle, Faust? Is it gonna be you, or is it gonna be me? The circle's gotta close."

"Here, Curtis, we're just people with guns. We're just solving problems."

He's gone against his loyalties.

"But the circle's gotta close."

His recklessness has put Blackpeak – and the Well – at risk.

"Maybe some other day, Curtis," I said. "Maybe not today."

I can't forgive this of him.

Curtis locked his elbows. The Gregdon inside of him started to awaken. "It ends today, Faust. It needs to. I killed the Arbiter of the Well. They'll be out for blood. They'll have me. Sooner or later, no matter where I'm at, they'll have me."

There has to be an accounting. He stole from me. My son sought to steal the Well from me.

I ground my teeth until my jaw shot through with pain.

Curtis tilted his head to the side. "How long has he been talking to you?"

I reached, very carefully, into my breast pocket.

I showed him the Eye.

"Not long," I said.

"He's inside you, Faust. You ain't even touching it," the Magnate's son said, "and he's got hooks under your skin. God. *God.*" He swiped his hand down his face, then turned to the wall and drove his head against it several times, until a hearty gash smiled on his brow. "I never let him. I never let him. He didn't own me. He never will. You don't own me. You hear me? Now it's all just circles, isn't it?"

I swallowed. "Come with me, Curtis. There can be a fair reckoning. A fair accounting. Let me help."

"No," Curtis said, tone as sharp as a knife. "I told you Blackpeak runs you foul, Faust. I told you it does. Place fucked me up, fucked up all the Gregdons. Fucked up the Magnate and Rufus Oarsdale, too, and now it's on the way to getting inside of you, too, not letting go. Thought I'd try to give you a warning, but it's like talking to a goddamn rock. But I'm stronger than that. I refuse. I'm my own man. I'm my own circle."

Curtis lowered the gun. He examined the pistol from a distance. Seemed to settle up and relax. He looked at the Eye.

"Steady hands," said Curtis. "Steady hands."

He opened his mouth like he was going to say something. Curtis angled his wrist, crammed the .44 Russian into his mouth, and pulled the trigger.

A volcano of blood exploded out the back of Curtis's head. A slaughterhouse splatter whipped across the wall and ceiling behind him. A whole mouthful of smoke rolled out from around the barrel. He didn't fall over back or forward or even to the side, but instead right down like an accordion crushed down by two meaty hands.

"Curtis," I shouted, because for a minute I forgot words ain't as fast as bullets.

I stood there with one hand out. Two dead bodies, one on the other, lay right in front of me. Burnt powder. Scorched hair. A few shards of skull like broken porcelain littered the floor around him. A half-lidded eye, blown out, still fluttered.

The Magnate came to me like a lightning-storm, crashing into my mind.

What have you done?

The room swam. Heat pressed into me. Heat and stink and there was so much blood and his head was just a crushed gourd. I fell back against the wall and closed my fist around the silver ball-bearing, trying to blind the Eye with the darkness of my hand.

"I tried to stop him," I said.

You didn't.

Illness coursed inside my gut. Curtis hadn't had another option. Torn between obedience and choice, he'd taken the worst third option of the two. With Rufus dead and the Magnate's access to this Well destroyed, he'd no place in Gregdon's syndicate. As I looked down at the mangled remains of a still-warm man, wondering if any part of him still clung on, numbness washed over me.

Curtis had wanted him to watch.

This, the Magnate said, *changes everything. You understand that, don't you?*

"Did you know? Did you know this was a possibility?"

Curtis...never functioned within the rules. Billy knew his place. Billy paid attention. Billy saw the larger possibilities. He trusted in me, in the Well, and in what could be accomplished with it.

A morsel of anger sprang up in me for the boy laying in pieces on the floor. A boy I'd damaged and then sought to deliver from damage.

Curtis suffered perpetual myopia. It limited him. It limited us. If I am to function within a cage, Faust, then I'll make that cage for myself, break it, and bend it as I see fit when the time is right.

"Your son is dead. Did you see? Your son is dead."

I'm growing used to it.

"Is ambition worth this blood?"

I'll need to make new plans, certainly. But the Well's worth every drop. This is a distraction, but I'll not abide having my attention divided. Elias Faust, know my gratitude—

A hail of gunfire ripped through the side of the shack. I felt a pull at the front of my duster, ripping through one lapel and launching out the other. I dropped to the floor. A steady rain of bullets chewed through the shack's wooden wall.

You have my truest thanks for your willingness to help my boy, lost as he was. You could have turned your back. You didn't.

While I was on my stomach next to the two corpses, I heard an occasional warning shot ring and felt the whole shack shudder as the bullets bit away at it. The stream of fire soon slowed. I kept my head covered. Something trickled down my arm like a warm razor.

"What the hell is this," I asked the walls.

The next step. Improvisation. A little something to push us forward. We're bound now, Faust. You and me. Circles and circles and circles...

29

WHAT A DAY. ME, SPRAWLED NEXT TO TWO BAGS OF HUMAN LEATHER talking blindly to the voice in my head about Arbiters, Wells, and fatherhood. Gunshots stopped. Down below the shack, somewhere near the train-tracks, I heard the metallic noises of guns being reloaded. Someone spoke, but the voice was wet and ragged, as rough as a scorpion's tail. "We should check to see if it's taken care of. The Magnate will want proof."

"He will have his proof," said another, struggling over what sounded like a throat full of phlegm.

"You sent them to kill me?" I whispered into my shoulder.

Please. I'm not that spontaneous. My neonate sandshades have been on your tail since your run-in with the coyotes.

One said, "Did you check their horses?"

"A repeater and a shotgun. A bit of ammunition for both. Slit the necks when I was done."

Damnit.

The first cleared his throat. A repeater racked below. "Go up, see what you can find. I'll cover you from down here."

I elbow-crawled closer to Curtis's body. I grabbed his .44, stuffed it in my belt-loop, and began to sift through Oarsdale's clothes to see if there was anything of use.

I pulled up his shirt. Tucked against his cold skin and expanded belly was a white bone handle. There were designs on it, inlaid with something shiny, probably gold. I grabbed the handle and yanked it out of his pants. Rufus Oarsdale's so-called lucky pistol hadn't done shit to keep him from getting shot in the back. It was an antique, a flintlock that looked more for decoration than for practical use, though my leg knew otherwise.

Though his skin had turned to grotesque rubber, I noticed a curious etching on his stomach: a wild, unnatural scalework, all scarred symmetries and shapes, a galaxy of geometry sprung up from underneath his skin. Nothing about it was organic. It reminded me of the branding on a cow's flank. It trailed up, up along his skin, until I discovered, right at the meeting of his ribs, a coin-sized pustule. Not round, the way you'd expect a swollen abscess to be, but shaped like a jagged cube pressing up from beneath his skin.

"Can you see this," I asked the Magnate. "This scar?"

Show me with the Eye.

I opened my palm. A long pause. Then:

The Arbiter's Mark. The Well chooses as it desires, even if the justification for candidacy appears...unclear.

Unsteady boots crunched up the stony hill, getting closer to the shack. I crammed Oarsdale's flintlock into the back of my pants. Was this what they were after, then? Kallum and Magnate and, hell, Curtis, too? To have this brand, be this so-called Well's chosen piss-boy? I didn't know what kind of power or influence such a mark would have afforded them, but it was clearly enough to die over, or destroy families and towns and livings and lives over.

"Call off your men," I said.

That would be disingenuous.

There were at least two – the one coming up to the shack and the one still down below it – and that meant I was already outnumbered. If Goon Numero Uno opened the shack door and found me, he'd unload, and the rain of gunfire from below would start again. I'd be cooked, dead as my two new bunk-mates. Couldn't let that happen. And they had my guns. I swallowed down all the little bits of sour fear in my throat, weighed my options, and—

Well, I went with the idea that would get things over quickest. Could've meant the situation. Could've meant my life.

The wall of the shack faced the train-tracks and the hill below it. Just a few seconds to act, to make a good first impression. "Let's get this over with," I said, drawing both of my Colts.

Breathe.

I sprinted for the shack's brittle wall.

I smashed through the bullet-weakened wood and shouted, throwing myself out and over the down-slope of the hill. I was in the air, my legs circling wildly. The world around me spun in a blur of color and scenery. One of the gravelly voices barked in surprise. The slope was too steep to get footing on, so I slid, spraying wood and dirt everywhere. Goon Numero Uno was just in front of me. He raised a long, silver-mouthed revolver.

I careened into him. Him, and all his strange-shaped limbs, more bone and spur than skin and muscle.

Several black-clad figures at the base of the hill reared their horses around to face the commotion. Their guns came with them. They all fired blindly. Goon Numero Uno started to convulse as bullets clapped into his back. Bullets meant for me. He made a few choking, gagging noises in his throat. I grabbed the chest of his black clothes and yanked him with me like a shield as I readjusted my momentum and threw myself behind an outcropping of stone.

Bullets in search of me slammed against the boulder I hid behind, throwing little white chips down on me from above.

Goon Numero Uno, still laying on the hill, started to crawl up to his feet, despite the holes in his back. His body, all exaggerated and wrong, occupied some space between *human* and *shadow*. His pointed chin turned. His eyes, both silver as nickel, fell on me.

There it was, that wave of discomfort inside me, coming to life.

Sickness. Dread. Acid bubbled into my mouth.

I leveled my guns on him. "What the hell is so wrong with dying lately?"

After his lead backrub, I was starting to think bullets were taking a holiday. Without a pistol, he had to dig into his coat to find another option – though his coat wasn't a coat at all. It was long, black, and layered like loose robes and tattered upholstery. I couldn't see his legs, and my assailants' pale faces seemed to float in darkness underneath their brims. Their heads were covered on the sides and backs with fabric, sort of like nuns.

Uno wrenched a sawed-off shotgun out of his robes. "Say your prayers, Faust, because—"

I shot him in the forehead.

The bullet blew him back, a black dot stuck between his eyes. I shot him again. His skull caved. The black hat went flying. I chambered, shot, chambered, shot. Puffs of dirt from his skin shot up into the air like little geysers. He fell, robes fluttering in the wind.

I reloaded as quickly as I could. The second voice, Goon Numero Dos, came up over the rocks. "Faust, we can do this simple or we can do this hard. It's all up to you. Throw out your guns. There are three of us left and one of you."

"That *is* simple." My heart slammed. "You're outnumbered."

An echoing shot. A bullet smacked against the boulder behind me. It ricocheted, howling off into the hills. "Gregdons," shouted Dos to his associates. "Go drag that hiding pig out from behind his rock. Let's get bloody."

So much for negotiation.

Hooves thundered up the stony hill, grabbing hold with almost human precision. Dos sent his two other henchmen – Tres and...Seis, let's say – up toward me. Being hunkered behind the boulder left me only one exit.

Had to move. Had to move, or had to die.

I rushed out from behind the boulder and onto the hill, which rolled like a beige carpet down to the train-tracks. Goon Numero Tres, mounted on a horse as dark as night and gleaming like a streak of thoroughbred oil, thrust a bony hand out in my direction. His fingers snapped into odd shapes like broken branches. I dove. A hum rattled in my teeth. I heard a sharp *crack* and squinted against two rapid flashes of white light.

The ground right where I'd been standing smoked like a stifled candle. My hair stood at attention.

His lips peeled back so far, the skin split wide and wet. Teeth the color of cork formed a jagged smile. The skin of his fingertips, sooty and black, continued to smoke.

"Did you just shoot lightning at me?" I roared.

I scooped up Uno's sawed-off from the dirt and unloaded both barrels not at Tres directly, but at his mount. A fat, fist-sized hole blasted in the mount's chest, spewing oily blood onto the dirt. It fell.

Tres landed on his feet. He drew a small revolver.

I threw the sawed-off at him.

He whipped his fluttering sleeve. Unseen wind deflected the weapon and sent it crashing across a nearby stoneface.

Tres's revolver burped fire at me as he took off, meeting up with Seis, who still stood atop his horse with a rifle. I squeezed off two rounds from my sidearm as I skittered down the hill. Stinky dust sprayed off his clothes. Flecks of gleaming sand splashed out of the wounds as he dropped to the earth. He didn't so much fall as he seemed to fall apart like a burlap sack torn apart at its edges.

I was on him in a breath. I wrestled the repeater out of his hands. I slammed my boot into his jaw. My mind screamed at me, told me to turn and run. But I racked the rifle instead and loaded a round from the magazine.

Like Uno before him, Tres wasn't done yet. I whirled toward him. He stood, as firm as a half-deflated mannequin. He raised his hand, preparing some destructive force.

The rifle-shot hit him in the left side of his chest, knocking him back like a sledgehammer. His spine smashed against the rocks behind him.

Which is when Seis flew in on me.

"Pain in my *ass*," I said. I pulled the rifle back, grabbed it by the barrel, and swung it at Seis's chin before he reached me. The chin and neck snapped. Mismatched teeth scattered across the sand.

Beneath, I felt a tattoo pounding against the sand like a drum, getting closer and louder. A shrill, happy whistle cut through the air from somewhere far off. The chug-chugging of the pistons got louder.

The seven-fifty from Crown Rock. Just like Gregdon said.

An escape.

I dropped Seis's rifle and reached up to grab the reins of his confused horse. If I could get into the saddle in time, I might be able to intercept the train, might be able to hitch a ride...

Goon Numero Dos, though, had other thoughts.

He didn't shoot at me. He didn't even raise a hand. Instead, with mountain-cat speed, he launched himself at me. I swear to God the bastard covered ten to twelve yards in less than two seconds. He was a flash of black like a soaring crow. He crashed into me. His forearm cracked across my throat. My feet went wild in the air; my back smacked flat across the sand. A flash of steel glinted in the sun. He swept a talon-shaped knife down at me.

I rolled. The knife hooked into the side of my duster and shredded it. When I came up, I swung for Dos's chin. He came up underneath with the hilt of his knife, crushing my teeth together as he smashed my chin. Little universes exploded in my eyes.

"You've dodged death way too much, Faust," he said. "You're losing steam. Getting tired. You don't have much strength left." His form flickered again with insane speed, swinging the knife down.

I caught his bony wrist in my left hand. The knife-tip edged close to my eye. I couldn't place the smell, but it made my nostrils flare and the gorge rise in my stomach. Breathing him in made me hurt.

"The Well won't be yours," he said.

"I don't want the damn thing."

The knife-tip pressed against my cheek and started to bite.

With a desperate heave I pushed the sandshade's form aside. I jumped for Seis's horse, grabbed the saddle-horn, and threw myself up onto its back. I was barely in the stirrups before I kicked it into a run. It shot off with insane speed. Every sinew in the horse seemed to be made for running, and it did exactly what I wanted it to. Along the back of its neck, a whole line of bony protrusions stuck up from the sleek, hairless flesh, breaking the field of blackness with spines of white.

I ran out parallel to the train-tracks, looking behind me. The engine was a monstrous snake rolling through the arid fields. Its steam carried high into the sky.

I wondered if Curtis knew we were being followed. Maybe it was his plan, not surviving, but he didn't intend for me to die. The train wasn't dropping anything off. It was just passing through. I just needed to be quick enough to grab it.

Other hooves thundered behind me. I looked behind and saw both Seis and Dos on a single black horse, leaning heavy over the reins, giving chase. Behind them, Treis was running, his robes flaring out behind him like wings in the wind.

Let me repeat:

Tres was *running.* I distinctly remembered killing him. All the rules governing most living beings just didn't seem to be matching up lately. These sandshades and this Well were starting to rise to the top of my piss-me-off list. A bullet kicked up sand into my face from the left. On the right, the train picked up speed, almost overtaking me. Another thin *pop* trailed me – another shot – and it snarled past harmlessly.

I wrenched the reins to the right. The horse skidded. We leaped over the tracks just in front of the train. The whistle shrieked again. I looked behind me and saw Seis's horse manage to leap just the same. He and Dos were keeping up surprising well, driving their horse even harder than mine. Seis fired again. No success, but soon enough he might get lucky...

Tres, however, never did.

Surviving several gunshots to the chest finally caught up with Goon Numero Tres. God must've taken back all the extra chances. Tres was almost all the way across the tracks on foot when the front of the engine crushed him like a massive metal fist. His black hat flew off into the wind, his robes got plastered to the train's grinning grill, and he just...exploded. There was no blood, no cry of pain.

Sand sprayed into the air with a hiss. Tres vanished in a cloud of fluttering fabric and dirt, disintegrated by the engine's brute force.

Was that all they were? Sand in a skin-bag?

Seis and Dos, the saddle twins, were about fifty yards back. I went for my Colt, tightened my grip on the reins, and turned in the saddle. A round whisked past me, purring like a hummingbird. When I fired, I pulled the shot. It bounced off the side of the train.

Shit. I needed to make it count.

I flexed my fingers around the Colt's grip. For just a second, I stopped breathing. Loosened my arm to work with the gallop. Squinted an eye. Took aim.

Waited for them to get closer. Twenty yards. Seis called fire from nothing, burning in his palm like a torch. It splashed across the side of the train. Fifteen yards. Ten...

I fired at center mass.

I caught the mount right in its chest between where the muscles of the front legs tirelessly pulsed. The surprise of the shot sent the horse barreling face-first into the dirt. Seis vanished under its body, crushed by its weight. Sand blew into the wind.

Dos didn't meet so similar a fate.

Goon Numero Dos leaped. When the horse crashed, he had to have been twenty feet in the air, looking like he was shot from a cannon. He wrenched his talon-knife out of his sheath and plummeted from the sky right at me.

He collided with me. His black cloaks choked me. Darkness came. He surrounded me. He didn't so much join me on the saddle as much as float over it, swallowing me into his hideous robes. In that compact pocket of stinking darkness, he bent my head back, a hand of bones and flaking skin across my mouth.

He was some crude, stitched-together mash-up of living and dead. Being this close to him – to it – threatened to unravel me altogether. Like I wasn't supposed to be this near. Like the wrongness inside it awoke wrongness inside me. I choked on death. On that damn horse, running alongside that train, Dos manhandled me. Dark power crackled around him.

The gaping maw opened. Sand poured out likes waves between brown teeth.

"There's only enough room on this saddle for one of us, Faust."

He was gonna—

Eat me? Consume me? Rip me to pieces.

I was going to die here.

"You know," I said between breaths, "what you sons-of-bitches never remember when you start trouble?"

"Enlighten me."

I'd managed to eke the flask out of my pocket with my right hand and twist the lid between two fingers...

"I don't fight fair," I said.

I splashed whiskey into those silver eyes.

His violent scream pierced my ears. The limbs jittered and jerked like a stuttering machine. He fell away from me, the ball-bearings stuffed into his eye-sockets thrashing like angry silver insects.

I grabbed the talon-blade out of his grip and drove it into him.

It split Dos's clothing and skin like burlap, then spilled out a shit-ton of hot sand across my knuckles and the saddle. I just kept swiping at him with his own knife, hooking into his flesh and shredding him. I wanted the red stuff. Every time I cut him, he was dry. There just came more sand.

When he fell, I was alive again.

He hit heavy. The crumpled shadow disappeared far behind me.

Before I took too many chances and had more of the black-robed Gregdons popping up out of the sand to kill my ass, I kicked the black horse into a sprint just as the tail-end of the train toward Rouseville rattled by. I heeled hard until I was just even with the caboose. Sweat glistened on the horse's sleek neck.

When I grabbed the hard, metal railing, my duster cracking in the drafts, I loosened my feet in the stirrups and leaped.

If I wasn't humble, I'd tell you I mounted the back of the red caboose with pride and grace. No point in lying, though. I jumped and almost didn't make it. I wrapped both of my hands around the bottom of the rail and got a goddamn lot of sense knocked into me when my shoulders and elbows locked and my boots scuffed across the gravel and the tracks. I whipped a leg up, crawled my boot-tip to the bottom stair on the caboose, and heaved myself up to the car's back porch.

I lay there for what felt like a hundred miles, even though it was just a minute or two. The black horse finally stopped running, slowed to a canter, and vanished on the horizon as the train rode on.

I still had that talon-blade.

Everything was done. Curtis was dead. Rufus Oarsdale was too. I wanted to sleep. I brushed my sandy hands off on my duster, and reached for the caboose's little door. I pulled it open. I staggered inside.

The whole caboose shook left and right as the weight shifted on the tracks. When my breathing slowed, I heard clapping. I opened my left eye just enough to see a sleek figure sitting next to the caboose's only window.

"What a show," she said. "What a show."

She smiled at me. And I swear to God, I thought the coyote sitting next to her did too.

30

I DON'T THINK THE WOMAN AND THE COYOTE WERE CREW.

Though I couldn't see much of her, I'd rarely met a lady of such immediate radiance. She wore a dress made out of skins and hide. The skirt of furs had a slit in it that revealed high, dark boots. Her face, stifled by a hooded cowl topped by the head of a wolf, seemed simultaneously humorless and yet entirely charmed. She ran her fingers through the matted hair of her coyote companion, the lolling tongue dropping tiny specks on the floor as it watched me.

A stellar sense of style like hers could only mean she was a taxidermist or a sideshow manager. Around her neck, a necklace of what looked like bits of pemmican and jerky caught my attention. Ears. All sorts of them. Long and thin, some squat and fat. The nub of a boar's ear. The sharp point of a mountain lion's. The round, flappy edge of a man's.

She drew back her hood, showing me her crisp skin and the straight hair underneath, shining like filaments of steel. "Why, Mister Marshal," she said. "You've got quite a habit of staying alive."

"About the only thing I seem to be able to do with any kind of predictability, ma'am," I said.

"You're popular for it," she said with some admiration. "Renowned. Famous in these parts."

"Or infamous."

"That depends on the storyteller," she said. "Do sit down, Mister Marshal." She motioned to the chair across from a little table beside her. When I approached, the coyote gave a rumble in its throat. The woman's fingers sank into the nape of its neck. "Be civil, Constantpaw," she chided. Then back to me: "We couldn't possibly trouble you but for a few minutes of your time. A chance to talk. To parley."

Didn't like that word. But I clunked the sandshade's talon-blade on the table, withdrew my two Colts, their oils all gunked with sand, and set them beside it. I teetered over the chair, wondering how my body was managing to keep most of itself in one piece.

The coyote beside her sat on haunches coiled like springs. It perked. Its sickly gaze found my breast pocket.

I clapped the Eye down on the table.

It rattled into one of the gutters between the panels of the table and rolled, and rolled...

It fell off the table. And before I could react, Constantpaw snapped it up in its jaws and swallowed. I suppressed the instinct to go for the little scavenging bastard.

"We needed to see what all the fuss was about," she said.

"Worth it?"

"Still deciding."

"Cigarette?"

She shook her head.

I'd never seen her before. I don't think I would have forgotten that metallic hair, those gunmetal-gray eyes. I grimaced against the sharp reminders of pain that began to awaken throughout my body. "Have we met? Perhaps at a dance..."

"No. We've never met. Though we might oblige you in a dance if you so desire it. We're not against doing what needs to be done to get closer to a resource. Likewise, we're certainly not obligated to tell you anything about ourselves, Mister Marshal. Before you ask," she added.

"The hell you here for, then?"

Regardless of the wolf's cowl, she smiled the way snakes smile. "To congratulate you on your survival. To put our true gaze upon you. Any person willing enough to combat the Gregdons deserves a little attention."

"Your friend," I said, looking at the coyote, whose beady eyes never left me. "Maybe that's who I recognize."

"Perhaps. *She* doesn't like you, Mister Faust. You killed a good deal of our family, and while that's a regrettable act, it's certainly expected." Coyotes were unnatural beasts the closer you got to them. Like wasted sketches in a child's scrapbook, they might as well have been half-dog, half-fox, puppets of gray, brown, and bone that could blow themselves up to a wolf's width and shrink themselves down to slither underneath doors. Then, with simplicity in her voice, the woman said, "You didn't heed our warning, Mister Marshal."

"You mean the dead coyote on the path? I prefer notes."

The landscape whipping past the window outside must have reflected in at just the right moment, because I thought I saw the color in her eyes shift from gray to a mustard yellow. "Gravelfoot was an old soul, Mister Faust. She was ready to die and be of some use. We took no cheer in wielding the knife that killed her, but the early death was a kindness. Leaving her body on the trail had purpose. We wanted you to go back, to stay away."

"Why?"

"Curtis Gregdon was going to die."

"How do you know that?" I said.

"We were hired to kill him first."

When she deigned to look at me, it was from a thousand miles away, aimed just past my shoulder. Or through me entirely. "The mysterious woman has a story just waiting to come out. I'll bite," I said. "You did work for the Gregdons?"

"Occasionally. We gathered intelligence for them, patrolled the wilds, got our snouts wet with blood when it was needed."

"But what about Curtis," I said.

"We accepted the contract to kill him. Then we chose to break it."

"Imagine that went over about as well as a fart in church."

"We had every right to rescind the contract, Mister Marshal. The Magnate refused to inform us that a hit on Curtis Gregdon was actually a hit on his own son. We did not realize the relationship prior to accepting the job."

"It's sort of...right there," I said. "Out in the open."

Her eyebrow slanted.

"In the names," I said. "Magnate's a Gregdon. Curtis is a Gregdon."

"Human names are as deeply confusing as they are monumentally unnecessary," she said. "Regardless, as strong advocates of family, our pack retracted our willingness to complete the task. Killing one's own pup is a waste."

"But killing your Gravelfoot, that wasn't a waste?"

"Death is a suitable fate for the aged and the brittle, especially when that death brings both use and release."

"All this to tell me I should have turned back," I said.

"We were afraid your life would be lost in the fray."

"Obliged, though I admit, I don't exactly understand. All this talk about not taking the Magnate's contract and yet, your friends tried to chew on us last night."

The woman did not pause a beat. The coyote's tongue hung further out of its thin snout and it turned its neck to receive more attentive scratches. "You merely got in the way last night, Mister Marshal. You weren't our target. We were looking to eliminate Curtis Gregdon."

"I thought you were *opposed* to killing the Magnate's son."

She smiled again, but not in that way you do when you're amused. She smiled sort of like an old teacher, like she was frustrated with a stupid-ass attempt to do arithmetic. "When we retracted the terms of our contract with the Magnate, Mister Marshal, *all* Gregdons became our enemies. Those with whom we break our provisions run the risk of falling victim to our claws."

"Oh. Technicalities. You and I don't have provisions, I reckon."

"Not yet, Mister Marshal."

"That make me an enemy?"

"Undecided," she said, "though your violence last night does indeed make you less likely to win our favor. But oversights occur. You're but one mind and one mind alone, Mister Marshal. Some concepts will be regrettably lost on you."

For a minute I thought I'd really not mind being back in all the flying bullets. After all, bullets were honest. They didn't manhandle your brain too much unless they had somewhere to be that your head just so happened to get in the way of. "There's something in this for you too, about the Well that every Gregdon, Blackpeak's mayor, and just about the rest of the world seems to want to sniff out."

"Rest assured, Mister Marshal, we have very little investment or interest in seeking out the Shattered Well. Beings may choose one of two ways to be in this world: very alive, or chasing down the origin of a myth and ending up very dead in the process. We suggest a similar approach for you." Then she stood up. Her long legs drove her nearly to the cabin's ceiling. This nameless woman was a creature of damn near seven feet tall. "Disrobe. Quickly."

"'Scuse me?"

"Remove your clothes, Mister Marshal. We'd hate to ruin them."

The coyote's ears flattened against its skull. Its lips rolled back to reveal black gums. It ripped out a demanding snarl.

So I started to get undressed.

As I did so, Lady Freakshow crossed an arm over her chest, poised an elbow upon it, and tapped at her lips. "We do not envy your position, Mister Marshal. You have been tasked with a demanding responsibility: namely, to preserve the order in an increasingly chaotic world. We roamed these plains well before they sprang up into that which became Blackpeak, and well after Blackpeak is abandoned, we will roam them still. To entrust a man of limited potential and capability with such an enormous task is a cruelty."

"Real sweet of you to say." I swirled my tongue around, felt one questionable tooth start to wriggle, then spit everything there out on the floor. Constantpaw leaned over and sniffed the chunk of blood and spit. "You intend to throw your hat in the ring, too? Is that what you're here for, to announce your bid as new Grand Master of Everything? Emperor Supreme of this tiny one-intersection pimple on the ass-cheek of Texas?"

"You misread our intent," the woman said, gliding close enough to me to grab my chin in her pert fingers. "We want you alive, Mister Marshal. As long as you can be. Stability and peace ensures our continued prosperity. It benefits us. As we speak, Blackpeak teeters on the brink of destruction."

Normally, being this naked next to someone's body meant a whole other kind of day was in the cards. "How...how you figure?"

"You aren't there to hold it together." Her bony fingers crawled up to brush along the cut scraped on my face. "The Marshal of Blackpeak is little more than a man, it seems, capable of being harmed, of bleeding, and – as is the talent of creatures like you – of persevering beyond comprehension. If it weren't for your diligence up until now, we would have watched as that bastion of human indecency descended into greater disorder and destruction. With the Shattered Well so close—"

"That would be bad?"

"That would be bad," she agreed. "We have every reason to rally our support behind you, Mister Marshal. With Curtis Gregdon having drawn you away from town..."

Cold realization struck me. "You think someone's making a move," I said.

She nodded. "Which is why we are here. It's to our benefit that we aid you in quick return to Blackpeak, where your attentions are sorely missed." She applied a faint bit of pressure to my chest, pressing me back, back across the car, as she withdrew an object from the folds of her cloak and crushed it into my palm, all its bristly hair and strange, stiff coolness. "A gift for you, Mister Marshal. Something we think might benefit you. We had to meet you before we could know whether or not you would misuse it. For the moment, we believe very highly in the stubbornness of your integrity."

I looked down. My blood stopped in my veins.

A desiccated paw, gray and withering, lay across my fingers. Sun and heat had cracked the battered pads. A brown, cleanly-severed bone stuck from its cap.

"Gravelfoot sends her regards," Lady Freakshow said. "Her death was but one of many. It's our way: we live, we die, and we run anew, if not as our old selves, then however we must." She closed my fingers around the rotten object. "Our futures will find their ways close to one another again, and when they do, may they be amenable. If we meet you again as an enemy, then we will take pride in killing a local legend. If we meet you again as a friend?

"Then we will have a past like all good friends desire to have. Problems shared, problems solved." So close, she smelled like pinewood and rust. "For now, think of it as an even trade. An exchange. After all, that's what trains are for, are it not?"

"Even trade," I said. "But I didn't give you nothing in the first place."

"Yes," said the woman, another streak of yellow zapping through her eyes. "Yes, you did."

I looked out the window and saw figures dashing over the distant hills, running with the train. Coyotes. Faster than bejesus. They had their eyes on me, yellow as jealousy, knowing right where I was like they could see me through the walls. Following. Waiting...

Constantpaw crept forward, its elongated face rigid and restless. Its claws clicked against the wooden floor.

My legs shook. My palms clammed up with sweat. "One more thing, Madam Mange," I said. "I work better when business is casual."

"Names are useless, Mister Marshal."

"Sure," I said. "But if you want friendship, I'll want to know who I'm sharing it with."

"And if we have to kill you," she said, "you'll want to know who bested you."

"Something like that," I said.

This near, she overwhelmed me. Her high cheekbones, the cliff-ledge of her tan chin, the pale, dandelion color that bled across the surface of her pupils and consumed the tiny dots at their centers. On her breath, a whiff of steel, gorge, and blood. "They call me the Quicktooth."

She turned her head.

"Constantpaw," she commanded. "Now."

A blur of slobbering teeth and forty-some pounds of mangy gray-and-brown blasted into me like a sledgehammer. I crashed back, naked and tired, through the cabin's door. I fell and fell toward the tracks as the train toward Rouseville shot, bullet-fast, away from me...

I heard the Quicktooth's last command. It pierced me like an arrowhead.

"*Run.*"

EVEN AFTER BOUNDING off me like a stepping-stone, Constantpaw hit the ground first. When I struck a split-second later, it barely seemed to matter. Bones and skin, they didn't hold a candle to stone and steel and wood. I shattered into a million tiny pieces. Elias Faust, Black-peak's favorite broken porcelain doll.

I held tight to that putrid paw. For prosperity's sake. Good to have company when you're...

...unraveling?

Sky was up. Ground was down. Hit the ground. Found my feet. Did as I was told. Ran.

Ran fast, ran hard, ran because to run was as good as breath and as good as life. Ran,
tha-tha-thum
tha-tha-thum, ache was but an ache, for what I am is stubborn-rubber and
strong-as-bone
and Constantpaw, head-of-us, knew I was fresh-in-life and so she ran
tha-tha-thum
tha-tha-thum
and both of us, we ran, and ran...

She said to me this is One Great Run and glad you once again Run This Run and then

she bit-for-play and the world flew by underneath our two-by-twos until the

double-leg-lengths

melted away like fat.

Once I rooted-and-sniffed a Very Fine Hare, wire-haired and arrow-eared, and Constantpaw with her constant paws wore the hackles of a Huntingpaw until both of us, we bit-for-kill and crushed

and crushed

and crushed

but not so loud Constantpaw said you cannot

absolutely should not

chew-the-bones and so with belly full we

tha-tha-thum, tha-tha-thum, we ran.

Many double-leg lengths had we to go, but the Rotsmell-and-Blackstink pulled us. The Others caught up to us and as One we ran,

tha-tha-thum

tha-tha-thum

to join in our voyage.

First there was Spitjaw whose jaw ever-was-wet and on his head gleamed the ever-scab of a furious tooth, and too came another who was called Rat who sometimes lost-his-path and slept-too-long and weighed down he was

So greatly weighed down

with a bundle I

Bit-for-play

But he bit-for-kill

and Spitjaw said to him no for Rat burned with an anger so to blow it off we ran, tha-tha-thum, tha-tha-thum until the Burnball fell behind the great beyond and the Shimmerball awakened tall and fat—

So refreshing and so alive were we all on this One Great Run that Hill could not tire us and Stream could not slow for as

One

nothing could break us.

Greater and greater grew the Rotsmell-and-Blackstink until it was right before us.

Constantpaw said to me, it was good to Run This Run with you once more, Gravelfoot.

Spitjaw said to me, this was a fine way to live-but-not at your flank, Gravelfoot.

Rat said to me nothing, for Rat was very stupid.

Goodbye, they said, goodbye, until we Run This Run again—

—woke with a mouthful of sand and a headache that was brutal as a ball-peen hammer.

I peeled my damp face off the ground. I spit a bloody knot of hair into the sand. It was night. Like day had just vanished in a snap. My feet and hands wore tattoos of raw, wet blood, skin cracked from the heat. Trails of sand stuck to me. My knees were scraped to hell.

Gravelfoot's weathered paw sat on the ground beside me.

One of its clawed toes fell to ash, then blew away in the wind.

Shaking, I looked up.

Goddamn if I didn't see, just beyond the next hill, a whole horizon of squat buildings with withering facades and slate roofs. A steeple reached up into the night sky like a finger trying to pierce the moon.

Blackpeak.

I got to my feet. My spine and ribs and stomach all screamed at once. Then the cramping came, and I spent the next few minutes engaged in any number of violent unpleasantries as my body made damned sure I knew I'd put it through absolute hell.

When I looked up, three pairs of reflective eyes stared at me from a nearby hillock.

Constantpaw approached me first. I recognized her immediately, with her loping legs and rhythmic stride. Her tongue lolled out. She lowered down her head to the ground, heaved, and sicked up a puddle of foam and spit.

The Eye rolled into the dirt.

Behind her circled another coyote, its tired breaths blasting out as hot steam from its black nose. This one, more wary than the last, paced back and forth behind Constantpaw. In the starlight, I caught sight of a crude, hairless scar gouged in its forehead. Spitjaw, then.

Which left just one more, who sauntered like an off-balance ape, as though one of his legs was just a bit shorter than the others. "Rat," I said. But the poor bastard's yellow eyes seemed to look off in separate directions, and when I reached to him, he flinched and skittered. "Hey," I said. "Hey, it's fine, it's just—"

A row of hairs shot to attention on my neck. Instinct set itself aflame inside my chest. I spoke. But *she* spoke. Wetness cracked inside my voice. My throat scraped its way through the sounds.

"It's Gravelfoot. I'm Gravelfoot."

It...wasn't English.

Rat settled back on his haunches and dipped forward. On his back was a cumbersome load, like little doggy saddlebags. In the bags, carefully folded, were my belongings: my bloody trousers, my oiled duster, my leathers carefully bound up like a Christmas knot. The sandshade's talon-blade. Oarsdale's ornate flintlock. And of course my pistols, half-cocked, lathered with moist coyote-sweat.

I drew away from Rat, who suddenly snapped at me: not a warning, but gentler-like, if you can consider slobbery jowls and yellow jaws friendly.

Bite-for-play.

If I stood there too long and considered the nature of the boon the Quicktooth had given me, rest assured it'd damn well pull my mind to pieces. So I didn't. I'd gone from *there*, thirty miles away at the Western Elbow, to *here*. Miracles, maybe. Or just happenstance. Or sheer luck. Weirdness abounded. Sentient coyotes. Creatures of sand and fury. Men who chose to be forgotten by the world.

And a Shattered Well, that souls would scramble for and murder over and build a whole world in their image just to uncover.

Even a world had its skin, and the Magnate intended to peel it back to get to the heart beating beneath it.

Constantpaw, Spitjaw, and Rat slinked away from me. I wrapped Gravelfoot's paw in a strip of fabric and crammed it into my duster pocket.

Then I plucked up the Eye.

It's been awhile.

"I've been busy."

So have I.

"We have a lot to talk about."

I tried to keep it from you, Faust. Nothing exposes a man's hand like the reasons for his enterprise. Desire's a goddamn weakness, let me tell you.

"How've I gone this long," I said as I started walking toward my town, "without knowing about this Shattered Well, whatever the hell it is?"

Some barriers have to be crossed before you understand the world the way I do. You're seeing the world with one pair of eyes. I'm seeing it through a hundred.

The coyotes didn't follow. I felt emptiness behind me. They fled. They were right to. "What's this worth to you, that you play with all this dark shit just to make your ends meet?"

You haven't read the books. You haven't sought out the knowledge. You hardly have a stake in this, Elias. The Shattered Well – and any other Well like it – is a man's opportunity to submerge himself in elements and ideas entirely foreign to our natural brains.

"What makes you think you're the man meant to find it?"

Any man can find it if he looks long enough. I just intend to be the first.

"So it's about a thirst for power," I said.

It's more than that.

"Conquest?"

Over what? Blackpeak? I sensed his laughter. That's rich. That's real good, Elias. But let's avoid talking in extremes. I've got no interest in being embattled over this with you. There's no right or wrong here.

"Both your sons are dead, Gregdon. I'm not even sure why, really."

You have kids, Elias?

"I don't even have a dog."

Then I caution you in trying to moralize with me using my boys' deaths. I raised them up as well as a man could. They might have gone sour, but I loved them. Still do. Always will. Chrissake, Faust, what'd you even know about them?

"Nothing," I admitted.

I dragged my way back into Blackpeak on the tail of the Magnate's words. Before my eyes flickered morsels of my imagination: Gregdon boys like phantoms darting this way and that, pure and young and long-untouched by the same spite they'd carried in Blackpeak.

Things change, Elias. They will for you too.

I wandered up the middle of the main street. The moment I knew I was so close, fatigue started to tear me apart. I scuttled across the gravel, caught sight of the Crooked Cocoon, heard music and cheer, saw my office not far beyond...

Which is when the handful of oily shadows emerged from the alleys and started to walk in my direction.

The Magnate's voice vanished from out of my mind and echoed across the intersection.

"She was right, Elias. Somebody was going to make a move."

I stopped in my tracks.

Magnate Gregdon's boot-heels crunched in the dirt as he moved toward me. He swept a cowl off his bald and liver-spotted skull. This time he was clean-shaven. Meanwhile, his compatriots – three sand-shades, I realized, by the tightness in my bowels – converged on him. Couldn't see their faces, but I could see their silvers.

"Hello," he said.

Anymore it wasn't about broken laws or infractions. Frankly, I didn't know what it was about. Maybe a little bit of rage. Mostly a lot of confusion. A little pinch of surprise. All of them – Curtis, the Magnate, Nycendera, the Quicktooth – had dangled me over this pool of greater knowledge. To hell with sandshades. To hell with Shattered Wells.

To hell with the Magnate.

I went for my revolver.

I'd barely cleared the holster before, not even raising his hand, the Magnate clenched a fist at his side.

A shock of agony shot through my arm, deep as the bone. A hundred straight-razors cutting invisibly.

Slicing my nerves into frays.

I looked down. My fingertips jittered and danced like little bugs. I couldn't feel the gun in my hand anymore.

The Magnate raised his hand. He flashed his golden artifact: the gilded locust-thorn, its points bathed in his blood. His palm, littered with old scars and scabs, had endured that abuse before. His nostrils flared with exasperation. "You would, wouldn't you. You would try to end this with a gun."

The grip intensified. My arm went numb.

The sandshades, curious and enthralled, drifted closer.

"They were fine boys, once." The old man's brow knitted together. "You ruined them."

His palm turned upright. My elbow twisted. One of my fingers leaped out to lay against the trigger of the Colt.

My teeth mashed together. I stared at my arm, thought about the muscles, the bones, tried to shoot my thoughts into them, command them, will them to disobey him, *something*. "How did it happen," I asked, attempting distraction. "What made them go bad?"

"I did."

His pinky finger stuck out the way you might flick a fly.

Invisible force wrenched my jaw open, almost unhinging it.

I watched as the bones in my wrist flexed and my Colt turned to regard me.

Then I shoved my pistol between my lips. The sight scraped the ridge of my mouth bloody and raw.

All of it against my will.

The Magnate leaned close. I couldn't run. I smelled his blood. It ran as free as water. "My William and my Curtis were good young men, Elias Faust. They loved their mother. They loved me. They praised their God, they knew their letters and numbers. God, they were *good*," laughed the Magnate. "Before my eyes they grew up. Crown Rock's very best, one destined for preacherhood, and the other, if you believe it, for poetry. Maybe professorship. Smart boys. Prides and joys. But the Shattered Well doesn't open its gates to men who create good children. It opens for men who do what is necessary."

He hardened his stare. Looked not at me, but into me, past me, to old days.

"Better to break them down into people I wouldn't miss so bad when the time came for them to die. Better they be reckless, wasteful, abrasive; better they fight and spit and drink and fuck than cost me the greater part of my heart. I'd always love them – always – but not liking them so much?

"It made it so much easier."

The tiniest little cracks in his face. Wetness glistened on his palm as he wiped a hand across his eyes.

"All spellwork requires pain, Faust. Sometimes a man puts himself through the worst of it just to get what he most desires."

I stood in the middle of Blackpeak's lone intersection, a stupid puppet. Mouth full of metal. Tongue burning with gun-oil. The Crooked Cocoon Saloon rattled cheerful, drunken noise not fifty paces away. Their world was so small, those drunkards and miners and farmers, that not a one of them had dared to even look at the night beyond their bottles of beer and whiskey-glasses.

Magnate Gregdon patted my cheek, like a father to a son.

"Thank you," he said, "for being such wonderful help."

He let me feel the cold trigger.

I couldn't help it. I started to scream, a noise swallowed up by three-and-a-half inches of metallic cylinder.

My thumb reached up like an inchworm to the pistol's hammer. Drew it back.

A gray-faced bullet cycled into the chamber.

Longest four seconds of my life. *One. Two. Three. Fou—*

The Magnate choked out a laugh. Feeling faded back into my body. He pried the gun out of my fingers, which sprang to life, mine again.

"Christ almighty," he said. "You should have seen your face, Elias. That made my night. You should have seen your face."

Relief poured into me. My body was mine again. Mine.

I slumped forward, catching myself on my own muscles like a cap tossed on a hat-rack.

"I couldn't possibly be that cruel, Elias. Not to you."

He smiled at me. Can't shake that kind of smile. The way it disarms. The way it warms you from the inside out.

He rammed the Colt into my mouth.

He squeezed the trigger.

A burst of noise. Fire. A million pounds of pressure.

Then I—

NOW

"*Then you what?*"

Thirteen doesn't need me to tell him any of this. I know that. He knows that. He's just lining up facts in rows as fine as gravestones. The room's dull light turns sickly and pale, but it's not real; that's the worms, burrowing deep, finding levers in my brain — or what's left of it — and throwing them. It's the dusty, summer-night smell of crushed fireflies that comes next, sweeping over me. The sharp odor of combusted gunpowder, like sulfur and egg. He's going deeper.

Smells stirred from my darkest parts and brightest moments.

This is what he wants, somewhere floating just under the surface—

It isn't Nycendera. Or the Quicktooth.

A whiff of old beer. Then, clinging to the ridges at the back of my throat, a too-heavy smell of metallic blood, driving me to gag.

He doesn't want the Magnate either. They're all debris.

He wants what they lead to.

The voidworms—

(Did I create that? That name? Or has it always been there, just pried out of me before I remembered to call them that?)

—slither through me like I'm mud, because even Thirteen's subject to

*precious vanities: he wants the Shattered Well too, the way they all want the Well, because it seems the world bends in around the Well, and every-*thing – everything – *tumbles toward it before long...*

"Then I was gone," I tell him. "Quick as can be."

PART VI

THE WELL

31

So I died.

No muss, no fuss. I liked simple things. I liked smoking and bad books. I liked long summers and black skies pin-pricked with stars. I liked dust under my fingernails and the bleat of a harmonica four houses down. I liked mornings so bright, so sweaty, so new, that you couldn't help but bitch and moan about being alive when that sun beat down on you. I liked living. I liked simple.

So of course, dying broke the mold, because I didn't expect it to be so goddamn complex.

Don't believe them when they say it doesn't hurt.

I screamed inside and out. Every nerve in my body gave a right-eous howl. Sure, it might have only lasted a split-second, but what *they* refuse to tell you is this: time, to pain and agony, knows no boundaries. It stretches on like warm taffy, every piece of you begging, thrashing, praying to stay alive. It's *not* easy, because every instinct in your body explodes like wildfire and Regret and Fear and Could-Have and Never-Did, they turn tail and flee and crash into one another and...

And then it just stops, and you wonder if it ever *was* at all.

I was tranquil, like an endless black sea, windless and vast.

32

I SAT ON A CREAKING BENCH. IN MY THUMB, A SPLINTER, PRIED UP FROM the gray wood. I sucked at it. In my boots my feet swelled like sodden bags of sand. Underneath me a dinghy swayed, giving heaves and rolls. I grabbed the sides of the boat. It wasn't but a little slip of a thing, like an orange-peel cast into a sea.

A lone white sail hung above my head. No wind. Even if I was stranded, I at least had the time to take stock of my surroundings before the panic set in. In the flat, dark water, I floated. Not an island in sight. Not a speck of land. I was going to—

STARVE HERE? said the sky above me, as the words wrote themselves in lines of starlight.

I opened my mouth to respond, tasting saltpeter and fire.

Smoke curled out from my mouth.

I picked a grain of unburnt black powder from between my eyeteeth.

Was I going to—

WITHER TO BONES? the sky wrote.

I leaned out over the edge of the boat to look at myself in the water. What greeted me wasn't my face, but rather, a rush of vertigo so intense I thought I was about to keel forward and fall ass-over-teakettle straight into...

Nothing.

It wasn't water below me. Just hungry blackness, a void of far-Northern sky littered with twinkling stars and infested with swirling snakes of gaseous light, the kind that leads voyagers to ice and ruin. If I fell there, I'd fall for years, for centuries, into space and time.

I flattened myself like a child against the bottom of the boat until the spinning stopped and I stuttered, "Oh my God, oh my God." As I lay fighting back terror, my mother's voice stirred out of an old memory. *Feeling sick?* she asked me. *Gonna throw up? Hey, if you feel somethin' hairy tickling your throat, it's your asshole, swallow quick!* and we laughed and I didn't feel so sick no more...

I missed her.

I missed thinking of her. I'd almost forgotten...

Above me there was sky, but it wasn't sky. Like polished metal, it was a reflection of the expanse below me. I squinted my eyes, saw myself sprawled in the bottom of the boat, staring back. The mirrored sky rippled like melted steel.

A sea suspended above, the occasional light still tracing wordlike patterns.

WHAT COMES AND GOES—

It read...

—IS THE FUTURE AND PAST.

"Hello?" I cried out.

The fear set in, locking like a bullet into a chamber. Without wind, there was no way to push me to a distant shore. Standing was only a feat I managed for a few seconds before I had to kneel like a fresh-born foal in the boat. If I looked out much longer on that upside-down world, I might crack. Was this the end-goal, the Be All and End All, that *thing* you hollered for at church and sang all those songs for?

Hold onto your horses, Eliza.

What if the mercury sky fell down on me? Or what if the boat capsized and I plummeted into that endless expanse. This place's wideness and endlessness corkscrewed into my brain. I white-knuckled the boatside. I was stranded here. Couldn't swim out, couldn't call for aid, didn't even have a gun on my hips or a bullet to carve my name into.

A sobbing echoed out over the expanse.

Mine.

I caught my tears in my shaking palms, thinking maybe I could drink them if there were enough, and God, it seemed like they wouldn't stop.

I wiped my nose on my sleeve. "It's alright," I told myself. "It's alright, boy."

Raindrops from above began to fall on my hands. A cool wind cracked against the sail and fattened it. The boat gave a forward lurch. I cut a path through the sky. The vessel seemed to know where it was going.

Above me, the suspended ocean split in two.

Silver water peeled back like hide torn from a buffalo. With wonder I watched as a form emerged from the sky. The shape pressed out into the world, all sharp edges and perfectly-measured corners, a *thing* of absolute order. A great, metallic square, turned to its point so it looked like a diamond on a card-face, hovered in the upside-down sea. Must have been the size of a decent-sized house, give or take a few meters.

It hung in the air, dangling on unseen puppet-strings.

In the distance, where the mercury sky and the galaxy sea crashed against one another, a swath of pink light began to burn.

BEING BROKEN BEYOND REPAIR, said the sky, IS A NOTION RESERVED FOR THOSE WITHOUT IMAGINATION.

Compelled to look upon the cube and how it was both nothing at all and everything all at once, I turned my head. "You can speak?"

A TALENT LEARNED LONG BEFORE YOU EVER WERE, it wrote in light.

"This place don't make much sense to me."

LOGIC: THE LIMITATION OF FRAGILE MINDS.

"*Too-shay*," I said. "Is this how it ends?"

TO BE BROKEN IS NOT AN END.

"Not unless you take one to the mouth like I did."

WHICH IS WHY THIS MOMENT EXISTS BETWEEN BLINKS AND BREATHS.

"Am I dead?"

YOU ARE NOT ALIVE.

The chilly wind abated. The rain stopped cutting. A glittering path of sand emerged beneath the boat, a frail bridge springing across the darkness.

The boat rocked as if it'd hit land.

I disembarked. To my wonder, my heel didn't press right through the sand. It held firm. Gritting my teeth against vertigo, I proceeded to walk toward the gleaming bauble. The path vanished behind me and emerged in front of me, like an unraveling serpent tongue that just kept going and going. I shot my hands out to my sides. "Don't look down," I said. "Nope, don't look down."

So I did my best necessary-for-survival balancing act toward the suspended cube. As I meandered closer, guided by the sandy path, details started popping out to me: cracks sprawled across the cube's surface. One of its corners had taken a mighty blow, like a brick grazed by a bullet, or a fruit bitten into by a greedy mouth.

I picked up a fallen piece of the cube out of the sand. A little black shard, dusty as coal.

YOU HAVE BUSINESS YET TO PERFORM.

"Heavy lifting is a bitch," I said. "What do you mean by business?"

YOUR SECOND DAWN. AND OURS.

"Getting shot in the jaw ain't exactly a minor inconvenience." I rubbed my face, which here, seemed surprisingly intact. I needed a shave. "I get the sneaking suspicion that I'm about to grow mighty skeptical of these riddlesome suggestions."

THE OFFER IS SIMPLE: YOU ACCEPT IT, the sky wrote, OR YOU DO NOT.

"If I don't?"

A LOSS. NOT OURS.

"Okay," I said. "'Spose I find myself driven to accept. What exactly do I get?"

NOTHING.

"Then what do you get from it?"

EVERYTHING.

"Oh, so *I* draw the measly pair, and *you* get the royal flush." I was swimming blind. But with the last few minutes still mapped out in my memory – the rush back to Blackpeak, the Magnate turning my own weapon against me – it seemed like a good bet to presume my brain wasn't entirely cottage pie just yet. Of course, playing givesies-takesies with a floating box of magical cargo didn't exactly increase my chances of avoiding that fate, either. "Forgive me for saying," I admitted, "but this smacks of convenience, wouldn't you say?"

CONVENIENCE IS A REGRETTABLY HUMAN CONCEPT.

"Look whose shit don't stink."

A TOOL BY WHICH SMALL BEINGS LIMIT THEIR ACCOUNTABILITY. NOTHING MORE.

"For something without a head," I said, "yours is mighty big. What I'm going to need out of you is for you to talk to me like I'm less smart than you actually think I am. Simple questions, simple answers, you got it?" I cleared my throat. "Second dawn. You mean like, another chance?"

CONTINUATION.

"Reversal of death?"

MORE DENIAL THAN REVERSAL. IT MUST BE, it said, OR IT MUST NOT BE.

"You can make that happen?"

IT HAS HAPPENED MANY TIMES. FOR YOU.

On the surface of the cube I saw the rest of this abstract realm mirrored behind me. The pink sunlight splashed off other shapes emerging from the silvery sky: orbs, spheres, jewels, squares, whole planets, simple as cloudy marbles, some as tiny as fingernails and others swallowing up whole chunks of the skyline. *Many times*, it had said. The ache in my thigh came to life. And the remembrance of scorched skin smarted on my palms, burnt from the Fulton barn.

Eliza's tear-swollen face floated into my mind's eye.

He did what I wanted, didn't He. He protected you. So why don't it feel right?

I scrunched my brow and peered up at the cube. At myself.

"Banks, thieves, and con-men all got one thing in common. They don't give out loans without interest."

THERE WILL BE A COST. THERE IS ALWAYS A COST.

I turned to look behind me. The boat floated off, aimless and lost.

HALF-LIVES ARE LIVES OF IMBALANCE.

The boat receded to a pinpoint.

YOU WILL NEVER FIND TRUE FOOTING.

Then the boat was gone, sail and all.

YOU WILL EXIST TO DO THE BIDDING REQUIRED OF YOU.

Was this a normal thing? Was this the whole majesty of death, that you get shot, or take a tumble, or your heart gives out, and you meet this grand voice in the beyond that presents you with a choice to keep going or settle in? String yourself to a leash or shed the mortal coil? Pick one, step right up.

I knew a poor bet when I saw one. So, being pretty devoid of most sense of reason, I held out a flat hand toward the cube.

Only one way to solve this dilemma.

"You got a penny or something?" I asked.

I could lie and say I bellyached over the many implications – if I didn't go back, people'd be hurt, people'd die, all because I wasn't there – but this place made it simple. To be or not to be. Live and oppose, or die and sleep.

Cold metal materialized in my palm.

On one side, in sweeping letters, a proclamation: LIVE AND OPPOSE, the coin said.

I turned it.

DIE AND SLEEP.

"If this is death," I said, "then, say I flip this coin, how do you expect me just to start living again?"

BY FOLLOWING THE INSTRUCTIONS WE HAVE GIVEN YOU THESE PAST MONTHS.

Looking up from the coin, a pattern began to spread itself across the mercury sky: leaping out of one of the floating masses, a ribbon of light, lancing toward the others. It met another sphere, where it split off into eight directions. There were so many bullets of light, they started weaving a blanket across this strange other world.

Then one stream of light hit the cube, highlighted its cracks, and the whole beam of it flickered weakly, daring to smother out.

"What instructions," I said.

TO *BREATHE.*

So I did. One last time, for better or worse.

I flipped the coin.

33

*E*VERYTHING WAS SO SMALL.

At first it was a tiny colony, a diorama drawn in front of my eyes a thousand yards away. Closer I went, until I saw a flash of fire. A figure's head jerked back like it'd been hit with a hammer. The body fell.

Holding a smoking pistol, a robed man sucked his teeth. "End of that," he said.

The gunshot woke up the world.

Then there were more gunshots. A sturdy figure emerged from the saloon on the corner. Maybe it was just one second, I wasn't quite sure – time was rubber – but the man wore a bowler and spoke no words. He just raised the Yellowboy carbine he'd had at his side, racked a round, and fired. He didn't stop firing. He advanced off the porchway, his lower knuckles trilling the lever-action as the mouth of the rifle blew out burst after burst of smoke, flash after flash of fire.

His name was Grady Cicero, and he was my friend.

One of the sand-filled shadows jerked back once, twice, then hit a trough and careened over it.

Other slugs struck a field of glassy whiteness in front of the Magnate, whose trembling fist bled from its every crack. "You don't want to do this," he said.

Cicero said nothing. Just fired.

Another white flash.

Fired again.

Like shuddering pillbugs, hunk after hunk of lead trembled full-stop in front of the Magnate.

Another door opened. I watched it all, slow as molasses, like they were all just figures on a stage. Doc Levinworth emerged on the street in a pair of loose pants and a half-open vest. I saw the antique in his hands: a single-barrel shotgun, rusted but ready.

One of the sandshades slipped in front of him, opening its yellow-toothed jaw, to emit a banshee's cry. It took the brunt of a shotgun blast. But its hand didn't stop moving. Talon-bent steel winked in the air. Levin-worth's head leaned one way while his body leaned the other. His neck opened sideways. He fell dead to the ground.

No. No!

Breathe.

A greasy, curling smoke rose up from Levinworth's pores and spilled out of his mouth. Here, in this odd realm of sight, it shimmered like steam.

It coiled through the air and swept up into the Magnate's mouth and nostrils.

I didn't need to understand to know: *in the living world, nobody saw that ghostly vapor. The Magnate did, maybe. He worked his work; he squeezed his gilded thorn, and more of the silvery smoke sprang like night-fog from his flesh, clinging to his forearm until it crawled up, up, and into his mouth.*

Pain. The fuel for his craft. Visible in this place like desert heat.

Cicero might have had the Magnate at gunpoint, but the bullets rotated in the air and turned back to face the actor. Like wasps waiting to sting.

The rest of Blackpeak came to life around the town square. People poked their heads out and peered out from the cloudy windows. Miss Garland came darting up the street with her just-in-case leading the way. She scrambled for Levinworth.

"Doctor," she breathed. "Doctor."

"He's dead, Miss Garland," Cicero said through tightened teeth.

People congregated, forming a shadowy vicegrip around the square. God, you give them some blood, they swam in like snakes to lap it up.

A sandshade gave a rattling snarl and said, "Bitch," as it surged toward Miss Garland.

Her just-in-case gave two flashes. The sandshade's skull disintegrated. Sand whisked through the air.

"Marshal's dead too," I heard Cicero whisper tightly. "He's dead."

Miss Garland's hands tried to mop blood back into Levinworth's corpse.

The silvery smoke crawled off her, too. Drifting up into the air. Funny, because her face – stoic as a statue – never changed.

"You killed our people?" Miss Garland asked the Magnate.

"Your people made foolish choices."

Cicero trembled. He'd been framed something mighty in that iron smoke, so greatly that it formed a crude halo above his head. He might have been quivering, but his trigger-finger wasn't. "Are you him, then? Are you that Gregdon bastard?"

The Magnate clicked his tongue. Like a horse-cluck, giddyap. *One of the several floating bullets disappeared from in front of the Magnate. A streak of white shot across Cicero's left shoulder, biting through his sleeve. He gave out a furious hiss. The Yellowboy fell from his hands.*

Breathe.

The Magnate leaned forward, like a boxer ready to deflect oncoming fists. "I wonder if he told you. I wonder if Faust even told you what he did with the body of that fellow who tracked you down to this town, runaway."

A snap of his fingers. One of the bullets whipped toward Cicero, then stopped right in front of his face.

Breathe!

"Yeah," the Magnate said. "Your face is familiar. I've put together enough about you from stories. At least, all those I ripped out of that Alabamian's jittering brain before my shades put him down. Grady Cicero. Is that who you are here? Wish I knew all the names you went under before. Wonder how many Romans you've had to burn through, kid. New one for each city, I imagine. Is this living, man? Is it really living?"

"You don't know a damn thing about me," Cicero said.

"Dead men's brains are poor vessels for secrets." The Magnate jerked his

hand. Cicero collapsed to the ground as his feet were torn from beneath him. The bullet bore down over him, spinning violently in the air, hovering only a few inches from his left eye. "I'd break you open like glass just for the thrill of it.

"Which goes for the rest of you." The Magnate swept both of his hands out. The bullets fanned out like flower-petals and formed a hovering circle of bloodthirsty lead around the old man. Each one of them floated on a thin coil of silvery fumes, cast out from him, obeying him. "I find blood an entirely regrettable byproduct of irresponsibility. Of which, I presume, we'll have no more moving forward."

I watched, helplessly disembodied, as more cloaked beings emerged from the darkness and came forward, some wielding weapons, others handfuls of power: sparks of blue fire, globs of crackling force. Now the bastard had ten, then fifteen sandshades.

Revulsion rippled through the onlookers: some gasped, others surged back. Two – a man and a woman, curious lovers – tried to flee, but they ran face-first into a particularly spindly sandshade.

It stabbed. The man split open. The woman shrieked, covered her mouth, fell back.

"Stupid," the Magnate rumbled. "Stupid."

People stopped moving.

"Truth of the matter, Blackpeak, is this," he bellowed to the town. "Who I am is a man possessed of no desire to hurt you. The problem with men like Marshal Faust and Orations over here——" he thumbed toward Cicero, "——is that they presume all people fit into bottles: the good bottle and the bad bottle. Making the assumption we all want to be water, or we all want to be wine."

There. I thought I saw it...a spark.

Fluttering like a candlelight in the husk of my fallen body. A breath.

"You," The Magnate's finger leaped out toward a face in the crowd. Poindexter. "When the Prussians took Paris, and you fled with your wife to the coast, and then to Virginia, all you cared about was safety and opportunity. How is Carlotta, anyhow?"

Poindexter swallowed, wondering how this man saw right through him. How he knew so much. And yet——

"My Carlotta, she—"

"Don't say it," the Magnate sighed. "My God, man, I'm sorry. Consumption?"

Poindexter's shoulders dropped.

"No loss more painful," he said. "But she was like you, wasn't she? Did she fit inside a bottle, friend?"

"Non, monsieur."

It was Aremeda De Santos he approached next, his crown of bullets still hovering while he scooped up her hand and placed a gentle kiss upon it. "Miss De Santos," he said. "A lovely specimen. The wonder of the West, if men's loins were the measure of piety."

"Who are you?" she asked like a child.

"A man who needs neither a crystal ball nor a sixth sense to see a dreamer in front of me. A dreamer whose vision suffered when her quaint Ohio town, where she oversaw the finest children's dance academy, flooded itself right down the Cuyahoga River." In her fear, Lady De Santos flinched, seeing old ruins in front of her eyes. "When you lost everything you'd worked so hard to build, Aremeda, did you care – did you give a lick – whether you were water or whether you were wine?"

"I loved dancing," she said.

"Do you dance anymore?"

She shook her head.

"Do you want to dance?"

She nodded. The Magnate smiled. A warm, trusting smile. The kind that built bridges, despite the bullets around him.

"You'll dance again. We'll dance. What dreams there are to be dreamt."

And the Magnate went on and on, to almost each and every one of those frightened and confused folk, speaking prophecies into them as if he'd divined them right out of thin air. Like he knew their souls. Knew their desires, their secrets, peeled them open like so many cans of beans and made them feel like gourmet meals.

What a parlor trick, to win their temporary affections. Through what, force and stolen secrets? More sandshades began to appear, peppering the crowd. "Kallum believes he knows the ways to help you find these dreams—"

Breathe, Faust. *Goddamnit.*

"*—and yet, he spends too much time blinded by his own desires. Be with us, Blackpeak, clear of sight as we are: you have seen otherworldly occurrences, oddities of power and curiosity, and if I have succeeded in anything, it was removing the old guard that kept you from wishing and dreaming fully.*"

Breathe.

"*Marshal Faust believed you but criminals, outlaws, misfits, and vagabonds.*"

Breathe!

"*I see you as men and women who do not fit in bottles, but as those who break them.*"

They'd watched his crew maim and kill. I couldn't expect much from them. Eventually, somewhere along the line, everybody starved. Most for food. Some, just for purpose...

A stinging command tore like thunder through my brain.

BREATHE, *it commanded.*

So I did. I breathed.

I shot back into my body.

My eyes snapped open to see the spinning moonlight.

Blood rolled out of my nose like a rushing stream. I choked on the heat of burning metal. Realizing the *wholeness* of my body was damn near miraculous, but it didn't exactly promise comfort, either: I rolled over and spat out a mouthful of broken teeth, and likely would have expected more blood...

...if the damn gunblast heat hadn't already scorched the new hole closed.

Coming back to life wasn't easy. The effort of it nearly killed me.

I shook the rattling pain out of my head. I tasted lead. Flicked my tongue. Felt the flat edge of a bullet lodged into the top of my mouth.

Sight and sound and all the other senses hammered away at my brain. I pushed up to my knees, then to my elbows, and clapped my hands to my face. No permanent holes. No tears in my cheeks where I thought the gas and fire would've blown them right out.

I spit out a whole lump of wet, fibery junk. Ribbons of the skin inside my mouth, black and burnt to a crisp.

The whole town stared in my direction. The sandshades too.

Magnate Gregdon watched in disbelief.

One of the sandshades began to cut across the intersection toward me, talon-blade at the ready.

The old man flicked his hand. One of his bullets struck a silver eye. The sand-filled corpse fell to the soil.

"New plan," the Magnate said.

HE LOOKED at me the way hungry urchins fawn over food. The metallic halo he'd formed of Cicero's bullets came apart, falling harmlessly to the ground. The Magnate grabbed me with his free hand by my neck. His fingers dug divots into my throat.

Old bastard as he was, that hadn't limited his strength one bit. He smashed me back against the outside wall of the general store. "How," he said, frantic and wild. "Tell me. Now."

"Go to hell," I said.

Behind him, Miss Garland said, "You'd do damn well to unhand him—"

Never taking his eyes away from me, the Magnate lifted his gilded locust-thorn and squeezed it with such ferocity that I thought it'd split his hand in two. Miss Garland uttered a surprised "*Urp!*" as one of her reaching arms began to flake and crack. Like disease, wood-grain crawled up her arm underneath her dress-sleeve. Then it spread to her cheek, her chin, and she whispered, "I'm – I'm glad you're alright, Eli—" before her mouth locked into stillness.

Miss Garland became the only tree in the town of Blackpeak.

My heart punched a drumline in my chest. I tore my eyes away from my friend. "This what happens to dreamers? You turn them into your own personal topiary?"

"*It* touched you," he barked. "It's the only explanation. It's the only way you could have survived." Now he spoke to himself with a heated excitement. "God, it makes sense. It's the only way. Shades," he said, letting me go, waving my pistol like a rallying-cry in the air. "Subdue this trickster bastard. Now that he's shown us he refuses to die, I want him alive."

They were on me quicker than dogs. A whole gang of black robes poured onto me, all their teeth and black nails and stinking skin, all of them grabbing at me and hitting me.

"You break him," the Magnate warned, "and I'll give you back to the spirit broker to be shredded into little bits, you hear me?"

At least their beating was this side of gentle: their punches didn't unhinge my jaw, just shook it up a bit; their blows to my stomach didn't tear me in two, just knocked the wind out of my sails a few times over. They dragged me down. I saw the world in panels of stilled motion between their legs.

"The rest of these dirty pieces of garbage, round them up," the Magnate cried out. "If they try to flee, if they try to fight, end their lives."

On the ground, Cicero grabbed for his .44. A sweep from the Magnate's arm sent Cicero skittering across the town square until a cage of thorns blew up out of the sand and wrapped around him in a tumbleweed-knot.

He screamed inside his prison of briars as the thorns chewed into him.

The other sandshades – the Magnate's endless lot of them – began to go for the masses. Though they didn't wield the same power as their not-so-noble leader, they performed cruel work on those townspeople: they summoned up rings of fire to wrangle fleeing folk; they flung out whips of thorns from their hands and shredded up running feet. Others just shot.

They lifted me so I could watch as men and women and children were pulled from their rickety homes and flats and shoved into the dirt. Sandshades rushed the Crooked Cocoon and the Horseshoe Junction Inn, only to tear whole gaggles of the drunk and distracted from their pleasures and corralled them into the town square. The occasional denier or struggler took an executioner's bullet to the brain.

The sandshades came in droves, like bugs crawling out from a broken piece of driftwood. "While I'm gone," the Magnate commanded, "drag Kallum out of his fucking bed, even if it takes twelve of you to do it. And don't let these people get away from you. They're scared, and they'll continue being scared until they see what I've come for."

While the sandshades held me, Magnate Gregdon approached, then gave me a powerful punch to my stomach. I slumped. He stuffed my pistol into his belt, then grabbed up my right hand. Finding nothing there, he muttered, "It's here. It has to be," before he scooped up the left. "Ah. *There* it is."

He forcibly unfurled my fingers.

In the middle of my palm was a black blossom of ink. A perfect, painless starburst, and in its center, raised up like a faint lump, a tiny cube beneath the surface.

"Plans change. If I can't have *it*, Elias Faust, then I'll have you."

"Whatever you want," I said, "just take it. You leave these people their lives, you can have whatever you want, even if it means killing me a second time."

"Those aren't the rules, Faust. Curtis showed us as much. You can't just kill a man and steal what's been given to him."

He jerked his head toward the sandshades.

"Bring him home. Tonight, we reach out to the broker."

Systematically, the black-clad figures forced townspeople into the square at gunpoint. Several of the sandshades converged and moved their hands in jerky, wild patterns. Out of nowhere, a fire leaped up from the earth, set a prison of golden flame ablaze around the townspeople. They shrank away from it, piling atop one another, cringing like rats.

I'm not a smart fellow, but it doesn't take brains to see a ruse or a ploy: play with a man's mind, you got to play with his heart first, and to play with his heart, you need to slide a knife inside the creases of the armor to get at his softer parts. Blackpeak might have been on my shit-list after Nycendera, and while I knew that for every good soul there were ten more awful ones inside these city limits, I'd always been a damn halfwit at math. If I didn't own this, more people would die, like I almost had.

Like I should have.

For all the messages the Magnate had thrown my way in these past weeks, I didn't need the Eye or Billy Gregdon's spellcrafted paper to hear this one loud and clear:

Obey. Go with them. Or watch as he turned the town into his own personal death museum, filled wish ash-heaps proclaiming my failures.

"You want *me?*" I said. I rocked my head back and smashed it into the sunken nose of the sandshade behind me.

That one fell away, but two others leaped on me.

I kicked. I bucked.

They pummeled me, laughing and hacking the whole time, until the world faded in and out of vision.

The Magnate shouted out over the townspeople like a carnival barker. "Blackpeak bears value somewhere below her skin. I'll have my fucking Well, and I'll have my fucking Wish, and I will turn this place into cinders and mud around me to get it." Then he handed my pistol to one of his sandshades. "Edward Sloman," he said, staring over the rim of fire. "Is Edward Sloman here?"

Murmurs. Mutters. As they dragged me away, a silhouette stood. "Yeah. Yeah, I'm here," it said.

"Do you remember me, Mr. Sloman?"

"You don't look familiar."

"I wouldn't," the Magnate said. "Not to you. Do you know what the most wonderful part is, about having stolen any memory of myself out of your little pisspot of a brain?"

Sloman shakily shook his head.

"It doesn't leave much else left to destroy," the Magnate said.

My Colt, in that sandshade's gray hand, blew a slimy lump out of the top left-hand corner of Edward Sloman's skull. His body fell into the crowd.

They knew, now. They knew, and so did I.

No part of the Magnate's words were anything but promise.

They pushed me down until my face hit sand, then threw a rough whip of rope around my arms and belly, rolling me up tighter than a cigarette. As the reeking sandshades drifted around me and laughed with their horrible, dead-man breath right into my face, I took it.

I had to.

I was built for this, wasn't I?

They threw their rope over the horn of the saddle of a black horse, one that seemed to look at me with a surge of sympathy. But that was the way with all horses, loyal beasts.

I looked back at Blackpeak, tiny and insignificant and full of frightened people, as the butt of a pistol struck the side of my skull.

They dragged me through the night.

It was the laughter I remembered.

I DON'T KNOW where they took me. Sense of direction was shot to shit. Sense of time, even worse.

Blurry faces of smeared black and gray floated above me. Cold hands dug into my pockets, tore at my clothes, pulling at me like meat on a bone. A pat at my breast. "Tin cigarette holder. Some matches."

"Any other weapons? Don't want any problems from here on out."

"You see me looking?" The echoing words bounced all around me. "You want to be sure, how about you do the looking, instead of asking me over and over, 'Any other weapons?' like a pecking goddamn hen. 'Any other weapons? Any other weapons?'"

"Do as you're commanded, shade," came the order from the second voice, who drifted into my vision just long enough for me to see him: a spindly body, draped in robes the color of old red wine.

They found Oarsdale's pistol, tucked in the back of my britches. They slid it out. Another hand found something in my right pocket. It had to twist and bend the Bible-sized volume to get it out.

Red grunted. "*The Collected Works of Shakespeare.*"

"The Marshal's a well-read man." A pause. "You think it'll happen?"

"What do you mean?"

"The broker." Shining silver eyes stared down into me. "You think the broker will agree to it?"

"I think it's best we just stand by and support the Magnate in whatever choice he presumes is best."

Quietly: "You think he's losing his touch?"

"*I* think with talk like that, you best hope your skin stays stitched up tight to keep that sand where it belongs."

"I'm just saying—"

"And I'm just saying, you're still alive because the Magnate allows it, so if you have to fuse your lips shut to keep from saying stupid shit, then do it. This is the closest the Magnate has gotten to the Shattered Well, and the broker's got just as much invested in his success."

"You think the broker will agree to it? Faust's not like me or the rest of the shades."

"We'll work with what we have. Enough bullshitting. He got anything else on him?"

"Not that we haven't already found."

I tried, desperately, to pull my eyes all the way open. Blinding light forced me to squeeze them shut. My brain swam. A sea of dizziness overtook me.

"Ivanmore will be here soon enough," Red said. "When he comes, send him to me directly. I want him to examine Faust before we do anything else with him. The Magnate's been waiting for this day, and I'd prefer not to disappoint him."

I sank back down into unconsciousness, no matter how hard I bucked against it. It dragged me down like black oil, covering me.

34

Fading in and out. When consciousness came, it came with words. Words from other people. Again. I lay still, watching shadows flicker against a rocky ceiling. Whole body felt wooden, hollowed of everything except...pain? If it was pain, it was less the jagged bite of it and more like a dull warmth. I worked my jaw in circles, then opened my eyes and tried to find a pinpoint. An anchor. Anything.

"He's awake." Red's voice, who struck me as the leader of whatever group of dipshit ragamuffins decided to answer to him.

"He won't be for long," added another voice. I could see this new face more clearly. It was about as dead and waxy as alive could be: the fellow's white cheeks hung like loose fabric, and his eyes sat on crescents of black skin. His name was Ivanmore. Blackpeak's trusty undertaker. "Christ on the cross, looks like he took a beating."

"The sandshades got frisky with him," Red said. "What did you give him?"

They talked over me like I was just a puddle. Ivanmore's face began to melt. Red, like a bloody vapor, paced behind him. My heartbeat sang an anthem in the back of my head. I reached out, tried to grab one of them, but they all sank, drifting away...

"A little laudanum. Some methanol. Chemicals I've got are meant for the dead, not for the living."

"Just as long as he survives."

"If he dies, it won't be from what I gave him. But being a mortician doesn't make me a fucking doctor."

"Closest thing we have," said Red.

Red grabbed hold of my chin. He turned it left, turned it right, looking into me. "The Magnate's orders are to do what you need to do to keep him intact, keep him alive and hale, within reason. Please tell me there aren't any broken bones."

"Pain's a distant memory for him at the moment," Ivanmore said. "Corpses are my specialty. The living ones, that's where my expertise ends. The hell's Gregdon got planned?"

There was a pause until the leader said, "Magnate wants Faust to meet with Partridge," with something like disappointment, even regret.

"Is that right."

"Yeah," said Red. "Yeah."

"What's the use of that," Ivanmore said, "but to open up old wounds?"

"If you can't kill them, then you have to put them through their paces, or geld them so they don't buck. I imagine the Magnate's already conferred with the broker and struck a deal that suits them both. Faust won't be like the others." I felt a cold, bony hand pat me on the cheek like I'd been a really good dog. "Not every day you get to build something new out of a man while he's still alive."

"There's no coming back from this," Ivanmore warned.

They lifted my hand. Bent it back at the wrist. Ivanmore sucked his breath in through his teeth. They showered that blotch of blackness on my hand with their full attention. I turned my head. "The fuck you two gawking at," I garbled.

"A shiny new toy." Red jerked his gaze up – there were no bits of silver that I could see – and he stepped away. "Do what you can with him. Make sure he's clear enough of mind to think on his own. If there's anything the Magnate would want, it's his autonomy. For now."

When I felt my wounds being cleaned, my skin being wrapped up under bandages, the veil of the drugs splashed over me. Before I could do anything else, I was gone again.

———

I WOKE STANDING in front of a dead man, looking into the blank canvas of his face and wondering how long until I'd be next.

God, I felt like hell.

I'd lost a grip on time. Could have been out for five seconds or five years. Sensations came back to me little by little, spilled into me like color onto a painting. I could feel my heartbeats slamming, trying to split my skull in two. All of my veins were on fire. I had a bag of rocks in my stomach.

The chamber I was in was entirely dark except for three standing torches of flame that lit up the walls and floors. Christ, if the headache wasn't bad enough when I'd woke up, seeing those fires was like staring into hot suns. I expected the comforts of a home, like a hearth and a table to eat grub at and a pisscan.

But I was in a cavern.

Brown rock crawled up the walls and reached toward an unlit ceiling. Underneath my feet crunched little shards of stone. A tunnel with a black mouth led in from one of the walls. Place was stifling hot, like it hadn't gotten any fresh air in years.

Chained to the wall, the corpse might as well have been a curtain. Its scant clothes sagged in tatters off its thin body. A swath of waxy gray hair covered its face. The white cheeks wore a big, full beard that even death couldn't have thinned. When the haze blew away from my mind, I recognized that face, with its too-still grin of too few teeth.

"He took things further than he was supposed to."

A flutter of motion caught my eye around the entryway. A small figure took small steps in my direction until it stood right between the torches. I didn't see a face. Just a blood-red cloak and a tall, pointed hood that seemed to stand up on its own will. Hanging at his hip was some kind of cudgel, its head fat and adorned with decorative stones.

No, not stones. Pieces of teeth.

How inviting.

The man held up a hand gloved in black leather. "I'm not here to hurt you," Red assured me. "I'm just here to talk. And if all goes well, to help you understand the gravity of the situation."

"Who the fuck are you," I said, a regular master of etiquette.

"A man. No more, no less."

"You a Gregdon?"

"We're all Gregdons. He used to be too. Until the law caught up with him."

"Then why the hell's he chained to your wall?"

"Partridge had a lot to answer for. He got overzealous. He had his orders."

"Which were?"

"Not to get caught."

Red went into his robes and withdrew a sheathed talon-blade. He threw it on the floor in front of me. "We broke him out on his way to Huntington. You should have seen his face, Faust. He could have shit a brick. He didn't know whether to be pleased as punch or beg for forgiveness. He knew why we were there. Of course, now it's up to you to decide whether arresting Partridge was the kindest thing you could have done for him, or the cruelest."

Then Red tossed something else.

I caught it.

Cold as ice in my palm.

Shining like silver.

An Eye.

We really need to stop meeting like this.

I clenched my hand around the metal sphere. Since waking up a few hours ago with a slug of cooled metal embedded in the top of my mouth, I knew parts of me were missing: parts of my insides, probably parts of my outsides. Holding the Eye filled those canyons, and all I wanted to do was not let go...

Don't let my friend guilt-trip you, Faust. Partridge was bound to slip up one way or another. Brutes like him don't last too long in a world of civilized men.

A tug from within my hand. The Eye wrenched my arm toward the sagging form of Partridge Gregdon. Red lingered nearby. He raised his palm, and like a puppet's jaw, Partridge's head lifted at an unseen touch. The man's face was a misshapen prune of wrinkles and bruises. In the right eye-socket, a gleaming orb of silver. The left was just a little fleshy pocket, wanting for its sight. "Go on," Red said. "Put it in. Right where it belongs."

"Do it your own damn self," I said.

Don't be resistant, Faust.

Red's hood twitched. "It's not a difficult request. What was this man to you but a terror on your town."

A man who ruined a mother's life.

I said, "He worked for you. He did your bidding."

We are allies in this, Faust. Partridge disobeyed me, and he disobeyed the rules of your town. What honor do you have to give him?

They'd mutilated him. Just like Keswick Everett. They'd plucked out the soft dollops of his eyes. I noticed the hearty stitches crawling on his skin underneath his collar, keeping his flesh pieced together. Like he'd been peeled open, filled, and closed back up...

Revulsion came on with violence. I threw up. "You did this to him?" I asked. "You made him into this? Like the rest of them?"

If obedience cannot be encouraged, it will be forced.

"He suffered little pain as a result of it," Red said.

It's a kind ending for an outlaw, the Magnate said.

Partridge no longer breathed, but he'd dodged the full *look* of death, too. He resembled more a scarecrow than a man at all. Would he bleed sand, too, like the others? "What happens if I put the Eye back in?"

What happens for you when the rooster crows, Faust?

"Go on," Red said. "You know you're curious."

"Will it hurt him?"

"*He* doesn't exist anymore."

Partridge fled that form the moment I strangled the life out of him on that goddamn road, the Magnate added. *What we get back when the ritual is done isn't always the same. Bodies are just husks. Bodies are just there to be filled with one soul or another.*

I licked my lips. Surrendering the Eye would provide me with answers to questions I didn't dare ask.

So instead, "Why don't you just put it in yourself," I said.

I want you to see how it works.

Oh, I'd already had an idea. "S'all some kind of twisted skin-circus, and you want to make me a part of it, I wager. Can't beat him with a bullet, then make him join you with a yoke."

You're of indescribable value to me, Elias Faust.

"You were damn primed to put me down not too long back."

Red cleared his throat. "That was before he knew."

"Before he knew what, exactly?"

In the palm of my fist, the Eye gave a jumping-bean shudder and a faint surge of sweltering heat. Palpable anger. The Magnate's anger.

That the Shattered Well decided you were worth giving a Mark.

It was exactly as Curtis said, wasn't it? The more I communed with this Eye, the more I wanted it. The tighter I wanted to hold it. A whisper in your mind, no matter how kind or cruel, served a strange and constant comfort. You were a part of something. Something larger, something with purpose, even if you were blind to the beast. And in a too-hot shithole like Blackpeak, being a particle in a larger whole gave the heart a morsel of food it didn't have before. Now, more than ever, the hooks dug deeper; I didn't *want* to get rid of that Eye, because—

Because since the Well, I barely felt held together by threads. I floated somewhere between all these joints and skin, disconnected and lonely.

It made sense why a boy named Joshua found such comfort in such a tiny piece of metal.

"It took something from me," I confided. "When it spoke to me, it took...*something.*"

A pause.

Close your eyes. Feel for a moment. Reach into yourself.

"What do you want from me?"

A chance to trust in a future I see, Elias Faust. It requires sacrifice.

"I'm tired," I sighed.

Yet another thing we have in common. What did it take?

"I couldn't even be sure."

With time and patience, we could scour the maps inside you, all the nooks and crannies, and find out what it stole, Elias. I've already begun.

I opened my hand to look down into my rounded reflection in the face of the silver. Was he looking back?

You don't need the Eye anymore. I know you, and I will be with you.

Behind me, drifting closer, Red's voice came with smooth guidance. "Ours is an amazing world, Marshal. Live long enough and you'll see too many things that don't make sense to anybody but you. Cracks in reality. Rifts in the possible. Awesome secrets hidden away beneath the reasonable and the mundane."

The difference between you last night and you today, the Magnate added, *is that the you of today doesn't need to be afraid.*

Was it all it took? Just to slip it in, push it into the socket?

"Is belonging your only reason for being a Gregdon?" I asked Red. "Honestly, is it?"

"I've lived a hard life. Worked hard. Played hard. It's nice to relax."

"So what's kept him from turning you into one of his waltzing sandbags?"

"I listened, I said 'Yes,' and I learned how to shut the fuck up." He pointed two fingers at a nearby torch. He gave a flick. Orange fire sputtered in the bronze torch-bowl, then burped up a huge tongue of blue fire. He motioned to the other two torches. Sickly light splashed across me, across him, across the half-living, half-pin-cushion formerly known as Partridge Gregdon chained to the wall.

Go on, Faust. Get your answers.

Red nodded to me. I figured what the hell, this was all my second chance for some reason. I pinched the Eye, and then with my thumb, crammed it into Partridge's lonely, sagging socket.

The flaps of his skin *dragged it in*, the quivering lids of his eyes like clumsy fingers wrapping hungrily around the Eye. It vanished. Then Partridge's wrinkling face snapped to life. His mouth hinged open. The tongue lashed and licked. The silver orbs of his eyes spun and spun until they stopped and found me.

Partridge Gregdon lunged for me, both his fists shooting outright, palms open, wanting to tear me into fucking shreds. He screamed behind a blast of rotten breath, "You murdering sack of shit, Elias Faust. I'm going to chew you to pieces!" The chains locked, but his chest kept coming until, like a raging dog, I thought he was going to break them all.

"The hell you mean," I said, "this bullshit about *he* don't exist anymore? He sounds just about right as rain to me!"

The spark at the center of our being holds no dominion over memory. His mind, or what remains of it, is still as much him *as is his body. He remembers you. And he still hates you with a passion.*

"Then what's the use of waking him up?"

Partridge's snapping teeth crashed together like pistons.

So you can finish what you should have months ago.

"You see what they done to me?" Partridge roared. "You see what they done?"

Red's foot nudged the talon-blade toward me.

"Time's a-wasting," he said.

The words and sounds that poured out of Partridge might as well have been a hyena's chatter. He slobbered and spat, sprays of sand and filmy spittle. His dead muscles jerked and rippled, but not even those could snap the rusty chains wrapped around his wrists.

"You want him dead," I told the voice in my head and the voice in red, "do it your own damn self. I'm not one for bloody errands."

Of all people to hold fast to such righteousness...

"Killing half-men to satisfy your sick games ain't exactly my idea of a fun night."

Red hovered impatiently, walking paths behind me. "He can make you, if that was what he wanted to do."

He's right. You know that. With just the right application of pressure...

A charley horse throbbed right in front of my elbow. My arm

flinched out. Hand splayed open toward the knife on the ground. No. He wasn't going to do that again to me. My mind was my own. I ground my teeth and snapped the heel of my hand out so that it struck the wall not far from Partridge. "Get out of me."

But my fingers screamed silently, wanting the steel.

"No," I said. "*No.*"

I jerked my elbow back. A nearby wall in the cavern was there, just far enough away for my fist. Without thinking, I hammered my knuckles into the wall.

I want to see that killer in you.

"What will it prove?"

Another punch. Stone chewed into my knuckles.

I was mine. I was *mine.*

Elias Faust, capable of terrible things...

"Things I did because I had to."

Then how are we any different?

An unseen wind rolled across my arm, hooked me by the hand, and dragged me away from the wall. I skittered and slid toward the talon-blade, my feet and hands moving the way they wanted to. Trembling hands withdrew the talon-blade from the sheath, and Red, he was just laughing, loud as you please. Steel slid free. My fist gripped the handle. Commands bypassed my brain, slipped right by my inner wherewithal and shot straight into my limbs...

I gave it one last burst of will. Feeling sprang back into my fingers.

I screamed and pummeled my fist into the stony floor. Just to choose to do so.

Please, Elias.

"You can't take a man's choice from him," I said.

And yet you can take a man's children.

"It's not the same."

Of course they're not the same, but they're both equally heinous.

My knuckles left a lopsided smear of blood on the brown stone.

So the choice is yours, Faust: do as you're asked, or do as you are commanded.

Above me, Partridge continued to rant and snarl and twist like a bony storm. Red had come closer, a torch in one of his hands, its light a blinding ball of heat and fire. Do as another pleases, but not as they demand you, and retain responsibility. Do as you're told, as you must, and the heart suffers nothing.

Which man was I? Which Elias Faust did I want to be?

Bidden by a madman's magic, I raised the talon-blade. I might as well have been a million miles away, watching from afar. Partridge's silver eyes snapped left and right in a blind and bestial fit of madness. Flecks of stone and rust rained down on me as he wrenched at the chains. "You want him dead?" I gasped. "Is that what you want?"

I want to see you at your lowest.

"You have me. You have it. But not like this. You want me to bend and break? Then speak my fuckin' language, Magnate." I locked gazes with that half-man suspended in front of me. He deserved that steel. He deserved no explanation. I'd witnessed but one of the cruelties he'd done, among what I damned well knew was a list that defied numbers.

If what the Magnate wanted was Partridge's death, he'd have never wasted whatever craft he wielded on him.

If his greatest desire was to fully break my will, he'd have never teased me with even the slightest hint of control over my own body.

These were amusements. Testing the waters. Examining pliability. Chemistry, but with people and hearts and instincts.

"Take off his chains," I said, "and give him one last shot at me. For old time's sake."

That's not how this works.

"It's a risk. You not a gambling man?"

He could kill you. Right now, with that Mark on your flesh, I can't chance it.

"Then why play this game at all, with me and him?"

Silence. Nothing but Partridge's slavering breaths and Red's flickering torch. Just two steps and a flick of my wrist and I could have opened Partridge's throat without a second thought. I owed Miss Fulton as much.

But this wasn't about Partridge. He was disposable.

This was about me. My lengths. My limits.

The Magnate didn't have hold of me right then, so I turned away from Partridge, stared at the otherwise silent Red, and raised the talon-blade.

I slid its point right against the soft meat underneath my jaw. The point scraped my stubble, nearly pierced the skin like a needle popping through fabric. Red flinched like a squirming child. Instinct governed him. He went for something under his robes. The wooden handle of a – what, a pistol? A hewn shotgun?

But then, like a lightless strike of lightning, he went stark stiff. Dangling like a doll on an unseen string.

No. The Magnate's voice came with a warm wind of softness along the contours of my thoughts. *No, Faust. That's a foolish way to do this.*

"Is it? I reckon a little push, and I'll have another chance at this dying thing."

That would render all of this very useless.

"But you'd be one step behind."

It chose Rufus. Then it chose you. It would choose someone else.

"Not without delay. I could delay it."

You won't.

"Won't I?" I pressed the knife. Fluid crawled down the crease of my throat. "I got a hint on how the other side feels, thanks to you. I got less compulsion than anyone else to stick around. It hurts like hell, but only for a second." Even if that second never ended. "'Course, none of this matters, does it? Tweak reality; make me pull the knife away, if it pleases you."

I won't do such a thing.

"It didn't stop you before."

Before was before. This is now. For a moment, he sounded like his son. *Allow a man his vanities, Faust, for once in your life. I take no pleasure in forcing another's hand. Don't flatter yourself, Elias Faust. You are special to me – today – for convenience, and nothing more. You're less a prized possession and more...the cobbler's favorite hammer. A known quantity, but ultimately replaceable.*

We'll do this your way. The way I expected we would from the start.

A shuffle of robes. Red, now of his own volition, stepped back through the lone entryway, taking his torch with him. A parting gift, he threw his knotty cudgel from his hip onto the floor in front of me.

Spinning wildly in their sockets, Partridge's silver orbs had eyes for nothing but me.

The chains holding Partridge Gregdon crumbled away in specks of rust and steel.

Have your honor, Faust. Choke on it, for all I care.

35

WE BOTH WENT FOR THE CLUB AT THE SAME TIME. RED HAD THROWN IT
right on the dirt floor between us. When I moved, my whole body
revolted. My ribs felt like they were flapping around inside of me.
Legs felt like they were sprinting through molasses.

Partridge's first free strides were huge, leaping things, matching
two, even three of mine. Driven with animal power.

A split second before we collided, I dropped to my ass on the
ground and slid across the rocky floor. I grabbed the club in one hand
and came up double-fisting: a talon-blade, a cudgel, and every part of
me ready to—

The palm would have blown most of my teeth out of my mouth if
it weren't for sheer fortune. I stumbled back. "I owe you that," he said.
"I owe you a thousand more."

My talon-blade skittered across the cavern floor.

I was never much of a scrapper, which is why having a weapon is
good. Don't matter how big you are, you got a weapon, you've got an
advantage. I still had the club. After I got to my feet, I clobbered him
across the temple and cheek with the cudgel. It was like I'd just
smashed a sledge into a stone.

But whatever stuff the Magnate put in these sandshades of his,

Partridge barely seemed to blink. Like pain wasn't a factor. Just a distraction. He launched out a booted foot. It crashed into my chest, threw all the air out of me, and knocked me into a stone wall. I tried to keep my footing and suck in air at the same time.

"We should rethink," I said, holding my hand up in front of me, "how we're going to resolve these differences of ours, Partridge."

He charged me. I was waiting for him when he did. I set my feet and railed on him with the club. It *whapped* across his chest, just underneath the ribs and above the stomach. No bones collapsed, no skin broke. He folded like fabric, grinned his yellowed teeth, and hooked around with a fist.

His hand crashed into my ear. Needing no breath, taking no break, Partridge lunged at me. I grabbed the club in a horizontal grip and raised it. He bore down on me. His gnarled hands grabbed the middle of the club.

For just a second, being that close, I couldn't help but notice all the mysteries of him: his skin was leathery and putrid like a colicky baby, a being moving despite the inevitable laws of rot in its muscles. Where his torn shirt hung around his flat chest and distended belly, I glimpsed a scar on his chest.

And in its center, fused into his skin, winked a triangular coin.

"You want to live like this?" I asked. "Is this living?"

"It's whatever the hell I was given."

"You didn't ask for it," I said.

"And I didn't ask to die, so I'll take my chances," he said.

He punched me in the jaw overtop the club. Numb pain echoed in my bones.

The good news was that the nausea had mostly fled. Two cheers for Greater Problems.

He pulled the club out of my hands. Just like it was a twig, he snapped it in half. A spray of broken wood flew into the air. He hucked the two splintered halves over his shoulder. With one hand, he grabbed my collar, pivoted his hips, and threw me too.

I was in the air for what felt like an hour. Birds fly, I reasoned. Clouds do, too. I don't. About fifteen feet away from Partridge, I finally hit the ground in a heap and slid for several more yards. Skin scraped off through my shirt.

With busted ribs snarling at me, I tried to sit up. Partridge didn't run to me this time. He just jumped. He got into a crouch, slammed his brick-like fists into the sandy cave-floor, then leaped like a frog. A jump like that could have made him bound whole chasms. By the second, Partridge grew more used to his new strength and force.

A flashback in my mind carried me, for just a brief moment, to the Western Elbow, and those sandshades' defiance against gravity and reason. His loose-soled boots mashed into the ground on either side of me. Power hummed inside him. The Magnate's power. Partridge grabbed my hair with his hulking fist. "I could have liked you Faust, but you ruined me, and I'll break you for it."

Hair could grow back. My scalp tore like paper. I lunged for a shard of splintered wood. He clasped both of his hands together and swung them as one. I ducked under his wild swing, then came up and rammed the stake into his belly. The wood ripped through clothing, hesitated on hard skin, and finally popped through. Sand came dashing out instead of guts, splashing like sugar cane on the rocks.

Getting back out of Partridge's range wasn't as easy. Even doing his best impression of a broken hourglass, he didn't tire. He threw a hook at my ribs. I buckled over as he hit me.

So much for brief victories.

A faster-than-normal punch smashed my lips into my gums, made me bite down on my tongue. My already-weak legs became water. Partridge came in for the kill.

I flicked the broken club out to slice him. It ripped alongside his arm and opened up one of the stitches in his skin. More sand. He flailed.

I couldn't hope to last much longer, even with the advantage of movement. I turned and started humping it for the entryway to the cave where Red had gone. Should have thought of that first. If I put on enough speed, I might put some distance between me and Partridge.

Red was just beyond the exit, standing patiently beyond the cavern's mouth. He made a grand motion with his arm...

I ran full-speed into a brick wall.

Couldn't see it, of course. Even if I'd looked for it. The air of the cavern's mouth was as hard as old granite. Between Red and me, right on the invisible threshold that separated this cave from beyond, a black triangle had been scraped onto the floor. In Red's other hand, he waved a small piece of coal.

I threw a shoulder at it. I couldn't cross the triangle. My body rebounded off the empty air with as much force as I gave it, sending me to my ass.

"Surprising," said Red, though his voice was muffled like he was on the other side of a wall, "what a little bit of artistic talent can do, isn't it, Faust."

Above the ground, I knew how things worked. Don't get yourself killed. Don't break Poindexter's glasses. Don't piss off Peggy Winters. Down here, though, things seemed inverted. Sand for blood. Living dead men. Walls I couldn't see. What was next, lizards in dresses, bears that could throw a lasso? Partridge had his chance. I knew he was taking it. I rolled to the side. His feet thundered by me. His fist cut through the air. If I hadn't moved, it would have found its mark on my skull.

Instead of striking me, his knuckles exploded against the illusory wall right near where my head had been. His force had been ten times greater than mine. Ready to kill. A ripple of motion rolled through the skin and muscle of his arm, all but tearing it apart. I heard bone snap like twigs. Sand burst from the opened skin, spewing in a pressurized arc.

When the sand wafted across one of the nearby torch flames, the color of the fire changed. It blossomed up, leaping like an angry orange mouth. Some of the grains became hot sparks. They'd brought the fire to life.

Good news.

Sandboy was flammable.

Even with my brain thumping at the pace of my heart, I shot to my feet and ran for one of the torches. It had a long, bronze stick and a wide base. I grabbed the thing in both hands like a spear. Burning oil seeped out of the wrapped end, running down my arms, splashing to the floor.

With my left hand wrapped around the shaft of the free-standing torch and the end of it propped under my right elbow, I went for him. For the first time in my encounter with him, Partridge didn't come for me. He ran from me. I swept the torch left and right. It made a fluttering noise like flapping cloth. He hopped out of the way of each swing.

"I want information," I said over the torch. "I want to know more about what he did to you, Partridge. I want to know about this place and what the hell is going on down here."

He kept backing up as I jabbed the fire at him. I could see fear on his stiff face, twisting his lips up like rawhide. "What do you expect me to tell you," he said, flattening himself against one of the walls. "You think I'm tuned into this whole operation?"

I took a step forward. Some of the fine sand that had fallen out of him crunched beneath my boot. I brandished the fire just to the left of his cheek.

"You killed a boy," I said.

"You really think I give a damn? Those Fultons are no different than a thousand others like them, just good-for-nothings, boring and alone and..." Flame came close to him. The fire flashed against his silver, the lifeless reflection giving him the look of a molting snake. "Look, all I know is that we're built to serve the Magnate. Our own ambitions are moot."

"So you're slaves," I said.

"Disciples."

"You do his bidding."

"A purpose that feeds the whole. I've got no love for the bastard anymore, but given what he's put inside me, I think I could start getting used to this—" he showed me the sand still pouring out of his deflated hand, "—and all the advantages that come with it."

"Until what? He doesn't have use for you anymore?"

"That's life," Partridge said, "ain't it?"

I took a few steps back, not really knowing what else to do. Out of the corner of my eye, I saw Red wave one of his gloved hands. The way that neither Partridge nor I could, he stepped across the threshold of his coal triangle and smeared it with a boot-tip. A low hum accompanied the motion, then a pop like a bursting bubble.

When he came into the cavern, six other robed figures swirled into the room with him. Their cloaks looked exactly like his, pointed top and all, except that they were black. They floated like bad nightmares, surrounding me. They possessed a grace and ease that Partridge, in all his lifeless newness, hadn't yet adopted. He was a clumsy child; they were otherworldly, engorged with unnatural potential.

"You're hard to crack, Marshal Faust," Red said. "I half-expected to be in here mopping up what was left of you."

Red pushed aside his cloak and unholstered his sidearm. A sawed-off double-barrel. Red jabbed it into my ribs, smashing it into the tender spot where they'd been broken.

"Kill him," Red said to me.

Partridge was stuck between a rock and a hard place. Wall behind him, fiery torch in front of him, black robes everywhere else. "That's not how this works," he said.

"That's not a job I'm willing to do," I said.

"Your antics in Blackpeak have proved otherwise. More dead bodies every day. Don't try to reduce your accountability. He's served his usefulness." Red motioned with the shotgun to all of the black cloaks around him. "There are plenty more where he's come from, Faust. Consider this a formal invitation to join us."

You know where the Well is, the Magnate said. *This is an opportunity to embark on an endeavor that will benefit the world.*

"As a locomoting sandbag?"

Limitations have to be set. Every dog needs its lead.

Partridge licked his dry and cracking lips. "You don't want to do this, Faust."

"The problem," I told the Magnate, "is that the only way to get to the Well as I know of involves riding a bullet pony. It didn't exactly give me a treasure map."

We'll forge our way. Maps can be made. Trails can be found and discovered. Ours is a country of pioneers, Faust. Why should the next horizon be any more difficult to find?

"You can't force loyalty out of me."

But I'm going to. That's a matter of fact. How much of you you retain is really up to you.

Six sandshades. A whole room full of invisible power. Red and his tricksy coal tricks. I considered taking a gamble, turning around on them, letting the torch do its business on their sand-stuffed carcasses. Maybe Partridge would appreciate it and join me. We could crush sandy faces together and find out what was under Red's hood. Sure, Partridge wasn't Cicero, but I suppose I was in the market for new one-time friends.

But the lucky rabbit's foot had been shoved so far up my ass as of late that I was afraid it was nowhere to be found.

What the hell was I thinking. Partridge probably didn't even know who Shakespeare was.

I spun the torch and lunged its fiery edge down onto the floor.

The sand Partridge had dropped was as volatile as gunpowder. A darting snake of fire shot across the cavern's floor, following the path he'd left. I heard Partridge let out a frightened shout before, like a rag dipped in oil, his whole body went up into bright, orange flames.

The burning skinbag that used to be Partridge Gregdon withered into a pile of loose ashes on the ground. Little glowing embers winked in and out of the gray dust.

When the show was done, Red held both of his hands out in front of him. A strong burst of air whisked through the cavern's interior, kicking up Red's cloak like he was standing in the middle of a storm. Wind bellowed out of his hands at the ashes, scattering the pile into nothingness across the rocky floor.

Red leaned over where Partridge's ash-pile used to be. Between his fingers, he picked up a small piece of metal that had been left behind, flipped it like a coin, and caught it in his leather glove. He marched over to me and slapped it in my palm.

"This was his," he said. "And now, Marshal Faust, it's yours."

All the pain in my body sunk back into me. I became aware in an instant of my bruised ribs, my near-to-exploding head, all the countless other nips and scrapes and scratches I'd endured. I dropped the torch.

Still hot from the fire, a tarnished medallion in the shape of a triangle sat in my grasp. Flakes of burnt skin clung to it. I closed my hand around it.

"I want to see the Magnate," I said.

36

THEY OBLIGED, BECAUSE OF COURSE THEY OBLIGED. RED WRANGLED MY arms and slapped some rusty shackles around the wrists. He nudged me on with the barrels of his sawed-off and trucked me through the bowels of the caverns.

"You won't shoot," I said as we rounded a corner lit by a blue flame.

"Protocol. Just playing it safe. You're a slick one. People around you wind up dead."

The black-robed sandshades fluttered and slipped and slithered in a diamond formation around me. The rocky halls were as windy as a snake's spine, damp as hell and lit only by an occasional torch. The world was just a bunch of shadows, silhouettes, and flickers of light.

The corridor opened up into an adjacent cavern lined with barrels, bags of feed, and crates full of whatever trade-goods could be stuffed in them. More sandshades, dressed just like my escorts, milled around, moving some of the stock into different locations. Silver flashed under their hoods. Some stacks of crates and barrels had to have been four or five men high. I smelled cedary pipe-smoke, the tinny aroma of fresh whiskey. On the side of one of the crates, there was a painted stencil that read, *Crown Rock General Goods.* "Kallum alright with this, I suspect?"

Control the trade, control the people, the Magnate said.

"I thought this was about the Well, not the town. This like some kind of double-or-nothing?"

Only a damn fool takes one approach. Distribution of influence. Choke it, burn it, make friends, murder enemies, I don't care what I have to do. Be a good boy and I'll keep feeding them, the Magnate said. *It's all up to you.*

The sandshades all looked at me as I walked by. I gave them my best stink-eye, squeezing my fist tighter around the hot triangle-coin still in my palm. A few more windy halls, a couple of rocky corridors held up by strong, wooden beams. Sometimes the earth rumbled like the whole place was going to come down. There were spots where moisture squeezed through the rock like blood through a towel.

Finally we came to a door. It was heavy, tall, fastened into the rock with rusty hinges. Looked like something from the Middle Ages. Red bashed a black-gloved fist against the fortress-like door. There were triangles etched all in it, looking like they'd been burned in the wood with a hot stick.

A metal eye-slit whipped open. Two beady eyes stared out.

"Let us in," said Red.

Ivanmore's voice carried through the crack. "Do you have the package?"

"Hey, Ivanmore," I said. "I'm right here."

Deadbolts slid, scraped, screamed, and the massive door opened. I saw the undertaker standing there, decked all out in the same reddish robes that Red wore, pointy-topped hood and all. "Sandshades," he barked, and all the black-robed folks around me snapped to attention. "Drag our guest in. We've got a place all ready for him."

They converged on me like vultures on carrion. Despite the shackles, they all grabbed me by the arms, the elbows, and the shoulders, pushing me in front of them. One of them hammered me in the ribs with an elbow. Again with the damn ribs. Ivanmore snared me by the hair. "Don't be shy. We're not going to hurt you too much."

His nails dug like little rocks into my forehead. I might have noticed the pain, but to be honest, I was too busy staring in amazement at the place around me.

The dull browns and bleak grays of Blackpeak had made me nearly forget matters like art and architecture. I stared like a kid seeing lightning-bugs or shooting stars for the first time. The cavern's ceiling vaulted fifty, sixty feet above us, chewed right out of the stone. The rocks of the floor had been smoothed down to a vague shine that reflected the thousands of candles flickering all around us. It was a circular chamber, walls bastioned by firm beams shaped up against the countless tonnage of earth. A stone altar jutted up from the middle of the floor.

There were two levels. Between two shoulder-high torches was a channel of steps carved into the wall-stones, winding up to a terrace where wooden pews sat in rows. Onlookers saw everything from that angle, like an audience to a medical theater. There had to have been thirty pairs of silver jewels leering at me, watching me like beasts in the shadows. I felt like the main character of a traveling show.

But when I looked beyond the altar, I realized that I wasn't the main character. I was just the supporting role.

At the other end of the room was a platform like at the front of a church, where a priest would give his homily. There was a chair there carved out of sturdy wood. Next to it was a little side-table where there was a bottle of alcohol, a little glass, and a musty old book made of fine vellum.

"You have a habit of exceeding expectations, Elias," said the familiar man sitting on the chair, one foot casually thrown over an armrest. "I take it you enjoyed the gift?"

"You've been too kind. You've given me so many, I can't even remember which one you're talking about."

He dipped his chin toward my fist. The coin.

"A chance to settle old debts," he said.

The Magnate, who wore the same bloody-colored robe, drifted with preoccupation. He took up the glass and pushed himself to his feet. Underneath the wrinkles, I could see the strength of his youth, the hardness of fieldwork and farming. He wore a pair of copper-rimmed spectacles this time. His jowls looked like an angry dog's. "Shades, put him on the altar." He waved his glass like a wand. "Elias and I have a lot to discuss before we get down to business."

The sandshades took their pains to yank me up by the collar, twist me around, and sit me on the edge of the stone table like a doll. Even though my head was spinning, I tried to stay balanced. I squeezed my fist around the triangular coin.

The Magnate finished his drink, then grabbed up a small tin next to him and stood. His limpy swagger made him look both dangerous and feeble at the same time. As he descended the platform, the ocean of sandshades around me broke apart and gave way, though Red and Ivanmore stood at attention. "The best part about convincing dullards like Partridge to join your cause is that gold and money blinds them outright, and when they die the first time, you just raise'em right back up for a second try."

"And then you let your new friends burn them alive for amusement?"

"It's flattering you think of us as friends at all," the Magnate said. "There's good reason I've been in your head this long, Faust. I'd like us to know each other better."

"I reckon you already do. I'm not complicated."

"But you're loyal."

"To Blackpeak."

"Why?" he asked. He knocked the tin against the palm of his hand, drawing attention to it.

It was mine. That was my cigarette holder. "Because everyone needs someone else to make mistakes on their behalf," I said.

"Aren't you tired of picking up the pieces?"

"It's the only thing I'm good at."

He opened the tin. A stern row of rolled cigarettes, each laid next to one another like white-wrapped corpses, drew my gaze. "If you're under the impression that my purpose is to terrorize the town or claim some semblance of power, I apologize for being so opaque. In recognizing my whole menagerie of oversights, I imagine a part of that your perception's in my title. In the end, I can't ever live up to expectations. But men listen to titles where they might never listen to names. Magnate. Mayor. Marshal."

"The all-mighty *M*."

"If it weren't for our movement in the shadows, Blackpeak would wither up and die," he said. "It's damn hard work, running a syndicate under everyone's noses. Which brings us to the main problem at hand." He held a cigarette between two fingers and tapped its edge against my chest. "You."

"Don't see how me doing my job has become such a problem for you, Gregdon."

"Magnate will suffice," he interrupted, putting the smoke in his mouth and lighting it with a match off the altar. "Or Father, if you so choose."

"You want the man who killed Billy addressing you that way?"

"It's just a name. At times, one of endearment. At other times, one of loyalty and respect."

"Got none of that for you."

Puffs of smoke started curling out of his nose and out of the corner of his mouth. I could smell the tobacco, ripe and sharp, like it had little fingers trying to beckon me. "Give me an hour's work with you, Faust, and you won't have any choice but to call me by that name." I wanted a cigarette bad enough that I thought I felt my knee starting to twitch.

"Some family," I said. "Your own son was afraid of you. Afraid enough to put a bullet right in his own head."

"I have many children."

"Sandshades," I said. "Whatever the hell they are."

"All my children, if not from the womb of my dead love like Billy and Curtis, then from the industry of my own hands. And a little outside help." Still casually smoking his cigarette, the Magnate circled me, tossing his gilded locust thorn in the air, catching it with no fear of its bite. "I'm too old for games. Forcing your obedience suits me."

"And you think that'll let you control my town?"

"*Lookit* that," he sing-songed. "A man proclaiming ownership. As a badge-wearing man of the law, there's some part of you that's invested in Blackpeak more than anybody else, I wager. That's what I think I'll need," he said, jabbing a finger against my temple, "to bleed the Shattered Well's location right out of you. It picked you because you care."

The Magnate, between puffs of his cigarette – of my cigarette, stolen right out of my own tin – tilted his head. Listened to nothing, or to something only he could hear...

Then, to Red, he commanded, "I think you can unshackle our guest. I don't foresee him being much of a problem at the moment. I'll need his hands."

"As you wish."

Red came up behind me as I sat there. I felt the cold metal slide away. I immediately brought my hands out in front of me and rubbed my wrists.

"Here." He threw the tin in my direction. I caught it between my hands. He threw the matches next. I took out one of the heartily-rolled cigarettes, lit it, and leaned back, taking in the coarse smoke.

Could you buy time? I wondered that. It was a damn fool's phrase. You bought things with money. Sometimes with blood. Time wasn't something you could put in a bag. In this place I felt time pressing down on me like a fist. Not much left. "What made you like this? What forced you to live like this?"

From a glass decanter on the table beside his chair, the Magnate poured himself two more fingers of whiskey. He lingered, opened his fancy book, thumbed through a few pages. "What I experienced was a revelation. Maybe you've never had a moment such as that, Faust, but I have. For some people, it's the sudden discovery of God, the occurrence of a so-called miracle. There are events we witness that seem magnificent, unheralded by anything but the existence of something wholly beyond our conception.

"They change us. Some for the better. Me," he said, "for the worse."

An underhanded toss. The shining locust-thorn flew through the air. I caught it.

"Understand," he said.

Memories bled from it, right into me.

She was gold as an idol. I loved her. I loved her in that way you love all beautiful objects: with a complete abandonment of reason, and the sheer satisfaction that possession alone provided you some stunning advantage over the whole world. I won her. Her heart. Her eyes. Her mouth. I won her.

God, my head. Throbbing. Swimming in a strange sea...

"Come with me," she said, and I said to her, "Where," and she touched me and we were in love, and all the pure Gregdon futures my father had forged for us blew away like old dust. A future in railroad steel trickled away. I saw no future that included me.

But her. My God, she was the whole future. She was the World.

"Come with me," she said, and I said to her, "Where," and she touched me

and we – I knew –

could be

one.

A hot storm of words, ideas, notions, feelings. Tore me into pieces, reknitted me, made me forget I was Elias Faust—

Her name, Illemone, came to me like smoke. I knew her before I knew her. She was soft as a silken wrap. She whispered dances in my ear and blinded me with the music of her being. I'd found her bathing in the brown and putrid waters of Shelburne Bay, naked and alone and gleaming like carved metal amid the film and flotsam and foam.

"Tell me," she said, kissing me.

"I need you," I said.

The miracles she drew with her fingers from the air looked like perfect triangles. I traced them with my eyes in childlike wonder. I could never go back. Lights shone inside her and outside her. The sky bent and almost shattered under the power of her voice.

When she wafted like a vapor toward the center of the country, she beckoned me to be the downbeat to her pounding heart, to leave it all behind: the preordained legacy, the promise of affluence and steel carved out of ore and industry in my father's footsteps...

A flicker. Me again. All me. In my shuddering hand, the locust-thorn burned. "What are you trying to show me," I growled. "What are you trying to—"

In the hot Midwestern plains, where the earth cracked like reptile skin, she summoned the stalks of green flowers from the soil. She stepped from the back of our wagon and ferns and blossoming life sprang up in the wake of her every step. I said to her, "I love you," and she breathed into me and said, "I know, I know," and across the World, we

left

traces of

Her,

multitudes of verdant green, endless miles of sprouts and shoots and rolling nature birthed from the bosom of a dying world—

I wanted to know how. She wanted me to want to know.

It was under the gold Texas moon that I begged her, "Show me," and she did. In the shade of a tree, she broke off a branch with thorns like a spider's feet. The gold of her skin bled into the thorny branch, gilding it, gilding me, gilding us,

making

us

one.

"Stop," I gasped, realizing only too late that my hand clenched violently around the locust thorn, and if I didn't watch out, it'd pierce right through my skin, right out the back of my hand. "Get the hell out of me."

Her belly grew fat and large like a hill on the dryland horizon and I told her, "I love you," and she said, "You must," and I followed her, chained by unseen bonds, addicted to her. Outside her, I yearned for her; inside her, I found wonder. Her triangles became mine: all the unseen rules of the world in absolute order, functioning in unison when I demanded them. When we hungered, she summoned gardens and orchards from marks drawn in the sand. We slaked our thirst with the juices of otherworldly fruits. And when our minds wanted for the softness of another dimension, we awakened poppies from the sand and milked them for the wonders

hidden like liquid

pearl

inside their bulbous eyes.

My skin wanted to crawl away from my bones. My head and mind swam in a sea, barely holding on. My cigarette, burnt to a blackened nub between my knuckles, crumbled into ash. The Magnate's smile stretched in a vicious, liquid crease across a face that wore decades like armor and paint...

"How was that cigarette?" he asked me, knowledge in his voice—

—as she scooped handfuls of the crumbling Texas soil into her ancient palms. Illemone gleamed in the sun and our children – our boys, our twins – toddled like clumsy ogres through the too-tall grasses. Grains fell between her fingers, and she said, "Do you want me to teach you," and I said, "Always," and she said—

"Do you want to learn how to bring life from death?"

But we both knew the answer, for women gold as idols turn men into fools as thick as stone.

"I love you," I told her, because it had always worked before; "I love you," I told her, because it had always kept her so near, but she was slipping, slipping, slipping, and the gold in her skin wore the pale fire of a dying star. "I love you," I said, I screamed, "I love you, I love you," weightless and unfeeling, just noise to fill the air where silence would be, an honest-to-goodness lie...

"Xa'anshangerrad," Illemone said to me, filling my hands with her sand before she clasped my cheeks in her golden hands—

Before I lost her.

"Come back," I begged.

But she left me with sand. The bitch, she left me with sand, and faded like a laughing dream.

I fell to my knees, my hands, my coin clattering to the cavern floor. I clenched my teeth so damned hard I feared they'd shear themselves to nubs. The walls of the world flickered like water. I opened my mouth to suck in breath, to be sure it was *my* breath, though God, as near to those moments as I'd been, I swear Illemone's palms still warmed me. "She wasn't...human," I said.

"When your mind starts thinking outside the boundaries we're born to respect, you begin realizing that things around you aren't as they seem," the Magnate assured me. "She was far from human."

"You want her back," I said. "That's why you want the Shattered Well. That's why you want your Wish."

A momentary tremble rolled through his body, enough to set his robes alive with motion. Bloody, lonely, and unoccupied, his fist, scarred from a thousand clutches around that gilded thorn, crashed against my temple.

I crumbled. He picked the thing from my grip.

The memory turned cold and melted like ice.

"To presume the weaknesses of a younger man are reason enough for him to set the world on its head when he's an older one is pedestrian thinking. No, Elias. Love and infatuation belong to lesser men. She gave me boys that were half hers, bred from me like...like fucking prize cows, and then she *left me* with them." His words came out with frantic, manic energy. "Left me nothing of her, and yet left me with everything to *remember*." His pointer-finger knocked against his forehead.

As he spoke, I formulated possibilities in my head. But every time I looked, the sandshades were still staring. Red and Ivanmore were still behind me. Getting out of this compound was going to take exactly what Gregdon blabbered on about: a miracle. Especially with my vision wavering like smoke, and my brain half-scrambled, half-firing.

"Existences are being wasted in Blackpeak. People live shit lives of regret and sorrow. But I refuse," he said. "The Well's here, somewhere in these mines, somewhere beneath them, somewhere around them, and if I have to turn you into a motherfucking slave just to rip it out of you – to get to it, and get to *her* – I will do so with sheer happiness."

When he turned around to me, his red robes snapped around his ankles. In his right hand he squeezed the thorn. In his left, he held a curved knife like the ones I'd seen Uno, Dos, Tres, and Seis wield. A talon-blade. He pointed it at. "Returning to the ordinary after you've witnessed the extraordinary is just a waste, Faust, unless you can bring some of the extraordinary back with you."

I looked down to the triangular coin still clasped in my palm.

Life from death.

His hairy nostrils flexed and closed. "I'll ask the Well for my boys again, shed of everything that made them hers. I'll ask for Illemone, who gave me a morsel of her power, and left me, *fled* from me, before I even knew what questions to ask about the wonders she'd given me. I'll extract her from whatever pit she dwells in, whatever piece of the universe she calls her own.

"I'll drag her to me and tear the rest of the magic in her veins out of her."

He didn't stop walking in those energetic, wild circles, like a raven trying to find a perfect perch. Blood plopped from his hand. He went back to his drink in Poindexter's glass, emptied it, then let the glass fall from his hands. It shattered against the smooth-stoned floor.

"I want to show you a trick, Faust," he said. "I want to show you the power she gave me. I want to show you the power that will turn you into one of my sandshades."

His boots scuffed across the floor. His shoulders, set for conflict, swayed forward. He gripped the talon-blade.

The Magnate came for me.

He never lunged, never ran. Just kept striding, fierce-like. Chin bent down, knife out, thirsty for blood. When he got within several feet of me, I made my move.

I thought at first that I slipped. A surge of warmth ran down my legs and it felt like bricks had been dropped on my toes. They didn't cooperate. I wobbled. I put my hands up. My arms stretched out, turned to responseless ribbon. Too late...

The Magnate reached up and struck me in the throat with the base of his palm. His red robes became like living streams of blood. They writhed in the air and dripped all around us but never left stains. The rocks had become a black ocean. I thought I saw stars twinkling on the ceiling.

I fell to my knees. The Magnate rammed his knee against my chin. Pain was somewhere else, like I'd all but forgotten how to feel it.

He grabbed me by the hair with the hand holding the knife. He forced my head down flat on the altar.

"Soaked your tobacco in formaldehyde," the Magnate whispered in my ear as he raised up one of my rubbery arms and lay it on the altar beside me. "It hits you like a stampede, runs right over you, and you don't feel a thing until it's too late for you to realize what's false and what's true."

He yanked my index finger out and pressed it down on the altar. A million multi-colored bugs crawled in and out of the cracks in the stone. I could feel them crawling on me too, inside my clothes, inside my brain...

"I want you to understand what I understood."

He adjusted his glasses with the edge of the knife. Then he over-extended my left index finger and poised it underneath the shiny crescent-moon of the talon-blade's edge.

The weapon smiled at me.

The Magnate jammed his hand down.

The blade slit through skin.

Metal crunched through a meaty joint.

Blood everywhere.

It took me just a few seconds to realize my finger was gone.

I screamed. I didn't feel the agony at first, but there was a deep throb pulsing through my bones. Blood ran from the knuckle like a butcher's stream. The digit that used to be mine just sat there until the Magnate picked it up between his thumb and his own index finger and examined it. The Magnate's face still looked like fleshy mud. He had four eyes and a serpent's tongue. Or did he?

Like a child playing in sand, the Magnate used the severed base of my finger and drew on the smooth stone altar like it was paper. My stomach started to dance like a jumping-bean inside my body. He drew a sloppy triangle with my blood.

"There are two essential components one needs to perform magic, Faust. It's a surprisingly simple equation, and Illemone, my fairness that she was, had it *in* her like second nature. One—" he tapped my forehead with my severed finger, "—a constituent, a gate, a portal – an aid of sorts through which to bring magic into our reality. And secondly, the desire to do so. An emotion strong enough to break through that gate and bring the power with you.

"Why the drugs," I said, trying not to focus too much on the blinding sunlight in the Magnate's eyes. "Why'd you lace my cigarette—"

"I did it with no intent to offend or disarm you," he said. "Really, it's a gift. For Illemone and me, it was opium. She demanded that we modify our perception when I was learning how to break down the barriers of the ordinary. It's just a component, an opportunity to glimpse the world through new lenses. But we work with what we commonly have, don't we, Ivanmore?"

"We make it work," the undertaker said. "However we need to."

The Magnate reached across the great seas that separated us to pat my cheek like a doting parent. "I need you ready to shed your understanding of the ordinary. The mind doesn't take kindly to... intrusive ideas."

Which is when it occurred to me: the Magnate had been intending this end for quite some time for me. "You groomed me," I said. "The paper. That voice of yours in my head. Little hints and slivers of *your* world peeking into mine. You want to turn me into one of those goddamn shade *things*—"

"But those *goddamn shade* things," he said, "were quite good and dead before I got my hands on them. You're different."

"'Cause I'm alive?"

"Because the murderer of my sons deserves special treatment. Revenge may be primitive, but it's also satisfying. Not to mention, making you one of my disciples waylays the only opposition in Blackpeak that might have been a worthy adversary. You haven't been easy to overcome, Faust. I'd like to use that to my advantage."

The Magnate grabbed me by my hair and wrenched my head down above the little triangle he'd drawn with my blood.

"The triangle," the Magnate said. "Illemone introduced me to them. For her, for *her*, it was all so natural and effortless, but I needed a harness, a gate deliberate enough to serve its purpose. Put too much power into something unsure, think of it like a cracked gun barrel: it can backfire, explode in your face. Control is essential. Humans like you and me, we weren't made to dabble in this kind of power.

"I've perfected my use of magic in the ways even Illemone hadn't. I've turned something unpredictable into a science."

He pulled my head away from the triangle. Just as he did so, the edges of the bloody drawing started to smolder. Smoke curled up from its curves. I turned my cheek. It was searing, almost unbearable.

"Heat. Cold. Impenetrable barriers. Illusions. Vast possibilities," whispered the Magnate as he grabbed my blood-covered, four-fingered hand, "all from just a tiny little triangle."

He jammed the stub of my knuckle down into the middle of the triangle. The drawing glowed with hot, orange fury, like dying fire. I tried to pull my hand away, but the bastard's grip was iron. The skin seared, bubbled, even started squealing like moist beef on a griddle.

Ivanmore, Red, and the Magnate were all on me, holding me still. The two or three seconds he held my hand above the triangle turned into torturous years. Finally, when he pulled it off, they stepped away. I cradled the blackened place where my index finger had been.

What a way to burn a wound closed.

"We're not quite through yet, Elias," said the Magnate from above me. The Magnate manhandled me again, but this time sat on my back and peeled my other hand from behind me. He plucked up my right index finger and pressed it flat next to the still-smoldering triangle.

"I want you to learn," he said in my ear, "so you remember my sons. Carry Billy with you always on that scarred left hand. On your right, carry my Curtis. My *children*."

There was anger inside of him that he had subdued, but only now – with the excitement of the blade, the wretched scent of blood – the father in him came out, overwhelming the magic-addled zealot, the whack-job, the Magnate.

"Gregdon," I said. "Don't do this. Please."

"My sons didn't have a choice."

"They did."

"You made it for them, Faust."

"For Billy," I said. "But I was just quicker. Nothing more than that."

"That was more than enough."

Like a butcher cleaving off a hunk of loin, down came the blade. I tried to jerk away, but no hope – too sluggish from the formaldehyde, too weak.

Blinded by pain, I twisted and screamed. Hot blood ran through my palms.

I could still feel my fingertip. God, I could still feel it...

I twitched it, thrust it out—

Saw it there, disembodied, my second lost finger unwilling to move.

He crouched down on the floor again. Grabbed the finger. He started painting another triangle with it. Darkness knocked at my mental back door, asking to come in, to take over...

"You're a...fucking lunatic," I said.

When he leaned down and grabbed me by the hair on my scalp, he pulled me over and all but pressed my face down into the middle of the triangle. "You're angry, Elias. You're not absorbing what I'm trying to tell you. And if you don't understand it enough when you become one of my disciples, that lack of confidence in the powers I possess could put the whole ritual at risk. How could I expect to create a being out of magic," he asked, "that doesn't believe in it?

"If I'm going to pull power into our reality from another where such forces exist, we need a battering ram. Something strong enough to make us *want*."

The Magnate went for my right hand again. He grabbed it by the wrist and pressed the very tip of the talon-blade's edge into my finger-stump.

"Pain, Elias. One of the simplest, most powerful emotions."

The knife gouged my finger-stump. I bit my tongue so hard my mouth filled with blood.

The prodding sent lightning-bolts of pain through my body. I wailed like a child.

"Focus it all on that triangle, Elias. It doesn't matter who made it, doesn't matter why it was there. Make it yours. Make it do what you want."

I could barely see the smudged drawing through my tears. My blood. It was *my* blood.

"Chaos and order, Elias. Symmetry." He whispered in my ear, proclaiming all the virtues of the stupid little triangle. "A portal to the extraordinary. Pour your pain into it, Elias. Make it burn." Another twist of the knife. "Do anything you can with that pain except feel it."

That was part of me there on the ground, that triangle. Something from inside of me. Every time he gouged me, it felt like my eyes were bulging out their sockets. I wanted to get rid of the pain. I wanted it to go away.

Is this how it was like for him, losing his sons? But deeper, sweeping into trenches I couldn't really fathom? Wasn't that what he needed, what he wanted?

To find the Well.

Find his way back to Illemone.

I'd never stared that hard. Never screamed so loud. Never asked for God to take pain away that much before. I searched for Him in that bloody scrawl, and just when I thought I could almost feel the blood with my eyes, the strangest thing happened.

I thought of burning coals and sweltering breaths of wind. I asked for Hell, because that's what the Magnate deserved.

Underneath me, the smooth stone within the boundaries of the triangle ran through with a spidery crack. A spark or two belched up from the tiny rift. A little tendril of blue fire leaped into the air, bit my nose, and then vanished. The blood dried instantly. I was left staring at a mottled, ashy triangle.

And just like that, the pain inside of me was gone. Poured somewhere else. At least for a moment.

The Magnate stood. "Boys, pick him up. Cauterize that other finger and bring me a barrel of sand. Throw him on the altar and let's get the last step of this task underway."

37

RED HEATED A BLADE OVER ONE OF THE TORCHES, THEN CAME TO ME and seared the stub where my right finger used to be. The pain fell away into the damp, oily haze of the formaldehyde. That had been *my* blue fire, and while it had been a limp dick next to what the Magnate could do, I'd called it. Me.

He said he couldn't create a being out of magic that didn't believe in it.

My life was his to forfeit.

The Well would be his.

They dragged over a keg of something and set it by me. Blood was in my palms. Place reeked of the rubbery, hot mist of burnt skin.

Red pushed me over on my side. He bundled my wounded hands behind me. He clamped the shackles and rolled me so my palms and wrists were between the small of my back and the stone under me.

"This is so you don't cause trouble," he said.

While they prepared me for...whatever it was, the Magnate, Red, and Ivanmore bustled all around, their words an indistinct cloud sparking across the air. The sandshades up on the balcony above observed silently. Me, I conserved my energy and tried my best to hold fast to consciousness – and the liquidy, seeping froth of reality.

"Ivanmore," said the Magnate as he lifted the wooden cap off the barrel, "Prepare the triangle. Can I trust you to measure it perfectly?"

"Twelve feet on each side."

"And the placement?"

"The altar and Faust directly in the middle."

"You're learning quickly."

"It's not that difficult, Father."

"Not too difficult to do adequately," said the Magnate, lifting his hand from the barrel and letting sand spill from between his fingers, "but almost impossible to do perfectly."

"Then let it be your hand that draws it if you don't trust my judgment. I'm just here because you needed bodies."

He unsheathed his talon-blade and held it out to Ivanmore. "Let's do this quickly. I want a celebratory drink."

"As you wish."

I watched as Ivanmore drew back the length of his red sleeve, raised his gnarled hand, and gouged the tip of the talon-blade between the bones in his wrist. The skin split open. He walked over to a clay vessel on the ground and squeezed the red stuff out of himself like he was wringing a rag.

When he was done, he stood and brought the bowl with him. I could see him staggering weakly. He looked ready to keel over. Then, with a bone-handled brush, he walked in a wide berth around the altar, drawing a triangle on the floor. He measured feet and distance under his breath. At each tip of the triangle, he swept a broad circle around his feet.

While Ivanmore worked, the Magnate approached me. He hummed under his breath. Red stood on my other side. I still couldn't see the bastard's face, but I could see the Magnate grinning, showing me his teeth.

"Blood and pain go hand-in-hand," he said to me, before telling the others: "Open his vest and shirt. I need his flesh."

Out came Red's talon-blade. He hooked it under a button and just yanked my clothes apart. Meanwhile, the Magnate pinched my bloody hand in his fingers and examined the Mark crawling like a stain from my palm toward my wrist. "I need his head lifted for the ritual. When the spell hits him, I imagine he'll seize. Granted, I've never done it on the living before. I'd rather him not clobber his brains out on the stone if something goes awry."

I said, "That'd be unfortunate."

"And messy," he said.

Red removed a thick volume from his pocket and fanned the pages. It was my *Collected Works of Shakespeare.* He grabbed me by the hair with his gloved hand and slid it under me.

"Good?" said Red.

"Good," said the Magnate.

"What, no pillows," I said.

The Magnate watched me. I saw little shadow-dancers in his eyes. "I'm looking forward to the time when you're able to speak only because I allow you." He smiled. "You're going to live anew today, Elias. Are you paid up with God?"

"I still owe him a bit of attention," I said.

"You're a man of conviction. Don't tell me those morals of yours have been arbitrary."

"Faith never really mattered much to me until I was staring death in the face."

"Fair-weather Christian, then."

"Still alive," I said. "I never took you as a religious sort."

"I'm not." The teensy grin kept growing. "But that doesn't mean I don't believe in God. It's just that maybe the one I know isn't the same one you're familiar with." The Magnate's cheek twitched, like his eye was trying not to spasm. He scooped out a bunch of sand with the wooden trowel. "Open his mouth," the Magnate said to Red.

Gloved fingers pressed into my cheeks and forced my jaw open.

"This works out for both of us," the Magnate whispered next to my ear, "I gain a new son, and you, a whole family. And when the time comes, I will stare into the heart of the Shattered Well and take back what's mine."

Red yanked my mouth further open. The Magnate nudged the

trowel against my bottom teeth and poured the sand down into my throat.

"You think this will work?" Red asked over me.

"It had better," the Magnate said.

"The spirit broker won't wait much longer for us."

"He won't need to."

"I dislike risks," Red admitted.

"You let me worry about the chances," snapped the Magnate. "The spirit broker knows what I've brought him; he knows I need this one to *live*. Do you doubt me?"

"No. But—"

"You cannot doubt me. Not now. Do you? Does doubt linger in your heart for what I plan to do, and what we plan to accomplish?"

"I trust you," Red said. "It's the ritual I question."

"I've come too far to harbor weaklings and simpering fools. Be silent, do your task, or step aside."

But Red remained. Loyalty's loyalty, I guessed.

The sand filled me up. It clogged in my throat and turned into moist lumps under my tongue. It had a taste like salt and sulfur. My throat and nose burned in the back. Every time I tried to spit some out, more slid off the little scoop.

"My own mixture," said the Magnate. "Various minerals found here in the mines. Do you like it, Faust? It took me years to perfect it. Very volatile, but very potent when ground up and mixed in the right amounts. An efficient conductor and insulator of magic and power. Might not taste fantastic, but it'll do the trick."

I couldn't help but swallow some of it. It laid on my stomach like bricks and granite. The Magnate shook several scoopfuls of sand across my body and onto my chest. He crouched down on the floor, picked up the triangular coin that I'd gotten from Partridge's body – I couldn't remember when it had fallen – and placed it right in the middle of my chest.

"This tells the world you belong to me," he said.

After he was done distributing the sand, Red drew two tapers from his robe and gave them to the Magnate. He lit them with a snap of his fingers. He placed one above my head and one near my feet.

"Let us take our places," the Magnate said. "I'm through dragging out this process. Elias Faust, it's a shame we need to finish things this way."

By some magical influence, the ambient light of the cavern faded. We were left with the wall torches and the candles to light the way. Red approached the triangle – the point at my right shoulder – and stood facing me. Ivanmore did the same at the left. The Magnate took his place at the point of the triangle facing my feet. In their red robes and darkness, they looked like spirits waiting to devour me. The tension in the cavern started bubbling. The sandshades leaned over the balcony, all staring at me. The Magnate never looked away.

"When we open the gate, gentlemen, remember: There will be more power than any single one of us can handle. Manage what you can and diffuse the rest across the triangle. Nobody alone can manage this much force."

"Just like all the other times," said Red.

"Only this one's still alive," said Ivanmore.

"Silence," said the Magnate.

And there was.

A gentle gust whisked through the cavern as the Magnate raised one of his hands up in the air. The candles flickered. A few grains of sand blew away. He opened his mouth. A sound started rolling out of him: a hum, a deep chant. The rest of the place went dead silent. If only I had a gun, something to aim at him and pull the trigger.

Christ, if only I had fingers to pull a trigger.

The temperature, like a tide, began to rise. Sweat trickled down the sides of my face. The blood on the floor steamed. I couldn't tell you what it was, couldn't really find words to do so, but there was *something* in the air. A presence, an interloper, a weight like iron. It was invisible.

If you ever stand still and let a train pass you, there's this split-second after it passes where the wind cracks, the world bends, and everything's quiet. Like it's sucked the life out of everything, and you realize a true power – a thing that could kill you without flinching or caring – just passed by and let you live.

This feeling wasn't passing. It was hanging in the air over me.

Watching.

The bloody triangle began to boil. I heard wet pops from the bubbles. The coin on my chest seared against my skin.

Inside my mind, the Magnate appeared one last time.

And so it comes to this.

Like he was throwing a ball, the Magnate tossed air in Red's direction. Red caught it in his gloved hands and spread his arms. He started moaning out the same kind of noise. The blood of the triangle steamed, glowed, like metal heated up over a fire.

Red started to shudder. He made a throwing motion toward Ivanmore, who caught what I couldn't see. He too spread his arms and began to howl.

An invisible weight pushed down into my chest. Unrelenting power.

Death.

The three of them stood at the points of the glowing triangle of blood, their arms outstretched as if they were holding hands from long distance. They completed the triangle. They all hummed, each at a different pitch but all together in a perfect harmony. Their song was a single sound made of smaller, uglier sounds. A chorus. Three things as one. Chaos becoming order.

"Well, shit," I said, right before the spell crashed into me and broke the world in half.

———————

Blink.

A landscape of white. Pure emptiness. No color. Horizon to horizon, just *nothing*, and in the center of it, where everything congealed together as one – reality, consciousness, laws both physical and not – was me.

I gasped for breath, but it was all poison. My lungs sputtered, shrank, refused to cooperate.

Where was I?

The air in this place was a miner's sulfur nightmare. I felt like a goddamn canary with its wings clipped and its beak viced shut. Couldn't scream to warn the world, couldn't thrash.

A pressure filled the air in front of me. A presence. A thousand-million screaming voices, clapped together like a lone railroad-spike, drove through the space where my brain should have been.

BLINK.

They dragged an invisible mountain-range down on my chest. The triangular coin started to jitter. My skin smoked and smoldered. Like hot little cinders, the sand began to dig into my pores. Trying to get inside.

The Magnate broke the chorus, saying something new. He said it over and over. It sounded like gibberish to me, a bunch of syllables thrown together in a mish-mash, but he spouted it like Cicero would a Shakespeare soliloquy.

"Xa'anshangerrad." He kept screaming the word over and over until he had his hands in the air. *San-shanger-rod.* "Xa'anshangerrad." His sleeves fell to show his veins almost bursting out of his arms.

Then he got struck by lightning.

BLINK.

The white world came pouring back into me.

The Magnate's chant, like a muffled gunshot, hovered overhead.

Displeasure ripped through me, an arrow through animal-hide, almost turning me inside-out.

Something *else's* displeasure.

And when it spoke, it wasn't in words or ideas, so much as in bone-deep truths: communication plucked out of previously-built ideas in my head, and rearranged in front of the vision of my mind's too-damn-blind eye.

He asks a great boon. On your behalf.

Speech wasn't so much an action as it was a *happening*. The words simply were, things felt instead of heard...

Too much thinking. Too much. Chatter, chatter, chatter...

Slimy yet warm, a stinking palm brushed across my chin, my lips, and began to pry my teeth apart...

Chatter, chatter, chatter...

BLINK.

The darkness above the Magnate cracked open. The whole place went wild with blue and white light. The lightning didn't stop with the Magnate. It bounced through him, shot in an arc out to his either side, and struck Red and Ivanmore, too. They were ready for it. Nobody should have been able to live through that kind of lightning, but they did. They persevered.

Like they'd practiced it in a dance, they all pointed straight at me.

I found out what the triangular coin was for.

From the three magicians at the three points of the triangle, three bolts of lightning lunged at me, leapt into the air, then clapped down into the coin.

I started jittering. Sand dug into me; lightning burned me from the inside-out. One of the candles tipped. A hot flash of fire swept across the sand spilled along my pantleg.

Shit. *Shit.*

BLINK.

A heartbeat. Its heart still beats. Its heart still beats.

Oily tendrils sucking at my mouth. At my lips. At my skull, my brain, slithering into me, inside me, piercing every pore, pushing through every membrane you could imagine.

It pulses with warmth. It breathes from within. It operates.

The presence crashed across me, not like a wave, not even like a hurricane, but like a whole planet rolling over me, across, me, through me.

I lived, right then, only because the spirit broker allowed it.

———

BLINK.

I tried to sit up. The blinding lightning kept blasting into me, drilling the coin into my skin. I was being scraped clean from within. My stomach was a puddle of lava. My brain was a screaming pocket of sparks. The Magnate kept saying that word over and over.

"Xa'anshangerrad. Xa'anshangerrad!"

Moments slipped away. I writhed, smashed my legs on the altar. The lightning had me pinned like a cockroach under a bootheel.

The Magnate yelled into the air, "I've my offering to give you."

———

BLINK.

Split in two. Right in half. That was me. One foot in that pain-addled world, and one foot in this one. All that I was in *this* place, this crude, flat, paper-thin sliver of existence, were thoughts that might as well have been cinders and smoke.

Is this the offering? This occupied vessel?

Shouting across planes, across worlds and existences, the Magnate said, "He is as we discussed."

A tongue lashed me. Slithering, wet, hungry.

It tastes of...dominion. It tastes of other power.

"But will it satisfy our bargain?"

It belongs, it breathed, *to Something Else.*

———

BLINK.

"It's a body, Xa'anshangerrad," the Magnate cried to the ceiling, "but this one's different than the rest. You know the bargain: I give you free rein over the shell, and in turn you ensure the spirit conforms to my will and wishes."

Couldn't remove the coin. It was seared in. A part of me. My fingers gripped at the side of the altar until I felt my nails start to crack.

"This one's special," the Magnate said. "This one's still alive."

———

BLINK.

Chatter, chatter, chatter. Humans wear a thousand faces. You do too.

"I am who I have always been," the Magnate said.

Illemone's favorite bauble.

"Her lover."

Her vanity, Xa'anshangerrad thundered, for in this fold of time, it was everywhere, was everything. *That is all you amount to. But a bargain made shall be honored. Show me it.*

"Must you always?"

Show me it.

"You know I—"

SHOW ME.

———

BLINK.

Even in the true world, up and down went topsy-turvy. Xa'anshangerrad's fury filtered with such deafening power through the cavern that tiny flecks of stone rained down from above.

"What are you waiting for?" Ivanmore snarled.

"Give it what it wants," Red said.

"It's *mine*," the Magnate said.

Red, still managing his conduit of power, snapped, "It just wants to see!"

"She's mine."

"Then goddamnit," the undertaker said, "show the proof! Either way, this power's gonna come full force, and you need to be ready—"

A sputter, a flicker in the beam of lightning. One of the pulses burrowing into my chest fizzled.

I could move. Just a bit...

The Magnate, his palm gleaming red, thrust high his right hand toward the gaze of an unseen eye. Buried in his grip was the gilded locust-thorn, glowing hot and glistening with his blood. "Here. It's here," he said.

BLINK.

There it is.

"Is that all you wanted to see?"

A beacon of light flickered into being in the distance, bleeding color across the lifeless span. There, like a blurry memory, was the Magnate's hand and his beloved locust thorn, bleeding droplets of blood into the air.

Here, though, the gilded thorn was...not the same. Countless golden tendrils, each a writhing snake, cast out like a net from its liquid-metal surface. They lanced into the great beyond, and floating at their ends were shadows, each one twisted up and gnarled in the most heinous kind of way. Sandshades. Held in place. Imprisoned.

So many of them. Lifeless. Aimless. Tethered.

Illemone's Heart weakens little by little, human. The gift she has given to you tires like a withered old cronc. You neglect it with misuse.

"I'll forge it anew when the Well is mine."

With what power? You borrow it from her. You are but its custodian.

"She granted it to me fairly. Out of love." A flare of light shot up across the wires of gold. The shades shuddered in response.

Can it handle the strain of one more shade?

"It has never failed me."

You traffic with fragile magic, human. Illemone's Heart struggles. The burdens you have placed upon it threaten to unravel it altogether. Your citadel nears its fall.

"Do you threaten me, Xa'anshangerrad? Do you threaten my life? My purpose?"

Even powerful spellcraft, when stretched too thin, promises to shatter like glass under the fist of any other magic turned against it.

"Then I will be wary and vigilant to a fault."

How long do you think you can abuse Illemone's gift? Look at yourself, human. At the sweat on your brow. At the pain underneath that little seed you call a heart. You age too quickly. A hundred years is but a breath for me. You're but an imposter. Magnate! A fool's title for a kingdom built on fool's gold. Your sandshades exist because of Illemone's power – and her power alone.

"I have built this with my own blood."

It's human, the being croaked, *to swing at the world with weapons forged by other hands and proclaim themselves destroyers, rebuilders, and saviors all at once. Will you risk all of this, human? Truly?*

"If I must. Faust will lead me to the Well, Xa'anshangerrad, and what I've destroyed in that search will return whole when I lay my eyes upon it."

I have never been fond of the stink that results from the crude mixture of human ambition and recklessness. Will this one pay the price for your desire?

"A hundred times over, if he must."

To call her power yours?

"It has always been mine."

No, the presence corrected. *It has not.*

Parts of me broke away in this world. I was a spider's web coming apart, wrapped around Xa'anshangerrad's invisible fist like a bit of old cloth. Every time he squeezed, layers of me sloughed off like old flakes of skin. Days, months, and years came crumbling away.

Or was it that I shot forward through them?

Illemone's Heart beat with hungry excitement.

From the nothing, there emerged a smoky, black smear, coming toward me.

I provide a spirit to fill the vessel. And the one that we're to remove...

"You keep it. An equal exchange."

A coiling snake of golden thread shot out of Illemone's Heart, spiraled into the air, then skewered the unsuspecting shadow. It writhed, howled, thrashed, but like a fish on a hook, it only slid further, further down...

They were going to take the *me* out of me.

And replace me.

The spear-point of gold flinched in the air. Then, with an oily spirit still impaled, shot straight toward me.

BLINK.

When I tried to sit up, I swear I felt skin pulling away from my elbows and back, like I was an egg on a hot-plate...

And that's when I realized something: the shackles weren't around my wrists anymore. My hands were free. The chains were still under me. I'd wrenched my way out of them, but it hadn't been too hard. Effortless, actually.

Red hadn't fully closed the goddamn things.

The lightning kept punching me in the chest. I howled, trying to push against it, meanwhile sifting through everything in my brain for a solution, a way to get out.

The spirit rushed down into me.

Pressure fused us together.

In both worlds, my heart jumped a beat. Two beats. Ten.

Death and life, simultaneous.

Time was ticking. I was burning. I thought about what the Magnate had said to his pals.

There will be more power than any single one of us can handle. Manage what you can and diffuse the rest across the triangle.

I couldn't really adjust my body. Unseen here, Illemone's Heart still pinned me, impaled me, but my arms were free. I could swivel my head just enough to get a solid glance at the Magnate. I thought about his last warning.

Nobody alone can handle this much magic.

I grabbed my copy of *The Collected Works of Shakespeare* from under my head. Heavy little book. Hard enough to hurt, maybe even knock somebody out.

Had to have good aim. The best. No wonder I liked shotguns.

I threw the book as hard as I could.

The Magnate saw it coming, but he managed too much power. Probably have thought I shouldn't be able to move. I barely could – the pain was like a blanket – but I'd done dumbass shit before, so this was no different. Pages fluttered. The book soared like a bird. It smacked the Magnate in the face and knocked him back.

I'd have to thank Cicero for the gift.

With its foundation pulled from under it, the spell broke apart and went wild.

———

BLINK.

Suppose a little bit of the Bard never hurt nobody.

The Magnate, with a fury that trembled the world, let out a cry of desperation. Illemone's Heart, thrust into this white plane, spasmed and flickered like a blown candle. Pressed almost entirely into me, the spirit Xa'anshagerrad had summoned tore at the core of my being: arms of black tar and smoke shredded me, desperate to hold on...

Pulling time from me. Pulling from me what *could* have been—

Pine trees shooting up into a cool blue sky.

A warm home, budding with life.

Clogging my nose, a hint of hearty stew. Onions, maybe. Bison. Pepper. Heaven in a kettle.

A smoke-covered mantel, and perched on it a brown daguerreotype in a copper frame. A family, all unsure shadows burnt there by mercury and patience, captured in a frozen moment.

Evidence of a life well-lived. Of fulfillment. Of happiness.

And there in a rocking chair, an old man, his skin as fine as paper and his eyes as deep as a rheumy sea. He cradled a weathered guitar. The music whispered with a beginner's beauty from his yellow fingers.

His name was Elias Faust, and he was a happy man.

The spirit dashed away, tearing it all from me.

The white world fell away for the final time in a scream of noise and blindness.

BLINK.

Once the book hit, a whole bunch of shit happened at once. I guess when you fiddle-fuck around with that much power, mistakes absolutely shouldn't happen. I heard Ivanmore gargle just a second before the lightning lashed back into him. His head blew apart like a rotten fruit.

Red must have been more trained, more prepared. He staggered out of the triangle with his head between his hands. Smoke poured out from under his hood. He was trying to handle the energy Magnate Gregdon had dropped.

A flash of green shot out from the darkness, almost fast as a bullet. It whacked into Red's chest and blew him back to the floor.

A jade knife, lodged to the handle in his chest, stole all his attention.

"Sandshades," the Magnate roared as he stumbled back. "Put the bastard down like a dog!"

I suppose you're only worth as much as man's patience.

Countless guns discharged at once from the balcony. Arc-lights of fire and energy splashed down at me. I rolled off the altar and behind it. Bullets pecked into the stone but didn't get to me. A spray of tossed flame flashed across the edge of the stone.

A round whisked off the top of the stone table. I didn't have no gun, no way to defend myself. From the rattling of magic and electricity in my veins, to burns on my chest, even so far as the formaldehyde still playing around in my skull, I didn't have much of a chance.

"Plan," I said to myself. "Plan. You need a plan."

I peeked around the corner of the altar. Some of the sandshades jumped to the floor. Others took the stairs.

A silhouette ran out from the darkness of the chamber. It ran, planted its foot on a stony wall, and bounded into three or four of the sandshades. Their attention shifted toward it. So did the muzzles. Gunfire didn't seem to touch it. It had a single knife, glowing green, that moved like a predator. It stabbed, sliced, and sprayed sand with every motion as it cut through skin and robe.

I scrambled out from behind the altar.

Crossing almost ten feet toward Red's shivering body took a damn lifetime. I grabbed the red-robed magician by his wrist. Even though every muscle in my body told me not to strain, I had to. I yanked him with me back behind the altar.

The shadow still wasn't dead. It kept fighting.

Buying me time.

"Faust," Red said, belching blood.

"The sawed-off," I said. "Do you have it?"

"On my belt. On my—"

"Shut your mouth," I said, sifting through bloody cloth. The sawed-off was there. A bandolier, too. And a talon-blade.

"I hoped you'd notice," he said, shaking all over like winter had just come over us. "I hoped you'd feel how loose they were..."

I unholstered the shotgun and opened the breach. Loaded. And there were about ten more shells in the belt.

I pushed his hood off his head. I nudged his chin with the shotgun. He looked at me. Red was an older man. Entirely unremarkable. A face even a crowd would forget. But not me. His eyes were soft. They were familiar. Gentle. And though what wisps of hair remained on his bald head had been burned black, I recognized him.

The foreman of the mine, Mr. Bisbin, lay dying right in front of me.

"Hello, Elias." My middle finger paused on the back-most trigger. "A part of me hoped you'd never find out."

"You're part of this goddamn madness?"

"I had no other business options. No spine, either. But your shackles," Bisbin said, "weren't an accident. You'd either notice or you'd die a free man, even if you didn't know it."

More gunshots. Several buzzed above us, raining rock down from the wall behind us. Bisbin grabbed my collar and pulled me down.

"Things in Blackpeak haven't always been easy, Faust. Men who don't have a hope in the world, we'll go where we know there's money and power, even if it kills us."

"We're in the mines," I said. "In the coal mines?"

"More than just coal down here, Faust." Blood started bubbling on his lips.

"Why didn't you stop him," I said.

"Afraid. Scared."

"He's eating Blackpeak alive."

"I kinda hoped you'd make sure he didn't."

"You almost got me killed."

"But you're not dead."

"Almost," I said.

"If I fell too far out of line, Faust, he would have known. I'd be dead, and so would lots of others. And if you'd died down here, you'd just be another black mark inked on this darkening heart of mine. But you didn't." He pressed a finger against my chest. "Not yet. You still got a chance." Then he fell into coughing, and ribbons of blood spilled out of his mouth.

"And how the hell am I going to get out of here?"

"Mine's a mine," he said. "Every way leads out in the end. Be fast and you can make it."

"Fast isn't really my forte at the moment."

"Ignore the pain. It's temporary. Death is final."

"And what about you," I said.

"Do you think I want to go back up there and see the sunlight? Do you think I'd be proud to live in a town I helped terrorize? I belong here. I deserve this."

"Then I'll bury you as right as I can."

"Don't you dare. I don't want a grave up there, Elias. I don't want to be remembered."

He reached down and gathered my hand in his. Then he placed my palm on the handle of the glowing knife.

Another bullet winged by us.

I heard the Magnate roar like a beast: "Don't you worry, Elias Faust. I won't let you die. Not until I pry those secrets right off your useless hide, and make you feel every exquisite ounce of agony."

I looked up, but Bisbin grabbed my face.

"I've barred the entrances to this room and all around the mines with triangles," he said. "They're impenetrable, just the way they were in the killing room with you and Partridge. No flesh can pass; no bullet can break them. As the creator, only my hand can undo them."

"Then do that," I said. "Let me out of this pit so I can make you feel better about yourself."

"Do you think I'm really going to be able to get up and walk over there?" He motioned to the single doorway of the Magnate's chamber with his chin. "But the minute I'm gone, Faust, so goes the power I called on."

"So go the barriers," I said.

I heard the roar of a shotgun. Pellets snarled around us and vanished like a haze against the wall.

I know I could have used the shotgun. The blade, though, felt right. It was meant to happen this close, this brutally, this personally.

And any ammunition I could save would make what was already impossible a little more bearable.

"Elias," he said. "Don't tell anybody about me. Please."

No more time. I wrenched the blade out and heard something crunch. My whole shoulder screamed with pain. I brought down the blade. You'd think it would've been harder. In the darkness I couldn't really see the blood, but I felt it. I hacked again. And then a third time. I kept chopping.

I screamed so I wouldn't hear the noises he made.

You don't kill a man because he asks for it with words. You kill a man because he asks for it with his actions.

When it was done, I stood up. The nervousness faded. I could have been sick, but I didn't have anything to throw up. I buckled on the bandolier with the shotgun and the talon-blade.

Just in time. The shadow that had swooped in ran in my direction. It had a face masked with white and black paint. Skull-like. Hiding golden skin. Behind the figure, a whole swarm of black-robed sand-shades gave chase. A few muzzles flashed.

The Magnate's voice rang out through the cavern.

"Enjoy the breath you have, Elias Faust. It's the last gift I'm giving you."

Throbbing inside my head, and dancing like a surge of electricity along my wrist and palm – right where the Mark blackened my skin – I felt the Shattered Well speak inside me.

RUN, it said.

So I did.

38

I WASN'T GETTING OUT OF THE PLACE WITHOUT FIGHTING. I KNEW THAT. And I was ready for it. As ready as you can be when you're missing two fingers, silver-dollared by lightning, and suffering a brain full of smoke and visions.

The nimble shadow ran straight for me. It planted a hand on the altar and leaped over it. When it landed, it grabbed me and pulled me down behind the cover of the stone table. Another hail of bullets buzzed through the air. We crouched together. Our eyes met.

They blinked. Twice. The way normal eyes blink, then *flick-flack*, sideways.

"Herald," I said.

A bullet screamed against the stone.

"Dead Man," she greeted.

I didn't know how she knew to be here, or how she'd even gotten here. Underneath all the pain, I tapped into some small well of hope. "Snowball's chance in hell," I said. "But hey, nice make-up."

She wiped a summoned knife on her black robe disguise. "I am clever."

"Think we can take a few before we eat dirt?" I said.

She nodded.

"I'll give firing cover as we retreat to the entryway. You take any of them that get close. Funnel them through the doorway. Then we beat peat and find our way to the surface."

Silence.

Good enough for me.

We both leaped up at the same time. I unloaded both barrels over the altar one after the other, a little slower than normal since I had to use my middle finger. There was a wall of sandshades there. Pellets ripped into three in the front, staggering them and spraying sand.

One of them leapfrogged over the others, launching into the air like an eagle. It bounded across the altar and came for us. Nycendera threw her knife underhanded. It clapped into the jumper's forehead and stuck. He spun and fell to his spine on the floor, and the weapon was already back in her hand.

When we were about five yards away from the entryway, two others rushed toward us. The Herald met the one that came for her toe-to-toe, deflecting a talon-blade with her jade knife. With inhuman speed she sidestepped another stab, ducked a slice, then jammed her blade up into the hooded bastard's chin. She smacked the hilt of the blade with her palm, a final *take that*, then wrenched it out.

The one that came for me had lost its hood. The hair was stringy and wet. It had a black hole in its throat that looked like it'd been made by a bullet. A memory nagged me as I took aim...

When the sandshade's two silver eyes were only a few feet away from my barrels, I got a chill.

And I'd seen her get shot before. And die.

Her name was Knox.

The right barrel of my sawed-off boomed. She ducked down just in time. Behind her a sandshade's face blew up into a fleshy mist. I tried to readjust to find her, but she'd vanished back into the crowd. Three more came for us, rippling and black.

Nycendera spun and dove through the entryway. It didn't refuse her. Bisbin's spell had fallen. I kept backpedaling and fired off my other shot. Right before I passed the threshold, I looked down and saw a black triangle drawn on the floor.

I had no problem stepping over it.

Relief distracted me. Another sandshade was in front of me. Before I could reload, he had me by the throat. His fingernails dug into my skin. Blotches of colors started flaring in front of my eyes.

I slammed the handle of the shotgun down on his scalp. It crunched in like a dry sponge. He went at me with his talon-blade, right for my eyes. I wrenched my whole body to the left. I rammed my boot into his stomach and pinned him to the wall. I cracked the barrels of the shotgun open.

No time to reload it. I improvised. I smashed the open breach against his throat then pushed forward to close it. The mechanics weren't forgiving – they bit out a whole chunk from his throat. Sand started spilling out of him.

A flare of blue light from within the cavern caught both of our eyes.

The Magnate had his hands in the air. His thumbs and forefingers touched in a triangle shape, Illemone's Heart between them. A stream of cobalt fire sprayed into the air, jumping over the sand-shades. It dove toward me.

Nycendera grabbed my arm. She pulled me back through the door and out of the cavern. When the fire hit its mark, I wasn't there. The magical flame turned on its closest target and swallowed the throatless sandshade alive. He went up like oil and ran around with his arms flailing.

The flaming robes fluttered off him like burnt paper. When he got near some of the other sandshades, they lunged away. The burning one blindly stumbled into the altar.

Nycendera tugged at me. I shrugged away.

"Wait," I said, sliding two shells into the shotgun.

The Magnate's barrel of magical sand was only a few feet away from the altar. I watched it until the burning sandshade came danger-ously close to it. Then I raised the shotgun and squeezed the back-most trigger. Most of the spray got him. His smoldering arm flopped off. He wailed, then pitched right over against the barrel.

Not sure what kind of minerals were in that sand, or why they were so flammable. But once one grain in the batch had gone up, the rest of them flared. It was almost like black-powder – there was a hot *whoosh* as the heat spread. Then, like a bunch of fireworks, the whole barrel ignited.

In such close quarters, the explosion deafened. A wave of force hammered Nycendera and me to the ground. There was an orange flash, then smoke. Several other sandshades were consumed by the spreading flames. Several chunks of stone started splitting away from the cavern's ceiling and smashed to the floor, crushing several others beneath. A wave of smoke and dust billowed into the corridor.

We turned and fled.

Every time we passed a torch on the wall, the Herald waved a golden hand. The fires died. Leaving darkness behind us meant making it a bitch to be followed. We'd also know where we'd already been.

"You know how to get out of here," I said. "Right?"

The caverns were like the guts of a snake, winding up and down, leaving someone to wonder which way was up. Sometimes the ribs of the rocky caverns got too tight and we had to slide through sideways. When we came to a wide opening, we hugged the opposite walls. The cave beyond was brightly lit, and while it wasn't as elegant as the Magnate's chamber, it sure was a sight. It was the storeroom I'd been escorted through earlier. Bags of grain, kegs of beer and whiskey, sacks of tobacco leaves. Anything you could think of was there.

And it all belonged to Blackpeak.

Tried to keep the whole place from spinning inside my head. My sweat was like ice. I could feel my limbs shaking. My whole body and brain ran off a single desire: the need to live. Nycendera steadied me.

"I ain't dying," I said. "Not yet."

She did not seem convinced.

Behind us, thundering up through the caverns we'd come from, a rumbling like a train shook all through the stone. The odor of burnt flesh and gunmetal blew up through the corridor like it was a funnel.

No time for dying. They were coming.

Panic pinned me to the floor, but just for a second. We could run to the other end, maybe get free, but I didn't know one damn way from the next.

Running will only get you so far, the Magnate said.

We skittered behind a bunch of boxes just as the figures poured into the storage chamber, some running, some floating up like wraiths on the strings of power.

I see what they see. I can sense you, Faust. This is futile, even with your...friend.

I peeked around a box. A skeletal, long-dead face grinned at us from on-high, leveling a Henry rifle at us from twenty feet up.

A cold hum of fear exploded in me. It fired.

A lance of pain shot across my cheek. A bullet snarled into the rock behind me. I fell flat.

The rest of them came pouring in.

A rain of magic and gunfire tore the boxes to splinters. Reeling from the graze, I was slow as hell. Nycendera wasn't, though. She shoved me toward more cover and flapped her golden hand in my direction. A crackling ball of energy splashed against a blurry barrier thrown up between me and a casting sandshade.

Henry already had a bead on us, I was sure. I dove for the nearest cover – a pile of grain-bags that looked like they'd already been riddled with bullets – and dropped flat after I fired Red's shotgun at him. A rifle-round popped into the grain-bag behind my head.

"Harman," Henry shouted. "Scare that scoundrel out so I've got a shot."

A younger shade wielding a pistol obeyed. I heard hammers get pulled back. I hugged my shotgun to my chest, breathing hard.

Footsteps to my left. About to come around the bags...

If I fled, Henry'd have a clear shot, unless—

I leaped up and blindly fired. Don't know if I hit Henry or not, but I only needed a second to distract him. It must have worked because I didn't get shot. The sandshade that had been sent to hunt me down was right there.

"I'm gonna kill you, Faust. You," he said, "and then that Fulton bitch that ended me the first time."

When silver-eyed Harman grinned, I thought I saw pastry-powder on his rotten beard. I swung the sawed-off at him. It cracked off the side of his skull and sent him staggering. Then, without thinking, I leaped for him, grabbed him by the hair, and started trying to choke him with the sawed-off by pulling it back against his neck.

"You think that's gonna do anything, you dumb shit?" he laughed.

"Only what I need it to."

I spun him around and hid behind him. Split-second later would have been too late. Henry let go another shot, but it lanced right into Harman's chest. He jerked in my arms. I pushed him away from me, but before I did, I grabbed him by the cold-skinned hand. I pushed the shotgun against the inside of his elbow and pulled the trigger.

I was left holding his limp arm and the revolver he'd shot at me.

I pried the dead fingers off the revolver.

Then I swung the severed arm left and right like a floppy sausage at the rest of the sandshades, who stared at me like I'd gone absolutely crackers. "*En garde*," I said, which, as far as last words go, were dogshit.

The Well sparked to life in my brain. TRUST HER, it said.

Wasn't bad advice.

"Come on," I said to the group. "Come *on*."

So I hucked the arm at them.

I fired Harman's revolver, unsheathed Red's talon-blade, and took them all on.

Well, not exactly. The sandshades came at me and just overwhelmed me. Their hands burnt with fire and power and I guess out of interest to preserve my skin for the Magnate, they didn't rip me apart instantly. I stabbed and sliced; I fired until the revolver emptied. It was enough time, though. A golden flicker shot through the air above and crumpled Henry in half in a flash of airborne power.

Nycendera tore the crack-shot sandshade apart, stole his Henry, and before she even landed, started firing.

Heads, skulls, and rotten brains blew up in a wild confetti around me. Some collapsed on me while others went for cover – the baby shades among them, still holding onto whatever human instincts for survival they possessed.

I stabbed one right in the cheek and yanked up until its head fell apart into porcelain-like pieces. Scrambling free of them, I started to run, trying to find my bearings. Nycendera bounded down a pile of boxes like a deer. There was another corridor on the other side, leading into other sectors of the old mine. It was our only exit.

Elder sandshades, with their rattier robes, their gray and flaking skin, their yellowing teeth, called terror out of their palms and tossed smoking bolts of power at us that seemed to tear the air in two. Bottles of whiskey blew apart. Grain coughed into the air. A white flash snarled by. Every one of my hairs leaped to attention. My eyes nearly boiled in their sockets.

"Flee or die, Dead Man," the Herald said.

So together, we jumped out from behind crates and barrels. Bullets flew by like leaden bees. Nycendera stopped now and then, set her feet, raised the rifle, and gave off a shot. Even with all that, she still managed to keep up to me. She tossed me a rusty six-shooter.

I fired the revolver twice behind me.

The fact that we kept standing meant we weren't dead.

But luck only favored you so long as it deemed you were worth the effort.

Next to the exiting corridor, I saw a crate that piqued my interest. I slammed my boot into the wooden side. One of the panels came free. Inside were a series of glass jugs with cast-iron tops and handles, each of them filled with a yellowy liquid that sort of looked like piss.

Among goods for trade, tobacco and beer were both fun and necessary. But lamp oil, that was a midnight vanity. And anything flammable was a godsend. "Boom," I told her.

Nycendera's gaze fell to the jug, then me.

"Bring it," she said, and then darted for the nearest exit.

I hugged the jug, as if shielding it with my body would protect it from one slip-up of a well-placed bullet. The supports in the mine-shafts flew past us as we ran. The air was getting damper, heavier. The tunnels narrowed and curved like knotted snakes and the walls gleamed with an ever-running wetness that rubbed the stone smooth and shining. Just as we passed another tunnel, my foot skidded through a streak of mud.

Nycendera, neck bent, examined the low ceiling.

A few drops of water fell from it, clean and crisp. She let one drop fall to her palm. Condensation rolling right off the stones above. Underneath our boots, chewed by what must have been years, was a divot gnawed into the earth, and in it, a tiny stream of water that crawled on the floor toward some unseen destination.

"You know where we're going?" I breathed. "Please, tell me you know where we're going."

Shouts and an errant shotgun-blast roared down through the tunnel behind us.

She licked her palm. Seemed satisfied at the taste, whatever it was she tasted.

"We go," she said.

We tumbled like a pair of kids into the damp offshoot. Our shoulders and elbows smashed against rocks. Their voices rolled behind us in a wild wave.

Right behind us...

When the tunnel opened up like a mouth, first thing I noticed was the cool whiteness of natural light pouring in from a ceiling that only time itself could have carved. This chamber wasn't like the others: no picks or stone-hammers had formed this place. This wasn't work done by dedicated miners, but instead chiseled out by the power of the most patient element.

The cavern's floor might as well have been a smooth mirror. Water, silver as a polished dollar, splashed beneath our feet.

And in the ceiling, perfectly round, was the source of the ambient light.

A hole. Ascending up, toward freedom.

A ladder, all rope and old slats of wood, waited for us.

The Herald jerked her head toward the ladder, shouldered her stolen Henry, and stepped into the corridor. Her first shot lit the whole place up. For just a quick flash, I saw everything.

Including the figure leaning in the darkness, waiting for us.

The body smashed into me and sent me sprawling to the wet floor. Hair like musty seaweed clogged my mouth. The attacker was on me, hammering punch after punch into my jaw. My jug almost slipped from my hands. "Should'a known there'd be somebody waiting for you, Faust," Knox said, her voice coming out of her neck-hole with a wheeze. "You don't know all the tunnels in this place like we do."

She reared back and balled her fist again.

"Hey, Knox," I said.

I swung the kerosene jug up. It whacked her in the skull and tossed her aside. I lumbered to my feet. Nycendera looked back.

"I got it," I gasped. "Just hold them off while I—"

Knox sprang like a jackrabbit, giving me a kick in the gut that threw me several feet back. When she moved, she didn't seem to care much about physics. She ran after me on the tips of her toes. When she got close, she grabbed my head between her hands and blasted death-breath against my cheek.

"Glad I got another chance to meet you," she said. "The first time came to an end so fast."

Her head snapped forward. My nose met her forehead. Blood started pouring down the back of my throat. I swung a fist for her. She caught it, twisted my arm, and drove me to my knees.

Her elbow didn't taste very good when it crashed into my teeth. "I want the sly motherfucker that shot me."

"Cicero? How do you know it was him?"

"Because it wasn't you."

She bent my arm almost to a breaking-point. I crumbled.

"He's...he's in Blackpeak," I gasped. "Dead, for all I know."

My elbow screamed. Her other hand raked at my face, my forehead. "*She* came for you. Why didn't the bald one?"

"What do you fucking want me to tell you," I growled. At her. At the pain. "He's not around here, Knox. He's gone."

Nycendera shot again. Then she shrunk back against the wall, worked the action, and looked at me.

I could have asked the Herald to drop Knox, but I didn't. I actually held up my bloody other hand to her.

"You sure he's dead?" Knox said.

"Last I saw of him, the Magnate had him twisted up in his own personal tumbleweed."

Knox's bulldog face flashed through a whole caravan of thoughts. "Still gonna kill him. Maybe bring him back like me," she said, "then kill him."

"He was doing what I asked him when he shot you," I said.

"His trigger. His finger."

"My command," I said.

"Don't try to reason with me, Faust. You find his ass alive, you tell him I'll find him. You tell him I owe him."

Sure thing, I thought. Telling a dead man that a dead woman was going to come after him. I'd deliver the message with bells on. I half-expected her to pummel me again, but instead, she just let my hair go and stepped back. She grabbed the kerosene jug and hefted it in one arm. Then she swung it high and brought it crashing down to the stone floor. Glass sprayed out in shards. The tinny stink of kerosene filled the little room.

The oil spread across the thin layer of water, casting a rainbow's reflection if the light hit it just right.

"Tell him," she said, pulling a match from her pocket. I remembered right then that she'd been a pretty poor smoker in—...well, in life. "*Tell him.* Even if you tell just a corpse or a coffin, you tell him."

Knox flicked the match with a mossy thumb-nail. Orange light flared between us.

She handed me the match. I took it.

"What about the Magnate?" I asked over a flickering flame.

"I've got more loyalty to my memory of the man who ended my

life than to the greedy prick who gave part of it back to me. Gregdon's a dying name. I serve me."

She pried out one of her silver eyes, and threw it with disgust on the floor.

A moment later, she vanished.

Truth be told, I didn't know what the hell was happening anymore. Like dying and living, I assumed it was best to fall back on simple before my tiny brain decided it'd had too damn much and just fell apart of its own accord.

Today I'd died.

Today I'd come back to life.

I'd seen another world. Two other worlds. I had the coin to prove it.

But I had a match. And kerosene-water. And a ladder.

Nycendera shot again. Another muzzle-flash lit the place up. The smoking cartridge ejected. When she fired again, the trigger just clicked.

A spray of bullets danced into the stony floor right next to her feet.

Time to go.

Nycendera threw the Henry to the ground, darted past me, and leaped with silent grace toward the ladder, her cavalry boots never brushing water. She made it look easy. When she grabbed the ladder, she started hoisting herself toward the light.

I dropped the half-burnt match to the kerosene.

In a blue wave of fire, the whole floor of the cavern burst into flames. The oncoming sandshades froze when they saw the flames.

I jumped for the ladder too. You'd be surprised at how much you need index fingers. Almost didn't even make it. I grabbed a rung and started to slip, but I told myself that I wasn't gonna make it if I complained about things like missing fingers and tired shoulders.

With smoke billowing up beneath us and the oil-fire raging on, I looked up – two-hundred feet up – to what looked like sky.

I took a breath and savored it.

I started to climb.

39

CLIMBING A ROPE LADDER IS HARD ENOUGH NORMALLY, BUT WITH EIGHT fingers, it's a whole new struggle. Being in a rush certainly didn't help matters, with the thing swinging like a drunken bar-brawler and a swath of kerosene smoke rising from below. Daylight beckoned.

It was a manmade hole, augured deep into the earth, but barely the width for a quaint fellow, let alone me. The shaft gave way to sides strengthened by patches of crude brick. The muscles in my shoulders and arms had been torn to shreds. Any second, a bullet or spell from below could have ended it all. But none did. When I got to the top, Nycendera's face appeared above me. She pulled me out.

"Kind of you," I muttered, pouring over the edge of the opening like water. An orange evening sky stretched out like tanned leather from horizon to horizon. A falling sun burned bright, casting the long shadow of a house.

I was outside.

Imagine my surprise when I crawled to my feet and found myself standing outside the abandoned Simpkin farm, staring at the half-crumbling well we'd just crawled up.

Nycendera already set to work, sawing the rope of the ladder where it was tied to the stakes. When it frayed and gave way, she let the tangled mess fall into the tunnel. It vanished below. Still, she had poise and readiness to her. Damned prepared to spring into action.

Tethered not far away from the crumbled well was a horse, a sleek, brown, forgettable creature. Blanketed, impatient, ready to ride. "Yours?" I asked.

"We must go. Time flees," she said. "Town's in danger."

What else was new?

"These mines," I asked. "They extend this far?"

"A spider's web underneath our feet. Miles upon miles."

"How'd you know to find me?"

"You make noise," she said.

Focused, she started for the horse. Me, I lumbered behind her, glancing behind me at the well. Suddenly, it came clear as day: the abandoned Simpkin stead wasn't just the Gregdon Twins' little holiday house, but their back access to the father's network of tunnels and secrets.

Nycendera pulled the reins off the rusted peg and gathered them up. She took to one of the stirrups, tack rattling and squeaking. "Why are you helping me?" I asked.

"Any man with his heart set on the Shattered Well is a far greater threat than any cruelties your town can offer. I am resilient. I will endure."

"I can handle the Magnate if he comes calling. This isn't your fight."

"I am not here for him."

"Then who are you here for?"

She raised a finger at me.

"I owe a debt. I will see it repaid," she said.

"He had a hand in it. In freeing you."

I reckoned as far as conversation went, I was getting the most of what I'd ever get from her. She curled the corner of her lip. "The works of his talent mean less to me than the labor of an honorable heart. I grant you this boon of my blade, and if necessary, my blood. For your town. For your—"

The thunder of a shotgun caught us both unawares.

A rain of pellets ripped through the ragged gray-black folds of Nycendera's stolen hood and robes. Mercurial blood, fine as mist, belched into the air. She dropped off the horse. The beast twisted, swayed, all confused.

I dove for the well. From behind the protection of old stone, I saw the gunman standing like a statue on the edge of the Simpkin porch. A brisk memory played across my brain. I slingshotted back, back, to a hotter day, and to a simpler one. I'd been here before.

Billy Gregdon, cloaked in black, standing dull and silent and powerful, held a smoking shotgun and surveyed his kingdom.

NYCENDERA DIDN'T MOVE. The wind dashed across her but didn't stir her. The horse stirred, flicked its neck. Sure, I could have rushed the Gregdon on the porch, but two details locked me into place.

One, the shotgun.

Two, the burst of sickness that flooded me.

Maybe being down there, among all those shades, I'd grown used to it. Maybe up here, not so much. I could feel those cold, silver, steely eyes boring into me. I peeked back around the well. Dry, dead flesh sat in flecks on his clumpy beard. With a face like a melted candle, he wasn't at all alive – just something sort of close to it.

Elias, came the invasive sigh. *Running isn't like you.*

From the mouth of the Simpkin home, as if he'd lived there all along, walked the Magnate. He patted his son on the shoulder, nudged past him, and held high Illemone's Heart. "I expected a stand-off, or a proposed duel, or even expected some kind of brave, self-sacrificing death more suiting your past escapades. But I suppose all men have their limits."

When shit's already rolling downhill, you learn to stop trying to push it back to the top.

"Billy," said the Magnate. "Throw the marshal his pistol."

The brute did nothing.

"Billy," said the Magnate.

Nothing.

So the Magnate looked in my direction with apology scrawled all over his face. "Newer ones, they're remarkably resistant to encouragement. We're all works in progress, I suppose. *William*."

Whatever spirit was tethered to Billy Gregdon's shredded body must have only then realized what its name was. From his hip he drew a weapon in a twitching and unresponsive grip, then jerked his arm out toward me. One of my Colts landed in the yellow grass.

"Pick up the gun, Elias. I give you permission. Then forget whether your Herald friend is still breathing. Her kind are hardy people. Now come look me face to face like a man with purpose. Billy won't shoot."

"You some kind of bloodhound, sniffing me out?" I asked. "You mind enlightening me how you managed to get up here so quickly?"

"You're remarkably dull for such a smart man, Elias Faust. Don't you remember the lynching? I came to *you*. A little squeeze of Illemone here, and one step of mine can cross a hundred-thousand of yours. Now quit stalling. Pick up that gun."

I was outgunned. We both knew that. I could run again, but luck would have it that without the Quicktooth's blessing, I couldn't run faster than shellshot or spellslinging. "What if I don't want the pistol?"

"Then I put a bullet in you one more time for not dying the way the marshal of a town is duty-bound to. I hope you haven't forgotten about your jurisdiction."

"And the Shattered Well?"

"I've broken rules before. I'll skin you alive, peel that Mark off your flesh, and find a new way while your dead ass bloats under the Texas sun."

I leaned out and wrapped my remaining fingers around the butt of the gun. My pointer-finger stump was a black, burned lump, throbbing with every beat of my heart. It felt good to hold my own gun again.

When I got to my feet, he clamped his fist around Illemone's Heart. I *flew* toward him like a bullet. An unseen hook in my breast dragged me his way. My feet scraped two snaking lines through the dirt. When I struck the stairs of the porch, I rolled over them, smashed in through the ragged front door, and came to a bleeding stop in the foyer of the house.

He liked playing with me. He knew and I knew that with the right application of willpower, he'd grind me to powder. Boots clicked on the floor. "Priorities," said the Magnate. "A marshal needs to live his life by them. Do you remember this game? You played it with Curtis. Get on your feet." The man spoke fire. Spittle foamed on his lips. "Point that gun of yours right at me."

I was only too happy to oblige.

The room spun like a tumbleweed around me. On the ceiling and floors and walls, the triangles – all shapes, all sizes, scattered like kiddie fingerpaint – defaced what seemed like every inch of the world.

The Magnate stood there in his red robes, looking over the rim of his glasses. He gripped Illemone's Heart at his left hip. His nose was just a spattered lump, courtesy of Shakespeare. Billy, the resident skin-carriage, stood beside his father with silent obedience, holding onto his shotgun almost like he didn't know how to use the damn thing.

"I kill you," I said, raising my weapon, "your Billy kills me."

"To clarify: You *try* to kill me, but I shoot you before you make a move. I can almost guarantee I'm a faster draw than you'll ever be, Elias Faust. I've had practice. And when we're done, I invite Billy to rip your friend in half – whether or not she's still alive."

"This is between you and me, Gregdon."

"It won't be anymore. A Herald will be a unique addition. And so will every other senseless lump of skin in this shithole town."

Because if he couldn't have his Well, he might as well make it personal.

Because if he couldn't have his Well, he might as well burn it all down.

Nero, a golden fiddle, and lots and lots of blood.

"Bringing your children back from the grave," I said. "Assembling a group of misfits from the flesh of dead men. No matter what lengths you go to, you'll still be a big fish in a little pond, Magnate. What you've done is inhumane. Unnatural."

"Laws no longer hold importance to me."

"You could have strangled me with magic," I said. "Abracadabra'ed my brains into mush."

"That would be fun, but certainly not as satisfying. I haven't shot a man in years. I think you're a good opportunity to reintroduce myself to all of the fun I've missed."

Billy Gregdon drew back both of the hammers on his long shotgun and held it to the side. I flinched. Turned my pistol toward him. We met eyes. I snaked my middle finger up inside the triggerguard.

"Antsy," said the Magnate. "Too jumpy. You just need to relax, Elias."

I was slow, that's for sure. My senses were dulled from the drugs. My timing hadn't been on for what seemed like years. Just as I turned my eyes back to Gregdon, his red cloak flapped aside. I watched him move like a professional. He drew his pistol, faster than you'd think a cheetah could move. Shoulders forward, but not beyond his hips. Interested. Ready to play. On his terms, of course.

He never intended for me to have a chance.

His left hand raked across the flintlock's hammer the minute the barrel cleared leather.

It was Rufus Oarsdale's flintlock. The one Bisbin fished off my body.

A hot tongue of fire flashed out of the flintlock. Smoke filled the room.

The Magnate shot me right in the stomach.

My back crashed into the wall. I sunk down to the floor. My guts twisted around the hole that had been blown in me. For a minute I was somewhere else, my brain swimming to hold on.

Well, that was that. Round two, I suppose. You only get so many chances to bounce back. I'd had a lot. Sometimes you just don't get them.

I crumbled to the floor. Blood was everywhere. I pressed my palms against my stomach. It felt like trying to keep water in a broken bucket.

The Magnate took the long shotgun from his sandshade son and came up to me. He held my chin up on the edge of the barrels. He crouched in front of me. "Too slow," he said.

"Wasn't...one of my better days."

"Think of it as revenge for bringing Shakespeare into this." He tapped his nose. "I guess you're dead, Elias."

"Just about."

"It's a shame. You would have been the first one I'd ever converted alive. But now I suppose we get to watch your Blackpeak burn together in the distance as you bleed out in front of me."

I was surprised to be still holding onto my pistol. I raised it up and pressed it against the Magnate's forehead. Billy made some kind of grunting sound and strode forward.

"Stay, Billy. Let the marshal have his revenge."

"Eat shit," I said.

I pulled the trigger.

Nothing happened. Not a click, not a blast, not a jerk of the gun.

"Don't you see?" Daddy Gregdon just plucked the Colt from my fingers and threw it out one of the shattered windows. "What I will to happen becomes real. That gun refused to work because I willed it so."

"With her?" I said, nodding toward Illemone's Heart. "With your stolen power?"

"Have a deft hand at them like mine, and the fantastic is limitless. In this case, I just unloaded it before I gave it to you. Stacking the deck is still playing poker." He leaned forward and whispered in my ear. "Doesn't it bother you to lose?"

Every muscle in my face tightened against the pain. I clenched shut my eyes. I reached out for the Shattered Well, but found silence.

The Magnate lifted up my jittering, spasming hand, soaked in blood, and wiped Bisbin's blood and my blood away from the Mark under my skin. Then, with a knife, he pierced my skin. Began to fillet me like a fish. Redness ran free. Spilling out.

The pain was there. I just couldn't feel it.

I sucked in a few breaths. Then I rolled my head back and looked at the ceiling, at the walls, where there were triangles painted all around the place in old blood and coal. Some of them were incomplete, but most of them were well-drawn, very specific and precise, like they almost had an artist's touch.

I thought about the pain.

With what I could swear was going to be my last breath, I said to Gregdon with a smile, "I might have reminded you of some of your old tricks," I said, "but you taught me new ones."

I jabbed my remaining fingers into the damaged gun-shot hole ripped in my stomach. I grabbed the hole and pulled, squeezed, tore until I felt the skin rip like fabric. This time, I was in control of the pain. I knew it was there, so I brought it to the surface until I screamed.

I pulled it out of myself with invisible hands.

Pulled it out of my broken stomach.

Ripped it out of my forearm, where, like a sloppy surgeon, he cut in greed.

I didn't stare at him as I did so, but up at the ceiling, at all the triangles I'd seen the first time I'd ever come to the Simpkin farm to encounter Billy and Curtis Gregdon.

Just like the Magnate taught me, I launched my pain like a hot, invisible ball of emotion toward the triangles.

I thought about destruction. Dreamed about chaos. Thought about those triangles spitting fire and brimstone. I willed my fury and agony into them. I fucking screamed.

I believed in strength. I believed in something like miracles, but this one was an evil kind of miracle. Just wanted to balance the odds, then tip them a little bit in my favor. But I guess you think about that kind of shit enough, it starts getting otherworldly, starts making you believe in the impossible...

I was desperate. I was sure.

I'd done this before.

I unleashed the triangles.

One by one, like a whole posse of gun-toting madmen were outside of the Simpkin farm, the triangles started blowing inward, spraying rotten chunks of wood. The wallpaper tore apart. I could start seeing sunlight coming in through the holes. The whole room started to shake.

But I knew it wasn't just the room. It was the whole shebang.

The triangles painted on the rafters above started popping. Whole fistfuls of the supports came raining down. The Magnate stumbled along the quaking floor. Billy, too. Gregdon dropped the shotgun, but he scrambled for it.

I realized there wasn't any reason to ignore the pain. Against every ripped muscle and wound, I stood. Entire time, I thought about those triangles. I snatched the shotgun out of Gregdon's reach.

Billy came diving for me, but I blew him in half before he got there. Sand sprayed all over me. He fell apart like a ruined old doll, split in two. With a sound like old cracking bones, one of the beams broke free of the ceiling. It smashed down to the floor only a few feet away. The building shifted. It was starting to buckle. The walls cried.

The Magnate pitched forward. In desperate need for balance, he fell to his knees.

Illemone's Heart, like a fallen gem, slipped out of his fingers. Bounced, *clack-clack-clack*, across the floorboards.

On a whim, I reached my free hand out.

The gilded locust-thorn could have just kept rolling toward the wall, but it had other plans. So by some miracle – and I knew, I *knew* it was because I reached out – Illemone's Heart, gold and shining and covered in the blood of fallible men, shot through the air and landed in my palm.

"Gregdon," I shouted, turning the shotgun toward him.

In his hands he molded some kind of fireball, like he'd just pulled it out of midair. The last threads of whatever power of Illemone's he still had...

"Give her to me," he boomed, eyes bulging, spit spilling free from his mouth. *"Give her to me, Faust!"*

I twisted my middle finger around the other trigger and let him have the shotgun's remaining barrel just as the swirling fist of flame and force pounded me in the chin. It lifted me up in the air, knocked me back into the wall, and set me aflame.

The brittle wood of the wall's panels buckled behind me. I flew out of the Simpkin house as a burning man. My spine smashed into the porch-railing. I flipped over it, ass-over-teakettle, and pounded into the earth. Inside, the Magnate let out a wet, guttural scream.

The walls gave out a final moan. The top floor of the farmhouse became too much of a burden for its brutalized belly to handle. The structure imploded, spilling onto its own guts. A plume of dust and dirt belched into the air.

I didn't hear the Magnate anymore.

Maybe I was burning. Maybe I wasn't. The sunlight beat down on my face and scorched me like I deserved it. The vision of thousands of little triangles, scalded into my brain, blinded me.

Priorities, I thought, before I went numb.

Yeah, I had a sense of those.

40

BEING DRAGGED BY MY ARMS. THE WORLD FLICKERED IN AND OUT IN front of me. Somewhere, I'd lost my vision, but it wasn't that I'd gone blind.

It was that my eyes weren't mine any longer.

A hardwood floor covered with mushed-up peas and crushed red potatoes. An overturned table. Good dishware was just a thousand little white pieces broken all around.

A man kneeled on the floor, his hands tied behind his back. Lots of black dirt under his fingernails spoke of a hard day's work. Name came to me like a feeling, an instinct, like he was a part of one of my own memories. Galbreth Simpkin. Crop farmer. One wife – Alberta Simpkin. Two young girls, Nell and Maddy Simpkin. Hard-working family, cut from fine stock, loved the Lord, toiled hard to make a fortune out of a tiny chunk of land – this land – in the Midwest.

Good people. Knew them as well as if they'd been stitched into my heart.

When was this going to stop. This fiddling in my brain. This weaving realities in the meat that drove my limbs, my feelings, my soul.

Somebody had a gun held to the front of the man's head. The gunman was a blur. Alberta and the two girls – one of them, Nell, was probably nine

or ten, Maddy about fourteen, fifteen – were kneeling too, blindfolded. Big
blotches of tears wet the burlap over their eyes.

I knew the boy with the gun.

I'd killed him. Twice.

I tried to move, but couldn't. Couldn't talk, couldn't change anything,
like I was reading an awful book I couldn't put down. I was trapped behind
wallpaper, held hostage.

"There's nothing you need on our property, William," said Galbreth
Simpkin. "You can see it for yourself, can't you? No crops are growing. The
earth's as fertile as sand and as wet as ash."

"It's about what's under the soil." Billy Gregdon angled the barrel of his
revolver down to the floorboards. "Few hundred feet below is something my
father's got some interest in. Ain't that right, Curtis."

"S'right," Curtis said. While his brother did the dirty work, he was
scraping black triangles onto the wallpaper with a fat piece of coal.

"My family and I, what is it you want with us, William?"

"We're taking your land."

"Your father and I go back a long way, William. I'm willing to listen to
whatever he might have to—"

Billy silenced him with a flat hand. "There ain't no niceties here."

"My daughters are afraid. Maddy's slow, William. She doesn't under-
stand what this all means, why you're here scaring her father, her mother,
her sister. Put down the gun and we can discuss this calmly."

Billy aimed the gun at the two girls.

Somewhere outside the vision, my body got tossed like a sack of
meal. Hooves pounded the sand. I tried to stir myself out of it, but the
scene knitted itself like a blanket before my eyes. One I couldn't shake
or pull away...

"Please," said Galbreth.

"Which one's the idiot," said Billy.

"We can work this out, William, between your father and I. We can
work this out."

Billy blew out a breath. He tromped over to Alberta and the girls,
crouched in front of them. He put the cold steel of the gun on the little one's

cheek. She flinched, made a little sound, looked around frantically as if she'd be able to see around the blindfold.

"You got a name, kid," said Billy. "Don't'cha?"

She leaned away from the gun. Alberta started breathing in little gasps.

"Yes, sir," said the girl. "I'm Nell."

"You do arithmetic and all? You read poetry?"

She nodded.

"And your sister, is she an idiot, Nell?"

"Father says the Lord gave her less than the rest of us, so it means we have to do just a little bit extra."

"You scared of this gun, Nell?"

"I'd like to finish dinner, sir."

"Poetry's for damn fools. Your Papa tell you that?" He jabbed the gun against her forehead. "You tell her, Simpkin. You tell this girl words and rhymes, they're for dumbfucks and dipshits."

If I could've moved, I would have done anything for her. Would have smashed his skull into the floor.

Galbreth started trying to scramble to his feet. "William, you sick bastard, you get that gun out of my girls' faces before I—"

The horse was riding fast and hard. Woodsmoke clogged my nostrils. But I didn't want to go back there, not to reality, not yet.

Billy stood. He raised the gun a few inches from Maddy's blonde head.

And then, carelessly, he fired, and—

God, I'd never wanted to kill a man more than twice.

The teenager's body rolled back, collapsing with one elbow in a lump of spilled yams. Thick, black shoes stuck up in the air from under her skirt. Her right knee bent, unbent, bent again, before she went flat.

"Jesus," Curtis said. "Jesus."

"You see what happens when you act out of line, Simpkin?" said Billy as Nell blindly howled and Alberta crumpled over. The murderous kid's eyes were on fire as he shoved the gun at Nell's little brown-haired head. "You could have made it simple, old man," said Billy, cocking his pistol, "but you didn't, and my old man, he'll tear the thoughts of you right out of Blackpeak's mind so they never know about this. So they never know you ever lived in the first place."

Billy flinched. The gun barked. Nell fell still. The mouth of the gun adjusted. Alberta made a sound like a blatting sheep. Gregdon reworked the hammer. Another blast. Alberta fell over on her two daughters and never moved again.

Galbreth never made it to Billy. He dropped down to his knees, his hands held out before him like he could just pick the pieces of the world up again. His mouth dropped open, noises that weren't words scratching in his throat.

"Curtis," Billy said, leveling his gun at Galbreth Simpkin's forehead. Curtis forced steady breaths as he stared at the slaughter. "I want to cover this place in triangles. I don't want to stop until the walls are covered, until there's no more ink left. I want to leave our mark, for you and me." He walked around behind the kneeling Galbreth, whose eyes were locked on his family. "For the Magnate and the Gregdon name. Our spot. Our world. Our future."

"We don't have any ink, Billy. I just brought coal—"

Billy crammed the revolver into the back of Galbreth's head.

"When this Well belongs to the Magnate, it'll all be forgiven. We'll have done the right thing, and this place will be a monument to it all.

"Use their blood," said Billy Gregdon, "and draw triangles until there's nothing left to draw with."

Galbreth Simpkin died with his family. I watched.

God, I watched.

HATE IS a poor man's emotion. Take away a man's belongings, a man's family, even a man's soul, and what he's got left is that little walnut in his heart: that too-hard bit of hate that drives him to breathe, to take another step, to go to the edges of the earth just to soothe that burning coal inside him. Hate is a poor man's emotion, and while it doesn't need to squeeze a man's wallet dry, it'll wring him out like a rag. Right then, with my mind lingering in some folded pocket of space, watching a family die, I knew hate. It carved itself into my bones.

Give me one wish, and I'd ask right then to bring him back. To bring back Billy Gregdon, so I could pry my fingers into his cheeks and rip him in two. Tear him to ribbons. For what he did to people I didn't even know. For the simple things he had the capacity to do, and the nerve to stay alive after doing them.

IT IS A DESIRE WHICH CAN BE GRANTED, said the Shattered Well.

Galloping. Up and down, up and down, like a body on a wild sea. Vision faded back into my eyes.

I was slung, like cargo, across a horse's backside.

Nycendera heeled the brown beast like a bullet toward the streak of Blackpeak on the horizon. She'd shed her black cloak. The shot from Gregdon's weapon had ripped a wild galaxy of metal skin off her back and shoulder, and some off her neck, but still, she gleamed gold. What was left of her right ear sagged like wet fudge.

"You...you *alive*, Skullface?" I asked.

"Should I be dead?"

"Shotgun's a shotgun," I said.

"Stop talking," she commanded. "Do not allow stupid words to be your last."

And it was a good time to revel in silent amazement at the fact that I was, mostly, still alive. There was a lot of blood, but that was to be expected. Don't get much done without a lot of bleeding. Good to feel accomplished.

We crashed into the town like a wave, but it was already a shambles. As the light of a new day streamed across the ground, I smelled powder and fire and blood. There were gunshots, too. The popping gunblasts had a heartbeat rhythm. Woodsmoke was in the air, but I knew it didn't come from a hearth-fire. It was death-smoke. *Town's-on-fire,-get-your-ass-in-your-hand-and-run* kind of smoke.

Welcome home, Elias Faust.

I suppose it's not worth the time retelling how it all was when me and Nycendera flew into the town's limits. The Magnate's sandshades were destroying everything they could reach: popping shots at innocent folks, calling down their flashes of thunder, and setting fire to pretty much every damn thing they could.

In front of us, with Blackpeak burning like Hell itself had jumped up to eat it, there wasn't much left to do but bring these shades to meet their maker.

Die and sleep, or live and oppose.

You can imagine which one seemed like a better option.

Nycendera, painted up with her crude skull disguise, took an arrow, then threw me to the ground off her dying horse. She killed some. I killed some. You remember...

But it wasn't enough. There were so *many* of them.

There was no time wasted on trophies of flesh or blood. The mass of them was a machine, powered solely for the swift destruction of everything that flickered in front of their eyes.

We'd be next.

The thunderous crowd came closer. I didn't hear so many people screaming anymore. Made me think most of them was dead.

Nycendera sifted through the dirt. When she found what she wanted, she lifted it up and showed it to me.

"Did it speak to you," she snarled, her English rolling out with all its sharp edges and crude angles. "Tell me. Tell me now."

It was a rock, about the size of a fist. Round. Just the right size to—

"The Shattered Well. Did you hear its voice?"

With fading strength, I lifted my hand.

I clenched my fist. Around Illemone's Heart.

And showed her the risen lump of blackness that had started, since I'd taken a bullet to the mouth, its slow crawl up the skin of my wrist.

The Mark. My Mark.

She raised her arm, gritted her teeth, and swung the stone down at my face.

What a prick.

I fired, mostly on instinct, right from the hip. I felt the Colt jerk, but I never saw what happened. I got clobbered in the forehead with the stone anyway. I was thrown into a black sea and floated further and further away. The cold sensation of wood and metal in my hand started to vanish.

I don't remember my head hitting the ground.

I don't know if my shot landed—

—right where I wanted it to, but I *do* remember seeing the sand-shade behind Nycendera stumble back, its face hanging open like an old torn boot where my bullet had cut it right in half.

I tip-toed that line again. The line between life and death. That edge where I could have just fallen forward into darkness and turned to look back at life as I fell away from it. Slingshotted forward into that bleak place, it was only a tug at my heel that kept me from plummeting all the way in.

NO, the Well said. NOT YET.

Then Nycendera's voice broke through the veil of death.

"You are one of the Magnate's children, now."

I'd survived a goddamn bullet; I'd survived two. Hell, at this point, I'd survived three. No way I was planning to let a rock push me that final few inches into the afterlife...

I think the Herald knew that, too.

"Whether or not you want to be, he gave you a particle of knowledge."

But I hadn't wanted it. I didn't ask for it.

"It's yours to use as you see fit."

Triangles began to emerge in front of my eyes, dragging me from unconsciousness. Glowing, brilliant, silvery, beautiful.

"Yours to use as you deem necessary. So use it. *Use it.*"

A firepit of agony exploded in my brain. A delayed reaction.

New pain.

What I remembered next was being on my feet, screaming, *screaming*, and witnessing a world around me that moved with agonizing slowness. I balanced somewhere between this world and what felt like ten others: that of the Shattered Well, Xa'anshanger-rad's white abyss, and that of death, the longest dirt nap, the final sleep...

The Shattered Well slipped me back into my boots, stood me up, brushed me off.

DESTROY THEM ALL.

A town on fire. Sandshades dashing and slashing through buildings and people. I cast my hand out at one of them, and wild power filtered through my veins: I shot it, not with bullets, but with invisible force, and it disintegrated, just wind and ash. Another on the top of the livery caught my attention, and I slung my finger in its direction. A faint feather of power connected us for just a split-second before its body simply fell in half. Sand rained to the Blackpeak town square.

All around me, drawn out from my own pain, silver triangles floated in the air, unseen to anyone except me. And they were all mine to channel, to tear in half, to rip asunder...

In the center of the town, a mangled tree – it had never been there before – stood, leafless and half-alive, a mouth-sized knot in its trunk open in a silent scream.

I threw my will at it.

The bark exploded, shredding another sandshade nearby. Out of the crumbling branches, Miss Lachrimé Garland fell to her knees, gasping for breath. She tugged her skirts out from around unnatural roots. A sandshade fell on her, talon-blade winking.

Without missing a beat, her little pistol found its voice. *Pop, pop.* "Elias Faust," she shouted. "Well, I'll be *damned.*"

HIS WORK WAS FRAGILE. IT IS YOURS TO UNMAKE.

Sandshades poured out of the alleyways, more and more of them. Nycendera, despite the arrow in her shoulder, came forward to slice her way through them. They fell apart around her. Miss Garland tangled with another, and its talon-blade leaped out for her, dipping for her mouth.

I couldn't get there in time.

"Lookit *may*, y' ugly sumbitch!"

From behind the sandshade, Peggy Winters's interlaced fists crashed down across its hooded skull. She grabbed it with her brute hands, and literally tore the creature like a rotten old dress. I grinned; God, I couldn't help but grin like a goddamn maniac.

I ran. I don't know toward what. I don't know why. Or I did, but I didn't realize it until my feet took me across the square. Another sandshade rushed toward me. "Come on," I roared, and took bead on its bulbous brow. "Come *on*, and try it, you damn hatrack."

Its teeth pulled apart. A black tongue emerged.

"You can't kill all of us," it teased.

Then it shouldered a shotgun and took aim.

I was quick enough. Just barely.

I rushed the sandshade. I checked the barrel with my shoulder from underneath just as it discharged. The world went silent for just a moment. I rammed my knee into the cold flap of its stomach, then pushed it back to the stairs of the Crooked Cocoon and leveled my pistol.

When Nabby Lawson came flying out from the saloon's doors with a fire-iron raised above her head, neither me nor the sandshade really expected it. So it took us by surprise. Me, mostly. Because the cast-iron hook fell across its nose from above and blasted the sandshade's face into powder, and I don't think much else surprised it ever again after that.

"Cissy," she barked.

"Excuse me?"

"Cissy!"

And she pointed with the fire-poker toward a massive, man-sized bundle of thorns and branches thrown up like some dried hairball against the lattice of the Crooked Cocoon's porch. Shit. It came back to me: Grady Cicero's thorn prison. With the remnants of the concussive pain still rocking around inside my head, I caught a glimpse of the thin threads of silvery power still binding the vines together.

I cut them apart with a frantic slice of my left hand, peeling the remnants of the Magnate's power away like the skin of a fruit.

Cicero crawled out a moment later. A bloody and punctured mess, he emerged from the thorny husk, staring at the world with confused and frightened eyes. He still had his Yellowboy cradled in his arms. Elation filled me up like good whiskey. I kicked his fallen bowler toward him. "You dropped something."

"You," he gasped, "look like shit."

"Charmed," I said.

"Down," he snapped.

Just as I squatted, Cicero slipped a round from his belt, racked it into the Yellowboy, took aim where I'd been standing, and blew a hole into a sandshade's throat. It pitched over me, flailing and howling.

ENDING THIS PROBLEM WITH MAIN FORCE, the Well said, WILL BE A FRUITLESS TASK.

"How many of these are there?" Cicero asked.

"Too many to count," I heard Miss Garland shout.

I crushed my heel down on the sandshade's head. "The Magnate was a busy man."

"He dead?"

"Close enough," I said.

"Precision work, as usual," Cicero said.

Pop, pop, pop.

A rain of bullets began to splash across the ground near us. I threw Cicero behind a stack of crates outside the saloon. Bullets snapped across the other side of our flimsy cover. Ducking my head, I said, "It doesn't make any sense."

"I abandoned sense a long time ago," Cicero said, "just about the time I wandered into this fucked up town. Hey, Nabby!"

"The hell you want," she said, squatting around the other side of the porch.

"Good to see you. After this wildness—" Two more gunshots tried for us, "—you want to celebrate?"

"Maybe they'll have lucky aim and save me from that fate," she said.

Cicero grinned at me. "Women." Then he popped up, got a glance, and fell back down. "Up on top of Levinworth's place. Two of them, taking as many pot-shots as they can."

"Think you can knock them off?"

"Eh," he said. "One round left."

It was, I realized, just a matter of holding out our hands against a tidal wave. With every sandshade that fell to the ground, two or three more emerged. Unfazed by the ringing gunshots from above, Peggy Winters continued to swing her wild arms, knocking them aside like tiny twigs, while Miss Garland fought off a sandshade's swiping fingers and jabbed a stolen talon-blade five, six, seven, ten times, into its guts. Then she threw the body into the wreckage of a burning building and watched as it went up like a flash.

But this wasn't right. It didn't fit the rules. Sure, not much fit the rules, but the brain couldn't help but try to piece together some logic.

"They shouldn't be alive," I told Cicero. "Power's supposed to fade when the wielder dies. Saw it with my own eyes when I killed—" *Bisbin...* "—one of the Magnate's men. So why aren't the shades falling to pieces?"

"You sure the Magnate's snuffed out?"

"Damn sure."

Cicero narrowed his eyes at me.

"Have faith," I said. "I pulled a whole damn building down on the bastard."

Nabby Lawson knocked another sandshade with her cast-iron poker. The moment I saw the crown of its skull, I took aim. It fell motionless.

The Shattered Well was right: they'd overrun us without much effort, and I imagine with enough time and stubbornness, they'd become more numerous and our ammo would become far too scarce. If destruction was the aim, I wondered, as another round flashed over my head and blasted one of Poindexter's windows out, then *how*?

I only had a few minutes. I lowered a trembling hand down to my belly to feel my gunshot wound.

My palm fell across a slight pudge of exposed skin.

I jammed my finger into my navel.

That was the *only* hole there.

What greeted my four fingers was the plane of my belly, completely unscathed from the Magnate's shot. The skin was as fresh as a babe's, and not even scarred.

I almost felt the Shattered Well smile.

ASSURING YOUR SURVIVAL IS OF MUTUAL BENEFIT.

"This is your doing?"

A TEMPORARY ACCOMMODATION.

Cicero snapped his fingers in front of my face. "You still with me, Marshal?"

CONSIDER IT POWER BORROWED. TO ENSURE BALANCE.

Balance.

And blood.

Playing proverbial mumbly-peg with powers far greater than I could ever be had already lost me two fingers and netted me an almost incalculable series of aches and pains. Whatever costs I'd owe when this was done, I didn't have time to consider. Not when I looked up and saw a stream of sandshades spilling into the Horseshoe Junction Inn and saw the flash of gunshots and wildfire.

Which is when it hit me. Like a damn brick tossed off the top of the building.

Why the sandshades still lived.

Why they hadn't simply fallen apart with the Magnate's demise.

"I need to run," I said to Cicero, preparing to sprint. "I've got an idea."

"Few words strike more fear in my heart."

"Your crack-shot all prepped and polished?"

"I won't miss," he said, "just as long as I know the target."

I nodded. Then I told myself something I hadn't told myself in quite awhile.

Breathe.

I ran, faster than I've ever run in my life, until my lungs howled in protest and the world exploded in tiny blurs in front of my vision. Near one of the alleys, I saw Emp trading blows with a sandshade. I could have stopped to help, too, if the target of my attention wasn't so close, laying in the sand...

Right next to Nycendera's wounded horse.

Illemone's Heart, winking in the morning sun.

Because it wasn't the Magnate's power at all that had given birth to the sandshades. It had never been his to begin with. He'd only been the channel for it, the living saddlebags of something else's influence.

Power borrowed. From the creature he thought he loved.

I plucked the gilded locust-thorn from the soil. The sandshades above the livery got a bead on me.

"Cicero," I shouted.

I threw Illemone's Heart up into the air above Blackpeak. It tumbled and gleamed.

A glint. The flank of the Yellowboy across the way. Cicero, cheek to the rifle-butt, followed his target.

Crack.

Illemone's Heart, as if jumping, leaped even higher. A ricocheting bullet whistled off past my ear. I expected those few moments to be my last: both of the sandshades wouldn't have had a problem finding my brainpan, and while I wondered if bullets travelled faster than murdered magic.

But their shots never found me.

A slobbering mass bounded with glee *up* the side of the livery. It leaped across the siding, to the awning, then up, up, until...

A bestial snarl ripped the air. A greeting. Then yellow jaws opened, snapped.

Spitjaw.

The second sandshade reared around to aim at the four-legged intruder attacking its friend, but lurched forward as another dog-like figure leaped on it, and together, my companion Constantpaw and the sandshade fell two stories to the street.

I don't know what it was that I expected. Maybe, with Cicero's successful shot, some kind of pressure relieved from the air, enough that those black-clad figures popped like blisters in the sunlight.

It didn't happen that way, though. In fact, nothing at *all* happened.

Shot out of the air, Illemone's Heart rolled harmlessly across the sand of Blackpeak's square, and landed right between my feet.

Completely unharmed.

Fully intact.

Shit.

Out of my peripheral vision, I watched as a sandshade dragged Nabby Lawson, her skirts torn and her boots flailing, into the street. Poindexter rushed it from behind, but caught a hammer of invisible force in the chin and flew back through the front doors of the Crooked Cocoon.

In desperation, I pulled my Colt, and unloaded the last few rounds right down at Illemone's Heart. It jerked, rolled, spun, but never suffered a blemish or a scrape.

The sandshades darkened the day. Blackpeak's defenses started breaking. A crowd of sandshades split Miss Lachrimé Garland and Peggy Winters apart, and a whole crew of shadows dragged the powerful fistfighter down into their midst. Miss Garland cursed at them, spit at them, tore at them with her hands. A cracking flash of thunder-and-lightning caught her in the chest. She crumbled near the town hall's grand black door.

It had all been worth a shot. Just hadn't been good enough.

One of the buildings came pouring down like liquid as all of its supports crumbled into ash and fire. Emp stumbled away from it, firing both of his pistols blindly at the sandshades bearing down on him. They took the bullets, jerking, flinching the whole way, but swarmed him, dragging him down to the earth.

Fewer and fewer people stood upright anymore. Even Cicero was up Shit Creek: he swung his empty Yellowboy at the nearest sand-shades. "Give me a fight, you *fucks*," he demanded, knocking a sawed-off shotgun out of one of their hands while another simply shuffled in, raised its gnarled fingers, and began to spit out a string of words.

Cicero dropped the rifle. He collapsed to his knees, eyes bulging, throat twisting in invisible hands.

IS THIS ALL YOU HAVE?

Three sandshades grabbed Nycendera by her head. They drove her to the soil. Too many of them.

"We aren't built for this. We tried."

They straddled her. One pulled a knife from its rotten boot.

AND YOU ARE SATISFIED WITH THIS?

"I'm tired," I said. "We all are."

The Shattered Well surged with displeasure at that response.

Fuck it.

Constantpaw put up a better fight than most. She howled, bit, snapped, swiped, but I heard a yelp as a gun discharged. The stink of burnt hair came floating through the air.

A talon-blade scraped against Nycendera's throat. She had nothing left.

Peggy Winters's cursing voice fell quiet.

I didn't think watching a town die was going to be so easy.

I had no means to change it – my veins had been milked dry of their temporary power, and no more triangles winked in front of my vision. I just sunk to my knees, waiting for Blackpeak to fall in around me. Nobody would remember these people, and even less would know exactly how they perished. History books don't catalogue horrors like these. Those, they reserve for tall tales, for gossip and rumor, all of which fall into obscurity at some point or another.

With Illemone's Heart between my knees and a sea of black-cowled sandshades turning their attention to me, I saw death...

...and on the black doors of the Blackpeak town hall, I saw a familiar jade knife, still stuck there, long forgotten.

Which is when Xa'anshangerrad's words poured into me from several hours before.

Even powerful spellcraft, when stretched too thin, promises to shatter like glass under the fist of any other magic turned against it.

My face went cold. My body followed suit.

If a bullet couldn't do the work...

"Lachrimé," I called out. "The knife. Get the knife. From the door!"

Her dress smoking, she reached for the handle, and with a tug, wrenched it from the wood. She threw it into the street. It tumbled, still fifty yards away.

But it landed at Cicero's feet. Even with his throat being crushed by the sandshades' power, the hard-headed bastard gritted his teeth, reached for the blade, and swiped his hand at it. It bounced end-over-end toward me, a little closer, before his final breath came whistling out of him.

Even with a hellish pile of bodies on top of her, Peggy Winters managed to crawl, covered in blood, the few feet toward the knife. With what must have been a legion of sandshades on her back, she grabbed it.

She threw it, too.

It *was* Nycendera's power, that blade, embodied and persistent, so when it skittered by her, instead of grabbing at the sandshade about to slit her throat, she pushed her palms at the air and blew the knife toward me with a last inkling of colorless, immaterial force...

It stuck into the ground ten yards away.

Dumb as an ox, Rat the coyote emerged from a mass of shades, loped up to the knife, and locked his jaws around the handle. Then, easy-as-you-please, just as every sandshade in Blackpeak seemed to collapse in on me, with their ripping hands and their knives and their guns and their reality-bending spells, it was Rat that dropped the magical knife against my knee and waited patiently for praise.

I took it up. I raised it in the air. I screamed.

Something else cried out in agony from across worlds.

Illuminated before me, imposed on a spiritual layer of the world, I envisioned the hundreds of golden tentacles lashing and snapping, connecting those brokered souls to this object, to this place. Anchoring them to their bodies. Tethering them to Illemone's power.

They tore the town apart. Tore my friends apart. Tore me apart.

I stabbed Illemone's Heart.

The magical blade broke Illemone's Heart into a thousand pieces. A flash of green blinded me, seared me like a flash of lightning—

Then everything went quiet.

NOW

WHEN I FINISH SPEAKING, HE HOLDS AN EMPTY CRYSTAL VIAL, HARDLY THE size of a finger. He stares at me through it with one of his thirteen eyes. "Doesn't it ever fascinate you, how fragile it all is? Just a few pounds of meat, some sparks of inspiration and thought. Everything you are hinges on the health of that nugget of fool's gold floating in your skull-water."

"It does its job best it can," I say.

"But does it?"

You think about that kind of frailty too much, it ruins you. One good bullet could slice through every happiness you've ever known. Take a bad fall off the saddle, and you might as well be busted fruit.

I tug at the thorn-shackles. Blood seeps free.

His voice dares a new kind of tone. Sympathy. "You really don't know, do you," he says.

"I know what I know."

A surge of pain sparks in one of my left hand's fingers. I glance down, only to feel a pinch of agony as my fingernail peels up out of its base, and from beneath it, a bulging, too-fat voidworm with skin like a wrinkled sock crawls free.

Thirteen plucks it up. He crushes it inside his fist until its innards blow out like curdled cheese between his knuckles.

Inside me, the other voidworms howl in pain.

"I can't blame you, Elias Faust. Or the tenderness of your mind. But what you've forgotten is how much you've forgotten. No weapon wields the sheer destructive capacity of a man given too much free rein. The Magnate was clumsy. Too much meddling, too little finesse. Murderers always leave blood," Thirteen says, "whether on the floor, or in the mind. The worms just follow the trail..."

He squeezes the juices from the voidworm into the vial. It fills with a putrid yellow. He shakes the fluid inside. It glows like crushed fireflies. Inside my head, a spark ignites: an uncanny recognition, like seeing your own smile on the face of a distant relative. Something mine, but belonging to someone else...

"What makes you think that when he stole Blackpeak's memory of him," Thirteen asks, leaning forward to place the vial into my palm, "he wouldn't do the same to you?"

The vines unwind from around my bloody wrist. I stare down at the vial. My blood becomes ice. It hits me. The realization.

"Is this mine?" I ask.

"It's what I could find. Even broken memories leave debris."

I stare at truth. A mind is a mind is a mind, as vulnerable as a newborn fawn.

The Magnate had done it to others. Which meant he'd done it to me.

"Why dig out this," I say, "and not whatever you want to find out about the Well?"

"You have to want to give me the Well."

"Why would I?"

"Because of all the beings you've ever met," Thirteen tells me, "I'm the one you can trust the most."

I pry the cork free with my thumb. It falls between my feet.

When I breathe, the liquid shimmies up the inner confines of the crystal, as if crawling through the air toward my tongue...

I drink it, not because I want to, but because I have to. It tastes like sunshine, like sweat, like—

—whiskey, clear as urine, in a tiny glass in my hand, and I wonder if I'm supposed to drink it or just stare at it, because (the pieces fall into *place like words in a memorized sequence)* I'm thirsty as hell from a long day baking out in the sun on a horse's back, and I hadn't even had the time to drop my shoulder-satchel before here *he* was, trying to get me tipsy.

"You know how to shoot, Mister—"

"Faust," I say.

"Do you?"

"Enough."

"That's encouraging," he lies. "Either way, you'll get practice enough here to get even better. Just try not to kill anybody without reason. Blackpeak's rowdier than hell." He tops off his own whiskey. His face (*it's a blur, a shimmering smear, and I can't quite place it*) catches a line of sunlight. "You can sit."

So I do. My feet are swollen lumps, bulging in my boots. Long day of travel. Long weeks of it. "Retirement?" I ask.

"Pursuing a passion," he tells me, then tops off his whiskey. "Heart's only got so many beats left in it. I'd prefer not to spend the ones that remain under Kallum's thumb. You met Kallum?"

"On paper."

"Keep it that way," he says. "Man's a snake."

When he stands, he stuffs his thumbs into his belt-loops. He unlatches a rusted key from his belt and tosses it down to the table. I take it. It's mine.

He surrenders it all. There's some talking, and some exchange over formalities as I finish a finger's worth of whiskey and he fidgets like an impatient meerkat in his seat, sometimes standing, sometimes sitting, but always watching me. (*It's an hour or two, but it snaps and flickers by in vague, unmemorable flashes. It stitches itself together into something-like-whole.*) The sun gleams orange, like a molten coin. The day is almost done. This is my first day in Blackpeak, and it's just like any other day, and it starts the same way—

"And always ends the same," he says. "Keys, rules, and whiskey. So that just about does it. I don't think there's much more I can pass along to you except the throne itself, Mister Faust."

He's at the front door of the marshal's office when he turns. From his chest, he unpins a battered star and places it in my hand. He shakes my other one with business-like firmness. We're standing, the tips of our boots touching, and I see the lines drawn on his face. We shake hands for what seems like years...

"I never got your name," I say.

"Fitzpatrick Gregdon," he tells me, and grips my hand with all the might of a gunmaker's vice. "*Former* town marshal of Blackpeak, Texas, as of this very moment."

"Pleasure," I oblige.

"All mine," he says. "Not that you'll remember."

He leaves me in that room by myself, with the taste of gold on my tongue and the after-pressure of his grip still aching in my hand. When he's gone, I look down at my hand to see a faint smear of blood where his thumb had curled around the back of my hand.

I sleep that night better than ever before.

ASHES

I REMEMBER THIS MUCH: THE MOMENT NYCENDERA'S BLADE STRUCK Illemone's Heart, the power within fired off like a primer. There was a flash, green and hot and blinding. All at once, the wailing cry of a hundred voices rose up in a storm as one magic tore into another.

It was Miss Lachrimé Garland who told me about the sand-shades. About how they screamed in unison, how they clawed at their silver eyes. How the flesh just unspooled and melted, and like boneless dolls, they crumbled away from their victims, all of them reaching out for something they couldn't see.

Grady Cicero told me about the silence, the deadlands quiet that brushed across the town in the seconds after they all fell. He told me it was because there were folk laying dead, clutching their guns or their children, and that while the world couldn't believe such creatures had come to be, it believed even less that anyone could have survived at all.

He said he picked through all of them, one by one, trying to find survivors. He told me later how Nabby Lawson slipped away in his arms, and he said to her, "I love you," and she smiled and they both smiled and she never stopped smiling, and of all the lies he'd told in his life, it burned like a red coal in his throat.

For two days after, deranged in a sleepless fit, Paul Fulton buried sixteen bodies – at least, that's what Aremeda De Santos said. Nobody could convince him to let them help otherwise, said he threw a damn riot and hollered, "I've got to bury *somebody*," and struck gashes in the hard, rocky Simpkin earth for hours on end until holes formed and he filled them with men and women.

Eliza gave some right nice prayers, somebody said, standing on the rubble of the Simpkin porch with her Sunday skirts snapping. But when the words came from her, they said, she stared at a spot in space, spoke wooden and quiet, and seemed just as happy to think of nothing at all.

Others said the town pulled together, mostly because nobody understood a damn word that came out of Emp's mouth, so they just followed suit and thought, to hell with it, let's just do what he's doing. So they doused fires and started putting boards on busted windows.

When word travelled, they said that you could see the smoke as far as Crown Rock, stretching like a smear across the sky. They said they blamed the chaos in Blackpeak on bandits, and that alone was enough of a reason to avoid sending help. Because the best thing to do, they said, was just to pray and hope for the best from as far away as possible.

And others, they said, told tales about a marshal coming back from the dead – *he ate a bullet,* they said – *he tore men to ribbons with wind from his hands,* they said – and it was worth a laugh, and that was all.

They said. They said.

They said they found me on the outskirts of the town, tossed out like garbage, my hand still clenched around the memory of a knife, but grasping at nothing.

They said Peggy Winters hoisted me like a sack of feed and brought me to the Horseshoe Junction Inn.

In the wake of it all, Blackpeak thrived. It took a few days to shake loose the darkness. They had to tell me all about it, about the clean-up, about the repairs, about the funerals, because I don't remember the aftermath. Not a moment. Not a hair's breadth. Not a blink.

I remember something else entirely.

IS IT DONE?

"As best as it can be."

AND YET YOU LIVE.

"Do I?"

AT THE BEHEST OF BOONS AND GIFTS.

The blinding flash faded. I was left standing on that sea of stars, looking up into the fractured edge of the Shattered Well. The pinkish light of an alien horizon fell across my face. If I could have slept for a thousand years, I would have. "Does this end, all this juggling about with my brains like I'm some kind of circus trick?"

WHEN IT MUST.

"He's dead. I saw to it. Whether or not it's what you wanted, I got it done. No more Magnate on your back, no more hound-dog sniffing you out. Christ almighty, did you put Rufus through this kind of hell?"

THE PREVIOUS SERVED HIS PURPOSE ADMIRABLY.

"Which was what, exactly?"

TO DRAW YOU INTO MY ORBIT.

There were lines that had been toed, crossed, then rubbed away altogether. I glanced down at my body – at the image of my body, it must have been, because of all the sensations in this strange plane, I *felt* almost nothing at all – and tightened my fist. Still four fingers. Still caked in blood.

The Mark, like a black sickness, crawled inside the prison of my veins, spread into the cracks of my palm, and coiled toward my elbow.

I sniffed. Burnt flesh still greeted my senses. Scorched black, the triangular coin seared into the middle of my chest refused to budge, even when I pried at it with a fingernail. "Blackpeak's got a short memory. It has to. Either it's a matter of survival, or the last hint of human hope too damn stubborn to break away. They'll move on from the Magnate. So, too, can you."

MORTAL RACES POSSESS INSURMOUNTABLE RESOLVE, IF ONLY TO DESTROY AND DEMOLISH INDISCRIMINATELY.

"Optimism," I said. "Try it sometime. With the Magnate gone, ain't nobody around to care much about you."

YOUR MAYOR KALLUM STILL IS.

"You really afraid of that lump of whale meat?"

HUMANS PRY.

"If your solution is for me to kill him," I said, "you can cram it wherever you manage to cram whatever it is you'd cram, if you can even cram at all."

The pressure in the air intensified. My lungs shuddered. Wasn't exactly a keen idea, I reckon, to piss down the leg of a...*being* such as it. But to hell with it.

IS KILLING NOT ONE OF YOUR FINEST TALENTS?

"When someone deserves it."

AND HE DOES NOT?

"Not by my measure. Not yet. Him being a bug up your ass or a bee in your bonnet isn't hardly reason to give him a leaden lullaby. Not by my standards. The Magnate, he took what didn't belong to him, and he damaged and destroyed in the process. Kallum, he's greedy, sure, but dangle a side of beef in front of a dog and kill it for snapping, that's not on him. That'll be on you. That'll be on us. That'll be on me."

I'd spent too many hours listing back and forth like a boat caught in the winds of these beasts and powers. I wanted a beer. And a goddamn cigarette. Simple man, simple pleasures.

WE WILL EXPECT MUCH FROM YOU. UNDERSTAND THIS, it said. BE EVER VIGILANT. OUR PRESERVATION IS YOUR PRESERVATION. SHOULD WE FALL, SHOULD WE BE CONSUMED, CONDEMNED, COMPROMISED, OR DEFILED, YOUR CONTINUANCE SHALL BE SEVERED. Like a tiny, black heart under my flesh, the Mark began to tremble. UNTIL WE CALL UPON YOU AGAIN...

"Wait. Wait." I held up my hand into the air. "What the hell you mean, my *continuance?*"

FOR A SHADOW TO EXIST, THE SUN MUST BURN.

A sucking, tugging sensation on the back of my neck, my spine.

Dragging me away. Dragging me away from it, away from this world—

"How close did he come?" I asked the endless beyond. "How close did he come to finding you?"

A begrudging surge of pleasure rolled through the air. A MAN CAN DIG WITH PICKS AND SPADES FOR CENTURIES AND NEVER FIND THE WELL.

For some reason, its easy confidence and know-it-all demeanor set my anger off like a match. Here it was, demanding protection, like I only existed to fulfill some watchman's clause.

IN ALL HIS LIFE, NO MATTER HOW DEEP THE MINES

GREW OR HOW POWERFUL HIS CRAFT, HE TOOK NO INCH
WHICH I DID NOT ANSWER WITH A MILE.

Everything faded from view. I fell back, like liquid, into the universe.

The Shattered Well's distant voice reached down after me.

HE NEVER EVEN CAME CLOSE.

MY MIND FOUND my body somewhere. I suppose it knew just where to find it. I heard voices across the way, so I drifted toward them until my eyelids opened, burning like blisters.

"—will have some volunteers in a few days, I imagine, to head back down there to gather what they can," said Miss Garland. "What wasn't destroyed, anyway."

"Much of it is still intact. And quite viable."

"What kind of goods?"

"Your kerosene. Your whiskey. Tobacco. Dried meat, salt, flour—"

"Any number of commodities that drive people to killing if they don't have their share, then. Is there any potential of danger if we go to retrieve the products?"

Heartbeat in my head, *tha-thum, tha-thum*, pulling me out of the valleys of sleep.

"You'll encounter no opposition."

"None?"

"The mines are the realm of dead men."

A marathon of cool water trickled down my forehead, crawled to my collar, silencing a wild, feverish heat.

The second voice, all sharpened steel – Nycendera the Herald – said, "Fire will serve useful should the Magnate's tunnels possess any stragglers. Tell your men to bring their torches. They're quite fond of those, after all."

"Reckon," said a third voice I instantly recognized, "I res' awn up a day'er two, I wone have ainy trouble tearin'em sandbags apart wi' my hanes, jes' you watch."

"Preserve your strength. There will be opportunity enough to bloody and be bloody," said Nycendera.

"Shaw." Peggy spit. "Shaw."

"In a few days' time, we'll reassess the state of things down in the mines," said Miss Garland. "I take it most of the men who worked in that vicinity won't want to return too quickly to their previous tasks, what, with the knowledge that their workplace was a glorified slaughter-pen. Regardless, Blackpeak is in your debt. Can we repay you?"

"Yes," the Herald said. "You can leave."

"Some'a us cain't jes' up and leave. We got thangs here," Peggy said.

"The Shattered Well cares nothing for your sentiments, your possessions, or your claim to land which has never been yours. This is poisoned land, dangerous and infected. The longer you linger in its midst, the greater threat it poses to you. Greedy souls with greedier desires will keep coming, drawn by the promise of what they've read in their books or heard carried on whispers."

Miss Garland's jaw clenched so tight, it rippled the blanket of darkness around me. "Then we will greet them as we must."

"We live heah," Peggy said. "Ain't no runnin'. Ain't no such thang."

In my brain, there was a little wink of light. Priests say that's the face of God when you're about to die, dragging you closer to Heaven. I waited a long time before I finally said *fuck it* and started swimming toward it...

I woke. Outside, day had given way to night, and only a dull oil-lamp flickered on a bedstand. I drew up in bed and goddamn if every muscle I had didn't scream a thousand curses at me just for doing so.

The sheets peeled back. I touched the skin where the flintlock had all but torn me in two. All that was there, though, was a pooch I could blame on too much beer and too much stew.

The Shattered Well could drive a hard bargain with clever tricks like this.

"She's not here," said a voice in the darkness. "She left. Hours ago."

By the smoke-stained curtains, I placed myself in one of the rooms of the Horseshoe Junction Inn. The fabric flickered in and out of an open window. From a seat in the shadows, Miss Garland threw me exactly what the painful moment needed: a little white stick. "Never met an angel so sweet," I said, as she brought the oil-lamp close to me so I could light the cigarette.

I smiled. She didn't. Her dark face, written over with too much thinking, might as well have been coal. She felt my cheeks, my forehead, looking for signs of fever. Unsatisfied, she went then for my jaw, my cheeks, pried my mouth apart like I was a child who'd eaten a rock. "The *hell*," I barked.

Her finger slashed along inside my mouth. "Hold still."

"The shit is this about?"

"Hold still—"

"You mind telling me—"

"*Hold still, goddamnit!*"

She rammed me back against the headboard and the pillow. She peered into my open mouth like a barber trying to find a rotten tooth. I could see her so close here, smelled the stomach acid and stale drink on her breath. Her eyes swam in pools of strange, confused tears.

Her finger finally found what it was looking for: at the top of my mouth, lodged there like a stone, was a misshapen bullet.

Miss Lachrimé Garland collapsed back on her chair and took a swig from a glass of bourbon. "She told me to pass along a message. When you were well enough to receive it." The cigarette seared the top of my mouth. "Are you well enough, Elias Faust?"

Whatever it was that made Miss Garland retreat into herself, I couldn't tell, but I was too weary to be frustrated. "Only as much as you think I am, Miss Garland."

She licked her dry lips and said over her glass: "'Other places, other beings, other worlds, they felt the rules bend here. Like a ripple in the ocean. They know there's a Well here. They know now,'" Miss Garland said, staring not at me, but at the coin burnt into the center of my chest. "'They know. And like all creatures hungry for hope, they make their way. They approach.' What in God's name is that supposed to mean?" she asked.

I couldn't answer. Her knee jittered under her skirt.

"What have you dragged us into," she asked, before spitting on the floor between her feet. "You should be dead. Now I'm here talking to you, delivering messages from one strange thing to the next. All the time wondering exactly what's been going on, or what even did go on, and why, when all the blood and shit rolls downhill, it always comes to stop at your boots. From Everett to lynchings to swarms of men made of sand and skin."

I swallowed hard. "Miss Garland, it's done. Whatever didn't make sense is dead and gone."

"You should be dead." She stood, clutching her apron so hard I swore the white bone would tear out through the skin of her knuckles. She shrunk herself against the door. "You turned me back. Just like *that*, you turned me back, tore me out of what he did to me." Behind her, she grabbed the glass doorknob until I almost thought she'd yank it right out of the wood. "It's not human, to live in spite of it all. In spite of lead and gunpowder. Living to end it all with a single blow.

"That's not natural. It's not human."

Drunk with trembling anger and yet coldly sober, she straightened her back. Her hand slipped into her skirt-pocket, feeling for familiar safety. Just in case.

Nobody got the best of Miss Lachrimé Garland. Nobody.

"What the fuck are you, Elias Faust? And why are you still alive?"

I never had the time to answer. She opened the door, retreated into the hallway, and vanished into that world where fighting pits were all she had to worry about.

I SAT IN THAT BED, staring at the Mark etched into my veins, filling myself with what remained of Miss Garland's bourbon. My cigarette ashes scattered like black snow across the bedding. I found a wrinkle in the bedclothes, traveled across it with my eyes, and didn't think of much at all. No Magnate, no dead things, no Well. So imagine my surprise when, from the doorway, somebody said, "I think it'd be in your best interest to stop doing your best impression of a side of beef."

A pistol-hammer jacked back.

"If you're gonna shoot me," I said, "then at least aim for something vital."

"Does that even work anymore?"

"We could give it a try."

In the door stood Grady Cicero, his .44 Russian held in the air beside him, muzzle pointed at the ceiling. His right arm was in a sling. His mutton-chops looked freshly oiled. He had a grin on his face bigger than a pig eating shit.

What I saw wasn't so much a whole man as it was a scabby puzzle-map of skin where thorny vines had torn perforated lines across his cheeks, his nose, and even along the backs of his hands. For a moment, my breath stuttered. I asked, "You have a date-gone-wrong with a broken pane of glass or something? If you think I look bad, you should—"

"—see the other guy, yeah, yeah," he said.

"How's the town?"

"Still terrible." He lifted the bottle from the table. "Want some more bourbon for that glass?"

"Any special occasion?"

"Winning. Skin of our teeth and all that."

We both drank. He curled his nose.

"Tastes like hell," he said.

"But it tastes," I said, "which means you aren't dead."

"Says the guy who makes it look easy."

I liked simple things. Cicero understood that. And yet as we sat there, drinking and talking like there weren't matters at hand, we could live the theatre of carelessness, like nothing else went on beyond that room. "How'd you do it," he finally asked, after a span of silence got between us and our smiles and our premature laughter.

"Crashed one bit of magic into another. Figured if a bullet couldn't do it, there had to be other ways."

"Fortunate guess?"

"Suggested course of action."

That, I think, was why I'd grown to like Grady Cicero. Because when there were questions that needed to be asked, he didn't always ask them.

I watched a ring of smoke catch the first rays of morning sun. A new day. The light, pink and blue and fresh, seemed like the run-off from another world.

Grady Cicero finished our last cigarette without asking if I even wanted a draw. He crushed it out with his fingers. "It's not just *your* responsibility." He flicked the paper out the window. It fluttered away, burnt and useless. "You shoulder too much of this shit and it'll just crush you. It's already begun. Don't make me watch. Christ, man, don't you dare make me just watch."

"Did you think I was dead?"

"You just don't assume a friend's dead. You make damn sure he is, and then you try to kill the sonofabitch who did it."

"And if he's not?" I said.

"Then you fight your way out of the shit with him when the time comes for shit to get fought."

I grinned for what felt like the first time in days. Dried blood cracked on my face. You don't miss a sunrise like the one that came reaching up over the peak of the Blackpeak town hall without, for just a moment, standing still in time.

He raised the empty bottle. "To living."

I raised my glass. "To dying."

"'Death, a necessary end, will come when it will come.'"

We drained our last drops of whiskey.

"This place needs you, Cicero," I said.

"So it does," he said with a smile. "So do you."

SUMMER STARTED TO WANE, but in Blackpeak, it was anybody's guess when it really stopped or started. Just hovered, mostly, like a ghost or a cloud. Life had come back to Blackpeak. Sure, there were some burned buildings, but it wasn't so bad other than that. The heartbeat returned. And the drinking.

Hammers and wood saws sang all hours of the day. Miss Garland, Emp, and a handful of others oversaw the return of Blackpeak's goods from the mines, and just like that, regularity returned to our dusty pit of a town. Nobody said anything about any odd encounters in the mines. No sandshades, no fights, no lingering threat. I guess if you cut off the head of the snake the tail doesn't live very long. Destroying Illemone's Heart had done the work that no amount of bullets or gunshots could. My body, still barely pieced together, was thankful for the cane I took from Levinworth's belongings, rest his soul.

Sometimes I drew little triangles on tiny pieces of paper. Every time I did I burned them up with a match.

One night I was busy on the saloon porch trying to find Orion in the sky when a pair of yellow eyes reflected the moonlight like precious gems. I felt them boring into me. When I blinked, they were gone.

I made sure nobody was around when I got up off the bench, wandered down the porch, and went across the street to the alley where I'd seen them. I held the wooden cane almost like a sword.

When I stepped into the shadows, a growl greeted me. A wolf-like beast was there, hackles raised like the tongue of a lumberjack's saw.

"Hey, Spitjaw," I said.

Its tall ears twisted. It turned and lumbered down the alley, bouncing with every one of its steps.

Every few yards, the impatient beast turned and looked at me, silently asking me what was taking me so long to follow. Obligingly, it slowed down, taking its occasional time to snuff at something curious on the ground.

It led me to the husk of one of the burned buildings on the edge of town. All that was left of the tanner's was a skeleton of black beams and old walls. My spine started to prickle. An audience of other eyes sprang to life, winking in the blackness. Watching me, remaining obedient. But something in the air whispered a breath of calmness. Calmed me, too. A presence, a chilling mantle of peace, like a mother's whisper...

The Quicktooth sat amid the ruins. There were four coyotes sitting around her feet. They raised their heads when I came near.

"We knew, inevitably, that we would need to speak to you again, Gravelfoot."

I sat down next to her, but not too close. She didn't look at me. Her silvery hair seemed to suck in the starlight and not let it go. "You could have just gotten me on a train," I said. "Seemed to work well enough last time."

"Friendly encounters are best engaged on familiar ground."

"I'd venture that 'friendly' is just the closest word for what it really is."

"We may have strikingly different definitions in mind," she said. "We thought it best to come to you and convey our gratitude. The Magnate is dead."

"I was there."

"We took it upon ourselves to retrieve his remains from the fallen home. To dismantle them. So he could not be reconstructed."

"How dare you break a trend," I said.

"We've brought you a morsel of his flesh and a sliver of bone to prove the deed's completion."

"Your social graces could use some work," I said.

"You have assisted us in killing the Magnate and removing one less threat from our territory. In turn, we have brought for you a portion of the kill. The bargain is complete."

"Spitjaw, Constantpaw, and Rat," I said. "They helped save my people." Three pairs of coyote-eyes flickered at the gratitude. "I owe them. I owe you."

"We are not predatory animals, Gravelfoot. We are merely protective of what is rightfully ours. Consider their assistance a contract of peace."

"Didn't we already have that? Or something like it?"

The coyotes circled. The set of her jaw became iron. "Much has changed since then. It behooves us to write new peace."

"Like you did for the Magnate before you turned on him?"

"You have intrigued us for months. The Magnate had been watching you for some time. We were his eyes. We witnessed your first gunfight with his sons from afar. And we later realized that you would be an invaluable asset in ridding us of our problem."

"Coal, silver, gold, platinum, and Faust," I said under my breath. "You sent me after him to cover your own ass. In case any of his boys survived, or in case the killing didn't go as planned."

"Better to send you than to bring a war upon our family if we could help it. You benefited. We benefited. The choice was clear."

"What makes you any different from him if all you did was use me?"

"Principle is what divided us, not lack of similarity."

Shooting a woman wouldn't exactly make the night much better for me, but I doubted it would do anything to make it worse, either. "I'm willing to call us Even Steven if you explain the triangles to me. The ones he performed all his powers with."

"A primitive visual totem used to draw supernatural power into the natural world."

"I used them," I said.

"Meddling with such power will get you killed."

"Sure, by people like me." I spun my cane between my palms. "How much do you know about these triangles?"

"A great deal more than we care to."

"I destroyed the Simpkin house with triangles Billy and Curtis Gregdon had used to mark one of the scenes of their murders. I pulled the place down around the Magnate. And after it was done, I saw something. I saw—"

"Visions," she said, turning to me.

"You know about them?"

"It is not often encouraged to use gates created by others, Gravelfoot. They leave hints and clues behind, information of the creator that those who access it can use to their advantage."

"Sounds like it could be sort of useful," I said.

"Or—" she reached down to stroke the snout of one of her coyote-children, "—those who access that gate may even absorb something of the creator, something they cannot shed no matter how hard they try."

"So use only your own," I said. "Right."

"Use none at all. It is best not to dabble in such nonsense." She took something out from her hide satchel. It was a small wooden box with a clasp on it. She put it in my lap. She tapped the box with a long fingernail. "The spoils of your campaign."

She stood. The threads and furs of her grand garments spilled down over her legs. The coyotes got to their feet and pinned me into place with their yellow gazes. When they circled her, they watched me with beastly caution, loping and slinking in subtle patterns around their leader. She stepped over the coals and the lumps of black rubble. Her pack jogged beside her, never straying.

"Quicktooth," I said.

The woman stopped. I raised the box. It was about the size of something you'd buy cigars in.

"The hell am I supposed to do with this?"

"Destroy the contents. Black secrets lie within. No human eye can be trusted with them. We trust you to know where the lines should be drawn between curiosity and greed. Perform your duties as marshal and we shall not need to speak again."

Some curiosities don't need feeding. Sometimes you just have to bury them away and hope nobody will ever come to nourish them. Good to live that way, I think. When she was gone, I opened the clasp with my thumb.

Inside was a book, a vellum volume with a triangle branded onto the front. It was the same book that had been sitting on the table beside the Magnate's makeshift throne.

I peeled open the first page. Tucked near the binding was a little shard of something I first mistook for a toothpick. It was grayish. Looked like it had been broken off a larger piece. The underside of it was dark and black. Next to it was a little flap of what I swear was pigskin, but at closer look I realized...

I dropped the book.

"Fuck me sideways," I said.

She hadn't been lying.

A MONTH LATER, Grady Cicero and I drank whiskey and sat on the hill overlooking the Western Elbow. We'd only brought one bottle. We were in the sun. Little wiggly mirages floated up from the train-tracks. Any hotter and I thought they'd melt into the ground.

"Time's this train supposed to be here," he said, passing me the bottle.

"You in a rush or something?"

"Tired."

"I-was-up-drinking-all-night tired, or stroking-it-until-dawn tired," I said.

"If I told you the truth existed somewhere in the middle, would you cease asking me questions?"

"I sawta wish y'all'd jes' stopped talkin' ten minutes back." Peggy, who was more brawn than both of us put together, had her arms crossed and spent her time sweating like a tired mule. Underneath her dress-sleeves, two patches of perspiration grew and grew. She shot a streak of brown tobacco out of her mouth. She'd come along too. She'd insisted.

I offered her the bottle. "Despite admissions, he's still drinking at ten in the morning. I guess we know which he did more of."

"Hair of the dog," Cicero said.

"Like yer one'ta talk, Marshal."

"Treachery, Peggy Winters, is punishable by a very sober and thirsty death."

We all could have taken the piss out of each other for hours, and we'd have known we meant nothing by it. They wouldn't have let me come by myself. Even though we'd organized a trade-schedule with Crown Rock, with Miss Garland taking over the helm of Edward Sloman's store, we had our work cut out for us. We almost felt normal.

"Miss Garland paying you for your work here?" I asked Peggy.

"Yawp," Peggy said.

"With money?"

"Nope."

"Tell her I said she's stingy," Cicero said.

"You do it cha'self, li'l man," Peggy said.

The ten-twenty from Crown Rock was just a few minutes early. It came chugging around the bend. When it stopped, we greeted the cargo manager and sweated for an hour or two lugging crates to the wagon we'd brought with us.

When the engine finally left, Cicero and Peggy and I watched until it looked as small as a snake sinking into the distance.

When it had gone and the wardrum beat of its pistons faded away, I started to turn. A long ride back to Blackpeak, after all. If we stayed any longer, we'd be drunk as hell.

"Faust," Cicero said, snapping his fingers. "Hey, you see that?"

He pointed. Sure as shit, something in the distance. It was moving. Something black like a blotch of ink with legs was marching down the side of the tracks. Not just marching, though. Galloping. And at a good pace. I heard hooves thundering against the sandy ground. A black horse came toward us.

"Wild," Cicero said.

"Maybe," I said.

"Rabid," Cicero said.

"Pro'bly," Peggy said.

"Shoot it?" Cicero said.

"You and shooting things," I said.

"Could punch it," Peggy said.

"You and punching things," I said.

I thought the animal was just planning to ride right by us, but as it got closer, it started slowing. No saddle that I could see. No bit. No stirrups. It had a tail that looked like black glass and a mane of thick, jetty hair. It stopped right in front of us. Huge, dark eyes took Cicero and me in from just a few feet away. It huffed out a breath like we'd gotten in its way.

"Now that's a horse," he said.

I scratched my chest through my shirt. I could still feel the ridges of the metallic triangle that had been seared into my skin. It felt right to leave it there. People weren't supposed to believe things like I'd seen in the mines. When I stopped believing them, I'd take my knife to it, peel it up by the edges, and put it up on my wall.

But until then, it'd stay. For now, anyway. I'd earned it.

The horse glared at the three of us. It kicked its hoof into the ground and blew up a ring of dirt and sand.

"Weird-ass animal," Cicero said.

Someone else, in what I swear was a vaguely English accent, said to us, "If you gents and the lady wouldn't mind moving aside, I'd appreciate it."

The three of us looked at each other.

The horse whipped its mane. It lowered its snout down in front of my face, pressed its forehead almost against mine, and studied me.

Then – I swear to God – the horse reared back and said in that same voice, "Wait a moment. You're *him*. Oh, thank goodness. You're Marshal Elias Faust, aren't you?"

Cicero, eyes wide, said, "As a matter of fact, he is."

"Bloody fantastic," said the horse. "I've been looking all over for you, Arbiter of the Well."

ABOUT THE AUTHOR

 Husband. Son. Cat-dad. Dog-dad. Self-professed synthwave addict. Podcaster. Moonlighting actor. Historical reenactor. Martial artist.

Rance's poetry, prose, academic publications, and journalism can be found littering the Internet like time-bombs. When he isn't writing, he is one-half of the podcast duo The Quarantine Book Club (http://www. thequarantinebookclub.com).

Rance lives in Baltimore, MD with his lovely partner and mountains of debt.

HTTP://WWW.ELIASFAUST.COM/

Printed in Great Britain
by Amazon

18896089R00243